MR. MITCHELL

BILLIONAIRES' CLUB: BOOK TWO

RAYLIN MARKS

Contemporary Romance Author

INTRODUCTION

Avery

I was going to miss my flight if this stupid Uber driver didn't step on it. *What the fuck, man?* I looked over at him, driving with great concentration. "Hey, buddy," I started as nicely as I could, "I am going to miss my flight. Can we go a little faster?"

"I'm going as fast as Chester can take us," he answered while petting his dash.

"Chester?" I questioned as he continued down side streets that I only prayed he was being directed through because his GPS had a quicker way to get us to LAX.

"The name of this little guy," he exclaimed about his tiny microcar.

"Ah," I answered. "Well, is *Chester* by chance small enough to fit down the back alleys of this neighborhood we're in?"

"Chester doesn't do illegal," the middle-aged man smiled.

Of all the Ubers I could've gotten, it's a guy who named his car Chester that will prevent me from my much-needed week-long escape to London with my foster sister.

"Here..." he said softly, turning to the right, "we...are," he stated nice and calmly. "You enjoy the flight, Avery. Keep the tip. Chester could've done better and gotten you here earlier. He doesn't deserve the good gas."

I looked at the man and forced a smile. *You're a whacko!* "I've got your tip—"

He stopped me from reaching into my purse. "No," he frowned, "You were too stressed. Chester and I would rather have a good review."

"Got it," I said, grabbing my carry on and taking off, never looking back at that crazy scene again.

I never thought I'd be sitting here, air blowing on my face and engines running on the plane. I closed my eyes, sitting in serenity only to have my neighbor—a two-year-old kid—poke my nose. I was never going to survive this ten-hour, non-stop flight to Europe.

Ignore him, and he'll stop, I thought, knowing this was not the solution. Trust me, I knew my three-year-old daughter would only take it as a greater challenge.

"Excuse me, ma'am?" My eyes snapped open to see a flight attendant on my left, "We have an opportunity for you to upgrade to first-class if you'd like to take it."

"Oh?" I said, knowing my wealthy sister had booked the flight on her mileage rewards, and I just hit the lottery. "I'd love to."

She escorted me up to where passengers were seated with more room and luxury.

"Right here," she directed me to the seat where a businessman sat, staring at his phone.

He glanced up, and brilliant green eyes framed by dark lashes met mine, throwing me completely off. Good lord, I'd never seen a man this handsome before in my life. Guys who looked like this modeled Gucci suits and lived on the covers of magazines for women to drool over. Now I was being seated next to this handsome man on a non-stop flight from L.A. to London. Talk about a first-class upgrade. Maybe I died from carbon monoxide poisoning when I was driving in *Chester?*

He smiled, stood, and allowed me into my seat next to the window.

So, this was awesome, now I was afraid I'd have to go to the bathroom the entire flight, constantly disturbing *Mr. Sexy in a suit* because he was too tall to shift his legs for me to get through.

"We'll serve drinks once we're in the air," the flight attendant said. "Anything you need, we'll ensure you're taken care of. Enjoy your flight, Miss Gilbert."

"Thanks," I said. My phone rang, and it was my sister—God love her. "What, do they instantly send you notification that I accepted the First-Class seating on your behalf?" I snickered.

"Hey," Britney said, "your dick-bag ex is giving mom shit right now."

"What?" I asked. "I don't have time for his bullshit. Period."

"You need to call him. I just left the house. I'll be landing after you, but the hotel suite is ready for us in London."

"Fine," I sighed and hung up.

"Please turn off all electronic devices…"

"Fuck," I whispered. Okay. *Breathe.* I dialed out anyway.

"Sup?" Derek answered.

"Listen, asshole," I growled into the phone, "Your parents aren't getting Addison until *after* I get home."

"You should've thought this through," he growled.

"I thought it *all* through, dick," I tried to keep my voice down. Swear to God this drug addict brought out the worst in me, and now I was going to get kicked out of First Class by Mr. Sexy himself. "My mom is staying at my place with her. You need to figure out your new drug charges before I let you anywhere around her again."

"Avery," he said in his manipulative voice.

"Don't *Avery* me, Derek. Your kid or not, Addison stays with Jill, got me? I don't trust your enabling parents, and I don't trust you. Please, God, don't do this to me."

"I'll do whatever I fucking want."

"I'm getting a lawyer…"

"You can't afford a lawyer," he sneered. "So what's next, Avery?"

A tapping to my right arm brought my angered expression to the man sitting at my right with a smirk, he rose his eyebrows and mouthed, *"I can handle this if you'd like?"*

I looked at him in confusion. I couldn't take off and leave Addison, my foster mom, Jill, or my mind in this state. Derek could screw me over hard in the week I was gone. I had no other option—either trust the man dressed like a lawyer sitting next to me to bail me out, or get off the plane. My life only led to option two, so I decided to go for it with this guy.

I handed him my phone—his hands were even beautiful.

"Excuse me, Derek?" he said in a commanding, confident, and supreme voice. "Yes," he paused, people staring at us while the plane started backing out. "I understand how you'd feel that way, yes." I looked at the man as he frowned, "Are you done? Good. Now, all of this has been recorded for my team and me. We will keep this while we continue to look into the custody and your sanity as the father of Addison. Now, I'll advise you to heed—" he looked at me and mouthed, *"your name?"*

"Avery," I said with a smile, knowing Derek—the low life drug addict—was shitting his pants on the other end of the phone.

"You will regard Avery's request in Jill watching over the child. If I learn that this has turned out to be more upon mine and Avery's return from London," he gave me a thumbs-up as if asking, *you are going there, right?* and I nodded. "Then you and I will be in court." He paused while I heard Derek kissing his ass. "That's fine. I would assume you would believe that. So, we're clear? If there is so much as one phone call toward Addison...er, excuse me, Avery, while she is away, then understand this will get extremely ugly." The gorgeous man who bullshitted my psycho ex handed me my phone. "Your friend hung up on me." He smirked, "I believe he got the message, though."

"I can't thank you enough for that," I said, my eyes captured by his, and his smile instantly made me grin like a girl, crushing on a Hollywood star.

"Not a problem. I couldn't help but overhear you talking to him—a drug addict?"

"Yeah, long story," I sighed. "And now I'm stuck with him because I was stupid enough to get knocked up by him."

"I believe it takes two to make that decision. I wouldn't carry the blame alone if I were you." He smiled. "You appear to be a good mom. I'm sorry if I was overstepping boundaries—being a stranger and all, but I do hope it helped?"

"I'm Avery," I said with a smile.

"I'm Jim," he extended his hand out toward me. "I guess we're no longer strangers, then?"

"Easy as that."

God, I wanted to join the mile-high club with this guy, but we just became friends over me telling him that I made the mistake of screwing a drug addict and got pregnant with his kid. I mean, that was three years ago, but still. I highly doubted *this guy* would stoop to anyone less than a socialite, much less some random chick who got upgraded to first-class that was drooling over him. Who knew, free drinks were in first class, and he just ordered two for us.

Please, God, don't let me start my trip off to London by screwing some guy while I was drunk on an airplane. I've done crazier shit, yes, but this trip was meant to be fun, but I suppose a girl could have fun, especially with a man like this dreamboat sitting next to her.

CHAPTER ONE

Jim

I sat in my office, going over the last of my emails from this long yet productive day at our London headquarters. My meetings with our associates and one new investor were finally over. The only shitty part of this day was that Alex and I couldn't come to an agreement and sign with a new business we flew out here to acquire. We could've offered them a million fucking dollars as a promise to his company's future success, and he still wouldn't have taken the deal.

We still had another week and more time, we would get the deal. I wouldn't sit here all night and worry over today's events. I learned a long time ago that *I* was running this business that I'd inherited from my father; this machine wasn't running me. That's what I always told myself anyway.

I weaved my pen through my fingers, reading the last of the man's prerequisites on his term sheet for Mitchell and Associates. This guy was a stubborn ass. I had to get together with Alex so we could find a way to close this deal. Our London employees had families too. They had to eat. All of that rested on my shoulders with every transaction we did.

A highlight of this particular trip to London was that my brother was here to bring more insight to our new program on behalf of Saint John's Hospital. Thank God he was not only a world-renowned heart surgeon, but Jacob was also a man who could charm a room full of snakes if need be. Jake was a genius with his words, and sometimes I wished he would have taken on the family business with me after Dad died. Then again, this was me at the end of a long-ass day, thinking selfishly. The world needed more heart surgeons like my brother and probably fewer corporate dicks like myself.

Jake had successfully pleased every investor in the room with his presentation to start up an online university, performing live surgeries and instructing students while doing so. With this first part of our plan moving forward, Jake was on track to have a new, innovative way to bring medical students and interns from the UK into his surgical room, looking over his shoulders while his brains and hands went to work on his patients for heart transplants. The Heart Institute was finally getting past the permits phase with the city, and once that was operational, Jake would be able to bring in more interns to work under the finest doctors who were ready to come to us.

"Mr. Mitchell?" my assistant called over the intercom.

"Yes, Becky?" I answered, pressing the button on my desk phone.

"I'm leaving for the day. Before I go, I just wanted to let you know that Adam is a bit concerned about today's staff meeting."

"Excuse me?" I said, picking up the receiver. "What did he have to say?"

"Well, you walked out of the room with a frown on your face during the acquisition questioning for Middle Group."

I rubbed my forehead and sighed. "I'll make sure to have another staff meeting with the acquisitions team tomorrow before I take off to work remotely. Have a good evening, and I'll see you on the next visit."

"Thanks, Mr. Mitchell. I look forward to it. Cheers."

Shit. Every expression that crossed my face was analyzed, even as I did mundane things like walk to my office. If I smiled, then someone took offense to that and found a way to link that expression to me having to fire someone. If I frown, everyone thinks things are going to hell, and they're going to be out of a job the next day. I'd dealt with plenty of that shit and had to quell rumors before they burned the place down.

This didn't just happen at our London headquarters; it occurred in the Los Angeles one as well. It was all part of the lovely job of being a CEO.

I picked up my cell and dialed out to the company's president, and my best friend, Alex.

"Hey," Alex answered, already at our usual dining joint. "Is your sorry ass still at the office?"

"Yeah," I answered. "Adam in acquisitions is concerned over a goddamn look I had on my face when I left the meeting this afternoon. I was taking off for the estate so I could work from there. I thought it would be nice to have some sort of reprieve after three days of living in this hotel and office. It looks like we're in early tomorrow for a six o'clock meeting."

"Good God, man," Alex responded. "Jake is taking off, and his flight is in an hour. I'll let him know. You want me to send out the message to the team about the meeting?"

"I'll handle it. My laptop is open."

"All right. Are you showing up tonight, or are we closing out the tab early?"

"I'll swing by for a bite and a drink. I'm sure the ladies are already entertaining enough for you."

"Right." Alex laughed. "Handle your shit, and we'll see you in a few."

AFTER SENDING out a quick meeting invite to the team to correct any insecurities over my expression in the meeting today, I shut the laptop. I was not going to leave for the estate with anyone in our London office feeling uneasy, so hopefully, the meeting would do the trick. I put the laptop in my briefcase, and a dark shadow appeared at the entrance of my door.

I glanced up. "Jules?" I questioned the knockout brunette I usually hooked up with when I came to London. "What the hell?" I smiled, and before I could walk over to her, she rushed to me. My face was in her hands, and her lip gloss was choking me as she impulsively kissed me.

She took my hand and walked me over to my leather sofa, which was positioned under the windows to give a sweeping view of London at night.

"Jesus." I chuckled. "Slow the hell down."

"It's been too long," she said, playfully pushing me to sit on the couch so she could straddle me.

Oddly, I wasn't in the mood for her or this for some reason. She loosened my tie, and I spotted a diamond ring on her finger. I pulled her hands down from where they fidgeted with my shirt.

"What's this?" I asked, holding up the evidence that she was obviously a married woman, unlike the last time I saw her a few months ago.

"Right now," she arched her eyebrow over her hazel eyes, "it's nothing."

"The hell it isn't," I said. "When did you settle down, and who's the lucky man?"

"It could've been you, you know?" she said as she gripped my shoulders and began massaging herself against my dick that was now hardening since it had a mind separate from my own. "But someone can't commit."

"Someone," I tried to control myself, "has a business to run. I couldn't have made you happy if I tried."

She licked her lips, slowly getting herself off on my hard cock. "You'll always make me happy, just like this," she said, biting her lip.

I gripped her hips, stopping her from making my dick take over my reason. "Hold on," I said, her eyes meeting mine in some daring and rebellious way. "You got married. You get what that means, right?"

"Yes," she said, rocking her hips against my lack of self-control. "It means you won't fuck me. If it helps, I didn't marry for love; it was definitely for his wealth. So, it's not a real marriage."

"The fuck it isn't," I said. I laughed in response, losing all sexual desire in that moment. "Glad to know the daughter of one of my wealthiest investors went out and married for fucking money."

"You expect me to marry a coal miner? I have a lifestyle that I need to maintain. Don't get self-righteous on me. Men and women have been doing it for centuries, so I'm not apologizing for anything." Her breath was ragged, eyes glossy, and lips on mine again. "Fuck, I'm going to come, Ji…"

"Jesus Christ." I stood up, leaving Jules on the couch and seeing a wet spot on my crotch. "Is this a goddamn joke?" I looked at her, disgusted with myself for letting her ride me like she did. "Things are over between me and you. You've lost your mind. Marrying for money and now getting yourself off on me like that? Fuck."

I was in a wretched mood after this day. Would it have been nice to go back with Jules to her hotel room and fuck it all out of my system? Yes, that's why we had this particular relationship. We both fucked for our own selfish needs. But this? No. I felt like a sick, dirty bastard now.

"I miss you, Jimmy," she whined with a sultry smile, showing me that she wasn't wearing any panties beneath her skirt. "I have a room at our favorite hotel. I left your name at the front desk. Go out with the guys, and I'll be waiting for you if you somehow get out of this shitty mood you're in."

"Shitty mood?" I said with disbelief. "You're the one who got *married*. I'm not fucking a married woman. Period. You ended our hotel nights together, so enjoy your room alone, and congratulations on the nuptials."

She rose and kissed me on my cheek. "I'll be waiting for you."

"Very well." Anything to get her the fuck out of my office. The very last thing I needed—especially after my brother's docuseries had thrown the media into our private lives—was this woman, *who married for money,* in my life. I didn't need her husband...*shit, who did she marry?* If it was someone who came from money and power, chances were, I knew him. He was probably one of our investors. Jesus, I had to get her and myself the hell out of this dangerous situation.

ONCE JULIA's driver took her away, I had my driver take me to Delia's. Thanks to Jules—um, *Julia,* now—I had to change into one of the spare suits I kept in the office. The suit was reserved for incidents like accidentally spilling soup down the front of my shirt, or having coffee spilled on me, or when a stark-raving mad married woman climaxed on my lap...things like that.

Once that debacle was behind me, I was at Delia's and walking to our usual table in the corner where the guys were. I sat at the table, grateful the waiter was already bringing my usual drink—the bourbon I desperately needed to help put the events of tonight behind me.

"Still pissed that you have to hold the impromptu meeting tomorrow?" Alex chuckled, running his hand over his smoothed-back, dark blond hair.

"When are you going to cut that mop off your head?" I asked, noting the new style he was sporting.

"Yeah, you're still in a pissy mood." He took a sip of his scotch.

I pulled my bourbon to my lips after ordering swordfish and steamed vegetables, suddenly starved by the aroma of food filling the room.

"Remember Julia?" I asked, eying him and Collin, my brother's closest friend. Truth be told, all four of us had been close since college.

"Julia Dunlap?" Collin asked.

"Yeah," I said, nodding toward the waitress in gratitude for my freshly poured water. "She stopped by tonight."

"Then why the hell are you so irritated?" Alex chuckled. "Did Jules break the cardinal rule of you not fucking chicks in your office?"

"Fuck off," I snapped. "No. She got married recently, and *then* she tried to break the cardinal rule." I half smiled at how stupid I sounded with my mandate that I would never have sex in my office. To do so seemed tacky on all levels, though, in my personal opinion.

"Married?" Collin practically choked on his gin.

"Um-hm." I took another sip, letting the warmth of the bourbon calm my nerves after sliding down the back of my throat. "She tried to act as though nothing had changed."

"Probably because you're the best fuck she ever had."

"Funny, Alex." I sighed. "She actually admitted that she married for money, of all the damn things."

"So, he cries into his bourbon because he can't fuck a married woman," Collin remarked sarcastically.

"Despite what the media blasted about my brother and me, one thing is certain. We *never* fucked married women."

"It's almost like a curse." Collin snickered. "A billionaire home wrecker? That shit would definitely swing the media back your way again."

"No shit," I answered while glancing around the room.

Holy Hell, I thought when my eyes caught the bright blue eyes of the girl with pitch-black hair who was on my flight from Los Angeles. Avery had a nutcase of an ex on her hands, but after she loosened up on the plane, I fell under some crazy hypnotism she worked with those eyes and the stunning sharp features of her face. I would be lying if I said she didn't stick with me, and I wish I'd taken her up on her offer to have sex on the plane. She was only teasing, but I'd fantasized about it more times than I wanted to admit since I'd been in London.

Now, here she sat—by herself—in one of the most lavish restaurants around, and one that was not easy to get access to. Especially for the type of woman she led me to believe she was. A single mom, getting away from her shitty life with a paid vacation by her foster sister.

"Jimmy." Alex snapped his fingers at me as I stared at the woman. "Are you checking her out too?"

I looked back at the table as my plate was being placed in front of me. "Okay, I guess tonight is a game of memory for the three of us, and I'm the one asking the questions."

"Don't tell me you know who she is," Collin said.

"Remember me mentioning that, on the flight out here, I ran interference for a chick with some douche, ex-fiancé?"

"I remember that it was fucking stupid, and the main reason we take the private jet. Go on," Alex said.

"That's her," I said, glancing over and seeing her saddened expression as the other place setting and glasses were picked up by the waiter. "Somebody stood her up?" I reached for my plate.

Alex grabbed my arm before I stood. "Hey," he said as I rose anyway. "Stop it with the charity cases."

"Yeah," Collin said from across the table. "Lillian—does that fucking charity case psycho-bitch ring a bell?"

I smiled. "She's not like that." I glanced over at her as she studied her menu. "Nothing like that. I highly doubt she's some crazy, gold-digging freak."

"The courts will decide that, Jimbo." Collin smirked, using the one name I despised.

"Calm down," I said. "I'm not going to let her eat alone in a place like this. I'm taking my food over there. I've had dinner with you two for the last three nights, so I think you'll live."

Both men looked at each other, and I knew exactly what they were thinking, but they didn't have the whole story. I'd sat with the woman and heard all about the shitty hand of life she'd been dealt. She was solid. If anything, she was a breath of fresh air. It was nice to talk about something other than women and work, or what got us labeled this ridiculous *billionaires' club* name—only entertaining wealthy women to protect our asses and assets. These two jokers I was currently leaving behind were the two who got that rumor going—though it was my ex, Lillian, who kicked the can of gasoline on that raging fire of bullshit.

Avery seemed like she'd been stood up, either by her sister or some complete idiot who would be dumb enough to turn down the most beautiful woman I'd ever had the pleasure of seeing. Seriously. Her black hair set off her striking blue eyes, and I swear the woman looked like the one of the pixies that my sister-in-law had painted for her art gallery. I couldn't take my eyes off her on the plane, and I couldn't take them off her now.

CHAPTER TWO

Jim

*A*very's eyes scanned the area, and she covered her mouth when I approached her table. I opted to not take my plate of food with me as if to appear like a high school kid in the cafeteria, wanting to sit by a hot chick who was eating alone.

I reached for the back of the chair and returned her confused smile. "Avery?" I questioned, not fully knowing what the hell I was doing.

I could feel the stares from Collin and Alex, burning a hole into my back as they watched me do the most uncharacteristic thing I'd ever done. This was unlike me in every way. Maybe Jules did fuck with my mind, and now I felt I needed the presence of a beautiful woman to blot out the disgusting reminder of a married woman humping my hard cock. *Disgusting.* Yeah, that was definitely it. That's why I was randomly leaving my dinner and joining a woman I'd met on a plane three days ago. *Fuck it.*

"Shit." She covered her smile and glanced around the room. Her cheeks tinted pink as she tried to control her laugh. "Sorry, I don't think this restaurant allows cursing." She looked around again, and I could tell she was entirely out of her element.

"It depends on whom you are offending," I said, taking the chair and sitting across from her. "Mind if I join you?"

Her perfectly shaped eyebrow arched over her long black lashes, and her blue eyes glistened like sapphires. "Well, I...um." Her scratchy voice was sexy as she laughed at this bizarre scenario. "Okay. I remember you from the airplane. You saved me from my ex-fiancé. I also remember getting a little too drunk and cried my sad life story to you the entire flight here."

"I'm happy you remember me." I smiled and motioned for the waiter. "Have you decided on your meal yet?"

"Sir," she responded, sitting back in her seat, "I'm embarrassed to admit that I can't remember your name when you remembered mine."

She had the cute yet sexy face of a younger version of Meg Ryan, my childhood Hollywood crush. This woman was a dark-haired version of her, especially when she pursed her lips and scrunched her face up in confusion like this.

"I'm Jim," I reintroduced myself. "Please, don't be embarrassed. I'm pretty good with remembering names," I said with a laugh, pulling the menu she'd given up on over to me. "Honestly, I'm only naturally good with names of people who've made an impression on me, be it good or bad."

She crossed her arms over the strapless top of the dress she wore. "And you remember mine because of which? Did I make a good or bad impression?"

"How could a woman as lovely as you possibly make a bad impression on anyone?" I smirked, only because this woman was amusing me with her rigid body language and charming facial expressions. "May I ask why you are here alone?"

"My sister's meeting got held over." She smiled. "She's a busy girl, so I can't blame her, and I won't. I'm here on her paycheck, not mine."

I wasn't going there with money or jobs. That was too personal, although I was curious. I hadn't forgotten the daughter she'd mentioned on the plane, or her asshole ex who was going to fight her to the death for custody. Obviously, I had only one side to this story, so it was better to remain silent about it. The guy did sound like a fucking dickhead on the phone, though, and I was pretty good about reading people.

"A shame." I smiled and glanced down at the menu. "What are you up for tonight?"

"Um." She pinched her lips together and squinted her eyes in humor. "I'm so hungry I could eat the entire menu if you want to know the truth."

"I'd like to see that." I grinned.

"I'm dead serious," she said, catching my attention with her lowered tone.

I licked my lips and caught my bottom lip with my teeth. "You're serious?" I leveled her with a gaze, trying to maintain my composure and not laugh.

"*Dead* serious." She leaned her crossed arms up on the table and smirked. "I can't afford more than an appetizer at this place. My sister is paying for the meal." Her eyes scanned the ceiling and back to me. "And this fifty-dollar-a-plate restaurant was *her* idea and not mine. So she's paying up, but if it were up to me, I'd be at some restaurant near the attractions I was enjoying touring alone and be just as happy."

"You do realize that even those terrace eateries can be quite costly, especially when you're out alone, and someone takes advantage of your purse, correct?"

"I know the rules." She arched a brow at me, her irises captivating me further. "I keep my passport hidden behind zippers and my cash separate in my wallet."

"Yeah?" I said, not really remembering what the hell we both were talking about.

"My point is," she took a sip of her Chardonnay, "I'm going to eat small here and go pig out somewhere else."

The woman was petite, but with strong, muscular arms. I couldn't imagine her putting away a lot of food as she was suggesting with this menu. The waiter arrived, and I decided not to question it further.

"We'll take two bottles of your finest wine," I said and then smiled at her challenging grin. "And it looks like the chefs will be busy tonight." I folded the menu and handed it to him. "We'll take everything they're cooking off the menu tonight as well."

The waiter's eyes widened. "Sir," he said. "We will need to move you to another table for that. Our tables are reserved—"

I pointed to where Alex and Collin sat at our usual larger-than-most table in the corner of the restaurant, surrounded by windows instead of walls. "Those two are my colleagues, and they'll gladly take this table and offer theirs up for the lovely lady and me."

"Sir."

I smiled at the man. "I know this is completely out of the norm for you, young man," I said. "However, the tip will be fine and should help with the drinks you buy all of your friends at the pub tonight when you find yourself telling them about the crazy man asking to switch tables with other guests."

He chuckled while Avery cleared her throat. "You're not doing any of that," she said. "I'll just take the fish."

"I have to disagree with my lovely wife," I said, watching her eyes bulge at the statement. "You see, it's our fifth anniversary, and we chose to come to London. I've had reservations since last year for this place. I also am fortunate to know those men enjoying a table that is quite frankly too large for them. Being at this place was the reason London made my lovely bride's bucket list, and I hate to disappoint her."

He looked at Avery. "I will speak with my manager, and we will do our best to accommodate you and your husband."

I whipped out my cell and opened my group chat with the guys.

Jim: *Hey, get your asses up and switch with us.*

Alex: *What the hell are you doing to that waiter?*

Collin: *What the hell are you doing, period?*

Jim: *Just do it. We don't have enough room for the food at this small table in the middle of the room.*

Alex: *Unless you're making a move on that chick, bring her to our table with us.*

Jim: *I'm not going to intimidate a woman I hardly know with your ugly mugs, watching her eat. We take the best seat in this place every time we eat here. Just do her a favor.*

Collin: *Her or you? Jim is just horny after Jules made the moves on him.*

"ARE you and your friends finished working out the eating arrangements?" Her voice interrupted our lame-ass banter. "Yes." I rose. "Follow me."

An extremely formfitting dress showed her well-shaped, muscular legs and wrapped tightly around her breasts, which were pressed together, pronouncing a cleavage that could only make me drool at this point.

"This is Collin and Alex." I introduced the guys, eying them, and as the casual guys they were, they were trading tables with us like we were at a diner and not a five-star restaurant.

"Didn't catch your name." Alex arched a brow at my lack of proper behavior.

"I'm Avery." She shook her head. "And I have no idea what's going on."

Collin grinned and took her hand next. "Make that four of us." He eyed me. "I don't think Jim knows what's going on either, and he's orchestrating this incident."

"These two are friends of mine, Avery. Forgive me if I mentioned how you and I met onboard the plane without your permission."

"Why would you think you had to apologize for telling a story about a crazy lady on a plane?" She smirked, and I could quickly tell the guys were captivated by the amiable and appealing nature of the woman—and those damn blue eyes. "I'm flattered that my story made it to your highlight reel."

Alex eyed me and smiled. *"Nice catch,"* he mouthed from where he stood behind the woman with a subtle thumbs up.

Once the staff turned our parade of chaos into a graceful situation that wouldn't disturb their customers, Avery and I were seated, and a candle was lit for our table.

"I almost forgot," Avery said, placing the napkin in her lap and smiling at me. "It's our anniversary dinner. I hope you plan to order the entire dessert side of the menu as well. You know I like variety."

"If you keep smiling at me like that, you'll get anything you want from me." *Fuck. Did I just say that? Out loud?*

"Is that so, Jim?" She hung onto my name in some taunting, yet suggestive way. "You're not actually going to order the entire damn menu, are you?"

"Language, darling," I said while the waiter approached. "We'll be enjoying the entire dessert menu tonight as well."

The man's lips pinched together in humor. "Excellent choice."

"My wife always makes excellent choices," I said, to which Avery's expression darkened some.

"What's with you?" she questioned. "Seriously. All of this. You are ordering everything off the menu and moving your friends out from their seats—I'm not sure I'm getting any of this."

"Well, I saw a beautiful woman sitting alone. I remembered her well from our flight together. I also find her attractive, and I couldn't imagine her dining alone tonight. Am I at fault for taking advantage of a situation with a beautiful woman left alone?"

Her lips twisted, and her eyes narrowed. "I'll give you that," she conceded. "I'll also not be a total bitch and refuse your generosity because you keep telling me how beautiful I am." She said the last part with a certain kind of sassy sarcasm that I adored. "The married part, though?"

"Yeah, I guess that was a bit over the top."

"Well, I pinned you as a stiff lawyer or something like that." She took another sip of wine, "It turns out, you've got an interesting sense of humor too."

"It's dry humor, but it works at times." I smiled and sipped my new glass of bourbon.

"Well, it worked tonight. I appreciate the company. I've had a bit of fun touring London on the two days my sister had off to spend with me, and now I'm pretty much enjoying the historical sites alone. So, running into a friend who helped me with my idiot ex on the plane is a welcome surprise. I have to say thanks at least—a serious thank you —while not drunk and spilling my sad stories to you. In fact, I'm shocked that after hearing about some of the shit I go through, I'm sitting across from you at the moment. I figured you'd be the last person on the planet to entertain my sorry ass again."

The appetizers came, and she lit up with excitement. "Enjoy some of the fine delights that England has to offer," I said after the waiter left. "Dig in, gorgeous."

"Gorgeous is starving," she said, filling her plate.

I casually added a few oysters and buttered bread, and I watched as she began to eat like we were old friends. How many women had I watched pick at their plates for fear of eating in front of me? I never understood that. Were they scared to eat? Get dirty? Nervous? Who knew; it always made me feel like shit, though. I had no idea how to make them comfortable enough to eat more than a few bites of protein and maybe a vegetable.

Avery, however, was the perfect date. The entire menu was being set on our table, and she was going for it without reservation. I had never met a woman who wasn't intimidated in front of me.

Goddamn, she was luring me in like a moth to a flame.

"What are your plans tomorrow?" I questioned.

"Well." She swallowed. "After my sister gets the bill to this menu extravaganza that you insisted we eat, I'm most likely going home."

"I'm paying for this dining experience as it was my idea to make up for you being left to dine alone."

"You can't pay for all of this."

"I can, and I will. I insisted on this, and I must see if you can fit all of this food into that tiny little body of yours. You're what, five-three? All of this food must weigh more than you do as it is. I've got to see if you're some kind of competitive eater."

She laughed heartily, and I loved her exuberance. "Trust me, I can throw most of it down," she said, taking a drink of water while I forked a piece of broccoli and placed it in my mouth. "Although, I hope they do to-go boxes here. If that's just an American thing, I'm going to be majorly disappointed." She started buttering a slice of bread. "God dang, this food is amazing."

"So now that I'm picking the tab up on this meal, you won't be leaving tomorrow. Do you have plans? How long will you be in London?"

She swallowed a bite. "Planning on giving me a guided tour?"

"I visit the city often, and I don't feel it's safe to travel or sightsee alone."

"And your suit tells me that you're here for work."

"Perhaps."

"Well, tomorrow I'll be eating in some cute place I spied today that everyone says is the best for breakfast food. If you're serious about joining me on another visit to the numerous sites I've enjoyed visiting more than once, I'll gladly take the company."

"Well, it might just happen."

She shook her head and laughed. "You must be one over-worked man. Perhaps we're at the breakdown part of working long and hard hours?"

"You're my wife, and we're celebrating our anniversary, remember?"

"Good heavens, Jim—" She scrunched her face up again. "It's Jim, right?"

"Yes." I smiled, surprised that she was still going hard on the delicacies surrounding her. Where the hell did she keep all of this food? "If you stay in this location, I might offer up another tour that might be more insane than this fake marriage and our fine dining experience tonight."

She set down her fork, and finally, in her private episode of *Woman versus Food*, it appeared food had won. "Nothing could be crazier than this night after you approached my table, Jim."

"We'll see. Meet me where the tours start for the Tower of London. Have you been there?"

"Twice, and I didn't even see any ghosts from all the stories. I was really looking too," she said with a smile.

I couldn't hold back my laugh. "Are you one who believes in the supernatural?"

"I have a very open mind, thank you very much."

"I can see that in you. You definitely have an intriguing side."

"If I weren't opened minded and adventurous, I would be scared as shit with everything you pulled off tonight."

"Then it's a date," I said.

"It's a date." She smiled. "We'll see if business holds you up like it did my sister. She's heading off to Amsterdam for the next week before we go home. Who knows where your job will take you?"

"I determine where my job takes me."

"May I ask what you do exactly?"

"I run a business."

"Okay. Well, boss-man," she teased, "we'll see how married you are to that. I don't date businessmen, so I'll warn you ahead of time."

That was a clean cut and a blatant reminder as to why I don't get caught up with women. Period. Now, here I was playing some flirty game that was entirely out of character for me, but I liked this woman. She had no idea the businessman I was, but the reason I was heading to my estate in the country was proof I wouldn't let Mitchell and Associates run my life. I ran it.

"Do you enjoy nature?" I had to feel her out first.

"I do. I love to hike and explore, but I'm surrounded by historical buildings, and I can't seem to get enough."

"What if I proposed a visit to my estate in the countryside, in a historical building? If your sister is taking off for the next week?"

"Yeah, we leave in seven days. She's gone until we meet up the morning we fly out."

"Would you care to join me at my estate? It's in the countryside and has a lot of local history."

"It's crazy if I say yes, right?" she said. "Fuck it. The life that awaits me when I get off that plane in the states is even more insane." She took another sip of wine. "Let's do it."

I had no idea what had possessed me to bring her back to the small castle that I had renovated. I'd never taken anyone to this place except for the guys.

This woman was entertaining on the plane and put up with this crazy shit tonight. Why not have a fun companion at the estate? Her sister was leaving her, and she'd be alone. Might as well enjoy my reprieve with someone I thought would make me enjoy work from the estate.

Besides, it wouldn't be a romantic affair. The estate had my horses and stables, plenty of farm life, and more than enough grounds for her to explore. Perhaps she'd enjoy that on her visit. Maybe I was a good guy by helping out a woman I felt for in my own way.

The estate itself was large enough for her to get lost in and filled with collected artifacts and priceless pieces of history from monarchs that'd traveled through the area. I had no idea if she cared about history as much as I did, but it would at least entertain her, especially since she mentioned she'd been to Buckingham Palace three times. This girl was going to hate London without a proper tour. I think *Adelaile Castle* would be a fun adventure. If not, I'd kindly escort her back to the city she came to visit.

CHAPTER THREE

Avery

The previous night was by far the weirdest thing I'd ever experienced. My sister couldn't make it to dinner, fine. I was cool with it, but a bit annoyed, eating alone in a restaurant that was priced off the charts. There was no way I was going to make my sister pay to fill my never-ending appetite.

I was sitting there, contemplating leaving so that I could actually eat something. Don't get me wrong, though. The food was indescribably delicious. Still, if the handsome man from the plane hadn't shown up from out of thin air and taken me up on me being hungry enough to eat the entire menu, I probably would've left hungry and ended up at the first take-out spot I found.

I couldn't get pissed at my sister for her choice of restaurant. She ate like a bird, and I ate like a freaking lion. Whatever. I loved food, I loved eating it, and I wasn't the type to become satiated at the expensive restaurants. The obviously rich guy in his perfectly tailored Tom Ford suit got to see that side of me too. What could I say? Food was my weakness, and I was pretty sure that after I ate like a starved homeless person in front of the guy—that and spilling some of my pathetic life stories while tipsy on the plane—he was having second thoughts about inviting me to his place for a week.

I should've scared the poor bastard off already with my drunken-fool monologue about the bullshit my ex was putting me through, but I guess I didn't. My money was on the fact that the businessman was probably bored on one of his many trips to London. He ditched his crew of associates to have a change of atmosphere, and I gave him one.

"All right, I'm leaving," my sister, Britney, said. "This has been fun...and that Jim guy?" She chuckled as she brought me in for a hug. "If he takes you off to the country, I want to know everything when I get back."

I picked at the breakfast cakes that were brought up by room service. "Seriously," I said, shoving another bite of cake in my mouth, "don't you think I should be a bit more cautious, taking off with a random dude?"

"You said he was a businessman named Jim?" she asked, checking through her matched, Louis Vuitton luggage.

"Yep. Jim."

"Hmm." She pursed her red lips. "That doesn't help. Maybe a last name?"

"No last name. Just friends he had with him."

"Maybe I know their circle," she said.

My foster sister ran her own skincare line and had become a self-made millionaire almost overnight. A company had come in and acquired it, taking everything on, and now, she toured the world promoting it all—that's when she became the wealthy woman she was.

Unfortunately, we still had some trust issues. Her mom tried her best to raise me, but I certainly didn't make it easy on her. Between doing drugs with my surfer pals and running away to live in a bus in Santa Cruz for a few months, my credibility was shaky as far as she was concerned. That life was far behind me, but relationships were complicated, especially the family relationships that define us.

My sister had warned me about Derek, but I just couldn't seem to stay away from the bad boy. His hazel eyes and dark hair pulled me in, and his sense of humor and charisma kept me around for too long. I only wish he could've given up the drugs when I did. His drug use took the darkest turn imaginable, and he couldn't sober up or admit that he had a problem.

"Avery." She snapped her fingers to get my wandering attention. "Who were the friends?"

"Um, two guys. One had dark blond, slicked-back hair, like a younger version of Johnny Depp. I think his name was Collin or Alan?" I said, rubbing lotion on my legs. "I don't know. I just know Jim could afford every item off the menu at your fancy restaurant."

"Collin, Jim, and Alan?" She sighed, "Damn. It doesn't ring a bell. However," she smirked, "I'm sure you have nothing to worry about. I know how you eat when you insist we go to those pizza buffets, so you'll probably never see him again."

"Well, I definitely made for an expensive date." I laughed, adjusting the towel that was wrapped around my head.

"Well, if you take off with the guy, let me know where the hell you are, please?" she said, grabbing the room phone and pushing a button. "Yes, I need a valet to bring my luggage to the car, please."

"I'll text you when I get there," I said when she finished calling for the valet. "It couldn't be worse than me running away from home and living on the streets, could it?"

"Let's hope nothing will ever be that bad again." She flipped her unnaturally red hair over her shoulder. "The man is American, and from what you told me about your small interlude last night, he seems like a businessman who probably wants you as his kinky sex toy at this estate."

"Oh, God." I rolled my eyes. "He watched me eat last night, so I'd be surprised if he had any sexual desire for me at all."

She laughed. "Okay, I'm out. Call me, update me, and keep your tracker on that phone, whatever you do. We already talked about my opinions of how odd this is, but God knows with your rebellious streak that if I tell you not to do something, you're going to do it just to prove I'm overreacting."

"I wouldn't do that. I'm not a teenager anymore, you know. Part of me wants to take him up on his offer, not just because he's sort of funny and stupid-fucking-hot, but because I want a crazy-ass memory to take home with me."

"Even if it costs you your dignity and life?"

"I'm not an idiot," I said, standing firmly, backing my case.

"One day you'll learn, Avery. Just remember, you have Addy at home. Feel this man out for safety purposes before you act like you're not a single mom, okay?"

We hugged, she left, and her words started to weigh on me. *Am I a complete moron for considering this?* I was getting way too caught up in my vacation, and I wasn't thinking about the most important person in my life: my daughter.

It was such a refreshing feeling to be here and make an impulsive decision, thinking of no one but myself. I hadn't had that luxury since Addy was born, and feeling so careless and free was intoxicating.

Shit. I might as well go home now that I'm fucking thinking about Derek again. I did not doubt that son of a bitch would find a way to get his family to back him, getting a lawyer so he could take Addison from me. He wasn't going to quit.

My problem was that I'd given his ass too many chances. I was a fool. How could I allow that piece of shit around my daughter for as long as I did?

Coming home from work and finding him passed out on the couch while he was supposed to be watching our then one-year-old child was the final straw, although there should've been so many last straws that came before. That time, I couldn't overlook the five fucking cigarettes that had been lit at the wrong end, sitting on my burning gas stove while Addy was in her room, and he lay unconscious as my house was an inch away from burning down. He had been so out of his mind that he didn't even know he was lighting his cigarette backward—five times in a row.

That situation created a terrifying question for me: what if the authorities took my daughter and put her in the system because I left her in the care of her drug-addict father? I allowed him to live with us. *I* did that. But there was no way I was allowing Addison to grow up in the system as I did. Over my dead body.

I had to stop thinking. I came out here to get away and take a breath from it all. I was heading right back down my self-destructive road of feeling like a shitty mom for believing my ex and all of his manipulative lies.

I needed to get out. I brushed out my hair and dried it as quickly as I could. I slid on fleece-lined leggings and an oversized sweater and flats, grabbed my purse, and headed for the door. I didn't even check the clock or finish putting on my makeup. Just a touch of mascara, and now I was heading into this luxurious elevator, standing next to a gorgeous brunette wearing couture—nothing like fancy ladies in high fashion to make me feel like a self-loathing, country bumpkin.

As I exited on the ground level of the hotel lobby, I found a chair in a private corner of a lounge and pulled out my cell phone to dial my foster mom.

"Jill?" I said when she picked up.

"Hey, sweetie. I was just getting ready for bed. It's morning for you, right? Did Britney leave for the Netherlands yet?"

"Yeah, she did. Sorry if I'm interrupting you trying to get some sleep, but I need some reassurance," I said, knowing I could use some of her hippie advice with the way I was feeling.

"What's wrong?"

"Just worried about Addy and Derek."

"Don't worry about it." She chuckled. "Derek stopped by, but I gave him a piece of my mind. I called his parents too. They understand that Derek needs to stay away until after you get back. They miss her, but they get it."

"Thank God." I blew out a breath. "Okay. I'm going to try and enjoy the rest of the vacation. You'll call if you have any problems, right?"

"Always. I told you I would. Stop worrying, and go enjoy yourself."

"Okay, I'll let you go. Love you."

"Love you more, kiddo," she said as she ended the call.

I thought I'd feel a little better after talking to Jill, but I didn't. I didn't get a chance to work out my anxiety in the gym this morning, and now my nerves were wound up. After ending my stupid drug addiction seven years ago, I wouldn't go near pills of any kind, so instead of taking drugs for my anxiety, I worked out instead. Shit, I could probably have entered bodybuilding competitions for all the working out I did just to shake out my nerves.

I stood up, shouldered my purse, made a right out of the hotel, and speed-walked through the streets of London, not knowing where I was headed or when I'd stop. I needed to fucking run through a field of daisies or some happy shit like that. Instead, these historic buildings that once captivated all of my attention were starting to close in on me. *Fuck.* I was going to burst into tears if I didn't get these feelings shaken off.

A river, a beautiful flowing river. I walked toward it and stared into nature, pulling the water in different directions. The crowd surrounding me was becoming too much, so I pulled my hair into a ponytail. I was losing my shit, and there was no stopping it. Tears started streaming down my face as I twisted and turned to get out of there. I should have gotten up earlier. I should have started my morning off with a grueling workout. Instead, I didn't.

Once I was down the road away from the crowd, my heart rate finally slowed into a regular rhythm, and that's only because I was coming off of the adrenaline high my body spiked into for no reason. Well, there was a reason, but I usually dealt with it much better. This time, I let my nerves bring me to a level of a panic attack, and now I was sitting on a bench, staring out at the walkway, trying to reset my tired brain.

"Avery?" I heard a deep voice ask. "Hey," he said again.

I felt him sit next to me, but strangely, like last night, I knew this had to be a dream. This guy was stupid sexy, and stupid period if he was real and trailing me for no good reason. Talking to my ex on the phone should have scared him off, on top of the fact that I was a single mom. I couldn't get dates, and even if I did, the pricks usually only wanted sex. No guy in their right might would gladly take on a case like me. Not that I ever divulged my entire dark past to them. I learned from that and moved on.

Maybe that's why I had this slight breakdown, bringing up the ghosts of the person I no longer was. Those days were so far behind me. They were stories about another girl, in my opinion—not me. Today I let them get into my mind and mess with me. No more. I promised myself that.

"You're not here. You're seriously not here," I said, half delusional and half hysterical.

"Well, that's news to me," he said, and I jumped when I felt his hand on my back. "You okay?"

"Bad morning," I answered as I looked at him.

How do his shades make him look even hotter after covering up those emerald eyes?

"I'm guessing you didn't get the fill-up of breakfast you desired so greatly last evening?" he smirked.

I couldn't take my eyes off him. His lips were framed by his perfect face stubble that, after seeing him in his gray suit, I would have assumed he'd have shaved this morning. His jawline was perfectly defined—hell, the guy as a whole was perfectly defined.

"Why are you here?" I questioned the man sporting yet another bespoke suit. "I don't get why you give a damn about me. After my—"

He smiled and leaned his elbows on his knees, then looked back at me. "You intrigue me," he simply stated.

I laughed, loosening up at that answer. "You must be one massively burnt-out businessman. Either that or you live a boring life."

"Some say both."

"Some?" I leaned back, more relaxed by the presence of this man, who seemed to exude power and confidence. "What do *you* say? You know, about being so obviously bored with life that you've taken some bizarre interest in me?"

"I say it's about time I opened my eyes to the world around me and do what I do best."

"What is it you do best, Jim?"

"She remembers my name." He chuckled and leaned back, stretching his arm on the bench behind my back. My eyes widened at the sight of his black leather shoes when he crossed one leg over the other.

"You made an impression on me last night. I won't lie. The way to my heart is through my stomach."

"Good to know," he answered. "And to answer your question, what I do best is going after something I want and securing it no matter how difficult that may be."

"Spoken like a true businessman."

"I'm more than that." He smiled.

"Doubt that," I teased.

"Well, if you've decided to take me up on my offer, I could prove that to you."

"Offer?"

"Staying with me at my place in the country."

"Right," I answered. "And how do I know you're not going to tie me up in a dungeon or something?"

"A dungeon?" He laughed a light and humored laugh that did something to my insides. "You, Avery, have been locked in the dark ages of London's history for too long. Two trips to hear the haunted voices of the princes who were locked away in that tower," he pointed back at the Tower of London that I'd ended up at, "tells me you need to learn the more current events of this fine country."

"Ah, so where's this place you have? Does it have cell service?"

"You'll be able to call your daughter in the states at any time, so long as you keep in mind the time difference, of course."

I let out a breath. "I've done some crazy shit in my life, and considering this idea might be up there with that."

"You don't have to come." He smiled sympathetically at me. "I will say this, though: if you enjoy nature, that place has it all. I will mostly be working from my study and out of your way. There will also be plenty of food," he said, and I could tell he was looking at my still tear-stained cheeks. "Up to you."

"Fine," I said, meeting his eyes with a little determination. "And if I need to get back here earlier than expected?"

"Then I'll personally drive you back."

"Personally?"

"Yeah, I have a driver." He cringed. "Is that a total turn-off?"

I laughed. "No. Somewhat geeky, I guess, but not a complete turn-off. Glad you value my opinion, though."

"As I said, I'm intrigued by you. That could be another turn-off, couldn't it?"

"Possibly, but only because I think you've lost your mind." I sighed and discreetly rubbed the back of my fingers over my cheek, making sure there weren't any lingering tears. "I am not afraid to state the obvious when I say that you could get any girl in the UK, and here you are somehow intrigued by me, of all people."

"I'll take that as a compliment," he answered. "And while you offered me one, I'll offer you one as well. I'm quite picky when it comes to the people with whom I like to keep my company. And here I am, begging to learn more about you and bringing you out of the city with me."

"That is quite the compliment. However, there's not too much to learn about me. Just an average gal, dealing with constant bullshit."

"Perhaps that's your opinion. I believe a woman like you has a better story than you give yourself credit for."

"A lot to assume since we just met, sir."

"Jim," he corrected me.

"Jim." I smiled.

"And since it is our fifth anniversary, I'd like to bring my wife to the house in the country."

"Where she'll be neglected while her husband works?"

He laughed, and I watched his eyebrow rise above his aviator sunglasses. "The last thing I would want is for my beautiful bride to be neglected."

"Make sure the fridge is full, and we have a deal. I had a partial city-life breakdown before you showed up, so I'm down for some of England's gorgeous countryside."

"And my dungeon, of course."

"Depends on what you plan on doing with me in your dungeon."
Shit. Too far. That was messed up.

He laughed that laugh again. "She loves food and the dark, kinky stuff. It looks like I might fear the dungeon of the old place."

"What time do we leave? I left all my shit at the hotel, and I have nothing on me."

"I disagree, you have too much clothing on you." He smirked.

"Flirting with me?"

"Perhaps. Hopefully, it's not too geeky for you."

"It's a good look on you." I stood, him following directly behind me. "I need to head back that way."

"Which hotel? I'll have my driver take us there," he said as he slid his hands into his pockets.

"The most expensive one in town. Forgot the name."

"I think I know where you're staying," he said, his tone drier now. "I have an old friend staying there. You won't mind if I wait in the car while you get your things?"

"Nope. Where's this driver at, Mr. Fancy?"

So I was going to stay in the country with some stranger, some very hot stranger who had a driver. The man oozed wealth, so why should I be surprised? Either way, after having a panic attack, I did need to get out into the country.

Maybe for once in my life, something would go well. I wasn't going to let this slip away. Most girls wouldn't do this shit—but most girls weren't me and hadn't been through the shit I had. I could handle myself with this man. If not, the self-defense classes I'd been taking since leaving Derek would be put to good use.

CHAPTER FOUR

Avery

$\mathcal{I}$ sat in awe in the back of the Rolls Royce as a blacked-out Mercedes SUV trailed us while leaving the city. Jim mentioned that his job prompted extra security, which made me wonder who the hell the man could possibly piss off in this line of work.

The men in suits who worked for Jim looked and acted like secret agents. Still, while I listened in on their conversations, I realized it was all reasonably casual and proper talk. I concluded that Jim must have just been some rich guy who was probably used to having superfluous things at his disposal, like a security detail. I didn't know about life as a socialite or a debutant or whatever-the-fuck you called living a lifestyle like this. Don't think I wasn't going to ask more questions, though.

For now, I was in a world of wonder, staring out at England's vast countryside of lime green rolling hills, rolling on into the cobalt horizon.

"Damn," I said while Jim had his head buried in his phone. "You're totally missing out on this."

He smiled while tapping away on his phone. "Stunning, isn't it?"

"Hey," I said with a laugh of disbelief, "do you live in that device? Planning on fully kidnapping me and throwing me in that black SUV behind us?"

He pulled his sunglasses off, and his green eyes seemed annoyed, yet somewhat amused with my interruption. "Planning out your kidnapping is quite exhausting," he said, then stopped while his eyes followed mine when we reached a village that belonged in a storybook.

I covered my mouth, completely overtaken by this scene. "Wow," I said in a breath of astonishment.

Jim's eyes locked with mine, and his expression tightened in an unusual, yet attractive way. "You're right," he said. "I have been missing the views."

The car slowed through the village, and now I was torn between staring at Jim's beautiful face and the cozy town we traveled through. "Where are we?" I asked, knowing I couldn't peel my eyes away from his endearing expression.

"Bibury," he said. "My place is out between Cotswolds and Gloucestershire. There is a ton of history here and a lot from the Tudor era. It's what makes this village so noteworthy, in my opinion. I love being out here whenever I come to London. It's almost as if time stops."

"Time can't stop so long as your phone keeps dinging." I smirked. "God dang, you are a burnt-out businessman, aren't you?"

"I just don't have a life." He chuckled. "Should I be bold and shut it off?"

I pinched my lips together. I didn't even know the guy, and I could tell the idea of shutting off the phone was like me losing Addison to Derek. "I'd rather you not die of a heart attack. Keep the thing on." I shrugged while looking out my window. "It's not breaking my heart."

"True," he answered. "However, I didn't bring you all this way to abandon you completely."

"Hey, it's your life, not mine. If that phone is what gives you the luxury of actually owning a place out in fairytale land, do what you gotta do."

"Hey." I turned at the change in his low and assertive voice as he spoke into his phone. "Yeah, turning in now. Listen, I'm going off the grid for a while. You got everything while I take a breather for a few hours?"

I watched his right hand as he ticked each finger against the tip of his thumb. Must be a nervous tick. I didn't mean to force the man to shut it down. I still had no idea what he did, but between the Rolls Royce, the bodyguards, and the thousand-dollar dinner bill, it all pointed to this man either having been born into wealth or, like my sister, he hustled up his money the hard way. The only difference between him and Britney was that he obviously made quite a bit more money than she did.

Must be fucking nice. The only rise to wealth I was experiencing was living on the second floor of my apartment, which I needed to move out of. I could live here easily. Addy running through those hills chasing those sheep? I laughed at the vision of that.

"Something funny?" Jim asked.

I looked over at him. "Just imagining my three-year-old running down those sheep."

"You miss her?"

"Hell yes." I smiled. "Maybe I'll get lucky and hit the lotto so I can bring her here, and we'll live with the sheep."

"Why would you care to live among the sheep if you have money to live in one of these adorable cottages?"

"You're too literal." I smiled, but then covered my mouth when the driver turned onto a long driveway, and we were traveling back in time to a massive estate. "Jesus Christ, is that the house from *Downton Abbey*?" I asked as I took in the sprawling estate...home...castle? Whatever the hell this place was, it sat imposingly on groomed lawns with a fountain as the centerpiece while a river wound down to the left of the area. This was in a world of its own.

"No, it's not *Downton Abbey*." He laughed. "That was filmed at another location. I've turned down quite a few offers because I prefer the privacy of the place and don't want it to have any publicity. You wouldn't believe it, but all of those gray stones that make up the house were nearly in ruins when I determined I wanted to keep this place and bring it back to life when I inherited it."

"Jesus Christ," I said as we stopped, and the staff walked out to meet us. "Sorry, change of subject, but are you serious? Is this place real? Are those butlers?"

He smiled and opened his door. "They're the ones who keep this place alive. Why they feel the need to walk out to greet me, I don't know. I don't request it, but they do it every single time. It is quite an honor, though."

"God dang, Jim, you're like a king in some castle out here."

"As I said, time appears to stand still when I come to visit the countryside. I do hope you enjoy a little history as I worked to keep this home as close to that as I could."

I stepped out of the car and suddenly felt like there was no way I belonged here. Or with him or anywhere near something this endearing.

"You hungry?"

Mind-switch. "Starved," I said. "Is food awaiting us, kind sir?"

"More food than what was presented on the menu."

"I could easily move in here. In fact, maybe I will let you kidnap me."

He chuckled. "Well, my phone is off, and my friend, Alex, is taking all of my business until further notice. So, I believe I can plan it thoroughly now."

"Funny," I said, walking up stone steps, watching the gentlemen take our luggage out of the trunk for us in disbelief. "Does everyone always do shit like that for you?"

He smirked as we walked into the house. "It's no worse than having a bellhop handle my belongings at a hotel, is it?"

"Guess not," I answered, fully engrossed in the era I felt I was thrown into by this place. "Oh my God. This place is like a museum."

"I'm happy you approve. Perhaps it will add to the sites of London I stole you away from?"

"That and then some. Never thought I'd be sleeping in one of these grand, historical places." I followed him up the carpeted steps, looking at portraits from another time that lined the walls as we climbed up. "Did the house come with this? Do you really own this place?"

"It was my grandfather's estate at one time, and mainly just a pile of old stones and a home that was deteriorating. My grandfather had intentions to renovate it once, but he never had the funding, I imagine. After he passed, I found the blueprints and questioned my father about our family having a place in England." We turned and walked up another story to this home. "My dad brought my brother and me out here after my mom left." He stopped and smiled at a portrait of hunters on horseback with dogs running alongside the horses. "I guess I fell in love with the potential. I told my dad that if he didn't renovate it as my grandfather had tried, I would."

"And so, you most definitely did."

"I believe I would have lost interest if it weren't for my dad saying it was a mere fantasy to take on something this monumental. I spent my vacations from school out here, helping with the carpentry myself."

"You flew out to help build this castle?"

"I lived out here while I attended Oxford."

That's when I knew this man was most likely born into his wealth. "Oxford, huh? As in the prestigious Oxford University?"

"Graduated first in my class. Damn American," he said in a dramatic voice. "That's what my UK friends say anyway." He laughed as he opened double doors to what could've been the fucking queen's bed chambers. He looked at me as I took in this room that had a bed bigger than I'd ever seen, "My friend Alex attended with me, graduating behind me. That pissed them off too, but after a few drinks at the pub, all was well again."

"So, you are crazy smart, went to a prestigious college, and strapped on a tool belt?"

Okay, this small gesture he hit me with more than once last night

—the tight smile while biting the inside of his cheek—it was sexy as hell. I already knew he was overwhelmingly handsome, but he had these expressions that made me want to impulsively kiss him more than once while I ate last night. He's lucky the food was a fantastic distraction.

"I don't like limits, and if there's a challenge, I rise to it. I also hate failing on any level."

"No wonder why you're in the businessman life. Careful of that, I saw you with your phone. That thing will have you failing at actual life if you're not careful."

"How so?" he said as the men brought in my luggage. "How can I fail by using my phone to keep me from being a prisoner behind office walls? It helps me get out and do things."

"Well, it's a matter of perspective, I guess. I'm not one to judge, and I'm not running a business. I can say, though, that by watching you stare at the phone for an hour and a half straight, it seems like you're in more of a prison than you think. It might be a virtual one, but you're confined nonetheless."

His face grew somber, and his eyes raptly studied mine. It was so intense that I had to look away, a bit embarrassed that I'd overstepped my bounds. "You can send me back to London if I'm pissing you off," I tried to tease.

His lips subtly pulled up on one side. "Why would you believe you pissed me off?"

"The look you're giving me," I said.

"Far from that." His expression recovered, "I'm sorry. Sometimes when I'm lost in thought, I believe I have my old man's expression. It looks like I'm irritated or angry, I think."

"Resting bitch face, huh?" I folded my arms. "Well, now I want to know what you were thinking."

"Yeah, a resting bitch face," he said, amused by my response. "Well, I was thinking that you keep surprising me. This might sound horribly conceited, but no woman has ever called me out on anything. I've never met a woman who was so genuine and authentic before."

"Well, I'm not afraid of you, if that's what you're getting at."

"Perhaps you should be."

"Gonna throw me in the dungeon?" I arched my eyebrow at him.

He laughed, slicing through this weird tension we'd created. "I might."

"Can I eat something before you get all medieval on me?"

"Lunch. Yes, right." He ran his hand through his hair. "Okay, quick tour. This is your room; do you approve?"

"Yes. I more than approve, and I might ask you to hire me so I can live here and keep the place up with all of those people who greeted us when we got here."

He grinned. "Well, they've been dismissed to vacation while I'm here, so I would never see you if I visited if I were to hire you on as Adelaile staff. I simply can't hire you."

"Damn shame," I said. "Food?"

"What are you up for eating? Everything is stocked and ready for me to be your personal chef during your stay."

"I could eat a cow."

He grinned and turned to guide me out of the room. "Let's see what I can pull off."

While I sat across the stone kitchen island, watching Jim chop vegetables like a top chef, I rested my chin on my palm, watching him throw pieces of cut meat into a sauté pan on the gas stove that was built into the island in front of me.

"So, what's your story, Jim?" I asked, watching him with adoration as he stood there with his sleeves rolled up and his tie thrown over his shoulder, and the most delicious aromas wafted up from that pan.

"My story?" he questioned, pulling out a pot, filling it with water, and placing it on another burner.

"Yeah," I said. "Sitting here and watching you cook is swiftly turning you into my dream guy."

He glanced up at me and smiled. "Do you like raw vegetables?"

"I'll eat anything right now."

He laughed that sexy-ass laugh, and my heart skipped a beat when he sliced off a piece of a yellow carrot and held it over to my lips. His thick eyebrow arched, his close-lipped smile popped a dimple in his cheek, and I opened my mouth slower than expected for the bite.

My eyes widened while I chewed on the carrot, shocked that it was sweeter and juicier than any carrot I'd ever tasted.

"My God," I said. "That's the best carrot I've ever tasted. It's juicy as fuck!"

His eyes glistened in humor, "We grow our vegetables out in the gardens. And yes, I enjoy their juicy as fuck flavors myself."

"Raw and unhinged juicy flavors," I pressed.

"Most definitely juicy, raw, and unhinged," he said, dumping his cut vegetables into the steamer-pot he had on the stove.

"Food can be a very sexual thing, you know?" I advised him with a laugh.

"I'm learning that swiftly by your reaction to a carrot alone." He chuckled, turning to wash his hands at the sink.

Damn. Nice ass, too. This was the first time I got a good look at his firm, sexy ass through his slacks. The suit jacket was off, and nothing but a fine-looking butt was on display for me.

"So, you asked what my story is," he said, drying his hands off. "I run a business. I was given sound advice today that even though I believed the phone to be a way to disconnect me from the chains of that business, it still holds me prisoner, and I love retreating to the country when I'm in England. I love it out here, but being that some decisions for the company need to be approved by only me, I have to be in constant communication even while trying to escape. I do my best, though. The phone is still off."

"Don't do that just for me," I said. "Honestly, sometimes I think and speak without giving much thought to things. I probably insulted you, and you're just too nice to tell me."

He worked with his sauté pan. "I don't get insulted. Unless I suck in bed, of course." He winked and then held the spoon up for me to taste. "Blow on it."

Getting strangely turned on by watching him cook, seeing his ass, and hearing his underhanded way of bringing sex into this, I licked my lips and then took a bite. All I could do was roll my eyes and moan in response to the tender, flavorful meat and the onions that he'd caramelized.

"Holy hell," he said. "Your moans are telling me—"

"That I'm having a *food-gasm?*" I swallowed the bite, and he laughed.

"New term, I like it," he said, turning to grab plates. "We might have to eat in separate rooms if you're going to make those sounds while eating."

"Let me help you with the plates," I said, coming around the counter. "Funny how I love food more than anything, but I can't cook worth a damn."

"Well, I'll make it my mission to teach you the art of cooking while you're here."

"That's if I make it through eating this without moaning through every bite."

"If you think moaning over my cooking is going to end you, trust me, I can make you moan over much more enticing things."

"Back to sex talking?"

"You're the one whose moaning is making it difficult for me to cook. My curiosity has piqued as to if I could beat your food-gasm sounds with something even more pleasurable."

"Yeah, hard to beat the food, buddy."

I had to feel him out. Was I only out here for his rich-boy, kinky fun? Not that I would be pissed about that. The dude was gorgeous, and I could only imagine what it would be like to sleep with him. I wondered if it would be like with Derek—when he actually could get it up—or the selfish assholes before him. It was never about me with any of them.

I hadn't had sex since before Addy was born, so there was the whole beggars/choosers aspect to the situation as well. Would I take this Jim guy up on using me for a week of sexual pleasure? Why not? I just hoped I was still good at it.

CHAPTER FIVE

Jim

$\mathcal{L}$ ast night was more of a get comfortable night, I believe, for both Avery and me. I felt strange ditching my connection to the company, European and American-based offices, but when I reconnected with Alex during my late night and his afternoon, all was fine. In fact, we both determined it might work for me to have a few days of not being glued to a phone or computer. I could check-in during the evenings when I felt Avery was okay with me disappearing, and if there were anything important to handle, Alex would contact me on my other personal line. The line that wasn't connected to my email or business.

God only knew how I'd handle this disconnect. I was a control freak with that company, and even though I knew that Alex could run it well, I had my concerns about pulling back like this. I didn't honestly know why I felt compelled to take this time away from work. I wasn't burnt out, but Avery had brought to my attention the fact that

I was chained down by the phone whether I was inside the office or outside, and fuck it if she wasn't right.

It was why I didn't have a life. It's why I had a driver take me everywhere, and it's definitely why I wouldn't be able to learn jack-shit else about this woman who seemed to lighten me up when I was around her. So, that was it. I was checking out, taking a mini-vacation, and actively trying to get to know this woman who'd captured my attention.

My morning sprint came to a halt when I spotted her, running on one of the hills. She seemed to stop at the same time I did, and we both jogged through the meadow of my hundred-plus acre estate.

"Did a ghost chase you out of the house?" I asked with a smile, catching my breath.

She laughed, leaning over on her knees. "Why would you ask that?" She turned her head up and squinted at me, smiling.

I loved her sexy, scratchy voice. "I believe it was you who called me a poor host to allow you to sleep alone in what you believed was a haunted room?"

She rose and laughed again. "That was the booze talking."

"And to think, I almost fell for it and took advantage of you while under the influence."

"Well, I wasn't that drunk. I might have been half-serious in wanting more than just your badass cooking."

Fuck me. "Don't tempt me." I smiled. "As I said, I hate to fail, and to fail in my new role as a host would piss me off."

"You're too much, Jim."

"Seriously, though." I looked around at the morning sun, spreading its light over the peaceful land. "What are you doing out at seven in the morning?"

"I was up at six, and I took off for a run if you couldn't tell by the sight of me." She looked around. "It could be the best morning run I've had in my life."

"Looks like morning runs are another thing I'll be sure to join you on."

"Yeah, of course. I'd like that."

"Here," I said, leading us over to a walnut tree. "There's nothing like experiencing a sunrise in the country."

We sat next to the tree, and I reclined against it.

"So," she said, not feeling ashamed to sit on the grass and dirt next to me. "I wonder what the history is with all this land. Like, if you could put on binoculars and travel back into time and see what was happening out in those fields."

"Time-traveling binoculars?" I chuckled.

"Why not?" She shrugged. "You look through them and see what was taking place during a certain period in time."

"Which time-period would you wish to look out and see on those lands?"

"They mentioned Henry the Eighth reigned in the 1500s; was he out here?"

I smiled. "Of all England's history, you seem to be fascinated by the tyrant King Henry the Eighth, eh?"

"Well, I think he wasn't horrible in the beginning," she said. "He just turned awful at the end."

"He wasn't horrible before or after he sent his first wife away in shame?" I smirked.

"I'm looking through my historical binoculars," she looked pointedly out to the lush hills. "It's the year 1500 and Henry," she pulled her lips up on one side and grinned—a grin so cute I wanted to capture it with my own lips, "sent his first wife away."

"Very well, then." I softly laughed. "Henry would have been young and fit, and since he enjoyed taking his court with him in his travels, he would have most likely been in your binoculars of time travel, enjoying a morning ride with his lover, Anne Boleyn."

"So fucking cool," she said. "You really think that?"

I laughed. "Who knows? I am merely assuming, but he was all over the countryside. He fled the city on numerous occasions to leave the chaos, to dodge the plague, or, more importantly, to flaunt his health and wealth to his people. He was a notorious show-off."

"Health and wealth. I like that." She looked back from where she sat up in front of me and touched her finger to my chest. "Sorta like you."

"Do not compare me to Henry the Eighth." I laughed.

"I'm comparing you to his young, healthy, and happy years."

"Awe, that makes it all the better. Even better for you keeping your head on your shoulders," I said with a wink.

She relaxed against the tree. "Do you have family out here? Or in the states?"

"Maybe it's best we put the time-traveling binoculars back on and search for another monarch."

"Answer the question, King Henry." She laughed.

If it weren't for her bold and adorable way of speaking to me, I would have clamped my mouth shut on something I'd never shared with anyone outside of my close friends and what my family knew.

"My father passed away after I graduated from college," I said.

"Oh, God." She covered her mouth. "I'm sorry. You look like you're maybe about five years out of college. Was it recently? I'm so sorry."

"Ten years now." I smiled. "It's okay. His legacy lives on well through the business he started. My brother and I have done everything we can to honor him through our actions. I think, hopefully, he would be proud of us."

"And your mom?"

"I don't speak that woman's name." The words came out harsher than I expected they would. "Sorry, I didn't mean to snap. She was and still is a nightmare at times. Jake, my younger brother, was too young to remember when she was physically abusive and brought drug-addict dickheads into our house, so I'm the one who got stuck with that."

"That's awful," she said, her eyes wide. "I'm really sorry. You both were young, then. Just you and your brother?"

"Yeah. I was seven, and Jake was five. I'm glad Jake didn't remember her as I did. Thank God my dad put us before everything. He had a surveillance system secretly installed and caught her fucking druggies in our home, forcing Jake and me to stay outside until she got her goddamn drugs and whatever the fuck else she wanted. It was a nightmare." I shook my head. "Sorry about that. I never speak about her to anyone, not even to my brother. She's a piece of shit, and I should've left it at that."

"Is that why you took the phone from me on the plane? I'm guessing you must've heard me mention Derek being an addict?"

"I heard enough to be reminded of a horrible parent with a poor kid involved to want to intervene impulsively. Again, I'm sorry I did that, and if it does cause you further issues with your ex, I'll be sure to give you my private number, and I'll help in any way you need."

"Derek's all talk," she said, but I could tell he was a lot more than that. I wasn't pressing, though. "I do appreciate what you did."

"I'm glad for that." I stood. "How about breakfast in the little town you appeared to be enamored with before we arrived here?"

"The storybook town?"

"Yes," I said, turning to walk toward home. "It's a lovely village, and after losing my shit about my dirt bag mother, I think you might need a cleansing that only the peace in that town can offer."

"Give me a break." She leaned against me as an old friend would, and I loved the gesture. "I get it. I'm just sorry you and your brother went through that. You had a great father to get her out of your life."

"Just like you're an amazing mom for working on getting an addicted parent out of your daughter's life."

"Don't go that far. In Derek's opinion, I'm the same piece of shit you see in your mom." She laughed.

"If *only* Derek's opinion were of any value to me." I smirked, prompting her sexy little giggle to lighten up the demons of my past I'd brought into play.

I needed to slow down, I was getting too close, and it was just through simple conversation with a woman I enjoyed.

CHAPTER SIX

Avery

*J*im brought me into the most adorable town, and I was at a loss for words. I couldn't speak for nearly twenty minutes as he trailed me, walking along the banks of the stream. Across from it were the most adorable stone houses. This place wasn't like anywhere I'd ever been.

"That's Arlington Row," Jim finally spoke. "That honey-colored stone is remarkable, isn't it?"

"It's all so beautiful. The mallard ducks." I chuckled. "Everything."

"We can continue, or perhaps you're hungry?"

I covered my stomach with my hand. "Wow, I think I forgot about food for once in my life."

"A small village steals her interest from food, and here I thought I could somehow do that."

"Flirting again?"

A mob of tourists—like myself—flocked over the short bridge Jim and I wound up on while I cruised through the area, taking in nature.

Jim seemed to grab my hand instinctively, and the romantic feel of this place had me falling into this gesture without reservation.

His steady hand sent some crazy vibes into my energy field through the contact alone. I smiled up at him and intertwined our fingers. "I thought you'd never bring romance into our special anniversary," I said after he gently closed his long fingers around my hand and looked at me in confusion.

"Forgive me, darling," he said after a man who was occupied with his camera shoved me into Jim. "Fucking tourists."

"You know I'm a tourist myself." I eyed this new expression I hadn't seen him wear. It was like the badass who hid behind the kind man surfaced, and anyone who met that gaze would end up in trouble. "Jesus."

"What's that?" he said in a low voice.

I tugged on his hand and pulled him off to the side. I couldn't resist but to stand on my toes and run my hands on his face. "You look like you're about to go scorched earth on someone out here."

His hardened expression softened, and I could swear I heard him softly sigh as if I'd exorcised a demon that hid inside, and I just hadn't met that side yet.

"Sorry," he said, his eyes turning back in the direction where it seemed a circus of people had shown up. "It pisses me off when people can't be considerate of others."

"I'm cool with it. Or are you the over-protective husband in this little game we're playing?"

His face contorted into a softer look. "Let's go eat." He seemed to force a smile on his face. "The lack of manners from those individuals is enough to drive me mad."

"Drive you mad?" I teased with a dramatic expression. We started walking toward another path, no longer holding hands, which sort of sucked. It felt nice to have that moment, but if the guy had anger issues, I'd rather push him a little to see what he'd do. It might not be the smartest move, but I preferred to know what I was dealing with sooner than later.

Jim surprisingly grinned. "Mad. You know, insane," he said.

"Yes, I do know insane. Maybe you're just detoxing from the phone. I haven't seen you on it since before we left the house, um, I mean castle?"

Jim shook his head and ran a hand through his hair. "Maybe that's the problem. I'm a bit of a control freak, and I'm sort of wondering if my business is falling apart by now."

"Is it a small, big, or massive-ass company that's worrying you?"

"It doesn't matter the size," he said as I tried to keep up with his long strides. "Things can go south with just a text, call, fax, or email."

"In three goddamn hours?"

He tightened his lips, and I saw the corners of his eyes crinkle in humor. "It could happen in three goddamn seconds." He arched an eyebrow at me.

"So, it's sort of like the bullshit that swings my way at any time with my druggie ex?"

"Possibly," he said. "Shit can go sideways, and it could be happening at this very moment while we walk up to this restaurant."

"Why don't you tell your driver to come to get you before the world collapses? I was only trying to give you a hard time, but it seems like you're not having a good day." I eyed him curiously. "Seriously, I'm not about to ruin this trip because of a guy who can't let work go for a few hours."

"Really?" He leveled me with a stare that made me take a step back.

I met him with a look of my own. "Really." I raised both eyebrows. "You don't have to stop everything you're doing to keep me entertained. I have enough money to get back to London. I certainly don't want to hang out with someone who's so stressed out that they're going to act like a kill-joy."

I watched him roll his tongue over his teeth behind his tight lips. "So, that's that, then?"

"I guess so."

"A divorce, and you're going to take half the company, I'm sure?"

I looked at him with wide eyes. "I'll take ninety percent."

I could see the smile he'd been trying to hide since the mocking started. "All over a fight about my phone habits?"

"The sex sucks too," I said.

Jim closed his eyes and worked to keep his smile away. I was cooling it because people were starting to take notice of us.

"The sex sucks?" he questioned much louder than I expected.

I glanced around, smiling uncomfortably. "Just drop it."

"How can I drop something that you were begging me for last night?"

Fuck. Jim, I mouthed with a smile of disbelief. "We're done here." I tried to diffuse him, though trying not to laugh now.

"Yeah, that's what I thought," he continued. "That's not the real issue here is it?"

"The real issue is, you're causing a scene," I said, eying the people sitting on the terrace with surprised eyes trying to conceal their own laughter and smiles.

"I disagree. You see, the real issue is that we're on our honeymoon, and you just declared that sex with me sucks."

Damn this guy. "The sex is nonexistent," I went for broke.

"Nonexistent?" He bit the inside of his cheek. "Well, it's not my fault you have had a goddamn headache since our wedding night."

"Hey, I told you not to take all that fucking Viagra, but I guess your performance issues got the best of you that night."

Jim licked his lips and that dark look—the one that made him look like a frightening badass, and one I never wanted to be on the other end of if he meant it—was back. "Well, if I hadn't found out you were screwing my brother, maybe I wouldn't have tried to overdose on his Viagra."

"Screwing your brother?" I laughed and couldn't keep this up anymore. "Can we eat something?"

"Not until you admit right here and now that I don't have performance issues, my darling bride."

"I think you have psychological issues," I said. "Let's get the hell out of here."

I walked past Jim, knowing lunch was definitely not going to happen at that place. Jim's heavy steps were behind me, and I couldn't help but burst into laughter and turn back to him.

"Hopefully you're not too upset with me," he said with a laugh of his own.

"I'm definitely taking half of your damn business, my darling husband, if you don't make up for the lunch you just shot to hell."

"Performance issues, eh?"

I planted my hands on my hips. "That one seems to have stuck with you. Is there a performance problem, Jim?" I teased.

"First of all," he said, his hand catching mine and pulling me against him. "Going back to what started our roleplaying; I'm not upset, but I'm sorry I let those tourists piss me off. I get annoyed easily toward rude individuals who selfishly push others around. You almost fell into the stream when that asshole shoved you."

"I can swim." I smiled up at his softer features. "Your phone problems? The company going to hell in less than three seconds? What's your reasoning for being obviously pissed about that?"

He grinned. "At first, I was responding with irritation because I do feel that way."

"And the reason you led me to believe I was ready to get my ass back to London?"

"That was all you." He smirked. "Talking about my business going south without the phone? I was merely riding on the fact that you were bringing up an excellent point. I'm too attached to all of it." He released my hand. "Then, the next thing I know, you're done and ready to bail on me."

"Your pissed-off expression helped motivate my bailing on your ass."

He stepped closer to me. "If I were angry with you," he swept my hair away from my neck, and my eyes couldn't leave his if I let them, "you would know."

Our closeness, his eyes, and the way his voice was so smooth when he lowered it? I felt my adrenaline spike in an exciting way. He was painfully beautiful and he held an expression that made me numb everywhere, except for between my legs. That part of my body was reacting with anticipation for more and feeding that hunger right to my brain.

Just when I got it under control, Jim pulled me even closer. He smelled intoxicatingly delicious.

I locked eyes with his emerald ones as his thumb grazed along the side of my neck. "The one thing I find more than attractive about you is the way you naturally don't give a fuck. I haven't met anyone like you. I do want you to know that there's something you mentioned that drives me crazy, though."

"And what's that?" I asked, my voice hoarser than it should have been.

"You said my expression made you want to leave."

"Yeah, you looked like you wanted me to leave if I'm honest."

"It drives me crazy when someone is disturbed by an expression I don't realize I have."

"Does it drive you crazy? Or does it drive you mad?" I mocked his wording from earlier.

"It drives me mad," he teased. "I deal with this daily at work. My expressions tend to concern or worry those I work with."

"Then don't give a scorched-earth look, Terminator, and I won't think you're in a miserable mood."

"Scorched-earth look?"

"Yeah, you're the most attractive guy I've ever met, and even your pissed off expressions make you look like an attractive badass. So, the best way to call it is your scorched-earth look."

He laughed and shook his head. "Fine. No more scorched-earth looks toward you."

"Or innocent people who threaten to knock me off a small bridge."

"They were assholes, Avery."

"I can decide for myself if people are pissing me off." I smiled at him.

His lips closed, and the last thing I expected was a raindrop to hit my nose, and Jim's hands to come up to each side of my face. "Very well, then. I've overstepped my bounds."

Just when I'd pulled myself back together, I was once again putty in his hands. "It was nice of you to care," I said, another raindrop falling on my face, but now I was lost in Jim's eyes. "But, again, you looked too pissed off for comfort."

"You remember when I said when I go after something I want, I won't stop until I get it?"

"Yeah?" I responded, remembering him saying something like that from our thousand-dollar-menu date.

"You're what I want. I haven't felt this way about a woman...ever," he said, eyes studying mine. "I believe I became too territorial."

"You mean jealous?"

"Either one." He smirked. "Damn, I'm truly sorry."

"Don't apologize. You made it fun when you realized you were an ass."

"You helped me realize that quite quickly. I admire you in more ways than one. I love your spicy spirit. If anyone went scorched earth, I believe you did when you put my stubborn ass into its place."

We both remained silent, more raindrops falling and threatening to ruin what I was hoping for. If this guy was sort of falling for me, then he'd better be impulsive and act.

"Damn it, kiss me, or get us out of this rain," I said, not knowing what he wanted but this closeness had me aching to feel his lips on mine.

"Kiss you?" he said.

"You heard me. We just had our first fight. We're apparently back in time by five years and on our honeymoon instead of anniversary and—"

My lips were silenced when Jim's covered my bottom one gently, and with some sort of passion that surprised me. I watched his eyes close as his lips gently massaged against mine. There was nothing crazy or intense about this kiss. What had me spinning—my head was actually fuzzy with intoxication—was the way he gently covered my lips with his own. Like two long-lost lovers reunited and savoring the beauty of the moment of their kiss, unifying them again.

My hands held his elbows as I worked to encourage more from him. Jim's lips parted, and his tongue swept gently into my mouth. I met his kiss with more urgency than he started it with. The rain began falling harder, and Jim pulled me in tighter and tilted his head, kissing me with more power and aggression than before. Holy shit, I had never been kissed this perfectly before. The man had class and a beauty that filled his entire aura, and this perfect kiss proved to me that I wanted more from him.

He ended the kiss and pulled me in tightly to him. That's when I felt how hard he was, and, Jesus Christ, how much more I wanted to have him inside me now.

"Well, well," I said, brushing my wet hair out of my eyes. "Sorry about the performance comment. That definitely shouldn't be a joke."

Jim laughed. "It's all my brother's Viagra." He pressed his lips to mine again. "I've wanted to do that since the moment you sat next to me on the plane."

"You're kidding, right?"

"I'm dead serious. The minute you caught my attention, I was at your mercy."

"Wait." The rain was pouring now, and I didn't want it to interfere with this revelation. "You mean you would have..." I bit my bottom lip.

"Yes, I should have taken you up on your offer to fuck you on that plane, but I was a jackass and too proper."

"And now, here we are. Out in the country, getting soaked—a second chance?"

"I'm hoping it moves that direction. Until then, you're going to ditch my ass and head back to London if I don't make up for lunch? Come on. I have a better pub you'll enjoy just the same, and I'll even order the whole menu if that's what works to make it all up to you."

"That kiss is holding me over," I said as we both jogged through puddles, seeking some form of shelter. "God, it's coming down."

"It's England. Awesome, isn't it?"

You're awesome, I thought, still enamored about the kiss, his personality, and the fact that I couldn't be mad at any of this. Even if he was pissed about the asshole who'd shoved us, that was cool—it showed his no-bullshit side, and I liked it.

I could take care of myself, but I imagined how Derek would've reacted in that same situation. Even if he weren't high—for some strange reason—he wouldn't have even noticed, much less gave a damn.

I could have fallen into the stream, and Derek would have laughed along with everyone else. That was how I was used to being treated. I wasn't accustomed to some knight-in-shining-armor, sensing the rudeness of someone toward me and it pissing him off. All of my life, I'd never had anyone come to my defense like that. I'd never had someone who gave a half a damn about how I was treated.

I felt some anxious nerves creep up as we walked into the pub, and he pulled my seat out for me, but I wasn't going to let my fear ruin this moment by overthinking it. Jim was a great guy.

Jim said that I intrigued him? No, that was quite the other way around. I was the one intrigued by him and fortunate to have met him, even if England was all we'd ever have. Trust me. My story? It wasn't made to end happily. At least, up until now, I didn't think so.

CHAPTER SEVEN

Avery

*J*im and I enjoyed our lunch at the pub, me sampling the
entire menu again. Well, not really. These places just
served up their delicacies in the smallest portions, so I
felt like I couldn't stop ordering. Of course, that was my never-ending
appetite talking because Jim was perfectly content with his sandwich
and soup, all while watching me throw it down.

Jim and I went separate ways once we returned to his estate. One
thing was for sure about this castle: you didn't need my dumbass idea
of time-traveling binoculars when you were here. The laundry room
and a sitting room that had been transformed into a theater were the
only two rooms in this place that weren't historically accurate.

While Jim disappeared to play catch-up with pressing issues for
his work, he showed me the laundry area, and I started sifting through
my clothes. It was something that needed to be done, and I hadn't had
a chance since I took off to the countryside with a complete and hot
stranger.

After dumping my dark colors in the washer, I ventured through the house. This place had it all. No kidding. There was an armory, bedrooms with antique, four-poster beds, and even a library that spanned three-bedrooms' worth of space. It was like those libraries from movies with the two-story ladder and all.

Peeking into rooms and exploring the world of history that Jim had salvaged for this house led me to see the man had a love for England's past. It was magnificent here from the floors, ceilings, carpets, drapes—every single thing. His armory even had knight suits, for Christ's sake. I smiled at the realization that, from the way he was attentive to my needs from the moment we met on the plane, he could definitely suit up in that shining armor. As cheesy as that sounded and felt, it was the truth.

When it was time for dinner, we ate in the main hall at a polished table that could probably seat at least fifty people. He sat at the head of the table, and I sat at his left. I couldn't help but be amused by how funny we must've looked, the two of us sitting at a huge, empty table. At least we weren't sitting at opposite ends, speaking to each other through megaphones like those comedy movies.

"So..." I said, slicing into my tender roast with delicious gravy spooned nicely over the top. I couldn't finish my sentence when the flavors erupted into my mouth. Damn, this guy could cook.

At first, I was afraid to touch the plate. Smashed potatoes were placed delicately under the slices of roast beef, a Yorkshire pudding was over that, and the dark gravy gently drizzled over the top of it all. Off to the side were long green beans and carrots.

"While I appreciate the compliment through your erotic moans," Jim interrupted my marveling at this dinner, "you seriously are about to have me dining in the other room."

I snickered while I picked up a green bean with my hand and crunched into half of its length. Jim's lips tightened in humor as he ate properly, and the pig in me acted like I was eating dinner with Addy.

I covered my mouth. "Sorry about that." I cringed. "You have this fancy dinner, and I'm slopping it up like I'm eating out of a trough."

"Never in my entire life have I been so aroused while dining with a woman," he mused, taking a bite of his roast. He swallowed and pointed his fork at me as I took another green bean with all of its robust flavors and chomped half the vegetable again. "That right there is why I'm not into oral sex."

"What?" I asked. "Why?"

Jim smiled. "The way you're eating those long beans and your sexual moans while eating them, well, let's just say everything is sexual at this point."

"No," I said with curiosity. "You just said, admitted, you're not into oral sex." I went back to eating, yet curious at this confession.

He shrugged it off with that handsome tightening of his lips. "Call it my fetish or whatever you like, but I don't trust a woman's mouth around my dick."

"And," I swallowed a bite of my Yorkshire pudding, "what about the other way around?"

He sipped his wine. "Too intimate. I have never been tempted to go that route in my sexual desire."

"Shit," I said with a laugh. "So maybe I was right in our fake honeymoon argument this afternoon. You do suck in bed."

He laughed. "Are you insinuating that I suck in bed because I'm not one to allow oral sex?"

"Allow?" I emphasized that word. "So, are you a control freak in bed?"

He looked past me to the window, rain still pouring down and complementing our dinner that'd just turned into inquiring about Jim's sexual preferences.

"Is that a bad thing?" His voice was lower, his eyes searching mine now.

"You keep staring at me like that, and we can easily go find out," I said. "But you cook so good that I'd rather finish dinner."

Jim's eyebrows rose in humor. "What about you?" he inquired. "The way you're chomping on that green bean, well, I'm quite surprised you haven't given your ex a blow job and bitten half his dick off. Easy way to solve your problems with him."

I nearly choked on the three carrots I'd forked and shoveled into my mouth. "Well, if Derek weren't constantly high, perhaps I might have. Dude hasn't been able to get it up since before I had Addison."

"Sucks for him, I'm sure."

"Sucked for me. I tried sticking around to make it work and was left to satisfy myself."

Jim's breath seemed to halt, and then he recovered quickly. "You're telling me you remained loyal to him and haven't—"

"Had sex in three goddamn years," I finished that truth with a laugh.

"Wow," Jim said. "Yeah, we might need to rectify that."

He gave me a look that made me want to jump over the table and rectify it all at this moment. That kiss from earlier was still on my mind, the way his tongue teased mine. How delicious he tasted and smelled. And I wasn't a jackass either; he was feeling me out and the glasses of wine we were having were helping it all come together for the better. To have this man of all people for the first time in years? Would I be able to contain myself in bed with him?

I maintained my composure. "We'll see," I said casually. "You just mentioned you're a control freak in bed."

"I've never had a complaint."

"Well, the way you kissed me today almost got your ass laid," I boldly said, letting him know I was all in, and mainly to see if I was right about him feeling me out for more.

Jim laughed, pushing his plate to the side, while I worked on finishing the last of my meal. "That video you showed me of Addison today—she's definitely your daughter."

"What makes you say that?" I answered. Maybe the subject change was a better idea.

He sipped his wine. "Well, aside from her lively blue eyes and her black curly hair, she's full of life. Just the will of determination in watching her swim for the first time in that video? She's pretty remarkable. How long did it take for her to learn to swim?"

"That very day." I smiled at the memory. "She was pissed at having to go through all of the technical lifesaving parts. Then the next thing we know, she's almost swimming the length of the pool."

"Adorable." Jim smiled, then we were interrupted when his phone rang. "Shit, this is Alex on my personal line. I'll take it in the other room."

"Okay," I answered. "I've got the dishes tonight."

He smiled back as he left the room to take his call, and once the dishes were done and the kitchen was cleaned, he was back.

"Are you up for chilling in the movie room for a couple of hours with me? My friend, Collin—you met him at the restaurant—well, I need to check out some video he's in before it gets sent over to some documentarians. He's kind of a hot-shot neurosurgeon. It's all very boring. Want to try to keep me awake?"

"Sure. I'll pop the popcorn," I said.

Jim laughed. "You're serious?"

"Well, something about that home theater and those couches that are longer than anything I've ever seen makes me want some popcorn."

"Well, you haven't seen long yet." He arched his eyebrow in a way that made me hope he would follow through on that.

"Funny," I said.

"Allow me to get the popcorn. Change into something comfortable. This might be a long, boring situation."

"Fuck," I said. "I completely forgot to dry my clothes."

"You can wear one of my shirts if you'd like. I'm sure they fit like a short nightgown."

"Lead the way, and we'll get this show on the road."

We were up in Jim's room, and going through his thousand-dollar suits and clothes. "These clothes are too expensive for me to even look at," I said with honesty. "Don't you have a T-shirt or something?"

"Here." Jim pulled out black and white pin-striped button-down shirt. "I rarely wear this. The button-down will be warmer than just a tee. You can keep the thing if you find it lounge-worthy."

"An ex-girlfriend buy it or something?" I taunted, taking the shirt.

"Nah, my design..." he stopped himself. "It was made for me to wear at an event. I never attended it, and truthfully, I just don't like the coloring."

"Well, I think you'd look damn fine in it," I said. "Either way, I'll change, and," I turned back before leaving the room, "do we even have popcorn?"

"I'll make some," he said with that dark, sexy look, studying me. Why couldn't I be a mind reader? He was complex, to say the least, but that's what made him that much more enticing.

An hour into leaning against Jim, my eyes were hurting from this dull interview. I was sitting here, wishing we were exploring whether or not we'd enjoy having sex after our dinner talk instead. After three years of not being intimate, I was down for this guy to take all the control he wanted while fucking me. I'd take dungeon sex right about now.

"What are you thinking?" Jim asked while both of us finished off the second batch of popcorn.

"Honestly?"

"Honestly," Jim chuckled.

"That I'd take dungeon sex right about now." I looked up, and his eyes caught mine.

I was leaning against him, my legs stretched out on the couch that extended from wall-to-wall in this room. I guess it was the popcorn and the two glasses of wine that had me sitting next to him like we'd been a couple for years.

"I meant about this boring documentary." He laughed, but his eyes were intently on mine.

"Your friend is sexy," I started. "He kind of reminds me of Paul Walker—RIP," I said, thinking about the handsome man who'd left this world so tragically.

"Great, this shit is going to backfire on us, too," he grumbled. "Well, damn."

"It's not bad. I'm just not into medical stuff, I guess." Jim's lips twisted as he stared at the massive screen like he could kill his friend himself. "You look pretty pissed."

He shook it off with a sigh. "Not pissed. Just a bit frustrated," he said. "We'll fix it. Glad I'm watching it, though."

"The neurosurgeon said some of the questions he's asked most about surgeries are his patients requesting information about sex afterward?"

"Most patients are young and healthy," Jim answered factually, still studying his friend on television. "Stands to reason why they'd be concerned."

"Yeah, well, I have the solution to that."

"Oh?" Jim looked at me. "I'm sure Collin would appreciate a little input. He does get this question a lot."

"Well, not engaging in sex, but instead just the…" I paused.

Jim tilted his head. "Go on."

"Well, you're not into oral sex, but, you know, handling it differently without engaging in the act." I exhaled. "It's probably not the solution, and who am I to talk? I've never had a guy get me off in my life." I shrugged at his mouth dropping open at my confession. "Hey, you confessed you're not into oral, and I'm confessing that if I don't handle myself, sex with a dude is basically just a dick inside me."

"You're fucking kidding me, right?"

"I could have responded the same way to your oral shit." I gave him a cheeky grin.

"You've only climaxed by giving yourself an orgasm? What the hell were your partners thinking?"

"They found a place to get their dicks off and moved on."

Jim pinched his lips together, and the voice of the interviewer and Jim's friend were now background noise.

"I could give you—right now—an orgasm that will have you begging me for more, and I wouldn't stop there."

"You tempting me?"

"I'm informing you," he said. "I almost feel it's now my duty as your host to ensure this issue is fixed immediately."

"We have to watch the interview," I teased with an arch of my eyebrow.

Jim inhaled deeply, and then brought his hand around my neck and pulled my face to his. He smelled like wealth. Whatever the hell his cologne was, it was assaulting me in ways that made me want Jim to show me what it was like to have a man get me off. His eyes moved raptly back and forth, looking at mine. His lips grazed over mine, but he never went further than that.

He smoothly maneuvered me to lay against his firm chest, my back against him, and now I was reclining between his legs. His lips touched my ear, "Would you like me to fix this blasphemy of not being properly taken care of by your previous lovers?"

I was breathless as his hand grazed over my nipple that swelled at his touch through the soft shirt I wore. "Yes," I said, drunk on this moment with this hot-as-fuck man who was willing to do something that no one had ever bothered to care about. I was already worked up just being this close to him; his sultry and smooth voice, and his hand massaging over my abdomen.

His lips grazed along my jaw, and he gracefully slid his hand over my panties. Shit just got real. I could have an orgasm right now as he massaged over my clit, slowly but firmly. I melted against his chest, letting out a whisper of a moan, and now my aching clit was swelling for more.

Thanks to the alcohol still working in my system, I was so relaxed and didn't have an ounce of concern about Jim getting me off like this. Actually, it was the main reason I was down for it in the first place, and thank God for that.

Jim's lips went to the top of my head while I moved my hips and spread my legs to grant him permission and full access to me. I slid my panties off, going wild in sudden ecstasy and molding myself back into Jim's arms.

"Jesus, you're sexy as fuck," he said as the shirt I wore fell completely open and now Jim had a full visual of my horny as hell body.

Jim brought his hand back between my legs and massaged over my swollen and heated clit. I gripped each of his legs, being so easily brought to ecstasy by his touch as he gently rolled my clit between his fingers, increasing pressure against my sensitive point. Having a man doing this, having *him* doing this to me...I was going to explode when I came. My breathing picked up as I rolled my hips while Jim conjured a deep sensation coiled up in my belly, working like sparks in my bloodstream.

As I rode his hand, Jim gripped my abdomen, pulling me up to where my head rested against his shoulder. His lips pressed against my neck while his tongue gently caressed my skin. While he tasted along my jaw and neck, he dipped two of his fingers into my wet entrance, using that to massage alongside my aching clit.

"Goddamn." I groaned as my fingers dug into his legs. I fisted his jeans tightly, feeling more build-up than I'd ever felt before while having an orgasm.

Jim's free hand went to my breast. "You're so fucking hot," Jim said, his fingers twisting my hardened nipple, adding to the ecstasy of my sudden bliss. "I know you're close. Your pussy is dripping wet. Fuck," he said in a raspy voice.

"This is fucking amaz…" It's all I could mutter while I groaned again. "Shit."

It was like there was a dam that was preventing the rolling sensation of climaxing and my entire body going into a spasm under Jim's control. This guy could control my ass all he wanted. My breath caught when his fingers began to roll my clit into circles.

"You're holding back. Let it go and come on me, gorgeous," he said, his lips touching mine when I turned to look up into the eyes of the man who was giving me a ride into ecstasy that most women would die for.

His tongue traced around my lips that were slightly open. After hearing his breathing go ragged, I had to see his face. I opened my eyes, feeling so fucking high on Jim working my body like this. His eyes were a swirling green—or maybe that was just my vision going while begging my body to ride out the orgasm Jim kept building deep inside of me. I gripped his legs tighter, opened mine wider, and nipped at his bottom lip. I needed that kiss from earlier today.

Jim only teased my lips with his tongue and his mouth tasting me while I sighed and moaned with every move he made with his hands, waking all of these sensitive parts in me back up again. Aggressive kissing or not, the way he was doing all of this was so insanely hot.

The perfect amount of motion and pressure to my clit, his other hand cupping my breasts and using his fingers to roll my nipples between them. And fuck, his lips and warm breath on my neck, behind my ear, my jaw and then brushing over my own lips...he was a master at this. I was his to do with as he pleased at this point.

"Let it go," he encouraged, nipping my ear.

"Tell me you want to fuck me," I begged, turning my lips back to his. "God, I need to be fucked."

Jim brought his lips to my forehead. "I'm definitely going to fuck this tight pussy," he said in a low voice. "But not before you come in my hand," he said, slipping his fingers inside me again.

"Fuck. Shit." I felt like I was exploding in ecstasy, my orgasm so powerful that I arched my ass into him, his fingers chasing my entrance and clit. "Holy..." I couldn't even speak. Did this guy just find my G-spot like he knew where it was all along?

I'd heard of this, read about it, but it never happened to me. The pressure swirled in my belly while his fingers strummed inside me, and his other hand now worked my clit. I felt his hardness as I stiffly arched into him. Jim's lips nipped behind my ear, his tongue gracefully tasted my neck, and the surge of power I didn't realize I carried while climaxing was now coming down on me with more intensity than I could ever imagine.

"Fuck yes," Jim said, my hands like claws on his legs and my heels dug firmly into the couch. "You're the sexiest woman I've ever fucking met, Avery. I need to fuck you more than you know."

"That's it, just like that," I screeched as the dam of sensations erupted out of my pussy, giving Jim everything he conjured out of me. I'd never known my body was capable of having an orgasm this powerful. "Jesus, you're so good," was all I could get out through pants of pleasure.

Jim's breaths were more ragged, and I felt his hard cock press into my back as I whined and moaned through the hardest and most intense orgasm I'd ever had in my life. "I'm going to take you to my room and bury my cock in you," he said. "You want that?"

I couldn't respond. My eyes were rolling into the back of my head, trying to respond to Jim sucking on my bottom lip as his hands worked every last sensation of this orgasm out of my body.

"Holy hell," I said, finally coming down and sensitive as fuck. I pulled Jim's hands away and managed to turn my limp body to lie on him.

I thanked him by aggressively attacking his mouth for a delicious kiss. Jim's response was his hands, pressing against my back—pressing me tightly against him. His hands cupped my bare ass as his tongue and mine danced in pleasure together. I moaned into his firm and possessive kiss, and his hands came up to massage my back.

"Your body is mine," Jim said, pulling away while I kissed under his chin and down his neck. "I'm taking it. Right fucking now."

As Jim pulled us both up from where we lay, making out while my body did another internal aftershock shiver, his phone rang.

"Fuck me to hell," Jim said, looking at the caller ID. "It's Alex. Goddammit."

"That was the best orgasm I've ever had. You can go to work now," I teased.

"I'm not done with your sweet little ass, gorgeous," he said. "I have to call him back. Things are trying to go south at work. I'll handle it quickly. If you'd like, I'll make sure I have plenty of condoms, and I'll join you in your room. I'll certainly make up for this fucking distraction."

"Don't make promises you can't keep," I said, sauntering past him and heading up to my room.

I was aching for more and shocked my body was in a state of needing to feel Jim inside me. I needed to know what it was like to be fucked by a man who, I had a pretty good feeling, knew exactly what he was doing.

I looked out the double glass doors in my room, watching as the rain poured down onto the balcony before I flipped on the flat-screen TV. I had to do something, or I'd be in misery as I waited for Jim to get back and give me more than the sample he gave me in the theater.

CHAPTER EIGHT

Jim

$\mathscr{I}$t took Alex calling in to instantly remind me of my conversation with Avery that my company could go to hell in less than three seconds. It was a fact, and here I was, reading an email string with a fucking asshole who was trying to back out of what he practically begged us for, acquiring *Knights Aware*, a new gaming company.

This dickhead was lucky I even considered this acquisition in the first place. It took Alex's convincing nature to get me to focus on their first, mind-numbing presentation to us. It wasn't sound, it wasn't catchy, and it wasn't going to fucking happen without serious help. I had no idea how they secured a meeting with us in the first place, but they did, and Alex urged me to challenge Mitchell and Associates by taking them on.

We had our teams put together a decent portfolio on them, and once my PR team delivered the new pitch to me, I was more interested. The investors didn't bat an eye at the idea of this new gaming company that was exploding with high-profile gamers. So, we made our pitch, the goddamn million-dollar acquisition deal, and now these sons of stupid bitches were backing out?

"I think there's more to it." Alex's words kept replaying in my mind as I continued to read the email string about their senseless reasoning for wanting to back out. All of this shit was almost as dry and witless as their first pitch to my acquisition team members and me.

I pinched the bridge of my nose, my eyes burning from staring at small words from dumbass college kids in an excuse to turn down our investors and my company. Then, she—Avery—and those glossy blue eyes came into my mind.

I didn't believe what she said about a man never getting her off until I watched the woman climax. It wasn't until I felt her clawing into each of my legs, watching her body stiffen, and seeing it in her eyes that I realized she wasn't lying about assholes fucking her for their own selfish desires. The thought of that pissed me off.

Sure, I was a man who was uninterested in relationships, and I had a bit of a history of bringing women to bed and moving on, but at least I made sure the woman got off too. Jesus Christ, all men were selfish bastards, weren't they?

Part of me didn't want to fuck Avery, because I knew exactly what I was doing. I was used to satisfying my own needs of wanting to get laid and never attaching to women beyond having sex. A commitment was a big-ass thing for me to consider. I knew all about it—that's why I wasn't up there in her room. Instead, I was sitting here, staring at the number-one commitment in my world—Mitchell and Associates— and someone trying to fuck us over.

My thoughts shifted back to when I kissed Avery in the village before lunch. I didn't kiss women like that. Ever. That particular kiss was right up there with my personal reasons for never having oral sex with women. It was all too fucking intimate. I could never lead a woman on to believe I was a man who could take care of them or do more than just fuck them. Then there was Avery. I felt myself drawn to her in more ways than I ever deemed possible with a woman.

I watched her take in the sights of the village like she was a celestial creature who'd brought me into this wave of bliss by examining her beauty and listening to her laugh. She'd freed my soul from these strange bondages of work that held me hostage, whether I wanted to believe my company did that to me or not. She hit me straight with facts. She smiled so beautifully she took my breath away. Everything about her was making it extremely hard to fight against these new and raw emotions I was having now.

I should've never let it all go as far as it did tonight, but I did without thinking. That's when, even though I knew it was a terrible idea, I kissed her when she asked. Her moans and bringing her lips to mine while her body was writhing in pleasure by my touch—that was part two of falling victim to this blue-eyed beauty. There was a cautious and caring way that I engaged in kissing her. It was intimate as hell, and I knew it. I savored her taste, her moans against my lips, and her body moving beneath me.

Goddamn I had to have her. Now.

I pushed back from my desk, got up, and trotted toward my room. That's when I realized it was three in the morning. Fuck me, had I been staring at that email string for that long? Shit. I grabbed one of the boxes of condoms I took with me from the states. I knew I'd get laid on the trip here, and two weeks' worth of condoms should've been enough—except the person I thought I'd be fucking turned up married.

My phone buzzed before I opened the door to Avery's room to check if she would accept my promise of fucking her before I lost track of time.

What the fuck is it now? I thought as I opened up the new text from Alex.

Alex: *Check your email. Dunlap & Son are pulling their investment and dropping stock. Fucking Julia!*

Jim: *I'll handle it and her.*

Son of a bitch! I knew turning that married bitch away in my office would spark this. First, we're on the brink of losing these college dip shits and their gaming company, but compared to losing Julia's father's company, that was inconsequential.

I wanted to text Julia and go off on the bitch for hitting me exactly where she knew she could. The woman could knee me in the balls and get away with it, but crying some bullshit to her daddy or goddamn brother? Un-fucking-believable. Now, we were losing a lead investor because I wouldn't fuck her.

I MUST HAVE SPENT an hour going through the email and hearing their bullshit reasoning for pulling out of Mitchell—after having been with us since my father recruited them—and also deleting my potential response email a hundred times. I was too fucking pissed to respond. Julia's brother, Greg, was being groomed as the next in line to his father's company, and he was the fucker who sent the damn email. I had to get in front of that smug little son of a bitch, and I would. Once I got home, I would handle this shit face-to-face and remind Gregory that his company depended on Mitchell and Associates. Not the other way around.

"A whole box of condoms?" The sexy voice of Avery broke through my thoughts, and I had to look to see if she was really there or if I'd fallen asleep at my desk. "Was there a party down here I wasn't invited to?"

Avery walked toward me, her full breasts partially hidden by my shirt she still wore, and her perfectly groomed pussy was still on display without her lace panties from our interlude in the theater room.

She walked in front of my chair, pushed my laptop to the side, and brought my face into her hands. "Chained down with work?" she asked, her blue eyes vibrant.

"Just ensuring you had a little catnap after that orgasm," I said.

"I'm fully rested," she said, pulling herself up on my desk to sit in front of me.

I ran my hands along the outside of her thighs. Her soft skin was silky smooth and my dick responded to needing more with her. If just the touch of her skin wasn't enough, she opened her legs and that's when I saw how wet she was.

"I could fuck you so goddamn hard right now," I said, my thumb rolling over her inflamed clit. She let out a soft, scratchy moan, and then her darkening eyes met mine. "But this desk is not the most comfortable place for that."

"You could fuck me on the floor," she said, biting her bottom lip. "I've wanted you ever since you started me off tonight."

I licked my lips, and I had to taste her kiss again. *Fuck me, why can't I resist this woman?* In a slow and fluid motion, I gripped her ass and pulled her closer to me. She ran her hands through my hair when I took one of her full breasts in my mouth. Feeling her nipple rise and harden against my tongue was building me into a desire to do things I didn't do with women I fucked.

"You're mine, gorgeous," I said as I rose up and lifted her off my desk.

She locked her arms around my neck and crossed her legs behind my back, then teased my lips with hers. As I went to take her to the closest room outside of my office, she pulled her lips from mine.

"Fuck me on your desk, Jim," she ordered.

"I don't fuck—"

"I won't let you fuck me any other way," she said, covering my mouth with her fingers. "If you want me, you'll do it my way."

Was this really happening? Did she mandate sex her way or no way? I'd never been told how I was going to have sex with a woman. I just did it, and any woman I'd been with never argued.

"You forgot the part where I told you I controlled the way sex went down," I reminded her with a partial grin.

Her lips twisted up. "I didn't forget," she said. "If you want me, I want it on your desk."

"Why is that?"

"Because you looked sexier than hell sitting there, and it seems like it would be more than arousing." She ran her fingers through my hair.

"Don't tell me this is another *I don't do sex that way* rule, like your oral confession."

I pressed my lips against her chin. "I don't fuck women where I do business."

She laughed. "Jim, I will let you have a pass on your preferences against oral sex, but I have a fantasy, and it's you fucking me on your desk. I believe you mentioned something along the lines of when you want something, you don't stop until you get it? Well, you wanted me."

"I said that, and I meant that, but I'm calling the shots now. I want you on a bed, not on that goddamn desk."

"Well, a little insight about me." She massaged her lips against mine. "When I want something, I fight for it, and I get it."

I saw fire light up in her eyes, and I was getting more turned on by the second with this woman, once again, taking control over my stubborn ass.

"Really?" I could hear myself concede in the sound of my voice. That's when I couldn't handle my aching and throbbing cock being denied her warm pussy any longer. "You win," I said and guided her back toward my desk.

She promptly went to work in helping me shed my clothing and stopped when she freed my cock. "Fuck me," she looked up at me from her long lashes. "I'll have to convince you of oral before this week is over."

I closed my eyes when she used my precum to lubricate her palm and began stroking my cock. "That feels so fucking good," I groaned.

Her lips were against my stomach and trailing up to my neck. "Imagine my lips wrapped around your long cock instead of my hand."

I smiled through the ecstasy of her stroking me. "Not after watching you eat that green bean, gorgeous."

She'd transfixed me and placed me under her spell, and I seriously couldn't remember how I ended up laying back on my desk while she brought her fingers to her lips. "You taste amazing," she said, licking my precum off her hands.

I went to lean up, but she held me down. "I'm not giving you a blow job," she said, tearing a condom wrapper open. "I'm going to ride your sexy ass into the same ecstasy you showed me earlier. I'm fucking you, Jim."

What the hell was this sexy woman doing with my mind, body, and —dare I even say the word—soul? There was no way I could be this fucking submissive to a woman. I couldn't be. I could never allow a woman to have any control over me, and yet here I was, watching her roll on the condom and putting way too much trust in her. I was at her mercy, and there was nothing I could do about it, and hell if I wanted to.

She climbed up on me while I pulled myself back on my desk. Thank God it was unusually long and nearly the size of a dining table, or this sure as hell wouldn't work.

"Are you done with this?" she asked, reaching toward my laptop that was close to falling off the side.

"Depends. You don't know if I can multitask or not," I said, feeling more vulnerable to a woman than I had ever been in my life.

"I'm moving this shit and fucking you," she said, her scratchy voice sultry and irresistible.

I smirked. "We'll see about—"

My eyes closed, and I was silenced while she rubbed her slick entrance over my abdomen. "Your body is sexy as fuck," she said, moving back to where my cock was fully erect. "You failed as my host, you know?"

"Is this my punishment?" I asked, trying to act like I was not under her seduction in more ways than one.

Her lips were on mine, and her kiss started with her gently biting my bottom lip and running her hands through my hair. My hands skimmed up her straddled legs, and I cupped her perfect, tight ass.

I drank from her tasty kiss, and then her lips roamed to my neck and then my cheek, then back to her enthusiastic kiss. I wanted to be pissed as she pulled away, but in reopening my eyes, she was positioning herself to slide down on my dick. I was going to come at the sight of her.

Her blue eyes were daring, and her lips turned up slightly while part of her long hair fell over her shoulder. I watched her gently rub my dick back and forth over her clit. My breath caught at the sensations of her bringing my tip to her slick entrance.

Avery's eyes met mine when she slid the tip of my dick into her. "Hell," I said, bracing myself by gripping her legs. "You're tighter than fuck," I said, knowing I probably wouldn't even be all the way in before I lost it early.

Think about the goddamn docuseries, Jim. The boring as fuck docuseries.

"It's been longer than I want to admit," she said. "You're about to loosen this tight pussy back up again, you up for that job?" she asked.

"More than, gorgeous," I said, not knowing if this would turn out to be the worst failure of my life. I'd fucked enough women to keep this premature ejaculation shit at bay. Now here I was, begging my cock to ride this out so I could enjoy the first time of letting a woman take control.

She bit her bottom lip as she slid further down my cock, and I groaned as I held back the cum that was at the brink of exploding out of me. This felt better than any fucking thing in the world. Her tight, warm pussy was clenched around my hardness, and her expression was indescribable.

"You're so fucking huge," she panted out, moving her hips in circles, and me coming out of my skin in sensations of pleasure and internal shivers of maintaining supreme control over myself. "God, you feel so good."

My lips were parched while I watched this beautiful woman plant her hands on my chest and move her hips up and down along my shaft. I fell into a daze of being high or something like that while watching my shirt she wore—now my favorite shirt in the goddamn world—slide off her shoulders and reveal her breasts, bouncing as she moved herself faster on my cock. Her eyes were dark after she found comfort riding my dick, and her breathing picked up. She was so beautiful it was almost as painful as holding back.

"Fuck," I stammered and closed my eyes in pain. "I want to come so deep in you, Avery," I said as she started moving faster and her waist in perfect circles to ride me better than any woman had previously done.

I reached back and gripped the edge of my desk, writhing underneath this woman taking advantage of my dick in the best way possible. I was in a state of bliss as my cock felt everything inside her. I started pumping myself up into her, needing to be deeper.

"Oh my God," she moaned.

"Harder?" I begged with a groan of pleasure, yet still the pain of holding myself back. I was going to come so fucking hard that I would most likely pass out from the sensation.

"Hell yes, lover," she said with a smile, and her eyes closed.

That pet name almost ended this that second, and not because I was throwing her off me. No one used that name on me. It was always James, Jimmy, or some other name, but lover? Strange how that coming out of her mouth was more sensual than anything else. It was the way she said it too. Her scratchy voice was sexier than anything and it strangely made me feel more apt to ensure this woman enjoyed my cock for as long as she needed.

I reached for her clit, and she batted my hand away. She stopped moving and rose up. "I want you to watch me get myself off with your dick buried in me. Deep," she said with an arched eyebrow, and what I assumed was a nervous bite to the corner of her lip.

"Fuck yes," I said. "Get yourself off on me, gorgeous. When you come, I'm taking you to that couch, and I'm burying my cock so deep in you that you'll scream for more."

"Oh, yeah?" she taunted, holding a breast, licking her lips and working her clit. She started moving slowly, working my cock however she wanted.

"Damn, you're beautiful." How many times could I say this truth? Did she have any idea how fucking sexy this was? Her confidence, her energy, and now her head rocked back with her mouth open.

I glanced down at her as she rubbed herself harder, and I reached down to feel that perfect ass while I watched her moan into a climax again. She cursed and practically howled while breathing out her spasm that was pulsating around my cock. That was all I could fucking take.

She was mine now. I sat up and kept my cock from slipping out while she dropped her face onto my shoulder, her teeth clamping down softly on it while she groaned. I could make it to the fucking sofa, couldn't I?

"You feel so amazing, Jim," she said, coming down.

"You ready for another one? Can you come on me again?" I asked, pressing our bodies together onto the sofa in my office.

I started thrusting myself into her hard until I saw her wince. *She's still sensitive. Settle for a kiss.* I did. I worked all of my energy into the kiss, forcing her to moan while I slowed my dick, sliding in and out of her still-throbbing pussy. I pulled away, breathless, and our eyes met in some moment of pure ecstasy.

"You're still coming on me, aren't you?"

"I want it harder," she answered with her hand on her clit again. "Fuck me deep, Jim."

"That's my girl," I said with a smile while she claimed my bottom lip and sucked on it.

I pumped harder and deeper. Avery let me go at that point, gripped behind her knees, and spread herself fully open for me.

"Fuck, Avery," I said, pumping harder. "You're unreal."

Her arms locked behind my back, and her lips were suckling under my chin as I found my greedy rhythm to claim this pussy unlike any other I'd ever fucked. I would never be able to outdo this, at least I didn't think so. So long as I was fucking Avery, I think anything would be possible. She was so tight that it had me pushing to bury myself as deep as I could. Avery confirmed this is exactly what she wanted, her lips sucking hard against my neck.

"Come inside me, Jim," she begged with a groan. "Fuck, I'm still going. You feel so good."

There was no more restraining my need to come and hard inside her. "I'm there, gorgeous," I drove my cock deep into her, the release more violent than I'd ever experienced. "Fuck, you're so tight." I kissed her forehead. "Goddamn," I said, catching my breath, while her lips swept across my collar bone and back up to my neck.

I felt another internal shiver of release, and moved my cock in her to feel the last of the sensations of her pussy clenching it. This woman not only had me by my dick, given the current situation, but she also had me ultimately at her fucking mercy.

Holy hell, what did I just get my ass into? I wouldn't be able to go very long without needing this—her—again. Her groans, expressions, tight pussy, and even her beautiful tits that I now sucked on while slowly pushing in and out of her. I was coming down but still feeling like I was coming inside her. This shit just wouldn't stop. It's like my dick was in control, and I was giving it the pussy it had waited too many fucking years to find.

Avery intrigued me at first. Her endurable and robust personality. Her sexy as fuck scratchy voice. Her smile and dazzling eyes. I knew I'd eventually wind up fucking her, but never imagined the sensations to be this incredible. I definitely knew we'd most likely wind up fucking each other, I wasn't that big of an idiot. We flirted too much and our sexual conversations seemed to steer us in this direction.

Even at that, it's not the sole reason I brought her out her with me. If it never happened—thank God it did—I would have been just as satisfied with having her company. Her personality was something I was becoming more and more drawn to since meeting her on that flight.

I found it soothing to my tired soul to be around her—no business talk, and not being treated like I was some god because of my position or my money. It sounded arrogant, I know. But I'd surrounded myself with women like Julia—God help me with that one—or fucking Lillian, who was insane and virtually planning our marriage after only a few nights together. This was the lonely life I'd carved out for myself.

Then I met Avery. It's as if my mind were starved to be around a woman who was down to earth and most of all? She was lively, strong willed, and had a mind of her own around me. I was just Jim to her, it was as simple as that. Not the intimidating CEO, the man who had so much wealth that rumor circles constantly questioned what I did with all my money. Avery never once made me think of that part of my life. She made me experience the normal part I'd been missing. The Jim I'd lost after taking over Mitchell and Associates.

With all of these thoughts and feelings surfacing, I felt like she should be afraid of me because, as of this moment, I wouldn't let her go—not if I could help it anyway.

CHAPTER NINE

Jim

*W*hen I woke up, I should have jumped from the bed and questioned *what the hell did I do?* I'd slept in, left my phone in my office, and had a dark-haired beauty draped around my body. Our bodies were still molded together where we'd both finally fell asleep after being fully satiated with fucking each other. Instead of fleeing from the bed in a panic, I did the opposite.

I shifted to where she rested her cheek against my shoulder so I could pull her in closer. After more rounds of sex than I deemed possible, and for the first time in too long, my mind was at rest. I shrugged off the immediate concern that was threatening to creep into my peaceful, rousing mind and thought only of this woman who made the impossible happen for me.

Last night was one for the books. She was a wildcat all night, and for the first time since renovating the manor, I put some of these museum-like rooms to good use. Aside from fantastic sex, the woman had a spark of energy that I didn't think anything could put out. This is what I needed in life, I suppose—a fun, wild, adventurous, and fearless woman.

Don't go down this road, Jim, I thought, but perhaps I could try to keep this going if she was interested. A relationship? I felt my stomach churn at the idea of letting her down. I pulled her in closer and kissed her forehead. I honestly didn't know if I could handle the commitment. I didn't know if I wouldn't hurt her, and needless to say, her daughter. Don't think for a second I'd forgotten she had a child while I lay here, contemplating if this could actually work between us.

I would never shy away from a single mom; in fact, I wanted to meet her daughter. That little girl was filled with so much life, and it made me smile when I saw her in the swimming video. She and her mother deserved so much more than a manipulative druggie in their lives.

I was going too fast and too far with all of this. It was how my mind worked, though. I had to consider everything before I took a risk on anything. With my company, it's who I was. I weighed everything before I allowed an acquisition to play out. It wasn't Mitchell and Associates first, though. A lot of CEOs wouldn't see it that way, but I did. I didn't run this business based solely on what was in it for us, but what was in it for the other company. Would Mitchell and Associates carry them into success or let them down? If the chances were that the business would fail, even with my company at the helm, I wouldn't allow the contract to take place.

So, shit. Here I was, weighing my new-found feelings like a business transaction. What was I going to do next, call up my risk assessment team, and ask them if the relationship would work? I had to get up and get my day started.

I slid my arm out from underneath Avery and watched her pull the covers up to her face and smile behind closed lids. She was gorgeous, even while she slept. I wanted to stay in bed with her all day. It was still raining outside, and I had plenty of other rooms to explore sexually and honor her request of fucking in every last room of this place before we left. Who knows; maybe that could be done. That was the easiest request out of all of them to honor.

. . .

AFTER A VIGOROUS RUN in the rain, a hot shower, and plenty of time to reset my mind while baking a quiche for breakfast, I was determined to enjoy my time here and ignore the bullshit that awaited me when I got back to the office next week.

"Hey, handsome," I heard the voice I'd been waiting for since waking at six this morning. "You let me sleep in."

I had just finished eating my breakfast and was working on a fruit dish I'd put together while heading toward my office. "I figured you'd need the energy for taking on the rest of the rooms in the house," I said with a wink.

She took the plate of food on the counter that I'd made for her. "I was going to wake you with that in bed." I shrugged. "So much for that one; I completely forgot, having too much shit on my mind this morning."

"So much for the breakfast in bed kind of guy I built you up to be," she said, smiling, her eyes still sleepy, yet more beautiful every time I stared into them.

"No shit. It looks like the honeymoon's over, gorgeous."

She covered her mouth as she took another bite and swallowed. "Last night told me the honeymoon better not be over. This quiche tells me we need to renew our vows too."

"But we were only just married, darling," I teased.

"Yeah, I think we should remarry, and this time, no annulment."

"You're still after ninety percent of my business, eh?"

"I might relax and just take the whole company like I took its owner last night," she teased with an arch of her brow.

"It's a double-edged sword, sweetheart," I said. "The money isn't worth selling your soul, and you might have had your way with me last night, but this company would definitely have its way with you."

"Goddamn," she said. "Maybe I'll stick to divorcing you, taking all the money, and leaving your butt to run the place."

"So long as I still had your sexy ass to fuck?"

She shrugged. "I guess. The sex could stay too. You're pretty good in bed."

"Well, now that all of the legal issues are out of the way, perhaps we will remarry." My phone rang, and it was Alex. Poor asshole tried calling me ten times, and I still hadn't gotten back to him.

"Better get that." She pointed at my phone with her fork. "I need a reason to divorce your ass, taking the money, and keeping the sex."

I grinned as I left the room and called Alex back.

"All right, did you handle the shit with Brad and Mark?" he asked, breathing heavily, and I could tell he wasn't taking things well.

I couldn't blame him; I usually shouldered all of this bullshit, leaving Alex to hunt down and maneuver his skill toward advancing business deals. Handling dumb, random shit like sudden pullouts and our top investor backing out because of fucking Julia wasn't in his wheelhouse. It was in mine.

"Alex," I said steadily, "take a breath. You sound like you're having a panic attack."

"What the fuck do you expect me to say? I'm not comfortable sleeping one more night with Knights Aware and Dunlap going to hell on us, and for no good reason."

"Calm the hell down. I'll handle it. Jesus, Alex, you act like this is the first time someone's tried playing games with us. We're not responding to this until I get back."

"Have you lost your goddamn mind, Mitchell?"

"No," I said in a lower voice. "But I will lose my goddamn mind if you keep this shit going. Calm the fuck down. If you want to keep them on the line and dangle the fucking carrot of wealth in front of their faces until I get back, then go for it. Until then, go to bed."

"This is not the James Mitchell that I know. You'd normally be ending your trip to London immediately and sit these people on their asses to fix this."

"I'm not taking that route with either of them. You and I both know there is no better company than ours for either of them. They're playing games, but I'm not playing along. I'm getting off this phone, and unless you have a fucking medical emergency or the building burns down, I want you to relax and not call me."

The other end of the phone was silent.

"Are you still with me, Alex?"

"I'm wondering if you are still with me."

"Can you just trust me on this? I'm not allowing anything to harm the company. If I felt concerned that everything was going to hell, you know I'd be on this."

"Right." He exhaled.

"Go to bed. I'll check in later and stay up to date with any bullshit they try and come at us with."

"All right. Then I'm going to get off the phone and do something I've never done before in my life—not give a fuck."

"You do your job, and I'll do mine. Right now, these fuckers can wait for my intervention on this bullshit when I get back. The ball is in our court."

"You're right. All right. I'll call if anything comes up."

"I'm checking emails, and then I'm out. Get some rest, man, because when I get home, we'll be going at this hard until it's resolved."

"Got it. Later."

Alex was pissed, and I knew precisely why—I wasn't acting like myself. As the words left my mouth, though, they made sense. If we reacted to this like we were desperate, it would only make us look like the fools these dicks believed us to be. They weren't getting responses until next week when I had them in my office to figure out what the fuck they were trying to pull on us.

I finished up as Avery walked out of her room, dressed in jeans and a sweater. "You up for a little tourist day in Gloucestershire today?" I asked.

She eyed me. "A tourist day? I think the question is, are you up for a little tourist day today?" She pulled her hair into a ponytail, "Last time we tried to go out, we almost got fake divorced."

"I have a driver waiting," I said with a smile. "I think you'll like this tour. It's about an hour away."

"Don't you have a car of your own?" she asked. "I mean, the whole driver thing seems a little over the top for us newlyweds."

My lips twisted. "I use my driver so I can handle business on the road," I answered honestly.

"Then I'll be the driver," she said.

"Avery." I smiled. "Are you forgetting that they don't drive on the same side of the road as Americans? The steering wheel is on the right side, not the left side of the vehicle. Your instincts will be completely turned around."

She met me with that challenge I saw all night last night. "I think if I can handle you and that long ass dick of yours after three years of not having sex, I can handle a drive. Do you have anything other than the Rolls that brought us here?"

"You want to go without a driver that badly?" I asked.

"I want it to be just you and me," she said with a smile. "It sounds fun, and your driver needs a vacation too. Why does he have to wait in the car while you and I go play?"

"He does whatever he wants after driving me—" I stopped myself, seeing her roll her eyes at my excuse. "All right. I have a few cars to choose from. I never drive the damn things, so maybe they could use some attention."

"Do they just sit out here?" she asked with a laugh. "Will they even start?"

I smiled. "My driver lives on the property. He handles all the maintenance on my vehicles while I'm in the states. They work. I'll even let you take your pick."

"I'll grab my purse, and we can get out of here. Damn," she said. "I should have taken a run before this."

I looked at her in confusion. She seemed to have a look of panic flash across her face. "It's raining. Would you rather go for a run first? I can join you."

"I'm good, taking off for a drive sounds like fun." She smiled. "I need to take the edge off somehow."

"Edge? Forgive me, I'm a bit confused." I could tell something was on her mind and didn't want to add to whatever it was.

"Yeah, it's the fun life of dealing with shit." She grinned. "I talked to Addy this morning, and it was lovely, but my ex was on one again last night. Long story. While I usually run this shit out of my system, a drive through the countryside sounds like it'll do my wound-up nerves some good."

"Perhaps we should get you behind a little horsepower? I was planning on taking you to Thornbury Castle."

Her blue eyes widened and her smile radiated excitement. "Shut the hell up," she said. "I saw that place in a brochure. It's a Tudor Castle."

"And supposedly haunted," I teased.

"Show me the way to our car, and let's go see a place that doesn't require my time-traveling binoculars."

"Oh," I said, stopping her, "if you can pack an overnight bag, do so. Or perhaps I might rephrase that. Would you care to stay the evening there with me?"

She narrowed her eyes. "Will there be sex?"

I smiled and slipped my hands into my pockets. "I believe I might continue our evening, minus you screaming out my name through the castle corridors, of course."

She looked at me in a way that I couldn't discern. Her eyes seemed to gloss over as she bit down on her bottom lip. She sucked in a breath, smiled, and walked away in what I assumed was happiness that we were taking this last-minute trip.

CHAPTER TEN

Jim

$\mathcal{I}$ took Avery's and my duffle bags to the garage, and I started to load them into the trunk of the car that I had hoped she would enjoy making the one-hour trip to Thornbury in.

"Holy mother of..." She covered her mouth as she walked toward where I was placing my briefcase in the back, which was insurance in case I needed assistance if shit went down that Alex couldn't handle alone. "That's a classic Ferrari, isn't it?"

"And my bride is a car enthusiast. If I would've known that, I would've married you earlier."

She rolled her eyes and snatched the keys from my hand. "Do I still get to drive this baby?" She dangled the keys in front of my face.

I felt my godforsaken phone buzzing, and I knew some company shit was busting loose again. I slipped it out of my slacks, which I'd put on out of habit—I could change into my jeans at Thornbury Castle.

"Is that phone buzzing in your pants the reason you need a driver?" Avery questioned with a devious smile.

"It is." I ran my hand through my hair, then smiled at her. "It also means that it appears my driver is now going to be you...since I just informed my driver that I wouldn't be using his services today."

She planted her hands on both hips and shook her head. "You're missing out, man. You have this classic car, and sadly, you can't enjoy it because if you don't answer that call, you most likely won't be able to keep and afford it."

"Just get in the driver's seat, gorgeous," I said, unable to resist brushing my hand over her tight ass.

I hit the call-back button. "What's going on, Dave?" I asked my public relations assistant, and the man could hardly get three words out before we were buckled up, and Avery brought the low growl of the engine to life and peeled out of the driveway.

I laughed at first, and then lowered my phone from my ear as Avery drove like a bat out of hell with its ass on fire.

"The other goddamn side of the road," I tried to say as calmly as I could.

"Christ. Forgot about that; sorry." She cringed with a sympathetic smile.

"Forgive the interruption, Dave." I went back to my phone once Avery got her bearings. "What can I help you with?"

"They need to know your take on the docuseries before presenting it to the London offices."

"Alex handled this," I said. "No." I rubbed my forehead. "Forgive me. You are correct. We'll be putting it on hold. I'm not entirely convinced this is the route I want to go." I glanced up, forgetting about the roundabout that Avery was entering. "Fucking..." I held onto the word after we were nearly side-swiped by a car and were now stuck in this roundabout, driving in circles, "hell." I let out a breath. "Dave, I need to handle some shit. Cancel any further viewing until I give the final word and get more info back from Dr. Brooks. Anything else?" I asked as Avery continued to look for a way out of the roundabout, but remained safe in the damn thing by the grace of God.

"That was it. Thanks, Jim," he answered, then we hung up.

"Avery," I said, watching her keep the car in low gears and us looking like the jackasses we were acting like. "You need to take that exit," I pointed at the upcoming turnoff. "Burford Road."

"How the fuck do I get out of this goddamn thing?" she asked with frustration and a laugh. "I hope the business is doing swell, but we're in this position because I have no navigation, and these people drive like lunatics."

"Avery," I said calmly, "merge onto the exit, Bufor—shit...it's 429. Right here, take this road. Avery, right there. Here, right here!" I was vomiting out directions like an idiot.

Avery threw her head back and laughed as she took the exit. We survived Avery's first roundabout in England, but we weren't finished yet. I knew the next one was less than a mile away.

"Jesus Almighty." She sighed. "That was insane." She sped up while I held her phone to her face and unlocked it. "Hey," she said, trying to focus on the road. "What the hell are you doing with my phone?"

"Loading your GPS in case the office calls."

"Oh, cool, good idea. What the fuck? Not another one of these bastards."

I glanced over at her. "Just merge into it like you're getting on a freeway in Southern California. This is no worse than the crazy drivers there."

The GPS was spouting off demands as Avery panicked in the second roundabout. "Shit, Jim, maybe the road to this castle wasn't the best route for me to drive."

"My driver handles these just fine," I said smugly while watching her frustration rise, trying to get out of this roundabout. "However, we didn't need him, remember?"

"I feel like a goddamn hamster in a wheel. Every time I go to get out, a fucking car gets in here."

"Slow the car and take the exit that your GPS is practically glitching as it screams at you."

"Good idea."

"Yeah, lead foot, it might help to keep it at low speeds to navigate."

"Hold on. Shush. I have to think," she said with a laugh as she turned the polished wood steering wheel and led us off on the exit.

"There's another one coming up. You're just going to merge this like you're getting on the freeway and hang a left onto Swindon Road."

"What is this, a fucking tilt-a-whirl for cars?" She blew her hair out of her face. "Hang a fucking left? How do I *hang a damn left* when I'm driving on the wrong side of the road, and I'm in the wrong seat too?"

"The same way you hang a right when you're driving on the left side, I suppose," I said as she flipped me off for my comment. "Hey, I was going to call the driver. You're the one who grabbed the keys, gorgeous." I chuckled, seeing another email pop in from my assistant in my London office.

"Holy shit." She raised her hands off the steering wheel and danced in her seat. "I fucking dominated that bitch."

"Only three laps this time." I smirked.

"If you can shut the phone off, you could be behind the wheel and driving this car. It's the most glorious thing in the world."

"Fine, you can pull over," I said. "Seriously, there are more roundabouts, and I'm in the mood to get to the castle, not spend my night going in circles."

She reached over and lightly punched my arm. "See, I knew I could get you driving again." She eased the car off the main road and stepped out. "It just took my pretending I didn't know what the hell I was doing."

I met her at the trunk and pulled her into my arms. "You weren't pretending." I lifted her chin to press my lips to her smiling ones. "Besides, it's raining, and the last thing we need is the GPS shouting, you laughing, and windshield wipers adding to all of that while we're dizzy from going in circles."

"Just drive my ass to this castle," she said with that damn smile that intrigued me from the first moment I met her on the plane to London.

"At least I learned something new today—when in England, don't drive like a crazy American." She laughed.

We sat in the car, settled, and took off. How long had it been since I'd turned it all off and drove one of my cars? This was somewhat healing to my soul. It was so relaxing.

"What do you know about Thornbury?" I asked, maneuvering the next roundabout a bit less theatrically than Avery would have.

"Well, from what the flyer said, it is haunted, and also, you can stay in the same rooms as Henry the Eighth and Anne Boleyn when they stayed here." She gripped my arm. "Do you think if we play into this lie, they'll let us stay in that room?"

"As much as the Tudor Dynasty is fascinating with the mark it left here, do you truly want to stay in the room that man stayed in?"

"When he was with Anne, he was cool, remember?"

"So, he only was not cool after he beheaded Anne Boleyn? I think Katherine of Aragon would disagree."

"I don't know when he went nuts. I know he suffered injuries and went crazy."

"Do you think that's why he killed Duke of Buckingham and seized this castle?"

"I know his uncle, Jasper Tudor, haunts the bottom floors of Thornbury because he hates women," she answered. "Henry killed the duke?"

"You seem to have a fascination, as most do, with this particular king. Can you guess why he charged him with high treason and had him beheaded at the Tower of London?"

"Well, if I'm honest, I got my obsession with the king because of a TV show." She bit her bottom lip.

"Interesting." I laughed. "Do you find it fascinating outside of that particular series?"

"It piqued my interest enough to know I wanted to see sights of the Tudors when I was out here. Little did I know I'd be going to a real castle—that is a hotel—and staying there, with a hot guy," she said and placed her hand over mine on the gear shift. I loved the gesture. "Tell me why he killed the duke."

"On top of the fact that Buckingham was going behind his back because he believed he had a stronger claim to the throne, owning nicer things than Henry wasn't something the king appreciated. Thornbury was just something else to stick in Henry's craw." I arched my brow at her, at ease from enjoying driving my car that I never took out. I was missing out on so many things in life, no matter how simple.

"Dude was a dick. Sort of like Jasper Tudor, haunting the bottom floor. I still need to learn why, though."

"That I don't know," I answered. "I've never gone down the paranormal route to the history of ghosts in England."

"This is the coolest thing ever, though." She unbuckled and brought her lips to my cheek, "We have to have sex there, and this will beat out every cool memory I have in my visit."

"We're most definitely having sex, gorgeous. I'm not that fucking stupid." I smiled at her.

Once we arrived, Avery was in awe of everything. Even I stood in amazement at the five-hundred-year-old castle. The history poured out of this place, but the only history I was attentive to was the history of the stunning woman who held tightly to my hand as we walked toward the main entrance.

I secured the room that Henry and Anne stayed in, believing that would add to the memory of Avery's visit. While she started taking pictures of the castle, our bags were taken to the duke's suite. I finalized our dinner menu—knowing these plates were deliciously smaller than Avery liked—and ensured our dining table was well situated. I wanted her to enjoy the candles, the ambience, and the feeling of being back in time that she was so fascinated with—all while the chefs took care of her appetite.

As we walked into our room, I saw that it was situated to overlook the best views of the gardens and lawns that, if this rain let up, Avery would be able to explore. I watched her take in the grand room, unaware this was the room that Henry and Anne had stayed in for ten days to avoid an outbreak of the plague.

Then my phone buzzed.

"Alex? You're either in the hospital or every last employee quit on us."

"The opposite. I have news you need to know."

"Jim," Avery said, picking up a booklet, "this is where Henry and Anne stayed. In this room! I'm literally in Henry the Eighth's room." She held the leaflet to her chest and walked toward the window.

"Did a woman just bring up Henry the fucking Eighth?" Alex asked, his mood lighter. "What the living hell are you up to?"

"Don't worry about it. Say what you called to say. Stay on topic."

"Henry the Eighth?" he repeated.

"Alex," I said, moving across the room. "What the hell did you call for?"

"Oh, that gaming company we lost?"

"Yes."

"Julia is married to one of the punks."

"You're fucking kidding."

"You're not surprised, are you?"

"She's a fucking predator, man. Dipping into the college-aged kids now? I mean, these kids are in their early twenties. She's thirty-two."

"You got passed over for some gaming kid." Alex laughed. "They're scared that leaving Mitchell and Associates might damage them."

"Good. Let them sit on that until I get back."

"Julia is answering your request to attend the meeting."

"You think I can't handle that crazy bitch?"

"No, I just want to be there when you do," Alex said with a smile in his voice.

"After fielding all this shit while I'm trying to stay off for a bit, you've earned the right to watch that show."

"All right, sweet. Who's the chick?" Alex pried.

"The woman I introduced you to at the restaurant."

"Oh, no shit? Goddamn, my mind is shot."

"Have you slept at all?" I asked, worried he might've been burning the candle at both ends without my help.

"I did. I just woke up to this email and couldn't believe what Scott found after I had him do a little digging."

"Well, tell him I appreciate it."

"Good call in not reacting and going off. You're right. Let's let them sweat it out."

"Glad that after all these years, you're taking my word on shit."

"You can't blame me. You were acting massively out of character."

"Yeah, perhaps. All right, we good?"

"Yep, I'll hit you if any other bigger news breaks."

"Got it. See ya."

"Well, well." Avery walked up to me and wrapped her arms around my waist. "I think we start this all off by getting busy in that bed."

I arched an eyebrow at her. "Thank God I took over driving, or we'd be off the optimum time I allocated for this all to work out with fucking first, tours, tea and cakes, then fucking again, roaming the grounds, fucking again, and then dinner?"

Avery stood on her toes and kissed my chin. "I might need to walk tomorrow. I'm already sore from last night."

"Quit fucking with me," I said, and she fumbled with my belt.

"We need to get on your optimum time schedule, Jim," she said with a sultry voice. "And I've been aching for this dick of yours since I woke up."

I captured her lips at that moment. This shit was fun. I was staying at some historical castle I'd never given any thought to, and there was no call for meetings and business for me to do while I was here.

Avery was somehow getting into my mind and soul and changing me. Now it was time I showed her how desperately I missed being deep inside her. The day was young, and it was time to christen the room and move along to teas, cakes, and tours of Thornbury Castle.

CHAPTER ELEVEN

Avery

I still couldn't fathom the fact that Jim had pulled off this trip, and I couldn't grasp why he would do this for me. I knew it wasn't right for him, but the smile on his face during the tour, the look of being the smartest kid in the group, had me wondering if he was enjoying this as much as I was.

Then came dinner. I felt like I was a queen in my own way. We had a lavish table, set for a king and her queen—I was so caught up with the Henry and Anne theme in all of this. Jim succeeded in having the entire menu served; at least, it was enough food in my mind for a whole menu's worth. Jim stuck to eating scallops and vegetables while I had to sample it all. I should have scared the guy off by now with this constant appetite, but I hadn't.

That evening, Jim and I snuck into the downstairs library. We held hands, only doing it as a joke after Jim announced we were husband and wife to everyone in our tour group, but damn it, it felt real. It felt so real that it started to fucking scare me to wonder what it was all going to be like when this week was over and we went our separate ways.

My mind was stolen from those thoughts after Jim walked me away from the doorway and pulled me against him for a kiss that I devoured like dessert. His groans were beyond sexy, and my body ached to ditch our library tour and head up to our room. His hands were cupping my ass—a sensation I couldn't get enough of while we had sex.

"Can we just head back to the room?" Jim asked, pulling away.

I smiled, breathless, with the tall man leaning over and kissing along my neck. I ran my hands through his hair. "It was your idea to tour the library," I said as his hand grazed over my breast.

He rose. God, he was so fucking gorgeous. His emerald eyes, this new smile, his lively expression. Everything. "I only determined the library to be a good idea because you wanted to see a ghost."

"That's what you get for determining things," I said, both eyebrows raising to challenge him.

"So," he took my hand in his, "we can get the fuck out of here?"

"Only if we play by my rules," I said.

He tucked his bottom lip between his teeth. "And those rules are?"

"I decide how the sex goes down the *entire* time."

"You want full control?" he asked, eyes dark, the *Jim is going to tear my ass up with his perfect fucking techniques* look.

"Full control."

"With limits, of course."

"Limits?" I questioned.

"You know what I'm not fond of," he said with an eyebrow arch.

"Oh, the oral stuff," I said with a laugh. "Fine. I'm down." I thought I'd tease this to see his expression. Poor guy had a fun day, fielding calls, and still managing to play the part of my newlywed husband. "Okay," I said softer, Jim's expression so hot I should just end the games and get our asses to the room. "Anal instead."

I pinched my lips together and did everything in my power to hold back the laugh after seeing Jim's eyes go as wide as silver dollars.

"Anal?" he choked out. "You're serious."

"Am I?"

"I have no fucking idea," he said. "Listen," he tried to level me with that voice I heard him use on the phone when he answered his calls today. "Perhaps that might be something we think about."

"Jim," I brought my hands around his waist and looked up at his concerned expression, "are you afraid of it?"

"Are you not?"

"You seriously sound like we're both virgins, and we're deciding whether or not to have normal sex."

"Well, this is one situation I might think—or hope, shit, I don't fucking know. Are you into that?"

I started laughing. "I'm into having your sexy ass in any way I want it."

"Well, gorgeous," he ran his knuckles along my jaw, "I think I will fight you on this."

"Don't say that," I said, walking away from him. "Or I'll suddenly have a headache and not want anything but rest all night."

"You're a goddamn tease," he said, following me out of the room.

His phone buzzed, and the older, gray-haired couple who were on our tour—giving us shitty looks all day, mainly Jim—walked with us toward the spiral staircase.

"You know, for a newlywed couple, he sure doesn't treat his wife right," the woman said under her breath.

What the fuck?

Jim got off the phone as quickly as he could, and I was confident that if his coworkers knew why he had been so short with them the past few days, they'd hate me.

"What did you just say?" I asked, stopping the couple walking near us.

"Excuse me?" the woman said.

"Avery," Jim questioned, looking at me as if I'd lost my mind.

"I just heard you whisper something about my husband to yours. What did you just say about our marriage?"

She narrowed her eyes at me. "Maybe it's none of my business, but

I think your husband needs to turn that device off and pay more attention to the woman he vowed to love."

"Wow," I said, seeing the fire in her eyes and feeling horrible for Jim. "That's honestly a very nice thought; however, you don't know us. You shouldn't judge him."

"I'm not judging. I'm just stating a fact about what I've seen with you two all day."

"Well, I'm glad we were more interesting than the history of the castle," I said.

"You both ruined our tour, young lady."

"Excuse me?" Jim's business voice leveled the woman, and I swear I watched her snotty face cower under his scorched-earth glare.

"You heard my wife. Your phone distracted our tour," the woman's husband piped up.

"Then I'll reimburse your stay," Jim countered.

"No, darling," I said, holding his hand. "You won't reimburse their stay. They're two nosy old grumps who need to mind their own business."

"Old grumps," the woman grumbled.

"What the hell else should I call you? You're out of line, and you both owe my husband an apology. You have no idea why he was taking calls all day, do you?"

"Seems like it was more important than paying attention or worrying about others on this tour."

I looked at Jim's livid expression. I had to end this, and the only way I knew how to do that was to freak these two rude-ass people out.

"Actually, it was," I said. "He's filing for a divorce."

The woman had the nerve to smirk. "Not surprised about that."

"You shouldn't be. Your wild imagination probably has him pinned as a man who fucks his secretaries and realized three days into our honeymoon that I'm some low-life that he shouldn't have married."

"You should watch your mouth, darling," Jim said, and I could see he was engaging because these people were out of line.

"That's another thing," I said with an exasperated sigh. "He's all about control. Censoring my foul mouth, knowing you both probably can't handle it. I embarrass him too."

"A shame," the man said.

"I'm the one trying to control things? Last I recall, you're the one who is trying to control our sex life." Jim smirked.

"Oh, you're going to bring that up again?" I turned to Jim. "Are you *that* afraid to fuck me in the ass?"

"Good God in heaven, young lady. This is disgusting!" the woman scolded, nearly shrieking.

I looked at her. "Hey, it's something I find arousing. I want it." I looked back at Jim's shocked expression. "He's just the one who calls all the shots. Not that it's a bad thing, but you've always got to be in control, darling."

"This is why he's filing for a divorce, young woman. So crass," the man said.

Honestly, I had no idea why the couple was still standing here. The anal thing should have had them running the other direction.

"No," Jim answered. "You see, I caught her screwing my brother on the eve of our wedding. I'd just gotten off the phone with her OBGYN because," he looked at me with an arched brow, "it's been going on for a while, and I didn't trust her stating she wasn't pregnant."

I grabbed Jim's arm. "What did he say?" I feigned excitement. "Am I pregnant? Are we having a baby?"

"We?" Jim said. "How can we have a baby when all you want from me is anal sex?"

"I just wanted to know if you were better than your brother. I'm not raising this child with the lesser of the two sex gods in my life."

"I won't listen to such filth a second longer. Howard, let's go. This is worse than the tour interruptions."

"No shit," I said, my eyes following her scowl at me as they shuffled off. "Probably shouldn't talk shit about people unless you want to really hear their story, eh?"

Jim grabbed my arm. "What the fuck was that?" He half-laughed.

"I can't stand gossip-drama fueled bullshit. That woman and her husband insulted you over nothing."

"My phone calls may have ruined their tour, Avery."

"Don't come at me with Avery in that boss-man voice. It was bullshit. I enjoyed the tour, and you didn't interrupt jack-shit. That old bag just felt she had to whisper her opinion loud enough for me to hear. I'm not okay with that."

"Well, I definitely think you scared their asses off." He shook his head. "Wow. Anal-fucking-sex. You're really down for that?"

"Are you?" I taunted him.

He pursed his lips. "I think that might be pushing it."

"Then we play by my rules when we head up those stairs and get in our room. At least the first part."

"Okay. Again, what the hell are your rules, my lovely bride?"

"I bring you all the way to the end. No jumping up and finishing yourself off by—and don't take this the wrong way—but nailing my ass while you're on top. I get to ride you and watch you come inside me while you lay on that bed."

"That's what you want?" He seemed to sigh in relief.

"I want to watch you come while I bring you there. Let me make you come."

He pulled me against him—this was a thing I was learning quickly he seemed to enjoy doing, and I loved being swallowed up in the muscular man's arms. "Very well, then. You can ride me into ecstasy if that's what you want. You could have just said that instead of scaring that poor couple out of their minds."

"They deserved it. It's not fair. You're a good man, Jim."

"I'm not your husband, and we're not on our honeymoon," he answered more seriously as we walked up the spiral staircase to our room. "I fear you'd agree with them if you were."

"You sell yourself too short," I said as we reached our room, and Jim unlocked the door. "You're a good guy. You didn't have to do any of this shit for me, yet you did. I still don't understand it."

"I'm extremely attracted to you like no other woman I've ever known," he said.

He was getting too serious, and I felt like the next words out of his mouth were going to fuck up the night ahead.

I reached for his face after he closed the doors behind us. "I want to watch your expression when I fuck you and bring you over the edge. I want to see your expression just the same as you've been fixated on watching me come."

His face turned into a smile. "I'm all yours."

"I want it on a blanket," I said, "and on the floor in front of that fireplace."

He brushed his lips over mine. "I only hope my expression lives up to this fantasy of yours."

"I have a feeling it will."

I WAS IN HEAVEN, my pussy clenched around Jim's cock, but dammit if I couldn't bury *all* of him in me. The guy was fucking huge, and I was still being broken back in—that's what I guess anyway. His body was perfect, and I loved watching his rigid and perfect muscles flex as I rode him. I loved his groans, but I'd never seen his face at his climax. He always seemed to bury his cock deep and then his face in my neck. Not that I didn't love that shit, his sensual kisses while he slowly pumped into me while coming off the orgasm high. Even so, after all these interludes, the one thing I never saw was Jim's face. I knew he had to look even sexier than this look of holding back—this painful, yet satisfied look of being fucked—but I wanted to see it all.

"Fuck, I'm close. Come inside me, Jim," I urged, rotating my hips on him, his thumb massaging my clit with slow and perfect pressure. He'd learned how to manipulate it in a way that sent me over the top, and he knew it. I pulled his hand away when I felt the energy release from my spine and rush down to my pussy. "Fuck me, goddamn, I love riding your huge cock," I said while my release came hard and fast. "Tell me you're coming in me." I was breathless, still feeling my orgasm clamping down on his dick that stretched my pussy with insane pleasure.

"Look at me, gorgeous," Jim said, sliding his hands from my tits and along my hips. He gripped me and pumped his dick harder.

I leaned over on his strong chest while his hands went to my ass. I gripped his broad shoulders and watched his eyes fade into bliss. God, he was mother fucking sexy right now. Jim press down on my lower back, all while he thrust himself deeper into me. A sexy grunt of pleasure erupted from him. I watched Jim's beautiful emerald eyes while he slowly closed and reopened them with each smooth thrust of his cock into me. His eyes returned to mine, and for the first time since meeting Jim, I saw where the man was truly and wholly—for this moment—at my mercy.

"Come in me, Jim," I whispered.

"Fuck," he exhaled, eyes rolling back. He bit into his lip, lifted his chin, and pushed his head back into the pillow. "You're so damn tight," he whispered while pumping harder and gripping my ass as he worked to cum inside me. "Your pussy is—" He stopped, licking his lips. I watched his upper body flex every last muscle, his mouth fall open in ecstasy, and then exhale the last of his orgasm of pleasure. Damn he was more handsome than ever right now. His dazed eyes returned to mine as my breathing picked up, another smaller orgasm rippling through me. "Your pussy is pulsating around my cock. It feels amazing."

He and I both collapsed. "You're the sexiest man alive," I said, molding my body on his chest, looking over into the flames in the fireplace we were lying next to.

I felt him kiss the top of my head while pulling my hair off of my sweaty back. "You're a wildcat, gorgeous. I've never just laid on my back and came like that in a woman."

"Oh," I smiled. "A first. How'd it feel?"

"Strange, but amazing to give that to you." I felt his hand stop rubbing my back, and he held me. "I don't give up control like that in any part of my life." He smirked. But I just gave that control to you. Jesus Christ, you're fucking amazing."

"I'll take the compliment," I said. "We're going to have to trade off, watching each other climax like this."

He brought my face into his hands and kissed my lips. "My God, what are you doing to me?"

"I'd like to ask the same about you. Let's go soak in that tub, what do you say?"

"I say if I'm not careful, we're most likely going to fuck there too."

"Is that another sexual thing you're afraid of?"

He sat up, bringing me with him. He locked eyes with me, "I don't fear shit. Nothing. I do, however, have my reasons for certain things. Fucking in a bathtub would merely be another first for me, but not crossing a line sexually for things I will and will not do."

I eased myself off of him. "You're a hard nut to crack sometimes."

"Perhaps you don't want to crack this nut?" He smiled. "Instead, you can just bust—"

"No." I held my hand up with a laugh. "Don't fucking say it."

"Bust a nut?"

I exhaled. "Go run the bath before you destroy my image of you coming with your cheesy phrases."

I watched his tight ass cross the room after a quick kiss to my lips. There was something up with him and his sexual preferences. It wasn't that he didn't like them; there was no fucking way that was the case. I followed him in, looking at his perfect posture while feeling the warmth of the water in the large claw foot tub.

This man was a sex god—he'd proved that at his home and the three other rounds we had here today. He did everything that would make any woman climb the walls, wanting more, but he had his limits. It's partially the reason I wanted to watch the man come. I wanted to see him climax and watch the beautiful beast of a sex god give me his most vulnerable side. I have no idea why, but I did. I wanted more now. Jim was a challenge, and it was beyond fucking weird that I would press for more or treat him like we were on a honeymoon.

He was a kind and caring man, he took an interest in me, and he fucked like a king. He was all of that, but something hid behind all of this. It probably was me, blowing things out of proportion because we didn't honestly know each other. Did I want more from him, though? Was he the kind of guy I could introduce to my daughter and trust him never to hurt us as her dad did? Those were the tough questions, the deep questions. I wasn't sure if I was ready to ask those, or just live out this week and look back one day and thank God

I met this man and enjoyed a week in England's countryside with him.

That was the road we were on. Enjoy the week and be okay separating, yet holding onto fun memories. That's why I had to be careful. This man was becoming my dream guy who was saving me from a world that was nothing but cruel to me. A world that treated me like trash and made me feel even worse sometimes.

I knew I deserved better, and what Jim was giving me was what I deserved, but was Jim a guy who could fall in love with a girl like me? I had hardcore baggage. I had severe issues with my druggie ex alone, and part of me never wanted to bring anyone into the world of shit I'd gotten myself into.

Fuck it. I was going to enjoy this bath. I slid in and reclined against Jim, and he started massaging my body and kissing my ear. This was the first time I felt him adoring my body as if it were his to cherish. His hands were gentle, and his kisses seemed meaningful.

Then he said the words.

"God, I never want to let you go, Avery."

CHAPTER TWELVE

Avery

The stay at Thornbury had me over the top with its Tudor Dynasty histories, and I was obsessed more than ever with King Henry and Anne Boleyn. I didn't care, though. I was having a blast. Jim and I traveled through the countryside on our way back, laughing and teasing each other, and it seemed that we'd easily fallen into some exciting—should I even curse myself with the word? —relationship.

As hard as I was pushing back the stirring feelings that I had been slowly developing, part of me wanted to think I didn't have to. Why the hell couldn't I have my cake and eat it too? I deserved someone good in my life, and I knew I wasn't the only one feeling what was happening between us. Jim felt the same. I could see it in his eyes and feel it in his touch and kiss. It wasn't just me, conjuring some wishful dream to come true, right? Was I fooling myself? Was this too much too fast?

I woke up at five, and all of these thoughts were on a loop in my head. I needed to get out and take a nice, long run. That would help me get my head straight. I wasn't surprised Jim wasn't in bed. It was about an hour ago that a text came through, and he'd had to wake up and deal with it, so I got up and put on my running clothes and shoes before I ran downstairs to let him know I was heading out.

"I already told you that it's none of your fucking business," I heard Jim say from inside his office. "Can we get off the girl I'm with and back on topic? I sent my corrections after going through the issues."

"Okay, okay. I'm just saying that you sound like you're breaking all your *Jimmy doesn't commit* rules," I heard the man tease him.

I stood frozen in the corridor outside his office door. Something told me that I wasn't going to like what Jim had to say to whoever was on speakerphone. I wasn't the type to eavesdrop, and I really had no idea why I was starting now, but here I was.

"I'm not breaking shit," Jim said, his voice seemingly arrogant and unashamed. "Fuck it. Maybe I have, but—"

"But?" the man laughed. "Did Jimmy finally have oral sex? Have we made it to second—wait, is it third base?"

"Fuck you, Jacob," he said.

"Is that any way to talk to your brother after everything I've been doing to help Collin with your demands for this film?"

"Listen, there is no oral—there is no commitment."

"Henry the Eighth?"

"Glad that made it to your highlights for the night."

"Imagine my surprise to find out you're taking time off at all, man? Then I find out you have some chick at Adelaile, and you're researching England's monarchy? I had no idea what the fuck to believe. A body snatcher could've gotten to you for all I know."

"It's nothing. It's a fucking fling," Jim snapped. "Once I get back to the states, I'll handle all the shit I let slip through the cracks while I enjoyed a little time off."

"It's okay to fucking let yourself go. I'm glad for you. My big brother is always taking care of everyone except himself."

"Yeah, well, maybe that's what I'm doing here too," Jim said.

"Because it's sure as hell not like me to shut it off and do these sorts of things. You guys are always telling me I'm picking up charity cases."

"You ever stop to think we're just giving your sorry ass a hard time?"

"Jacob," he said to who I understood was his brother, "there is no relationship, there is no commitment. It's a nice week with a hot chick I met on the plane. She's got her own shit to work out, trust me. And fuck you for nosing into my sex life and bringing up oral-fucking-sex in the first place. I don't do that shit unless I'm in a relationship I know will last."

I covered my mouth and turned to run up the steps quietly. *Fuck. Fuck. Fuck.* My heart and stomach sank. Why? Fucking why? I'd never felt more naive in all my life. Here I was, minutes ago, trying to convince myself that this man felt the same way I did. I tried to justify play-acting as though we were a couple, and we shared the same feelings. I couldn't have been more wrong. It was a slap across the face and a harsh reminder that I wasn't the type of girl who got a happy ending.

"Avery," I heard Jim call as soon as I reached the top step. "You're awake?"

"I'm wide awake now," I said as I spun around, furious at him but angrier at myself for letting my emotions getting the best of me.

"Looks like you're heading out for a run. I'll join you."

"You know what?" I started as calmly as my temper would allow. "I'm going to be honest with you and get this all out. I heard you speaking to your brother just now."

"Shit." I watched the man run a hand through his hair, and for the first time, Mr. *I don't fear shit* looked a bit scared. "Avery, half of that shit—"

"Save it," I said, holding up my hand. I couldn't listen to any possible excuse that would make what he said okay. "You were dead-on. I was the dumbass single mom who let myself get caught up in a fantasy. We both know this isn't real. I knew that, and I was too swept away to notice the fucking red flags you were throwing up for me.

Oral-fucking-sex." I laughed and shook my head. "Of course, that's why you weren't into that shit. You assume it's too intimate."

"Avery, it's not like that."

"Really?" I cocked my head to the side. "Then what's it like, Jim?"

"I just. Fuck. I do really like you."

"I like you too, Jim, but it's best to end this now before things do go in a direction where you're in some fucked-up position to feel like you need to commit to me. I've got a little girl depending on me to make better decisions in my life than going off alone with some goddamn stranger and fucking him all over his house. Games are done, and I need to get the hell out of here. I appreciate everything. You did give me memories to bring home from my trip to London." *Oh, shit.* I felt tears bubbling up. "I'll always be grateful to you for that."

"You don't need to leave," he said, his voice low. "Shit. I'm so fucking sorry. I'm just confused."

I smiled, feeling tears of sadness for me and, strangely, for him too. "There's nothing to be confused about. I need to go, and you obviously need to start being more present with your job. I'll send for a driver and be out today."

"My driver will take you."

"I don't need your help," I said, more bitterly than I should have. "I don't need anyone's fucking help. I'll find my way out of here on my own. I've crawled out of a lot of worse places than a beautiful museum in England's countryside."

"Please, drivers can be—"

"I said I'd handle it." His phone rang. "You should get that. Thank you." The tears were at bay, and thank God they never surfaced. "I mean that. You helped me shut out the noise for long enough. I needed the distraction."

"I feel the same about you."

"Then we each helped each other. We each know that even if somehow, in a perfect world, we wanted this to work, it's like you said at that castle—we aren't married, and we aren't on our honeymoon. I think that's the most confusing part. We pretended too much, don't you think? We acted like all of this was more than what it was."

"And what was that?" Jim's darker voice surfaced. "What was it, Avery?"

"It was a façade that we both played into. It was fun. It was a distraction. That's all it fucking was."

"It was more than that."

"No, Jim," I said. "It wasn't. I heard enough of your conversation to know that."

"You also didn't hear the entire phone call, Avery."

"Did I need to? Was there more evidence of reasoning as to why you can't commit to the chick you met on a plane who has issues to figure out?"

"Fuck me."

"Already did that," I said and turned to pack it up, pull it together, and get the fuck out.

CHAPTER THIRTEEN

Jim

Oscar Wilde once said, *"We are each our own devil, and we make this world our own hell."* He was right. I had created my demons a long time ago.

When my father died, I became the CEO of a multi-billion-dollar industry, and I focused on ensuring my father's legacy never fell. I loved my father, dearly—he was the one who made sure Jacob and I were shielded from our addict mother—but I wanted to do better than he did.

I was old enough to remember my mother's selfishness and neglect, and from a young age, I promised myself I would never be like my dad, chasing around a woman who inflicted maximum damage everywhere she went. I would never put my family through that.

I often wondered how my father got himself into that position in the first place. Certainly, he didn't show up at the nearest insane asylum and pluck her out of the bunch. Something had to have happened for him not to realize the woman he loved was the same kind of woman who would cheat on him and lock her sons outside in the cold, just to name a few significant offenses.

I wasn't going to pretend that my mother wasn't the reason for my commitment issues. Anyone within a thousand-mile-radius of me could point that out. I hated the woman for it, too. The damage she inflicted on me and my father was immense. Luckily, Jacob couldn't remember most of it, but she still robbed him of having a mother, whether or not he could remember the bad stuff.

I'd never minded the personal hell that my devils had created for me until now. I saw the look in Avery's eyes after she'd heard my phone conversation. I hurt her, and I lost her. I'd led her on, trying to hang on to the first authentic woman I'd ever met who could be worth my trust and more than just casual sex. I'd been guarded for so long that I didn't know if a commitment to Avery would work.

One thing was certain: she had a massive effect on me. She was different. I never once heard her mention my wealth, or pry into my business other than noticing how chained to work I was. Every other woman I'd encountered—inside or outside the office—saw a wealthy CEO and treated me as such. When I thought back to my pursuit of Avery, I realized all it took to win the woman over was food, not money.

It was so much more than that, though. Without even trying, she proved she wasn't the type of woman I should be afraid of committing to. She wouldn't be the type to hurt me as my mother had. I knew that because she was fighting the same battle my father had fought when he was trying to keep his sons from his druggie ex. She was living the same life he did.

Even with all of this knowledge, I couldn't manage to keep my particular demons from ruining it all for me. I destroyed what was probably my only real chance at happiness. Call me crazy, but something about her sang to me from the first time I laid eyes on her, and that was a fact I couldn't look away from, no matter what the reasons for subconsciously blowing it all up.

Had she overheard half the conversation between my prying

brother and me, and then figured out I was a piece of shit for not wanting more than sex? Yes. Half of that conversation was enough to let her see the asshole I truly was. Maybe that's why I let her walk out the door without any further explanation.

The worst fucking part was when she left. She hugged me and thanked me with all sincerity. She held nothing against me. She only realized what I thought I knew at the time—it was never supposed to be anything more than us enjoying each other's company for a little while. So, why couldn't I let it go? The weight of regret that hung around my neck was suffocating.

"Fucking hell," I muttered at my desk while I rubbed my forehead. "Focus, Jim!"

Damn it. I sat up and stared intently at the spreadsheet in front of me. I needed to straighten things up with this fucking gaming company. I was not in the mood to deal with this shit today, and that's precisely what this was. Bull-fucking-shit.

I'd finally agreed to meet with Julia and the woman's college-aged husband today. I'd put their asses off long enough, and now it was time to face the bitch and to listen to her stupid as fuck demands. A fun bonus? She was bringing fucking lawyers with her.

I had already handled Greg with Dunlap & Son as soon as I got back. It didn't take much convincing to let them know the millions of dollars they'd lose with the three companies Mitchell and Associates owned, and if they left us, they lost that investment too. So, for Greg to keep his cheap-ass Rolex and all the fun toys that went along with being one of the world's youngest multi-millionaires, he'd be dumber than he looked if he left Mitchell and tried another company. He was only doing this because his sister called crying after I refused to fuck her. Thank God she brought her husband and lawyers because the double doors to my office were never going to welcome her ass in through them again.

I stepped into the elevator and hit the button to get me down to the tenth floor. This was the floor where we had the largest conference room available to entertain two assholes, a manipulative witch, and their army of lawyers.

I walked past the glass walls, seeing dark suits and one shrew, served up ripe and ready in a red dress of all colors. To my left, heads were popping up and then ducking after I made eye contact with them. *Shit. Right. Expression!* I must've looked like I was going to fire the whole goddamn floor.

I let out a breath and relaxed before walking into the room. "Janice, darken the windows to give us our privacy from others on the floor, please."

"Absolutely, Mr. Mitchell."

An exasperated sigh came from Julia, staring at me while sitting upright like this battle was already won. "You'd think your staff would've given us the privacy we needed when we first walked in since you've kept us waiting for fifteen minutes, not to mention the additional two weeks since your return from London."

"Janice, send for Alex, please, and you may leave," I said, looking down at the portfolio she'd prepared for me. It took only a cursory glance for me to determine this was going to be over a lot sooner than anticipated. This whole thing was a waste of my time, and if I wanted to waste my time, I'd be scouring the United States for Avery. All that time with her, and I never even asked where she lived. Good God, why pine over something I'd fucked up from the beginning?

"Just Alex?" Julia answered. "What happened to your acquisitions team?"

I leveled her with the stare that Avery informed me was my scorched-earth look. "There is no need to waste their time. Alex requested to be present, or I wouldn't be wasting his time either." *Fuck, Jim, lawyers are present. Watch your fucking words.* "Allow me to rephrase that." I mustered a smile. "The acquisitions team is not available at the moment as they are working with another partner. Alex will be here shortly."

"And the powerful executive caves under the pressure of the lawyers," she snapped.

"The last time we spoke," I looked at the tall, lanky, overgrown child, wearing his comic book shirt, sitting between Julia and his gaming-company partner, "you and your associate requested that we refer to you with first names only, is that still what you prefer?"

"Brad is my husband," Julia said before the blond-haired guy spoke up. Jesus Christ, he and his buddy looked like they'd just rolled out of bed. How could she take this shit-stain seriously? "He and I are Mr. and Mrs. Jones."

"Very well, Mr. Jones." I looked at his annoyed expression. "That is what you'd like to be called, correct?"

"Actually, Brad is just whipped," the other bed-head spoke. "We're fine with you calling us Mark and Brad. Remember who bankrolls your stuff, Julia." He'd said her name as if he resented the fuck out of her. I guess I had more in common with these doofuses than I thought.

I pinched my lips together and closed my eyes at the mismatched pair, and I wished with all my heart that we could be recording this shit for Collin and Jacob to see with their own eyes. Alex walked in just in time. "All right. Five minutes early. Let's get this meeting going. Brad, Mark," Alex acknowledged them as he sat to my right. "Julia," he finished in a dry voice.

"Getting directly to the point," I said before Julia could respond to my Vice President and best friend. "Your company desires to withdraw from Mitchell and Associates' investment. At first, I thought this was a joke, but here we are."

"We've changed our minds about that," both gamers said in unison.

"What? Don't listen to them. They're children." Julia clamped her mouth as soon as she admitted what she thought of her husband.

The shock on Julia's face was priceless. These goofy little sons of bitches had ambushed her. I officially wished we had this exchange on tape now. Judging from the look on their faces, I had a feeling this was going to be fantastic.

"Children?" Alex said, clasping his hands and stretching them out on the desk. "That is quite a bold statement, considering your marriage and their wealth."

"If you've changed your mind, may I ask why we're in the presence of your lawyers?" I asked.

"Yeah, Jules. Maybe we can use them so Brad can get that divorce from your gold-digging ass." Mark cut off Brad by glaring at him with a look that was mixed with fear and confusion.

What a bunch of dip shits.

"I'm not trying to be rude," I started, "but can we not bring personal matters into the business at hand?" As much as I loved what was happening to humiliate Julia, I wasn't one to fuck around when it came to business. This unprofessionalism was wildly inappropriate, and it was ultimately affecting my business. And *that*, I would not tolerate. "Now, Mitchell and Associates are willing to grant your exit from our company. We are sad—"

"Dude. Come on, Mr. Mitchell," Brad said, elbowing Julia as she tried to stop him. "We can't lose you guys. If we lose your company, we lose the largest sponsors out there."

"I understand that. It is why I was genuinely confused about why you were leaving. We *were* covering all of your public relations and your marketing, as well as all advertising for you. We were also pitching you to even more investors and pushing you out further to more of the online gaming community. Due to our efforts, the gaming community has now taken more of an interest in your product as well."

"We believed when we reached this agreement," Alex said as I watched Julia squirm next to her man-child, "that it would help not only gain you money, but you would also be able to work on development with our hired staff, the building we just acquired for you to work wi—"

"We don't want out, goddammit." Mark slammed his fists on the table and stared at Julia. "Tell us what we need to do to make this right."

"Our offer was pulled after your letter of rejection. So we must draw up a new one," I said, eying Julia. "Mitchell will offer half a million as an advance now, to start. We will also keep the same agreements with investors, et cetera. After the advance, we expect seventy percent in earnings for Knights Aware. Will this work?"

Alex looked at me with some fear. This was a bullshit offer—an insult, really—to these two. An advance? No one took advances, and Mitchell and Associates never gave them. It was a goddamn joke, and I couldn't give a shit. They insulted my company and had the nerve to cross me.

"We'll take it," Brad said.

"Damn it, Brad," Julia snapped. "Can I speak for a moment?"

"No. You're the one who told us to back out," Mark said.

"Well, who the hell told you it was a great idea to take an insult for an offer to come back? We're here for more money last I checked," Julia argued back.

"Greg told us we were stupid for pulling out," Brad said.

Julia rose in a fluster while I covered my mouth, trying to keep my shit together. Nothing had ever happened in this room that had given me more pleasure than this entire exchange.

"I'm so done with you, *both* of you!" She seemed to have hit a level of outrage that was reserved for fifty-year-old men who were stuck in traffic. "My brother told you that?"

"After he spoke with Mr. Mitchell and decided not to pull your family from investing in this company. He said to stop listening to you. You're costing us money, Julia."

"What the hell?" she said, and I watched the woman almost melt where she stood. "You know my brother stole my family's company from me. Why would you speak to him behind my back?"

"Again," I said, "personal matters aside. Do you agree to our terms?"

"Yes," both gamers said at the same time.

"Alex, have Alicia draw up the new contracts. I'll sign them this evening." I stood. "Thank you, gentlemen. Good day."

I walked out of the office while Alex dialed Alicia to print up the new agreements.

"James," I heard Julia snarl from behind me.

I kept walking. There was no way in hell this nut was going off on me on this floor and in front of half of my employees that I'd never met.

"What?" I said, jerking my elbow from her as I quickly stepped into the elevator with her on my heels.

"What the hell was that?"

"What are you doing?" I hit the button to take us to the lobby level. "And why are you following me after trying to fuck my business over? Should've thought that shit through, Julia."

"This is crazy," she said.

"*This* is crazy?" I questioned. "You have gone off the fucking edge. Was this because I wanted nothing to do with you as a married woman?"

"No—I...I have no idea. You disappeared on me all week in London."

The elevators opened, and I stepped out, Julia following me. "You may wait here for your husband. I believe you're finished?"

"I'm not even close to being finished with you," she said.

"I believe you played your best hand, but, please, be my damn guest in trying to finish me, Julia. Will that still be Mrs. Julia Jones, or the former Mrs. Julia Jones. Best to go beg for your husband back."

"Why, because he wouldn't listen to me? You gave him a bullshit offer, and you know it. You offered him less than half of what your team offered the first time? Really? And now a shitty advance for him to sign with you? What the hell?"

"The new terms are with your team of lawyers if you'd like to go read what your husband is signing for your future." I glared at her.

"You're a bastard, Jim," she lashed out.

"And here I believed myself to be a fine ex of yours who escorted you off my upper floors and directed you to the exits personally."

"This is the end of us. You know that, right?"

Jesus, she's all over the place. "I understand completely."

I stepped back into the elevator, leaving her staring, mouth agape, as I hit the button to bring me to my office on the top floor. I was elated to be rid of her and was now even more motivated to find the one woman I couldn't shake. If only there were second chances. If only life were that kind.

CHAPTER FOURTEEN

Avery

I came to pick up Addison from her preschool, and I smiled when she held up her artwork while waiting impatiently in her class line for parents to greet the teacher and check out their children. I gave her two thumbs up, watching her small group of friends laughing and giggling at my daughter's enthusiasm.

"Thank you, Jeanine," I said when Addy jumped up into my arms. "Was she on good behavior today?"

"Always," the young teacher said. "See you on Monday, Addison."

"Bye, Ms. Jeanine," Addy said, hugging me tightly. "Momma, I made it for you."

I took the finger-painted project and smiled at my daughter's multi-colored, scribbled artwork on the coarse paper. "Wow, Addy. What is it?"

"Guess," she said in her sweet voice, trying to pique my curiosity by sounding mysterious. "You have to always guess, Momma."

I let Addy down and held her hand after shouldering her pony backpack. "Well," I said, walking swiftly toward our car to beat the parent pickup traffic, "I think it's a beautiful picture of palm trees and the ocean."

"No, silly," she scoffed. "It's your castle that you played in."

My stomach tightened. I thought I could come home with memories and move the hell on from what I shared on my vacation with Jim. In fact, I did pretty fucking awesome, and that's why my daughter knew Mommy got to play in a castle in England. I shouldn't have been surprised that Addy held onto that. We'd built enough sandcastles on our beach days for her to be excited that I stayed in a real one. Why did I have to remain emotionally attached to it all, though?

"I think it looks more like the sandcastles we make at the beach," I said with a smile.

"Can we go to the beach?"

"You get to go to Papa and Grandma's this weekend."

"Ugh," she said in annoyance. "I wanna go to the beach."

"You'll mind your manners, young lady," I said.

Addy pointedly ignored me after that. The one thing she hated hearing out of my mouth were those words.

"I missed you today, Addy," I said, bringing her over to the beat-up Volkswagen Rabbit I owned. Poor car was barely hanging onto dear life.

"I missed you, Momma."

I buckled her into her car seat, and we went for our usual Friday treat before I dropped her off across town at Derek's parents' house. Derek hadn't been on a bender for at least two months, and thank God for that. I didn't need his bullshit. We pulled into a drive-through and got soft-serve ice cream cones to last the fifteen-minute drive across town.

When I pulled down the street to where Larry and Annette lived, I saw a brand new—lifted—full-sized truck. *Fucking Asshole!* I thought, knowing this dick still lived with his parents, didn't pay child support, and this was probably an underhanded move to try and beat me out for custody if we finally did make it past threats and into court.

"That's Daddy's new truck," Addy said.

"I gathered that," I answered, but immediately feigned excitement. I wasn't pulling Addy into my drama. "I bet it's a lot of fun to ride in."

"Daddy says it's sixty billion dollars for it."

"Sixty billion, eh?" I said, getting out and pulling Addy out of her seat. "Wow, I didn't know Daddy had that kind of money."

Addy laughed. "Daddy says he bought it for me. It's big and fun."

"Hey, Avery," Larry said. "There's my baby girl." He squatted down and held his hands out to Addy.

"I'm a big girl, Papa," she exclaimed.

"Everything cool?" I asked, wanting to get the fuck out of here.

Then, out came my ex. He looked like death warmed over. His face was swollen, his once muscular body was overweight and bloated, and his formerly tanned skin looked pasty, almost ashen.

"Hey, Dad. Bring Addy in the house," he said, kissing our daughter on the head. "We'll go get ice cream later."

Addy didn't question her dad blowing her off. She happily went with her grandpa because the truth was that she hardly ever even saw this asshole. If he was at home, he slept all fucking day. How his parents hadn't kicked his ass out of their house yet, I'll never know. Addy only knew him as daddy, and I could see by her lack of wanting to hang back and reunite with him since my sister dropped her off for his birthday last Friday, she didn't give a shit. She'd rather be with her papa. He was more of a dad to her anyway. He was also the only reason I played along with this custody arrangement.

"Like the truck?" Derek asked.

"It's a truck. If it keeps Addy safe, then yes. It's also a nice way to bury yourself in debt while living with your parents."

"Do you always have to be a bitch to me?"

"What do you want? Your daughter is here for exactly forty-eight hours, and the clock is ticking on that."

"Who'd you fuck in London?" he asked.

"What the fuck did you just ask me?"

"You know what I asked. Britney said you were off with some man-whore in London. Who the hell was it?"

"You lost the right to ask those questions after we broke up two years ago. I'm leaving. You bring shit like this up to Addy, and it'll be the last time I play nice, dropping her off."

"So you did fuck some stranger then. You're such a fucking slut, Avery."

"I'm not listening to this."

"That's always the easiest way out for you, isn't it? Well, I hope you left that baggage in London because I'll kick anyone's ass you bring around my daughter."

"*Our daughter*, asshole, and I think I can make those calls in my personal life without your drug-induced, absent brain."

"Yeah, whatever, slut."

That's how I left the asshole—once again. Now, here I was, driving back to my apartment, my hands trembling, knowing that Derek was never going to let our relationship die. Ever.

I called out to my phone and asked to call Derek's mom.

"Annette?" I questioned once she answered.

"Avery, everything okay?"

"Keep an eye on Derek, please. He's already flaring up over my trip to London. Don't let him around Addy—or just call me if he starts acting weird."

"Everything's fine. You know Derek. He gives you trouble because he knows he lost a good thing."

"I'm just saying, it never ends well like this."

"We'll watch him. Besides, he's going out for some work party tonight."

"Wow. You can't be serious. He gets his daughter for a weekend and takes off on her?"

"He's playing with her right now."

"Good. Father of the year. Bye."

I hung up. Fucking liar. He's going out to get his fix tonight and get loaded. All he needed was to think I'd slept with someone to validate him going off the rails. At least his dad locked his ass out if he was like this. I *hated* being stuck with him, and I hated being paralyzed by my fear that the court would deem us both unfit and put her in the system.

I pulled into the driveway and saw my sister's BMW. She popped out as soon as I parked in my designated space. The place was a shit hole, but my OCD tendencies had my apartment so damn clean, you wouldn't know it—from my unit at least.

"I have good news, sis," she said. "Excellent news."

"I need all the good news I can get. I just had to deal with Derek finding out I slept with that Jim guy in London."

"Oh, God." She rolled her eyes. "Well, I'm sure he's excited about that."

"My daughter is at that fucking house. If he loses his shit on drugs and booze over this and she—"

"Annette and Larry would call the cops if Addy were in danger. You know them well enough to know that. Just because they don't like that you left him and aren't trying to help him overcome his addiction doesn't mean they'll allow anything to happen to Addy. They adore that child."

"True." I exhaled. "What's this news you have?"

"Let's get inside. No offense, but I hate this neighborhood."

"Sorry that my rich sister wouldn't hire me into her blooming business."

"Shut up." She laughed. "However, that's what this is about."

"You're hiring me?" I questioned.

"No," she said, "but the company that acquired mine is hiring. I just got out of a meeting, going over reports and shit, and on my way out, the head of their PR department, Stefanie—she uses my products, of course—she asked if I knew anyone who would be interested in being her administrative assistant."

"Where is this place? Isn't that company Mitchell Incorporated or whatever? Aren't they in downtown LA?"

"Yes," she said as we walked into my studio. "Listen, they have an advance they give to all their employees to help move them closer to the office. Their wages pay more than that company you work for."

"It's called Blessed Hearts Living," I said.

"Right, the convalescent home. You'll have eight-to-five hours, and," she pushed the paper across the desk, "starting pay for the position is five thousand a month."

"What the living fuck?" I answered. "I don't have a degree to warrant this sort of pay."

"You don't need one. I talked to Stefanie already. She even said that they have a preschool and daycare there. It's for working parents."

"That's wonderful," I said. "But Addy loves her school and friends."

"Avery." Britney stared at me dryly. "These offers don't come around all the time. Call me your fairy-fucking-godmother. The only reason I have this for you is that Stefanie is a friend, and she hasn't posted the job publicly yet. Yet! Someone will take this position in a heartbeat for the on-site preschool alone, not to mention the fact that most people with four-year degrees don't get paid this much. You've got to be out of your goddamn mind for even thinking of a reason you might not want this." She joined me on the couch. "Listen, this is life-changing for you and Addy. I even looked up living costs. Torrance is closest, and it's the best deal for you. It's also farther away for when Derek goes on benders and shows up here."

"Which could be tonight. Now that he knows I screwed Jim..." I looked closer at the brochure that she handed me about this building, the company, and its CEO. "Holy mother of fuck," I said in disillusionment.

"Pretty hot for a CEO, eh? I've never met him though. I'm sure I'd fall apart then and there if I had. God, look at his—"

"Brit," I said, stopping her as I pointed to the handsome man in the photo who was labeled the owner and CEO of this business. "*This* is Jim. My Jim, from London."

"James Mitchell?" She laughed. "Like fuck, this is the guy you slept with for nearly a week? The guy who spoiled your ass?"

"The very damn one."

Her eyes widened. "Get the fuck out of here! Do you *know* who that man is?"

"I'm getting a clear-cut idea and pretty quick." Jesus Christ, I guess I should have done the math on how important he was as a business man. The security detail he had follow us out of London. The castle he owned as a vacation home. The suits, cars. It was all in front of my face, but I was too fascinated with him and not all the company bullshit he was chained to. "Yeah, I can't work there. Not for him."

"The *hell* you can't," she said. "You'll never see him anyway. Trust me. He works on the top floors. I haven't even met the guy, and he acquired my business."

"Are you sure?"

"I'm not sure, but who cares if you see him again?" she said. "You both ended it, right?"

"On bizarre fucking terms," I said.

"You need to do this for you and Addy, period. You haven't had an opportunity for a win like this in a long time. Take it."

"You're right."

"There are two massive skyscrapers that Mitchell and Associates own. His office is on the top floors of the Howard Tower, and like I said, even if you worked in the same building as he does, you'd never see him. The place is massive, like sixty or seventy floors. Hotels are on the lower levels, with amenities like coffee shops, restaurants, and boutique stores…shit like that to entertain international travelers. It's enormous, so you won't see him. Trust me, they have those buildings set up to entertain and you'll be in a world of your own on your own floor."

"You do see how gorgeous the man is, right?" I asked.

She laughed. "Goddamn, do I ever. Now I really want to know what the sex was like."

"He was amazing." I smiled at the memory of seeing this face, laying back on the table—his look right before he came while I rode him. "All I can say was that the man I spent a few days with," I pointed at the picture, "smiled a lot wider than this, and he didn't look like such an arrogant dick the entire time."

Britney covered her mouth. "What if you see him again?"

"We *ended it*, remember? You keep talking like that, and I won't take the job."

"Get the fuck over yourself. You're doing this for Addy. Now, housing is so hard to find, but there is a studio available. Let's go look at it. I'll cover the down payment, and we'll get the process underway."

"What if I don't get the fucking job?"

"I already told Stef you're in. She trusts me, and I know you'll be a perfect fit. You're more than qualified for this anyway. There's no way I would let you pass this by."

"Stop trying to do shit for me," I growled.

"I'm helping you, Avery. Stop fighting people who want to help you. There's no weakness in saying yes. You have said more than once that you want out of this shit hole and a job that could fucking pay the bills. This is a golden ticket, and you know it."

I slumped against the couch. "Well, as long as you put the deposit down, you're out the money if I don't get the job." I pursed my lips. "What am I doing there, anyway?"

"Mainly paperwork and computer shit. You'll probably be setting appointments for Stefanie and doing personal shit for her too. Easy stuff."

"Fine. Let's go look at this place in Torrance you're raving about."

CHAPTER FIFTEEN

Avery

I went out with Britney and some of our mutual friends that night. We started with sushi, and then the celebration went on from there. Britney had reached some crazy-ass milestone with her company, and *Mitchell and Associates* were now helping her to open her first store in some ritzy area with an outdoor shopping mall.

If I was honest with myself, somewhere in the back of my mind, I think I'd always wanted my sister to bring me into her company. However, I figured that part of her still viewed me as the runaway who gave our mom hell when Jill fostered me, which is partly why I was surprised she'd name-dropped me to this Stefanie woman at all.

"Hey," Britney said, "you're not drinking."

"Four shots aren't enough for you?" I smiled at her.

"We have the party limo, and you're turning down a night where we can let loose?"

"Come on, Avery," Sarah said. Sarah, the straight-up, perfect wife—

until she got away from her husband and kids and drank with the girls, of course. "You're normally leading the way."

"She's probably fantasizing about her new job over at Mitchell and Associates." My sister winked at me. "She fucked the CEO, you know?"

"Shut up," Michelle said. Our lawyer friend's eyes lit up as she choked on her cocktail. "Mr. Fortune 500? Mr. Sexy himself—James H. Mitchell? You fucked him?"

"Yeah." Jim and I were pretty good at lying to people while screwing off together, so what was the harm in playing along when it was the truth? These girls were heading to blackout drunk—they wouldn't remember this anyway. "We fucked all over some castle in the middle of England's countryside."

"Oh, God." Michelle rolled her eyes. "You almost had me, girls." She started dancing in place. "Let's go. I want to dance."

Typically, I was the one to lead the pack in a fun night out, but tonight I felt off. I hated that Derek knew I'd been with another guy, not because I was afraid of him, but because I knew this shit would probably send him off the deep end. And he had my baby.

"Brit," I spoke up over the music. "Why did you tell Derek about Jim and me?" I asked, the girls already on the dance floor.

"Oh, Jesus," she said. "You're letting him ruin your night, aren't you?"

"I don't like it when he gets pissed off like he did when my daughter is there."

"Then why did you admit that you did when he asked you?"

"Why did it even have to come up? Why do you always feel like you have to intervene in my goddamn life? Shit like this always stirs the pot with that asshole."

"Sorry," she said, half drunk and half remorseful. "I guess I should've just told him you enjoyed touring the sites alone."

"You didn't need to tell him anything at all, but that version would've made my life a bit fucking easier."

"You need to find a way to cut his ass off. You say his parents enable him, but you also do. You don't see it, but you do."

"I'm doing the best I can with what I have," I snapped. "If my daughter gets—"

"We all know, Av. If she gets thrown into the system like you, right? When are you going to stop lying to yourself and face this head-on for Addy?"

"When I know for a fact that he won't bury me with his bullshit and lies."

"And what dirt does he have on you to do that with?"

"The fact that I have a DUI on my record and jail time for that shit. I was a runaway. The fact I did drugs too, and that's why I was stupid enough to get with him in the first place. He'll bring up all my history and paint me to look like the piece of shit *he* is."

Brit rubbed her forehead. "If you get a good lawyer, you'll be fine. They'll see that it was all six or seven fucking years ago."

"Are *you* paying for the lawyer? Michelle already made it clear that she wasn't getting involved, and she knows Addison."

"Michelle is a bitch," Brit said. "And no, I'm not paying for your lawyer. I paid to retain one for you already, and you fell for Derek's bullshit and trusted his stupid ass again. Never used the lawyer after he manipulated you the last time."

"Fuck this," I said, shouldering my purse. "Listen, thanks for the job offer, but I'm out of here. Tell your friend that I'm happy where I'm at."

"Don't do this, Avery," she said, stopping me from leaving. "Take the job. Take it for Addy."

"Throwing that back in my face again?"

"When you get pissed like this, someone has to help you see things clearly."

"Well, I'm half drunk and fucking pissed. I'm going home. I need to cool off."

I turned to leave, and there he was.

"So, I get our daughter, and you go out looking for someone to fuck tonight?"

"Get out of my way, Derek," I said, glaring back a Britney. "You smell disgusting. Drinking, pills, and smoking the good stuff again, dirtbag?"

"I've got your stupid ass doing it on video," he slurred his words.

"Tell me you narrated it because you sound like you belong in a hospital. What the fuck. How did you know I was here?"

He waved his phone at me. "Cell tracker, genius. You're still on my plan. Couldn't track you in London because you went international, and Brit gave you another phone, but I knew you'd be out looking for your fix tonight."

I thrust my phone in his chest. "Take the fucking phone. You offered this for me to stay in touch with our daughter. Now, I think I'll find a different phone." I looked at Britney. "Forget about what I said earlier. I'm taking that position, and I'm getting the fuck out of this godforsaken town."

A WEEK later and my interviews were out of the way. I was officially in as Stefanie's assistant at the company whose CEO I'd screwed like a wild woman, and today was my first day. I even used my iron and ironing board for the first time in a year when I had to get the wrinkles out of all of my pencil skirts and button-down shirts.

Stefanie's office walls were lined with magazine covers where the company had been featured, all of which had Jim's face plastered on them. If I was honest, I only recognized the sexy black, wavy hair, the emerald eyes, and that scorched-earth look in his photos. That was it. These magazines didn't do much to bring up happy memories of the times I'd shared with Jim, the man I'd had a blast with in London.

Addy was set to finish out the week at school, and we were going to be moving into our new place—the studio Brit showed me—over the weekend. Everything was in place, and Addy would be coming to work with me next week. I was feeling a lot of pressure fading just by moving this far from Derek. I'd like to see that asshole make it past security and come in here throwing a raging fit. Cameras were planted everywhere and for a good reason too. The place was fancy as fuck.

I was going to be working on the twelfth floor, and that helped me feel more protected. I would get my own cell phone with my first paycheck, and I was sucking it up without one in the meantime. It wasn't as hard for me to do as it might be others. I'd lived without one for almost all my life, and I'd rather take my chances with my POS car breaking down and leaving me stranded than having Derek stalking me on the other phone.

He had no idea where I worked, where my new apartment was, and I finally felt free of the abusive relationship. There. I fucking said it. Abusive relationship. Would Derek be out of my life forever? Not likely, but at least he couldn't stalk my ass anymore. One step at a time.

My desk phone rang, and I ran my clammy hands over my neatly pressed skirt before I picked up the phone. "This is Avery with Mitchell and Associates, Public Relations department."

"Hey, sis," Britney said. "I just wanted to make sure I could reach you. How do you like the job?"

"It's fine so far. I've been answering phones and directing calls to others on this floor, and stuff I can't handle goes to Stef."

"Sounds adventurous." She chuckled. "Listen, I just wanted you to know that Derek's trying to pressure us into telling him where you're moving and the new job."

"Pressure? Why is there any pressure?" I asked, almost growled, from my desk. I lowered my voice, "We went over this. Unless he holds a gun to your head, he gets zero info. Understand?"

"I know that."

"Does Mom know that? There's a reason I'm not telling Larry or Annette anything. I don't trust them. If I'm going to start over, it's not going to get fucked up."

"Chill out. Can people hear you?"

I glanced around, seeing my first fun co-worker, Amir, smiling at me and shaking his head. He already met the foody and sailor-language woman in me today at lunch. He was so damn cool that I'd actually want to date his ass if his preference weren't for men only.

"Amir says hi." I smirked at him.

He leaned back in his chair and raised an eyebrow at me. "You need to play nice."

"Sounds like you've made a friend already," Britney said.

I looked over at Alyssa, whose jade eyes reminded me of some eye model or any model for that matter. The girl was gorgeous, and, as usual, she was in LA to become an actress. She was super cool too. How I made friends so fast was beyond me, but I was genuinely happy about it. Maybe it was my fearlessly eating everything in sight—like I had done with Jim—that drew people to me? Hell, if I knew.

"Hey, sorry, but I've got to go," I said. "Stefanie's on her way over."

"No problem. I'm glad things are going well. Talk later," Britney said before she ended the call.

THE WEEK WENT PHENOMENALLY WELL. I couldn't have asked for a smoother transition into a new job—a new life. Amir and Alyssa were sort of my new crew, and I caught all the gossip on the floor from them, which was more than I expected. I guess a lot of behind the scenes shit went on down here.

There were two managers above Stefanie on our floor, but I hadn't had any encounters with them so far. They were stuffed away behind glass walls down the hall from my desk where about thirty of us sat and did the grunt work for the bosses in the PR department of this company.

Addy and I had officially moved into our new apartment, and it was her first day to come to work with me. I held Addy's hand, walking her into the daycare and preschool unit.

"You excited?" I asked, seeing all the kids starting to take notice of Addy—who'd dressed herself this morning. "It's a big day with new friends," I said as a woman approached.

"Can I help you two?" the gray-haired woman with a meticulous bun asked while another younger, beautiful redheaded woman trailed her.

"I'm here to bring my daughter in while I head up to work. Stefanie told me she was starting here this morning."

"What's the child's name?"

"The *child's* name is Addison Blake," I said.

After a whirlwind of bullshit, me turning over Addy's birth certificate, and all the other documents that came with enrollment, the woman refused my daughter. The sweet-looking younger redhead? She was a total bitch who helped escort us from the area.

Addy looked up at me, confused, and I did my best to keep it together. "The only way to get you into class is to give you a little experience, kid," I said with a smile, thanking God that she didn't get her feelings hurt.

"Sperience?" she tried to say the word.

"Yes," I said, punching the elevator button. "You need to learn a little bit about what Mommy does, and then you can go play with the rest of the kids and tell them what you learned about at work with mommy."

I wanted to cry. What the fuck was I supposed to do now? I pulled her out of a school with teachers and friends she loved. We were officially an hour away from that place now, and Stefanie had fucked me over by saying that I could just show up, and so long as I had my paperwork, Addy would be allowed in. Now, there was no fucking room? We'll see what Stef thought about that while Addy worked on her floor as a damn distraction all day.

"Hey," Amir said. "I bet you're Addison. You sure look like an Addison. Am I right?"

"Addy," she said, climbing into my seat. "I have to learn work," she stated thoughtfully.

I smiled at Amir's confused expression. "Apparently, there's no room for extras. That would've been nice to know last week," I said.

He frowned but kept his lips clamped while Addison looked at him. "Well, we can use your help here with us, Addy," he said.

"Oh, my God. She's your mini-me," Alyssa said, coming around in her tight-ass dress, long gorgeous legs, and breasts threatening to spill out of it. "You're a doll."

"I'm not a doll. I'm a person," Addy corrected her.

Alyssa looked at me and laughed. "She's got your strong personality, too, huh?"

"Yeah, and imagine two of us working up here together."

Everything was moving smoothly until three in the afternoon. Amir had even gone out and found a coloring book and colored pencils to keep Addy occupied. Then, Stef came onto the floor after being gone all morning.

"In my office, please, Avery," she said, half-smiling at Addy, who was sitting at my desk in a chair I'd rolled up next to mine. I followed her, knowing the woman was pissed. "Do you mind telling me why there is a child on this floor?"

"You might want to ask the lady in the daycare admin department who rejected my kid," I said, annoyed that this was blowing back on me as if I was trying to get away with something.

"You've got to be joking," she said, obviously irritated beyond belief that she had to deal with any of this.

"I wanted to say the same thing when they wouldn't allow Addy into their class. The last thing I wanted was to have my kid with me at my new job, but this completely blindsided me, and I had no other option. I was under the impression that this wouldn't be an issue."

"I'll handle this. Just get back to work. Supervisors will be on the floor."

I watched the woman scramble for her phone and try to work to fix the preschool problem. As I went back to work, I heard whispers and oh shits coming at me like friendly fire. I glanced around, trying to figure out what the hell was happening. It wasn't an earthquake. Addy was unaffected, scribbling on pages of a magazine, and I just shrugged it all off. That's when, from out of my peripheral, I saw a mob of suits.

"Amir," I said, and he looked over. "Are the men in black here or what?"

"Just work," he mouthed.

What the hell is happening?

I rose while everyone ducked and stared at their computers as if to beg the machine to pull them physically into it. That's when I noticed the tallest man out of the group. The onyx colored hair that hinted at the slightest natural curl if not tamed. The hair I ran my hands through and gripped in utter ecstasy. Holy fucking shit.

Our eyes met when he caught me staring at him in disbelief. Shit. I thought he never came down here. I broke eye contact with his emerald eyes after he gave me that look I thought I'd never see again. It wasn't a look that he was going to fuck me in every room in this building, but it *was* the look that he remembered fucking in every room in his castle.

I looked around at everyone who was hiding from him and the army of suits trailing him. What the hell? Was he that terrifying? Did I get out of that fake relationship just in time? Why was everyone working like they were robots?

I looked back at Jim, and his face recovered from the knowing grin and that glint in his eye that made me resist running out to him and holding the man who made me so happy in England. The dick look on his face now was that fucking scorched-earth look. Was I supposed to sit in my chair as he conversed with his men-in-suits? Was this his *fear the badass CEO* look?

What the hell ever. I sat down. I couldn't forget I had my kid here, and Stef was more than likely having a coronary attack that Addy was here too. That's when Stef went to Jim, interrupting him from his power-suit talk, and pointed in my direction.

What a goddamn bitch, I thought, knowing she was ratting Addy and me out. Now, here I was, watching Jim try and level me with that look I swore I never wanted to be on the other end of. Too bad that he was up against me protecting my daughter, and I wasn't going to allow him to say shit about her being here. I feared fucking nothing when it came to protecting her, even this CEO—who was sexier than fuck with the look on his face—heading my way. Time to meet the bastard side of Jim head-on, especially if he was kicking my daughter off the floor.

CHAPTER SIXTEEN

Jim

For the first time in my entire life, there was one employee in my building who didn't hide or giggle to their co-worker while I was in the room. Except Alex, of course, but he didn't count.

I know the usual expression I carried when I was in a room of employees that I'd never met—nor intended to—faded the moment she stood, and I saw those eyes that'd never left my dreams. Those eyes that glossed over when she climaxed while riding me into ecstasy. I recovered whatever expression I held when our eyes locked and forced it all down. I missed this woman more than I imagined.

Holy shit, she worked here? How long had she been working for me? Did she know who I was in London? There's no fucking way. She did role play well with me, though. Maybe she knew who I was the entire time.

Then I saw something I never thought possible—on top of realizing Avery was working in my building, and I never fucking knew it. I saw the black curls of a little girl who I assumed was her daughter, Addy, and I pinched my lips together to hold back the humor of what in the hell could have transpired to make Avery bring her daughter to work in her cubicle with her.

"Mr. Mitchell," Perry, my senior manager on the public relations floor, caught me as soon as I spied the adorable child scribbling on a magazine—ironically, the magazine that did an exclusive write up on me and Mitchell and Associates. "I assure you that we do not allow children on the floor."

I ignored Perry and went over to Avery's desk. Avery's eyes were fierce, and I knew why. She made it perfectly clear that *no one* fucked with her daughter.

"It's fine, Perry," I said, moving toward where Avery was staring me down like a mother bear watching over her cub.

I looked down at the magazine, which was written about my success as a young CEO of one of the largest companies in the nation. Addy wasn't aware of my approach, and I saw where she was intently scribbling over my face, and it was taking all I could not to laugh at how Avery must've loved her daughter doing so.

"Is something wrong?" Avery asked.

I didn't know how to respond to her. Shit, who was afraid of who?

"Mr. Mitchell," Stefanie started. I assumed Avery worked for her, given the placement of Avery's desk. "We're going to fix this issue of the child."

Addy looked up at me. Her bright blue eyes blinked slowly because I must've looked like a giant in her presence.

"Hi," she said. "Your face." She looked at the magazine, then back to me.

"Avery, I need to speak with you about your daughter," Stefanie said.

"That will not be necessary, Ms. Blythe," I said and knelt next to Addy. "Hi, I see you must not like my face?" I smiled and pointed at the sharp lines drawn across it.

"Your face is pretty," she said. "Why are you in my book?"

"I guess I got lucky," I mused. "My name is James. My friends call me Jim or Mitch."

I felt the anxiety of everyone in the room, and it was thick with fear and annoyance. All geared toward my being here and this sweet little girl.

"I like Mitch." She giggled and popped two dimples in each of her cheeks in doing so. "I'm Addison." She went back to coloring, "My friends call me Addy."

"May I ask why such a sweet girl like yourself is working today? You should be playing with the kids in the children's center, I would assume."

"Mommy said I have to learn work before they let me play," she said.

My eyes shifted over to Avery's, and hers were still ablaze. Though it was a short amount of time, I'd remembered these beautiful blue eyes well. All memories of this blue-eyed beauty pushed aside; I knew something must have happened to piss her off.

"Is Addy here because you do not trust the preschool? Perhaps a sick child wasn't sent home?"

"More like the preschool wouldn't allow her in," Avery shot back, eying me and everyone standing around me. "I told her that she was lucky and got to come to work with me instead."

I rose up and glanced around to locate Alex. "Mr. Grayson," I called out to my vice president.

"Right here," he said, walking over from speaking to someone in an office down the hall. "Wow, hey there," Alex said, his eyes meeting Addy's.

"Hi," she said, still working on dissolving my face with her colors.

"Nice to have you working in our public relations department, young lady."

"Alex, handle the issues with that video file and the advertisements that failed to send. I need to speak with the women in the preschool facility."

It didn't take much for Alex to do the math at that point. Typically, I would have called down and handled matters, but I didn't. His eyes went from me to Addison to Avery, and then his features went soft, and he nodded.

"We'll fix the problem," he said, then rounded up the herd and left me to speak with Avery.

I looked back at Addy and Avery. "Would you both mind joining me on a field trip?" I asked, trying to make this exciting for Addison. I didn't even need to. The kid wasn't frightened of any of us. I loved that fearless nature.

"Where to?" she questioned.

"Addy, don't be rude. This nice man, who you demolished with your colors, is going to take us down to where your school is."

"Good." She sighed. "Your work is really boring, Mom."

"I couldn't agree more," I answered Addy with a smile.

"I'll join you," Stefanie interjected. "Again, I'm so sorry about this, Mr. Mitchell."

"Why are you sorry?" Addison asked before I could dismiss the woman.

"Addison Jane," Avery scolded her daughter and took her hand. "It's rude to talk when adults are talking."

"Ms. Blythe, please stay. Thank you," I said, before the woman eyed Avery and rushed back toward her office. I nodded toward Avery, then smiled at Addison, "I believe our field trip awaits the three of us."

"Yes," Addison's smile beamed.

Avery and Addison followed me into the elevator, and I hit the button to the lower level, where our daycare and preschool was located.

"How long have you been working for us?" I finally broke the ice of quiet awkwardness.

"A week," Avery said flatly. "Listen, I don't need your help."

"I understand that. However, would you rather Addison work? She's already informed me it is quite dull, and there's the whole child-labor law thing."

Avery narrowed her eyes at me skeptically. "Fine, then. Maybe you can convince those women who run your cute little preschool and daycare to take her. I had no idea there would be a problem."

"Her records were turned in, correct?" I asked.

"Of course, I brought all of that. I'm not a fu—" She stopped herself, and I smiled, knowing the woman cussed like a goddamn sailor. "I brought everything required."

"Then let's find out why this super-smart little young lady isn't in preschool."

"I needed 'sperience," Addison spoke up. "Mommy said that's how I get in."

"Ah," I pointed toward her magazine. "Looks like you gained enough experience." I looked at Avery, hoping I grabbed the right word for Addison's excuse for not being in preschool. "You colored my face out like a champion." I laughed.

Addison giggled, and it was the sweetest sound. "I'm sorry, Mitch," she said. "Your face looked mean. Ya know?"

"I need to work on that, don't I?"

"Yes," Addy said. "You look pretty right now."

"I'm smiling," I responded.

"Smiling is pretty."

"It most certainly is," I answered.

After the elevator opened, we were soon around the corner where our Children's Center was located. When I walked in, Janice Spokes and her intern turned three shades of pink. Her eyes drifted from mine down to Addison, then Avery. That's when I felt Addison clutch my hand. I was shocked at the gesture, but then livid that the little girl would think to hold onto my hand in the first place. Was she scared of these two? What did they do to make her reach for my hand?

"Addy," Avery whispered, "come stand with Mommy."

I gave Addy a reassuring smile. "I'll take care of this." I knelt to where Addy stood quietly at Avery's side. "Should I use my smiling face or the face you scribbled on in your book?" I inquired when I saw her serious expression wasn't wavering.

"Scribble face," Addy answered and then looked at the two women who had plastered smiles on their questioning expressions.

I rose and turned to the women. Their faces were curious and confused, as well as they should be. "Ms. Spokes and Ms. King," I said. "Did Miss…"

Son of a bitch, I forgot Avery's last name.

"Miss Gilbert," Avery said.

"Yes, thank you. Did Miss Gilbert have any difficulty with her daughter's paperwork today?"

"No, Mr. Mitchell."

I looked at Addison. "It appears the children are having snack time. Would you like to join them?" I glanced to Avery. "Any food allergies?"

"None," she said. "Though she eats like her mother does."

I smiled, but Avery remained indifferent. "There's plenty of food. Try not to spoil your dinner, though," I said.

If I hadn't turned and knelt back down to reach Addison's eye level, I would have never had the smell of coconut and berries hit all of my senses after she hugged me. I patted her back. "Better hurry."

Addison scurried off, and I stood to bring my full attention back to the women. "While the aides assist the kids, I would like to meet with the one who refused one of our employee's children."

"That would be me," Ms. Spokes boldly spoke up.

I'd never been in this room, and I only knew the woman through staff meetings when we decided to open the preschool, but it was evident that the woman thought she owned the place.

"Very well. Where's your office so we can speak privately?"

I didn't fail to observe her glare at Avery before she motioned for me to follow her.

"Come with us," I said to Avery.

Avery didn't need the invitation. I could tell she wanted a piece of this woman herself.

"You will wait outside, Miss Gilbert," Ms. Spokes said.

"You're fucking kidding, right? That's my kid in there, and I'm not leaving a decision about her to be left up to you or him," Avery snapped.

"Excuse me?" Ms. Spokes countered. "You do realize you're in the company of Mr. James—"

"Mitchell," Avery finished for her. "Amazingly enough, Mr.

Mitchell is CEO of the company's preschool that wants to reject my daughter."

"Avery," I said, knowing I should have kept it formal with last names, but that slipped. "Please allow me to ask Ms. Spokes why Addison was..." I paused to ensure I heard correctly. "Addison was rejected?"

"Yes. Rejected," Avery confirmed.

"What is the meaning of this?" I asked Ms. Spokes in a demanding tone. "Do not even think about giving me any excuses either, Ms. Spokes, or this will be your last day watching over this department."

"We don't have enough staff," she said indignantly.

"How long has this been an issue?" I asked.

"At least a month."

"I've heard nothing of the sort. I haven't had any requests to expand this department. Did I miss something that you may have sent my way?"

"No." She stood solidly. This woman was an old crow. "We told the parents we were full."

"That is not your duty, ma'am," I said sternly, and the woman finally broke and sat in her chair. "Those are not merely parents. They are my employees who depend on my company's Children's Center for numerous reasons." I kept my gaze locked on hers, "I must know exactly how many children are in other daycares or preschools due to you not informing upper management there was an issue with a shortage in staff?"

"Eight, maybe."

"Eight, *maybe*?" I questioned. "Maybe is not a word I like hearing from a woman that my company entrusts with our employees' children and their safety."

"I can't remember," she whined.

"That is no excuse. That is eight parents—*my* employees, might I remind you—who have had to scramble to make other arrangements despite what was promised would be made available to them. I should have had something on my desk, informing me that more staff was required *before* the first child was turned away. I'm not quite certain I can trust you in such an important position, one that requires someone to look out for what's best for my employees and their children. You will be replaced."

"I'm fired?" She covered her heart.

"You will be transferred to a different role if that satisfies your needs. Currently, I do not care for your callous attitude or negligence. Until your replacement has been hired, I suggest you will work with your temporary replacement," I said. "An official announcement will be emailed to all employees, announcing their children are welcome back to our Children's Center. We have more than enough room here, so I know that space is not the issue. That is all, Ms. Spokes."

"I am so sorry, Mr. Mitchell."

"You might say that to the employees you've shunned; however, I do not see you as the type to apologize to the parents who've been placed in difficult childcare situations. I am thankful I found this child on one of my office floors with her mother, or I would have never known there was an issue. I will be working with human resources and our child development recruiters to find your replacement, and I do hope it's immediately."

"And where do I transfer to, Mr. Mitchell?"

I turned from where I was leaving her office. "Well, that's a question you might want to ponder for a while. Sleep on it tonight, perhaps? You see, the fear I see in your eyes is most likely the same that was in the parents' eyes who depended on this daycare and preschool for their children. It's in all their offer packages, and yet, here you are turning them away and making a liar out of me."

"My Lord in Heaven," she sat in her chair, frazzled.

"There are plenty of internal transfer positions available within the company," I said, seeing the woman was about to become my brother's heart patient if I didn't slow it down some on her. "Look them up."

"Thank you," she muttered.

I turned and felt Avery on my heels. "Ms. King?" I called out to the other woman who seemed to work alongside Ms. Spokes.

"Yes, Mr. Mitchell." She popped over to me as a young college intern would.

"We will be making changes to this department. Until then, no child will be turned away. You will find a way to ensure they're taken care of. The additional staff will be hired, trained, and working by the end of next week. You will also be reporting to someone besides Ms. Spokes." I saw her expression fall. "If you'd like to resume working here, I would like to know here and now."

"Absolutely, Mr. Mitchell." Her eyes darted from Avery to me.

"Very well, then," I said. "I should have never needed to accompany one of my employees down here to find our childcare facility wasn't operating correctly. The blame falls squarely on Ms. Spokes, but for the future, please know that there is a chain of command that ends with me. I decide the fate of every department, and I need to know what everyone needs. This all will be fixed, and I do hope you are more than welcoming to little Addison."

I left with a certain amount of bubbling rage inside that the old bag had made decisions for my company without telling me. Bullshit. It was unacceptable, and a horrible fucking way to reconnect with Avery. God only knew what she thought of my company after this debacle.

"You almost gave that woman a heart attack."

"My brother's a heart surgeon. He would've saved her miserable life," I said, angrier than when we left the daycare, but feeling more than familiar with Avery. I wasn't like this with anyone but Alex when I was this fucking pissed. I was, however, holding in more shit than I was letting Avery know.

Avery laughed. "She reminds me of that old bitch who gave you trouble on the tour."

I tried to smile at the memory, but I was too busy wondering how many other departments in my company were fucked like this.

"Possibly yes." I looked at her. "It is nice to see you again, Avery. I hope Addison enjoys her new preschool."

Avery was stiff, and I knew she was probably pissed off at the curt way I was responding to her. I couldn't mask my irritation, though. I couldn't bring her into my arms like I wanted to. I couldn't steal her over to the elevators that led up to my office and tell her I regretted everything—that I now made exceptions in fucking my employees, and that exception was her and her alone. I couldn't do anything but get my ass involved with these department heads and fix all of this shit.

When I was back on the top floors, Alex met my short fuse. "I want more surveillance on that daycare until a replacement is found."

"On it. Everything cool with Avery and her daughter?" he tried to probe, but I wasn't interested in small talk.

"Addison is in the facility. I need someone on those cameras. We can talk more about it later. I just pissed off the woman running that place, and I want her watched until she's replaced."

"I'll handle it now," Alex said, leaving and knowing we'd catch up after I cooled off some more.

What a fucking joke. In order to fix this, I would assemble a new team to inspect all of my departments. Never again would something like this go undetected. Of all places for things to go wrong, I couldn't believe it was with our employees' children. Good God.

I was embarrassed, pissed, and now fucking furious that I couldn't give in to what I really wanted—to express my apologies to Avery. To beg her for another chance. No, the asshole CEO had to leave and do his damn job instead.

CHAPTER SEVENTEEN

Avery

$\mathcal{M}$y mind was a shit-storm of a mess about Jim. Period. I was ready to rip his throat out when I assumed that he was pissed when he spotted Addy in the office with me yesterday. Then he knelt next to her. The James Mitchell façade that he carried—and everyone seemed scared shitless of—faded, and the Jim I'd been with in London, knelt to talk kindly with my daughter.

I watched Addy interact with him, all while observing Stefanie appear as if she was either going to pass out, cry, or hug me. I mean, I got it. Respect your boss, and follow the rules. It's as easy as that. At least that's how I envisioned working a job.

I could say with one-hundred-percent certainty, however, that even if I didn't know Jim from my vacation, I wouldn't have behaved the way everyone else seemed to when he entered a room. I wouldn't have hidden behind my computer, freaked the hell out if he approached me, trembled when I talked to him—all the shit I watched everyone, except for the suit-crew, do. I thought it was fucking weird, but maybe that's how all big businesses ran when the owner was around.

"So, he came to your floor," Brit said, "and then what? Finish your thought, Avery."

"Sorry. He brought Addy and me to the preschool that'd rejected her. He seemed pretty pissed that old lady had sent more kids than just Addy away."

"You think he remembered you?" She lowered her voice on the phone while I finished making Addy her breakfast.

"Finish, quick, Addy," I said, wanting to get our breakfast dishes in the sink before we walked out the door. "We're gonna be late."

"Avery."

"Jesus, Britney, I don't know. I'm trying to get out of here on time."

"Good Lord, he had to have remembered you. He probably wouldn't have done what he did if he didn't."

"Would it have mattered?" I said. "I mean, yeah. He remembered me. How could he not? He stared at my face for almost an entire week, so unless he's senile, he knows who I am. He asked how long I'd been working there, so it must've crossed his mind that maybe I worked for him all along." Addy got up from the table and slid on her red sequin ballet flats. She wore them with everything, no matter how much they clashed with her outfit. It was pretty adorable. "I don't have time to talk about it right now, though. I'm sorry. I'll call you later. Gotta go."

"Okay, okay. Have a good day, and call me later," Brit said before I ended the call.

"Let's hit it, kid," I said to Addy. "We're seriously going to be late if there's too much traffic."

"I work with you today, Mommy?" Addy asked as we walked out the door, and I locked it behind us.

"No. I don't think so. That nice man—my big boss—he helped you get promoted yesterday."

"Mitch," she said. "My friend."

We were at the car in record time, and Addy didn't give me any hassle when I buckled her in. "He's the boss too, Addy," I said, kissing her forehead and moving toward the driver's seat.

You piece of shit car, start already, I internally demanded. "Please, God, do not let me get fired because of you," I slammed on the steering wheel. "You stupid, stupid, car!"

"This car is stupid," Addison said.

"Don't say stupid. It's a bad word. Mommy shouldn't say it either."

"Oh, Mom. You say bad words, I don't."

The car started. "Thank God," I said.

"I know. God is happy that I say good words."

"God doesn't like Mommy saying the bad ones." I gave her a sheepish look while backing out. "I need to work on that. I'm sorry."

"I won't say stupid." She covered her mouth, "Sorry. *That* S-word."

"Don't say any S-words, how about that?" I smiled.

"I can't say silly?"

"You can say that one," I said with a laugh.

We were close enough to work to avoid freeways, which was a miracle in itself. We pulled into the parking structure, passed all the fancy cars, and found a place on the second level. "Sweet, right by the elevators."

That's when I saw the sign.

"Reserved for management," I said in defeat. "Well, maybe Mom will be promoted to manager one day, and this will be our parking place."

"Mitch will promote you. He promoted me."

"Addy, you don't even know the word." I laughed. "However, we need to work on our big words. We haven't done that in a while. So, our word for the day is promote or promoted."

"Mitch does it," she answered.

"Yes, he probably does. Other people do it too. It works in different ways and has different meanings, but for you and me, it means to get a better thing—to do a bigger job and to make more money."

"We need a new car, mommy."

"You don't like Bunny anymore?"

"Bunny is so tired, Mommy."

"Yeah, well, I'll need a really good promotion to get a new car."

"Daddy got one."

I rolled my eyes and slipped the keys out of the ignition. "He sure did," I answered, trying not to sound sarcastic. I was a lot of things, but I wasn't the type of parent to badmouth the other. He didn't need my help to look like a deadbeat dad to his daughter. "Come on, out of the seat. Where's your back pack?"

"Oh, no!" Addy clamped her small hands over her mouth and closed her eyes. "At home. Oh no, Mommy."

"My fault. I rushed us out. It's no big deal."

"Will I still get promoted from Mitch?" she asked.

"I don't think we'll see your friend today. We got lucky yesterday," I said. "Now, grab my hand. Let's go."

We headed toward the walkway that was erected over the street, leading us from the parking structure to my building. We always entered on the ninth floor, and today, we made it just in time. Instead of using the elevator, we breezed down the flight of steps to where the Children's Center was. When we got there, the kids were seated, and the old ninny was still present and in charge.

"I see you've forgotten your backpack?" she said to Addy. "How do you expect to learn if you can't remember basic things, young lady?"

"I won't—" Addy started making excuses for herself—a fucking three-year-old toddler—as the old woman towered over her intimidatingly.

"Addy, it's okay. Go sit with the others," I said, holding my arm up to back the woman away from Addy.

The fact that this bitch thought she could flex on my kid sent me through the roof, and I felt my self-control slipping away as Addy joined the group.

I took a long, slow, deep breath before I brought my furious gaze to meet the woman's eyes. "You have the fucking nerve to speak to my child as if she's the one responsible for her things? What the hell is wrong with you? You're already getting fired for acting like a miserable bitch, and you *still* can't help yourself?"

The look on her ashen face would've led anyone else to believe that I'd just ran over her cat. "Are you threatening me?" she said, flabbergasted.

"I'm serious as a fucking heart attack, lady. I can see the look on your face. Scolding a three-year-old for not bringing a backpack? Really? It's not like you sent her home with homework, is it? Did I miss that part after I picked her up?"

"Maybe you did."

"Bullshit. Listen up," I said, pointing at her. "If you so much as look at my daughter sideways and I find out about it, you're going to regret it. You have no idea what I'm willing to do to make sure my daughter is safe from predators like you."

"Well...I, um...listen, this is a complete misunderstanding, Miss Gilbert." She straightened her posture and held her head high with some level of righteous indignation that I had no idea how she had the nerve to muster.

"You're right about that." I looked over at the children and the aides who sat with them. Aside from this old nag, they seemed well taken care of, and that was the only reason I didn't march Addy out of that place right then. "I trust you'll make sure my daughter has a good day. I'll check on her later."

I turned to leave, and there was Jim with the young Johnny Depp-looking friend of his who I met at the restaurant in London. My eyes widened, and the Johnny Depp guy seemed to be covering his grin while Jim was looking past me at the hag.

"Excuse me, gentlemen." I plastered on the best smile I could. "I have to get to work."

"Is everything okay, Miss. Gilbert?" Jim asked, eyes still on the woman. "Ms. Spokes?"

"No problems at all, Mr. Mitchell, Mr. Grayson," she responded.

I stood at the preschool entryway and leveled the woman with my glare, and she didn't say another word. I should've left and headed to my desk, but I didn't want this woman spinning anything.

"Mitch!" Addy screamed, running over to greet her new friend. "I'm promoted today."

"Hey there, Addy," he said as he knelt to greet her. Certainly a good call, or he would've been doubled over by my daughter, ramming into his balls. She squeezed his neck, and I covered my mouth when he patted her back with one arm and remembered her name.

Maybe he did remember a lot more than our fake roleplaying. Wait, he was just good with names. Oh, hell, he didn't have to do this at all. It was the gesture alone that had me watching and wishing *Jim* was in my life for a moment. If only to see this smile on Addy's face.

"Promoted?" he asked after greeting her. "So that means you'll be working up in the top, boring offices with me now?"

"No, silly," she said. "I get to go in there."

"Why yes, you do," he answered. He pointed up to the man I stood next to now, "This is my friend. His name is Alex, and he's going to make sure you have fun teachers today. Sound good?"

"It does." She hugged Jim again and patted his cheek sweetly.

"Addy, go to class. Jim needs to go to work too," I said, and then nearly choked when I realized I'd said his name in a way that didn't fly around here.

"His name is Mitch, Mom," Addy said and then spun around and went into the classroom area.

"Jim and Mitch, eh?" Alex said, looking at me with a knowing smile. "I'm Alex Grayson." He reached his hand out to mine, "I believe we've met before."

I smiled after Jim walked with the woman into her office.

"Yes, in London, when we all played musical dining tables, I think."

He chuckled. "Do you always curse-out old ladies?"

"Just the ones who screw with my kid," I said. "I'm sorry, but I have to go. It's great seeing you again, Alex."

I left the man who'd blown Jim up the entire time I was with him in that castle, leaving him standing there and looking at me with great curiosity, I'm sure.

～

"Amir," I said to my co-worker, "are you gonna eat those fries?"

"God, what have we done all these years without you here?" he said, sliding the fries over to me.

"The crows are going to be pissed when they starve to death," Alyssa teased. "You want the last of this milkshake?"

"That's where I draw the line, my friends," I said, crunching into Amir's still piping-hot French fries. "I don't drink after others. Total germ freak on that one."

"Not like you'd have room for it anyway. All this food, girl," Amir said. "Your body can't process this food. You're too tiny."

"Guys, we have to get back. This will be the second time I would be late today," I said, checking my phone and seeing the time.

"Can't have that," Alyssa said. "Oh," she added like a mystery was being revealed, "want to know why the execs were on the floor yesterday?"

"Someone mentioned something about footage being erased from the company cameras after a sales manager got caught screwing a rep in his office," Amir said.

"Shut the hell up," I said.

"That's the rumor. I also heard the reason Mr. Mitchell was with them was because of the documentary on his doctor friend. I think he's a brain surgeon or something. They've been recording bits and pieces, but I heard it sucks. That's what Cary in media production says, anyway. Don't say I told you," Amir said.

Jesus, and here we were talking about the boring video Jim was watching in England, which led to him getting me off in the most glorious way I could have ever desired. I had to shut these thoughts down and now. My body was already aching for *that* sensation again —and from only him.

"Good lord, you two. Does the gossip run that thick in this place?" I asked, changing my mind's gears.

"When Mr. Mitchell comes off the top floors, yes. Everyone looks for some sort of reason he's on their floor."

"Goddamn," I said. "He's treated like a god here, isn't he?"

"He sure looks like one. A Greek god." Alyssa giggled.

Try seeing the man without his clothes on, I thought with a smile.

It was a lame way to compare a man with a perfectly chiseled body and a beautiful face of perfection, but hey, sometimes you had to call it what it was.

We were stopped when Stefanie met me at my cubicle. "I have no idea what's going on," she said. "Maybe it was yesterday, you know, with your daughter being here inappropriately, or something else."

"What is it? Am I fired, Stefanie?" I asked, cutting her off.

"Why would you think that?"

"Because you look like you're going to pass out."

"Well, I wish I could give you more information, but I can't. Mr. Mitchell would like to see you in his office," she said. "Follow me, please. I'll show you to the executive elevators."

"Should I be worried about this?"

"He's possibly addressing your daughter being on our floor."

"If he has a problem with her, maybe I do need to pay him a visit," I said, to which she eyed me in response.

I rode up to the sixty-fourth floor silently, and I walked out to floor-to-ceiling glass windows that overlooked downtown LA. I'd bet that without smog, you'd see the ocean from up here. It was exquisite.

Speaking of exquisite, so was the woman who stood in front of a massive reception desk, looking at papers on the counter. She wore a form-fitting, business suit with her red-soled stilettos, and had perfectly coifed hair, skin, and manicure. It was a much different world up here. Was Jim lying about not screwing secretaries or anyone who worked for him? This chick was drop-dead gorgeous. Her eyes were a brilliant blue, and they lit up when she spun around and saw me, or so I thought. She was actually beaming at Alex, who'd gotten off the elevator next to mine and was approaching me from behind.

Alex offered up a grin to her—one of *those* grins—and if this chick had been in a shitty mood before, Alex had changed it instantly.

"Miss Gilbert is here to see Mr. Mitchell," the elevator cop told her as he held the doors from closing. "How's your day, Miss Flores?"

"Great, Mike. Thanks for sending up Miss Gilbert." She took papers she'd been examining near a keyboard on the other side of the desk before turning to face me again. "Miss Gilbert, please follow me."

That was it for the sweet talk. I was walking the green mile down a hallway where fancy, English-looking artwork hung—the only artwork I'd ever seen, anyway. It must've been the hallway to Jim's office. Two double doors opened after Miss Flores ran a security card over a security pad.

She knocked as the doors opened. "Mr. Mitchell?"

"Yes, Summer?" he asked distantly.

"Miss Gilbert is here at your request."

"Thank you," he said.

I looked at her in confusion, and she just kept her poker face and walked away, leaving me to meet Mr. Mitchell in all his glory.

I held a hand over my heart, and it wasn't because of how gorgeous Jim looked, sitting in his dark gray, three-piece-suit either. The red tie set off the striking features of his face, but this corner office, surrounded by windows overlooking Los Angeles, was enough to bring me to my knees.

"Jesus Christ," I said softly, looking to my left, right, and back to where Jim's large, exquisite desk was. "No wonder England's countryside is in pictures out in that hallway. Where the hell would you hang a picture with windows instead of walls?"

"Nervous chatter?" Jim's voice quietly rang into my ears. "Since the first moment I met you, I would have never pinned you for having a nervous bone in your body."

I looked at him and grinned. "This is so beautiful," I said, ignoring him calling me out on rambling. "How do you get anything done with these views?"

Jim rose from his desk and pulled off his jacket. My eyes widened when I saw the shirt he was wearing under his black vest. That was *the* shirt—the shirt he hated. He fucked me in—well, I fucked him in. *Shit. You need to chill out, Avery.*

"Nice shirt," I said. "A little bird told me that you hated that shirt."

"Was that little bird chirping through a magazine article you read?" He smiled—the Jim smile. "Perhaps it was in a gossip column?"

"No. I think the bird told me first hand." I arched an eyebrow at him.

"A real-life speaking bird, huh? You must know a lot of parrots," he said. Then he grew serious, and that scorched-earth look was creeping its way up. "Will you please have a seat, Miss Gilbert." He pointed toward the luxurious leather seats across from where he sat in his billion-dollar, most likely Corinthian leather chair.

"The scorched-earth look doesn't work on me," I said, crossing my legs and trying to determine why I was here. "What do you need? Stefanie is pretty much packing my desk up right now."

He ran a hand through his hair and pursed his lips. "Did you have to cuss out Ms. Spokes this morning, Avery?" he asked, half humored and half annoyed.

"She was a bitch to my kid, Jim. Sorry, Mr. Mitchell," I said, my irritation beginning to grow. "That woman deserved a stiff slap across her face; she's goddamn lucky I didn't give her that instead of a few harsh words."

Jim glanced down at a piece of paper. "It also states here that you threatened to kill her?" He shook his head and licked his lips. "Why am I not surprised?" I saw the look on his face. This was him holding back laughing, but trying to remain serious.

"Kill her?" I rolled my eyes. "I'm not in the mafia, for Christ's sake. I told her she'd regret messing with Addy again, though, and I meant it. That bitch was completely out of line."

"You can understand why that might sound mafia-like to an old woman from Santa Monica, Avery," he said, trying to hit me with that look again. I noticed him rereading the paper in front of him, and then I saw that tick he seemed to have when deep in thought. He touched each fingertip, one-by-one, to his thumb while he read. "You've been here for nearly nine days, yes?"

"Yes," I said, angry that I'd fucked-up a new and excellent job. Jim was too serious, and I was too pissed that I'd let that woman get the best of me today.

"Well, I've never seen someone get reported to me in that amount of time. Honestly, I don't believe I've ever had anyone reported to me for their behavior ever. Not unless there's some sort of sexual harassment charges, but in your case," he looked at me, "it's regular harassment charges. It takes a hell of a lot to bring an employee past my HR team and directly to me. Would you know why that could be in your case and after only nine days working here?"

"I don't know." Tears were welling up in my eyes now. "Why don't you just tell me?

"Avery." He came across the desk and sat in the chair next to me. "I see that you are quite protective of Addison. I would have hoped you trusted that I was taking care of that woman after I talked with her yesterday. I didn't need your threats toward her this morning to add to my removal of her." He smirked. "I'm fairly sure you wouldn't have followed through on those threats too." His eyebrow arched, and damn, I missed him. "But it makes my case to remove her from that preschool more difficult than it needs to be."

"You have to understand something about me," I said, turning to face him and appreciating him coming to my side of the desk, perhaps as an understanding boss instead of the big exec standing imposingly behind his desk. "I've been in too many positions to protect Addy from the BS that comes her way. That woman started giving her the third-degree for forgetting her backpack. *She's three!* I wouldn't tolerate that from any teacher—here or at another preschool."

He took my trembling hands into his large ones. "My lawyers—"

"Your lawyers? Are you suing me for this?"

"No." He sighed. "Ms. Spokes threatened to sue my company over your behavior today. The lawyers were brought in with human resources and Alex late this morning. While we went through the surveillance footage, we noted a behavior with the woman that—well, let's just say, she's not suing anyone after the discussion we had with her. She signed off to leave the company."

"What the hell was on those videos? I have a right to know. Did that woman fuck with Addison after—"

"No," he said, rubbing the back of my tense hands. "She was negligent in her work. The videos also proved that she wasn't acting according to her job requirements. Thank God other teachers were in her company, or perhaps, children could have been harmed. She was getting paid to play solitaire on her computer. She was given the option to pay us back for lack of working for the two years of having her with us or leave without a fuss."

"So I'm not fired?"

"Actually, no," he said. "But I am kindly asking that if you are upset with staff, you do not threaten to make anyone regret it next time."

"If they come at Addy?"

"You'll come directly to me," he said with that CEO voice that was sexy until he used it on me. "I will handle it. We have security watching the preschool nonstop. No reason to go all Godfather and threaten to make anyone sleep with the fishes, okay?"

"All right," I said. "Is that it then?"

He pulled his hands from mine and stood and smiled. "Yes. I would like to say that I don't ever want to have to see you up here in my office again," he pinched his lips together as I stood, "but that wouldn't be true."

His face seemed pained like he meant something else, but—hell. I had no idea.

He did that sexy lip pucker thing while he bit the inside of his cheek. "Avery, let me take you out or something. Give me another chance. I know I fucked it up with the senseless words you overheard on that call with my brother. Truly, I never meant them. The second you walked out the door on me, I realized I was a jackass to even think like that, whether or not I was frustrated with my brother probing into my life."

"I have a hell of a life. You know I have issues. I'm a single mom who deals with a fucking drug addict for an ex." I laughed in disbelief that he was trying to have a shot with me. "I can't bring you into that. You knew that when you were on the phone that day. It's not a life you want, trust me."

"If it's too horrible for me, then why do you allow Addy to live in this life that is so terrible for you?"

"Good point." I blew out a breath. "But I can't explain it. It would be worse for you. Trust me on that."

"How much worse?" He waved his hand at his office. "I run this entire place, I have countless employees here and in my London office that I am responsible for, and all the shit that goes with keeping it all running smoothly. Why can't I have a chance with the one thing I feel might mean more to me than all of that?"

"You can't mean that," I said. "It was a fling, and you know it. You saw the good side. You saw the Avery that wasn't living in an average, bullshit day. And you never met the single mom Avery."

"I want to know that side of you as well. Just give me a chance and allow me to determine whether or not I want to be with the real you."

"Yeah, that smile." I shook my head, smiling back at him. "That cocky smile. It's going to screw your ass over, you know. I have a psycho ex who will despise you."

"Most exes hate themselves for losing the best thing they ever had, then project it onto the one who took their place."

"Oh." I planted my hands on my hips. "So you took his place? You're quite confident, Mr. Mitchell."

"Hopeful," he said. "And for the love of God, call me Jim."

"Okay, fine," I said. "You want a shot at my shitty life? Being around the bullshit? Because you don't look like you get dirty."

He held his hands out. "I believe I got this shirt quite dirty at one time." He smirked.

"You have no idea what the hell you're doing, do you?"

"I just know I want a chance with you again. I can't get you out of my mind. What I did to you." He ran his hand over the light growth on his chin. "I'm full of regret for hurting you and desperately sorry for those painful words. Allow me a chance to prove to you I knew I was foolish and wrong."

"Okay then, smart guy." I smirked at his lightened features. "Tomorrow night is big-mac night."

"McDonald's?" he questioned. "I can take you—"

I held my hand up. "It's Addy's night. You're welcome to join us if you want. She deems you are her good friend anyway." I narrowed my eyes at him. "I will warn you now, Jim Mitchell, if you hurt her—"

"If it doesn't work out between us, I promise Addy will still be my friend."

"I'm so serious. She's not to be hurt in this. Her dad's already doing a fantastic job with that."

"I understand. We'll take it all slow. I will prove to you I won't hurt either of you."

"Yeah. We'll see about that."

"Let me just kiss you or something."

Jim's cell phone rang, then his office phone, while his door opened to reveal Alex. Jim glanced at Alex with the startling act of all communication for the man happening at once. "What the hell?" he said. "Is the goddamn building on fire?"

"No, we just ran the first part of Collin's docuseries."

Jim looked at me then at his phone, which was still ringing off the hook. "Do I even want to answer that?" he asked Alex.

Alex laughed. "Let's just say Jacob will be quite jealous that he was a test subject. We were successful in ensuring better for privacy for Collin with the new methods used while airing this new series on neuroscience for Saint John's."

"Excellent news. Go ahead and field that out to the PR groups while I handle these phone calls."

"Collin and Jake are meeting us at Kinder's tonight. Nice job, man." He looked at me. "Nice to see you again, Avery," he said. "All right, my job here is done. I'm clocking out."

"Okay, I'm leaving too," I said.

Jim's phones were going into ringing frenzies. "Tomorrow night sounds great, Avery," he said, stopping me from following Alex out of his office. "So, I guess it will be a big mac for Addy and me, and I'm guessing three or four of them for you?" he teased, his phone still constantly ringing. "Dammit, I have to get this call. Your department might be insane, but just ignore it, and know that I'm going just as crazy up here." He winked, and I could tell he was my Jim from England again.

I had a responsibility to myself, my daughter, and really, any man that I dated—in that order. If I was a mess, it filtered in and hurt

Addy. I never brought men around her, but right now, she knew Jim as Mitch, her friend. So, a little fast food get together never hurt anything. Of course, I would ask Addy about Jim joining us first. She would have to be cool with the fact that we would have a new friend with us on her and mom's mid-week date night.

CHAPTER EIGHTEEN

Jim

I had no time to reflect on Avery being in my office, or exactly what I'd said to encourage her to allow me another opportunity with her. This day wasn't any less busy than my usual routine in the office. Still, by pulling recordings on my employees and going over them with human resources, Alex, and the lawyers, it wasn't necessarily an average day in the office either. It also wasn't usual practice for an employee with multiple supervisors above them to end up in my office, but I had Alex's intervention to thank for that.

Thank God Alex swiftly caught on to her being my Avery from England. Because of that, no one questioned Alex insisting that she was to report directly to me over her incident. In my opinion, Avery was justified in her actions toward the woman. How that old battle-ax made it through background was beyond me. Perhaps a psychiatric evaluation would have precluded her from even starting. There was no empathy or consideration for my employee's children, that was obvious from observing the way she treated Avery when we brought Addison into the preschool. Then her behavior toward Avery this morning? How many parents and children had she treated so rudely? It was unacceptable, and it wouldn't happen again.

I had Alex put together a strike force team that consisted of members that would begin internal investigations of all departments. This entire event with the Children's Center prompted me to ensure that all departments at Mitchell and Associates were functioning at optimum levels. After putting this new plan of investigation in action, I was feeling slightly better knowing we were taking steps to improve the quality of employment here at my company.

This day certainly did not want to end. Even after I packed up and left the office, my email was exploding. Thank God I had my driver today, or I'd be stuck in the office finishing this shit up. With my driver, Blake, at the wheel, I was able to keep my laptop open and answer pressing emails while he drove me to meet up with the guys for dinner.

Even with traffic tagging on an extra fifty minutes to my commute, it felt like I'd just sat in the damn car when we pulled up in front of the restaurant. "Give me another second to send off this last email," I announced to Blake.

"Not a problem, Mr. Mitchell," he said, getting out of the car and advising the valets that we'd have the Bentley out of the way promptly.

I worked quickly and once all the necessary items were taken care of, I stepped out of the car and headed into the restaurant. My muscles were tense and I was ready for a drink now more than ever.

"So," Jake said after I was seated at the table. "New rules for all of us, eh? No more fucking around in bars now that Collin has his docuseries out?" He shook his head at me. "Glad my documentary could be your test monkey to figure that out. You do realize that unexpected fame almost cost me my relationship with Ash, correct?"

I eyed my brother's cheeky grin. "You did that shit to yourself and you know it."

"Yeah, thanks to Jakey here using and losing the ladies, that stupid title we were given backfired on him after his interviews went out to the media outlets." Collin chuckled.

"Speaking of which," Alex pulled his menu open and smiled, "does Miss Gilbert know about this little gossip club headline of which you are an esteemed member? The Billionaires' Club." Alex laughed. "It has such an alluring ring to it. I personally think she would be impressed with your being a charter member, Jimmy."

"Order your goddamn dinner," I said, laughing off my best friend's remarks.

"Miss Gilbert?" Collin asked while sipping his gin. "Do you have a woman we don't know about? What the hell, Mitch?"

Alex chuckled and motioned the waitress over to him to ask about something on the menu. Meanwhile, I took a nice, long sip of my bourbon, something I'd needed for hours.

"Jimmy," my brother said slyly, "who the hell is Miss Gilbert? Are you fucking a teacher now?"

"Miss Gilbert has definitely taken my ass to school if that's what you're implying," I answered just before the waitress asked for my order. I glanced up and ordered my filet mignon, medium-rare, with steamed vegetables, and handed my menu back to the waitress.

"Just fucking tell them," Alex said when the server left. "Or I will."

"It's Avery."

"How in the hell did you manage to find her?" Jake asked. "Or wait, did she google you and stalk you out?"

"No," I said, rolling my eyes. "She actually works at Mitchell."

"So, she is a crazy-ass stalker, then, eh?" Collin tipped his glass to my brother.

"You both have no idea what you're talking about. It's not like that," I said.

"I'll agree with Jim," Alex snickered. "This chick is definitely not a stalker, though. In fact, it was more than obvious that she wasn't that impressed with Mr. Mitchell at all."

"You mean she didn't hide under her desk when he walked in the room?" Jake said.

"Nope. In fact, Jim called me over to her desk yesterday while he talked to her daughter, and she looked like she was going to strangle him if he made one wrong move."

"No shit? So, what's the deal? Are you finally ready to commit yourself to a relationship with a single mom?" Jake shook his head and sipped his scotch. "Last you told me, commitment issues were the reason you two parted ways."

"I'm joining her and her daughter at McDonald's for dinner tomorrow night. How's that for a commitment?"

Everyone laughed at that one.

"Let me guess," Collin said. "You can't afford to take another big risk by bringing her to a nice restaurant?"

"Her idea. I'm going for it. I've actually changed some things in my life after Avery gave me a few reality checks back in England. And now meeting her daughter? Jesus, the little toddler is just as adorable and strong-minded as she is. I can't seem to turn my back on either one."

"Okay, she's hot as fuck," Alex said as he looked at the guys. "She seems to be pretty feisty."

Jake's stark blue eyes never left mine as he interrupted Alex. "Not turning your back on these two is a very nice gesture, Jim. However, it's bullshit when it comes to a relationship with a single mom. She deserves a committed man, and we all know that is your biggest fear."

"Fact," Collin chimed in. "You're a chick whisperer, man, but that fucking company always comes first—or at least you hide behind it."

"The guys are right," Alex added. "You might be out of your league with this one, brother."

I should have been getting pissed by this point, but the guys knew me well enough to understand I'd most likely lost my mind. "That's an excellent way of putting it, Coll," I said. "I suppose I've hidden behind the company for long enough. I can't explain this without looking or sounding like a fucking idiot. All I can say is, I trust this one."

"Trust this one?" Jake said. "What the fuck does that mean?"

Our conversation ended when our food arrived, and our plates were placed in front of us. The waitress left after we were settled with our dinner, and I instantly carved into my steak and took a bite. Fucking hell, I was starving.

"Answer the question, Romeo," Alex said, cutting into his lobster tail. "Trust this one?"

"I can't explain it, or I would," I answered, forking through my steamed vegetables. "I'm a different person with her. At least I was in England."

"Okay," Jake said. "She has a kid, dick brain." His tone was sharper, and I got it. Jake went through hell and back to keep Ash after the press went wild, and a psychotic ex tried to ruin him. Ash was seven months pregnant with their first child now, and Jake—the biggest player of all of us—had changed significantly because of their relationship. He was the one who grew out of this lifestyle of using women for sex and not committing. He knew the drill.

"I know," I answered him with as much annoyance as I felt that he would question me being that *big* of an asshole.

"You know?" Jake said, taking a bite of his salmon. "So, you know what comes along with that, right? You hurt her, you hurt the kid. That's major."

Oddly, instead of fighting my brother's accurate words, I smiled. "That's the thing," I responded. "It's also the reason I'll be eating a big mac tomorrow night instead of taking the two to an ocean-view restaurant or whatever bullshit you all mentioned earlier." I took another bite of steak, and while I chewed, Alex spoke up.

"She threatened to kick your ass herself if you fucked with that adorable child." Alex laughed.

"Just like she did the woman that we fired today," I answered.

Collin laughed. "She threatened someone—and you fired the person she threatened instead of her?"

"It's not like it sounds," Alex defended me. "Trust me. We had a long-ass day, dealing with the old crone bringing in her lawyers and human resources. It's also the reason we're learning about Casanova getting his big mac date too."

"Exactly," I said, "and after asking her for another chance, we are both of the understanding that Addison comes first. If I am to try and make this work with Avery, I have to know it's not just Avery—it's Addison too."

"And Addison is already best buddies with your brother." Alex elbowed Jake, who sat to his left. "She calls him Mitch."

"You better know what you're doing, man," Jake said, ignoring everyone but me. "A kid is involved now. That is a road none of us have been down." Then he smiled. "I do trust you to know what you're doing, though. A single mom would've normally sent you running the other way; instead, you must have really found something in her—your dumbass only needed to get over your insecurities to acknowledge it."

"And who knows better than me that when you lose them, that's when you find out exactly how stupid you were to doubt yourself in the first place." I tipped my glass to my brother. "Thank God she's giving me another chance. I only hope she'll keep me around."

"Well, let us all know how your McDonald's date goes," Alex said. "You'd better pretend to love every last bite, or Addison will toss you aside."

"I should probably have her order for me," I smiled, imagining I was sitting with them at McDonald's and not here, getting my ass lectured.

"Good idea. Better dunk those chicken nuggets in the right sauce too," Collin added.

"Hopefully, Addison picks ketchup." Jake started laughing, dabbing the corners of his mouth with his napkin. "That would be ideal."

"Disgusting," I answered.

"The one condiment you hate," Jake said.

"Can we move off the McDonald's food menu, please?"

"So long as we get a detailed report from you," Alex chimed in.

The rest of the evening went off-topic from my personal life and back to business as usual. We mainly discussed Jake's video and Collin's interview, but my mind could hardly stay focused as I thought about Avery and Addison. I knew the guys meant well by bringing up the fact that fucking with a single mom was no joke, and I whole-heartedly agreed with them.

If I couldn't go all-in with Avery and her daughter, then I shouldn't do it at all. I had no idea what Avery's ex had put both of them through, but I understood well enough that if my bullshit got in the way, I could hurt them both. And hell if I'd do that to either one of them.

CHAPTER NINETEEN

Avery

*T*his day seemed to last forever. I hadn't been able to get Jim out of my mind since being in his office yesterday. Aside from the fact that he was gorgeous and stole my heart from the moment he first interacted with Addison, he wanted another chance with me.

I didn't even know what to do with that. I would have naturally turned it all down, but I couldn't get the way he and Addy interacted out of my mind. He treated her as if he'd waited all his life to meet her. He wore the same smile that I saw in England when I showed him the video of Addy swimming. So, seeing him being so authentic and sincere, I was willing to give it another try. I missed him. I missed England and us together in England. But I was home and in reality now, so I had to be cautious and smart about allowing this man into my life with my daughter around.

After work, I was highly interested to see how Addy's day went in school. I should have known it would be awesome when I arrived at the preschool's location. I stood silently in the doorway, my purse snug on my shoulder as I watched Addy rush around the preschool room, cleaning up to leave. The young blonde woman who was now in charge of the area was a breath of fresh air, and seeing the old, spiteful woman gone made this pickup that much easier.

I smiled when I saw my daughter's loose curls bouncing over her shoulders, following her teacher's instructions with her delightful and animated personality. With this sight alone, it was obvious little Addy had worked her way into being the teacher's pet. If that wasn't enough to make my heart swell with pride, I sighed with happiness while I watched her and the other toddlers interacting cheerfully. This is exactly what I'd hoped for when I pulled Addy from her other school and brought her here. I was so thankful she was happy with her new friends and teacher.

This week was going by too fast. Only four days until the weekend, and then it was her dad's turn again. I hated thinking about that. Why was I ruining this precious moment by thinking about her dad getting her this weekend?

The kids flooded out of the room to the waiting parents behind me. Addy was holding the blonde woman's hand while they approached me.

"This is my mommy," she announced.

I reached out to shake the woman's hand. "Hi, I'm Avery. I see you have a little helper here."

"Addison is wonderful," she said with a smile. "It's wonderful to meet you, Avery. I'm Lucy Stills. I came from Heavenly Love's preschool. It's my church's preschool from down the road. I have to ask—maybe beg?" She cringed.

"Go on," I said, glancing down to see Addy's devious smile. "I have a feeling Addy might have invited herself to your church?"

"No. Actually, we have a Christmas program that we're working on. After listening and watching Addy sing her heart out in the music portion of class today, I was wondering if you'd consider letting her sing in the musical? She's got some amazing talent," she said, smiling down at Addy.

I looked at my daughter's begging eyes. "Do you think you can stand in front of a lot of people and sing?"

"I love singing to people, Momma," she said.

I chuckled. "Well, Christmas isn't for three more months. When will you be holding your tryouts, or whatever you might call it?"

"I'm the director, and Addison definitely has the part of our singing angel," she said. "That's, of course, if you're okay with her going to the church for practices and doing the program. We start our practices early for the program, so that we're well prepared for the big day."

"I'm perfectly fine with that. God knows we all could use a little church in our lives sometimes."

"Mommy says lots of bad words," Addy said, while my purse dropped from my shoulder to the bend of my arm. She went on while she shook her head. "God doesn't like it."

I forced a smile. "I get a little wordy sometimes, and my mouth could probably use some holy water now and then."

"I'll say," a deep voice, filled with humor, said from behind me.

"Mitch!" Addison squealed, dropped the teacher's hand and rushed past me.

I turned back and watched as Jim knelt to greet Addy as she ran to him.

"Hey, kiddo," he said as if he'd known her for years.

I smiled at how adorable it all was. Addy was sort of blowing my mind with the way she kept reacting to Jim. She was an outgoing child to begin with, but when it came to her being around men, it took her a while to warm up to them, if she did at all. I would easily say that my daughter knew an asshole when she saw one. In the end, her papa was the only male figure she reacted to like this. That's why I stood in awe as I watched the way she treated Jim. This whole scene made me feel much better about being open to him wanting another chance.

I stood there, waiting and watching as Addy showed Jim her scribbled artwork for the day. God, how I wished her father could be that man to her—a dad that she would run out to and cheerfully tell him about her day. Every child needed that from their father, and Addy didn't have that with Derek.

"So, would that be a yes, then?" Lucy asked with a laugh, breaking through my daydreaming moment.

I turned back and tried to get my mind back on track with Addy's teacher. "When are the practices? She has to be at her dad's after I get off work on Friday. I can make an exception, though."

"We rehearse on Thursday and Friday nights. It ends at seven. Addy can come to see the stage, and we'll see if her outgoing nature is still up for it. No pressure."

"I think she'll love it," I said. "Seven is fine. It keeps us from sitting in rush hour traffic when we drive out to her dad's house in Orange County."

"This is excellent news. I'll see you tomorrow, Avery," Lucy said. "Good Evening, Mr. Mitchell," she acknowledged Jim.

"Good Evening, Miss Stills," he responded, rising up and smiling at her. "I trust your day with the children went well?"

"They were marvelous." She smiled. "If you'll both excuse me, a few more students are packing up," she said and then turned to meet with another student's father who'd just acknowledged Jim before he walked over to pick up his kid.

I turned and folded my arms at Jim and Addy, both now in a heavy conversation about what Jim would be eating at McDonald's tonight. "Well, are we all ready for our dinner? I know I'm starved," I said, interrupting the two.

Addison ran back over to me. "You can ride in my car, Jim," she said.

"Yeah, Jim won't fit in our car," I teased. "It's the McDonald's right before the freeway. It's a brand new one."

"Text me the address." He smiled. "I'll meet you two there."

Sounds great," I said, whipping out my new phone. "I need your number."

"Excellent point," Jim said.

After I added Jim to my contacts, we headed to our respective vehicles. I looked up the address and texted it to Jim before I fired up my car, and we headed out.

The thought of seeing this man at a McDonald's made me laugh. He was sporting some fancy designer, three-piece suit, a white shirt, and a burgundy tie. His taller than average height, the suit, and the painfully gorgeous looks of the man alone sitting at McDonald's would certainly make for an amusing night. Nothing like seeing Richie-Rich, slumming it at a fast-food joint.

Everything else aside, I was so hungry I could order the entire menu. The sandwich I'd ordered at lunch sucked, and the chips that came with it were all I'd been running on since noon. Jim was about to experience my wild eating habits again, and this time, it wasn't because of his mouthwatering gourmet cooking. Tonight, I was pigging out on fries, burgers, and milkshakes. I think Jim was in over his head, no matter how fancy he was dressed. Part of me was riddled with excitement to share this time with him and my daughter. I had to admit it, I was more than excited to introduce Jim to dining out Addy-style tonight.

We were parked and out of the car before Jim arrived at McDonald's. I would have been inside ordering while we waited for Jim to show up, but Addy insisted we stay outside just in case Mitch got lost.

Holy shit, I thought when I saw the black Bentley roll up like the president was paying this place a personal visit. The car parked in front of where Addy and I stood, watching as Jim stepped out from behind the driver's seat like it was any other day.

"You can't drive?" Addy asked with a laugh, poking fun at Jim as he walked toward us with a smile.

Jim's face creased in a way I'd never seen before after Addy called him out on having a chauffeur and not understanding it.

"I can drive very well, actually." He arched his eyebrow playfully at Addy after taking off his aviator sunglasses.

She pointed at the Bentley, slowly rolling toward a secluded area at the back of the parking lot. "Then why won't you drive your car?"

Jim glanced to where his driver was, then back to Addy. "Well, I must admit, I get a little lazy at times."

He looked at me for help in his excuses while being questioned by a three-year-old. I laughed and shrugged. "The crazy ways children view the world," I said with a soft laugh. "All right, let's go order. I'm starved, and Mitch is late for our dinner date tonight."

"Let's eat." Addy looked at me. "Be nice, Mommy. He said he's lazy. I think he'll get better though."

"Well, ladies," Jim said, "since I'm late, I'll be paying for dinner tonight."

"You're not buying dinner," I responded, walking behind where Addy was leading the way into her favorite restaurant.

"A real gentleman pays for dinner no matter what," Jim said, looking down at Addy, who stood next to him while we waited to order. "Never forget that." He winked at her with a playful smirk.

I smiled when I watched the two scouring the menu as if there were anything on it that everyone on the planet didn't know by heart.

"Well, since Jim is buying...thank you, Jim," I said after he glanced at me. "I'll take a big mac, a cheeseburger, a large fry, and a chocolate shake."

Jim's lips tightened in humor. "You sure that will hold you down?"

"Oh, and a coke." I smiled at him.

"Your mother is an expensive dinner date," he whispered down at Addy.

"Mom and me eats lots of food," Addy proudly proclaimed.

"That's good." Jim laughed. "It's healthy to have a good appetite."

"I'm going to go find a table," I said. "You two okay here?"

"We've got this, Momma." Addy gave me a wink and a thumbs up. "Get a big table too," she finished before studying the happy meal toy display.

I honestly expected Jim to look at me for help, being left with Addison, but instead, the two ignored me leaving, and I laughed at how brave the man was to handle the ordering with Addy. I knew if Addy was wise to Jim, she'd order the entire menu and try to get away with it.

While waiting at the table, I sat and thought about how this was turning out to be an enjoyable night. I was still in awe at how Jim was so taken with my daughter, and most of all, Addy was so accepting of him.

I could sit here and think Jim was only doing all of this to get laid again, but I knew that wasn't the case. Jim wasn't acting as if that were even a thought in his head. He seemed genuinely interested in getting to know this side of me and Addison too. My motherly instincts were definitely present as well, and I felt comfortable with him joining me and Addy tonight. Who knew, we hadn't started in on dinner yet—Addy and I could both easily send him running to that Bentley when we dug into our food.

"We have three trays, Mommy!" Addy shrieked while she and Jim came back with our food.

"Three trays?" I asked with a laugh. I stood to help Jim—who was balancing two trays with drinks, milkshakes, and food—then I turned to where Addy proudly held her tray that had two happy meals on it.

"Did you get a happy meal too?" I asked Jim while helping Addison up to her seat.

"Well, if I'm honest. We faced some difficulty, having to choose between two separate toys." He sighed and smirked at Addison. "Then the worst part…" he said dramatically.

Addison giggled at Jim's theatrics.

"I couldn't imagine anything being worse than having to choose between happy meal toys." I popped a straw in Addy's drink.

"Well, there was." Jim smiled at me, his emerald eyes dazzling in humor. "Addy couldn't decide between having a cheeseburger or chicken nuggets. We determined the best bet would be just to order two."

I rose my eyebrow when I looked at Jim in response. "Careful, Mitch, she'll play you like a fiddle if you give in so easily."

"Mitch is weird," Addy said, ignoring me and smartly changing the subject. "Mitch hates ketchup," she informed almost every family sitting around our table.

"I had to try and break it to her gently," he said. "I'm not a fan of the condiment."

"It's sauce, Mitch," Addison said, peeking into both happy meal bags. "It's good."

"I offered to dip my fries in the barbeque sauce," he said while I watched in humor as Jim opened his big mac packaging and tried to examine it while Addy was distracted.

"Scared she might notice you turning your nose up at that?" I asked, then bit into my burger.

He smirked, then took a bite. I watched him, knowing this man had to have been adjusting his taste buds. He swallowed then went for his iced tea. "Wow, Addy," he said. "I'm glad I picked the big mac."

She dipped her chicken nugget into her barbeque sauce and chomped on it. She nodded in response, but was fixated on her meal.

"So." Jim shifted to face me, ignoring the burger. "She's a lot like her mother when food comes into play."

"That's an understatement." I laughed. "In fact, she won't notice you're even here until she's finished eating."

"Fun date." He grinned. "God, she looks just like you," he said, picking up some fries and tossing them in his mouth. He swallowed. "She talks extremely well for her age."

"Well, I've always talked to her like she's an adult."

Jim's eyebrows rose in humor. "That could be dangerous, knowing how colorful your language can be at times."

"We read too and I do my best to keep my colorful language at a minimum when around her."

Jim only smirked in response, and then I noticed he was sticking to the fries.

"Afraid of the big mac?" I teased. I pushed my cheeseburger over to him, "Here, eat this. Some people don't like the sauce on the big mac, but I love it."

He opened the cheeseburger, and I laughed again when I saw the ketchup on the wrapper. "I'm not afraid of anything. I believe I told you that once?" He pushed the burger to the side and went back to the fries.

"Really?" I smiled. "You act like this food is going to kill you."

"I wasn't finished." He winked, and that did something to my insides. I'd seen that daring wink before, and after it happened—well, let's just say we were in a place where he and I could act passionately on it.

"Oh, excuse me for interrupting you," I responded.

"I think that statement was true at one time, and then I lost you." He took another sip of his tea, then his expression became serious. "It didn't take me long to realize that there's only one thing I do fear."

"And that would be?" I questioned while shoving some fries in my mouth.

"I'm scared to death I'll lose you again. I'll admit here and now, that is my greatest fear."

I smiled sympathetically at him, still trying to keep my composure at this confession. "Why don't we just play it by ear?" I smiled, then nodded toward Addy, the one I had to keep at the forefront of my mind when it came to thinking about rekindling what we had in England. "You're doing great, though. I think she's quite approving of you, Mitch," I reassured him.

"I'm happy to learn that," Jim said. "Hopefully this is a step in the right direction between you and me?"

I studied his curious smile for a moment. "I think it might be," I responded. I had to divert my eyes from his, before we got too deep with the conversation and Addy decided to chime in herself. That's when I started popping straws into our milkshakes. "Who got vanilla?" I asked in confusion. Then I pinched my lips together and looked at Jim. "Vanilla? Really?" I asked him.

"Addy advised that dipping fries in vanilla shakes is the best."

"They are the best. Try it." The word milkshake grabbed my daughter's attention while she'd been eating and coloring in her color book that came as her happy meal prize. "Do it, Mitch." She giggled while taking off the lid to his milkshake.

"Addison," I had to slow her down or Jim would be wearing the milkshake, "don't be bossy. Jim doesn't have to dip a fry in the milkshake."

"Sorry, Mitch," she said. "You don't have to do it. It's good, though."

"I'll give it a try." He stuck the fry in the shake and chewed on it. I watched and smiled at him, finally enjoying a menu item. "This is quite delicious. I haven't had a milkshake *nor* a smoothie since my trip to England."

Fuck. He's thinking about us tasting food off each other's bodies. Goddamn, I missed this look and this man. I was doing great keeping it together too.

"Mommy went to England and stayed in a sandcastle," Addy said.

"A sandcastle? That's intriguing," Jim said, eating more vanilla-shake fries.

"Like we build at the beach," Addy said, moving to dipping her fries into her shake now.

"Addy, it was a real castle. I showed you. A king and queen from a long time ago stayed there too," I said.

"And from what I recall, they enjoyed their chambers so much that they didn't want to leave."

Jim's eyes locked with mine, and I knew we were both back in that room, and I'm not sure which sexual routine he was thinking about, but mine was seeing him on his back with the roaring flames in the fireplace. The flicker in his glossed eyes.

"I could easily say they may have never wanted to leave," Jim said, then broke our stare and looked at Addy. "You mentioned sandcastles, Addy. Do you enjoy the beach too?"

Good job changing the subject. I was starting to get worked up just thinking about our time at the castle and knowing that our memories had stuck with Jim too.

"Love it, but can't go this time," she said, returned to her coloring again.

"She's going to her dad's this weekend. She only goes to the beach when I take her."

"Well, I would love to invite you and your mom with me sometime. My brother loves to surf, and I might try it if you think it's a neat idea."

"You surf?" she questioned with excitement. "I see the surfers too. They're cool."

"I used to. Quite a lot, actually."

"Mommy surfed a long time ago too."

"Well, then maybe if your mom thinks it's a good idea, we can all go to the beach."

Addy looked at me. "Can we go?"

"When?" I looked at Jim, whose face looked so soft, so young, so happy. Addy did bring out the youth in people, even when she was a spitfire.

"Whenever you would like. I have a home on the beach. If you're okay with it, we can spend next weekend there. I think it would make it all the more enjoyable."

"Mitch," Addy said. "Don't lie. No one lives on the beach."

"Some people do," he said.

"Next weekend works." I looked at Addy, "Do you want to go stay in a beach house like we're on vacation, Addy?"

Jesus, was I doing this too fast?

"Yes, Mommy, and surf too."

Jim laughed. "Wow. Perhaps we stick to sandcastles for now?"

He cringed at me as though he'd slipped up and started something with the whole surf idea. I grinned at how insecure the man was acting. It was another new side of Jim I'd never met, nor did I think I'd meet. I adored the concern and attention he gave Addy and me. He could've easily not given a damn about anything, but it was apparent he was trying hard to make it work with the three of us.

I respected him on a new level than what I had grown to admire during our fun times in England. He owed neither one of us anything, and yet here he was, in what I assumed was him trying his best to give us everything? Who knew? I never had anyone treat Addy and me like this. It was refreshing and a feeling that made me feel warm inside. The armored walls that I'd had up since before Addison was born seemed to come down more and more the longer I was in his presence.

"So, the beach next weekend," Jim said after we finished our dinner, and Addy went to work on dipping cold fries into her milkshake.

Addison smiled. "Sounds so much fun." She held out her chocolate shake toward Jim, "Try your fries in chocolate."

Jim was successfully eating cold fries and trying Addy's suggestions of dipping them into the flavors of the milkshakes at the table.

"Welcome to our world," I said, watching Jim play along with Addy.

"Your world is colorful, tasty, and adventurous." Jim nodded toward Addy, watching for his reaction. "I'm glad you invited me to dinner tonight."

"I'm happy you came, Mitch," she said.

After we finished, we headed out to our cars. "So, next weekend, then?" Jim knelt to Addy, and she put up a fist.

"Fist bump," she said.

Jim chuckled and met her tiny balled up hand and gently touched his fist to hers. "It's a sealed deal."

While Addy climbed into her seat, she worked on showing off for Jim, trying to buckle herself in.

"Thanks again for tonight," he said, reaching for my hand. "This was quite a treat."

I watched as he held my hand, staring down at it with that concerned look on his face again. "I'm glad you didn't run out of there after we started in on the French fry and milkshake experience," I said with a laugh.

He looked up at me. "I'll admit, I enjoyed the fruit smoothie I had with you in England much more," he said, his eyes searching mine.

I stood there, speechless, knowing what he was implying and remembering. He brought the palm of my hand to his soft, full lips. "I do wish to try that again and soon. Goodnight, Avery." He looked back at the car, where I definitely needed to help Addy with the harness of her car seat. "Thanks for a fun dinner, Addy," he said, and then he slipped his sunglasses on, smiled deviously at me, and I watched him walk like the million-dollar-man he was to his waiting car.

After I buckled in Addy correctly and sat in my seat, we took off and headed for home. That night—thanks to Jim, bringing up the smoothie from England—my eyes fell closed to that memory. The smoothie that started it all with us tasting delicious sweets from each other. Then I taunted him by spilling the smoothie on myself, and his eyes grew dangerously hungry in his kitchen.

One thing had led to another, and it turned out to be the most arousing and delicious sex I'd ever had. I had shivers of desire to feel his lips over my abdomen, my neck, my breasts—everything while he took and embraced my challenge of licking the smoothie off my body.

God, I sincerely hoped this all worked. I loved how Addy had taken to him. I adored the way he interacted with her, and I still couldn't get over the fact that we were reunited like this. I loved being with him in England, and now back in my reality, being with him like this at home. This was the real test for the man I walked out on that morning at his England estate. Mostly, this was the test of commitment because there was a lot Jim hadn't seen on my side of the fence. I was a single mom, yes...but there was more shit in my life and I wasn't quite sure that was something Jim would be willing to take on. We'd find out soon enough, I'm sure.

CHAPTER TWENTY

Jim

*M*y six o'clock meeting was going late as I expected it would. We were working with a challenging client, trying to go over final details for acquiring their boutique clothing line. Friday nights could be the worst, but as usual, I was prepared for it.

In my selfish interests, I would've liked to have skipped the meeting and ask Avery to spend tomorrow together, doing whatever she wanted. I didn't care what. I just longed to be in her presence and learn more about the side of her I'd met at dinner with her and Addy. Her daughter was an absolute gem and Avery's mini-me for sure. I had nothing of great importance going on this Saturday and was hoping that with Avery not having Addy for the weekend, she'd be free too. If this meeting ever could end, I'd text her and see if she was open to doing something together.

"Listen," I finally said, regaining control of the room, "while I would like to sit and continue the slides and presentation, I've noticed the expressions on your faces," I said to the two businesswomen. "I believe we've lost you both somewhere."

"We just don't feel comfortable having a company buy us out like this," one of the ladies responded.

Alex and I exchanged knowing glances. After going through it, I knew this presentation would hit a raw and very wrong nerve with these women. The presentation had not been properly researched, and it was not catered to their specific needs. Whoever came up with this needed to be fucking fired.

Alex read the expression on my face and instantly knew he had to find a better way to make this happen and immediately. If the person who was responsible for this didn't help Alex fix this embarrassment quickly, Alex would be personally letting them go. We were a better company than this, and I wouldn't tolerate people half-assing it with their jobs.

I watched Alex go directly to his phone—and until the solutions came in, I was speaking up. I couldn't sit in this room a second longer with these two women believing we were the bad guys, trying to steal their company from them. We saw value and we wanted to invest and help them grow their business to what I already knew it was worth. They needed our help in expanding like they wanted, and it was my job to take over and relay this information to them.

"I appreciate that more than you know," I said to both women. "While it may feel as though Mitchell and Associates are buying you out, I want to assure you that is not the case. In being up front, it is my job to ensure you know that we will be taking some proceeds after investing in the Chic Gals clothing line. With that said, you need to understand that we will also be assuming the risk and full liability as well." They looked at me skeptically, most likely for sounding like a dick. "Hear me out," I said with a smile. I used the keyboard to pull up their numbers onto the screen at the front of the room. "Those numbers you're seeing on the screen will not put you in front of the clients you're aiming for. My company has a greater potential to do so. We are also willing to use our investors to help you place your line of work in higher-priced areas to gather the clients who desire to pay over a hundred dollars for a shirt. We work in this area more than you know." Now was the time to turn into the dick, but only to allow them to understand the value in their own company. "Both of you, Christine and Gabby, would not be in this room if we didn't believe your company was worth our time, our investors' time, or my time alone. If Mitchell and Associates believed your company would fail our idea for opportunity and growth, we would not have extended the invitation to meet with you." I pointed back up to the screen. "Those numbers aren't anywhere near what a business like yours should be. In my personal opinion, those numbers should be double to triple of what I'm seeing on that screen. I believe you both understand that, yes?"

"Yes," they both answered.

"Yes," I repeated. "Your business deserves to return you both hundreds of thousands in at least one quarter, as we have already projected. In order for this growth, and for it to happen rapidly for you? It will only happen when we involve our investors, our sales teams, our marketing teams, and so on. You both saw how those teams would be working not just for my company, but mainly and exclusively for yours, yes?"

"Yes." Christine's features softened more.

"Yeah." Gabby sighed.

Okay, Gabby wasn't entirely with us yet. "Very well. I would like to ask you both if you believe you're willing to take this risk and go into marketing on your own, search for investors on your own, et cetera? Allow me to warn you, if choose to do this, it could cost you millions if you chose the wrong people. We have dealt with multiple clients who have sought us out after almost being bankrupted by falling into this trap. I'd personally hate to see this happen to either one of you. I believe your business should get off on the right foot with a company that uses investors who don't toy with their clients—a company that has your business's best interest at heart. I would assume you would believe the entire nation—to start—is missing out on your fashion line, yes?"

"Yes." Gabby smiled this time.

A solid yes from Christine, and I knew we were back in the game. I looked at Alex, who nodded in gratitude. The dumbass owed me a bottle of my favorite bourbon for saving his client.

"Then allow Mitchell and Associates to do the hard work for you and you can focus on your creative skill. We will have the clothing line pushed out to the entire nation, your brand buzzing across headlines, and a client base that you deserve."

My phone buzzed, but I ignored it while Alex stepped in from where I got the *yes* mentality going with these young and enthusiastic women.

Buzz. Buzz. Buzz. *Fucking hell.* I pulled the device out of my pocket and glanced at it from hiding it underneath the table. *Avery. Shit.*

I knew Alex could handle the rest from here, and I was more concerned about why Avery was blowing my phone up. I hadn't heard from her since the McDonald's date, so I had no idea what to expect, but the urgency with which she was calling my phone didn't make me feel at ease.

"My apologies, but you'll have to excuse me," I answered the phone and covered the receiver. "I need to take this in my office." I looked at Alex and smiled at Christine and Gabby. "I look forward to working with you both in the near future. Alex will present you both with more information that should help explain things further."

"Thank you, Mr. Mitchell," Christine said.

"Yes, thank you. It's much clearer now that you've explained it," Gabby said.

"I'm thrilled to hear that." All I needed was that lively *yes* from Gabby, and we had this company on board. I smiled, happy we saved them, and I walked out of the conference room.

"Avery?" I questioned, hearing her heavy breathing. "Is everything okay?"

"I'm so sorry about calling you, but I'm in a bad situation, and I can't pick up Addy from her church, singing-practice thing tonight," she said, sounding like she was in tears. "You're the only one I knew would eventually answer your phone because you pretty much live on the thing. I'm broke down. I was coming back from jury duty. Addy already likes you a lot and I don't want her going home with another kid's parent if I can help it. Fuck! Jim, are you there?"

"I need you to slow down. Do I need to pick you up too?"

"I need you to pick Addy up from her Christmas pageant singing practice," she said. "She's there for practice and has to be at her dad's like thirty minutes ago too."

"And what about you?" I asked, worried she was sitting on the side of the road while Addy couldn't have been safer, being at a church.

"I'm fine. And shit, I'm so sorry to put you in this shitty position, but I'm getting a tow, so I'm good. But having you pick her up will save me from another parent or teacher taking her because I'm too far to Uber back to get Addy and then drive to Orange County where her dad is."

"So long as you and Addy are safe, I will handle it."

"Okay, can you—damn it—do you mind picking her up and heading to her dad's house? I'm so sorry to do this to you."

"It's not a problem; send me the address."

There was a pause then Avery's heavy breathing slowed some. "Okay. I texted you the address, and I'll be waiting at the house before you and Addy get there. I just need Addy picked up and heading this way. They're closing the church early tonight too. Dammit, I should have started with that."

"Take a breath. I will handle it." I threw her on speaker, already packing my briefcase in my office, and heading to the parking structure. "I'm reading my text and it's an address in Anaheim. That's where I'm meeting you in Orange County, right?"

"Right. Hang on," she said. "I'm texting you the church location now."

"Try to relax a little," I said. "They're not going to leave a three-year-old standing outside a locked church."

"I know, but still. I didn't want to call you. I don't want you to have to see or deal with Derek, either."

"I can handle your ex," I said, seeing the address to the church had me about ten minutes or so away. "I'll get Addy, and I'll have her call you when she's with me, and we're on our way to Orange County."

She sighed a huge breath of relief, "Thank you. Can I say I love you for this?"

"You can say you love me anytime you want," I teased as I sat in my car, stuffing the briefcase on the floorboard, having no room for it behind the front bucket seats. "I'll call you when I've got the special package."

"I can't thank you enough for this," she said in a softer, more relaxed voice.

"There's no need to thank me. You just take care of you, and I'll make sure Addy is fine. I'm pulling out of the parking lot now."

We hung up, and precisely fifteen minutes later, I was pulling into a large church parking lot. Addy was swinging on a swing while a teacher stood by, watching her and three other toddlers in the playground area. A minivan pulled in next to me, and I smiled seeing that other parents also appeared to have been put in a last-minute predicament to pick up their kids.

I stepped out of the car, hoping Addy would recognize me. Thank God she did. I couldn't help but smile in response when she broke free from the teacher's hand, and scream my name with excitement.

"Sir," the woman called out to me after Addy came running into my arms. I loved the way this child seemed to admire me. I still had no idea what I'd done to gain her interest in such a way, but it was great.

"Yes," I answered the woman, taking Addy's backpack that she'd shoved into my hands.

"I will need your name before I allow the young lady to leave with you."

"I'm James, or rather, Jim Mitchell. Avery Gilbert should have called ahead informing you I would be picking Addison up in her place tonight?"

"Okay. Yes, Avery called to notify me. We must take safety measures; I'm sure you understand."

"I completely understand," I answered, while I opened the door to the passenger's seat for Addy.

"Hold up. That car—" she eyed my Aston Martin. "Darn it, I don't have time for this, but do you at least have a car seat in that? I'm pretty sure it drives itself and turns off the airbags, but it's illegal to drive a three-year-old in any vehicle without a car seat."

"Oh, gosh," Addy said, and I could have sworn she was trying to mock the woman. "He's okay, Miss Shirley."

"Addy." I smiled at her. "Allow me to work this situation out. She is correct."

Why didn't I think of the car seat? I thought, trying to come up with the quickest solution to legally drive Addison to her dad's house.

"I have an extra car seat," a woman's voice spoke from the direction of the minivan. "I still haven't taken it out since Connor grew out of it."

"I can use it and give it back," Addy said when the young woman came into sight.

Addison was so much like Avery that it only made my smile broaden in the midst of this sudden chaos. I couldn't get over how she was so outspoken, commanding and, well, just intriguing.

"This would be a lifesaver. What are the chances of this? Really, thank you," I said, following the woman to the back of her vehicle.

She smiled back at me. "Do you know how to put it in your car?"

"Not exactly."

Her chocolate skin glowed and radiated with her humorous expression. I understood why she found this funny too. I looked like a total dumbass.

"Well," she started after I took the seat she offered, "safety first with children, of course. Always." She winked while the other woman seemed to collapse in some sort of relief.

I tried to smile at the spectating woman, but that wasn't breaking through the stress I'd caused her after not being prepared to pick up Addison safely.

She sighed loud enough for me to wonder what I should say to help ease her distress. She eyed my car like it was Satan's personal vehicle. "Well, I hope her mother knows about this car. It doesn't seem too child-friendly," she said, rightfully annoyed.

"Miss Shirley." Addy planted a hand on her hip and faced the upset women, while I tried to work with the helpful one that was occupied by installing the car seat into my car.

"Yes, Addison." She tried to smile past her stressful appearance.

Addy kept her sass going. "You've met my mommy. You know she'll yell at Jim if she doesn't like his car."

"Well, it's safety first and—"

"Children first," I said, feeling like I would have to pass a safety exam next in order to leave with Addison. Hell, this whole thing was turning into a movement that was about to go up against me and this stupid car I'd decided to drive to work today of all days.

"Very good. I need to leave, and you were the last two parents." The woman, Miss Shirley, finally gave up.

"Okay. Very good," I responded. "Addison will be driven safely to her mom."

Shit. I'd closed three, multi-million-dollar investments today, and I dealt with bringing in a new investor to Mitchell and Associates, and yet, here I was, feeling like a total deadbeat who had no idea what the fuck to say. No matter what smile I held, I was still getting an evil eye from Miss Shirley.

"I'll drive slowly," I said, waving her off as she sat in her car.

"You're all set," the woman who saved my ass said.

"I'll have Avery return the seat to you," I answered. "I truly appreciate this help."

"Just take it slow," she said with a laugh.

"We'll be heading out on the 405 and at this hour, that freeway will likely still be a parking lot." I grinned.

"Traffic on the 405 or not," she arched a motherly eyebrow at me, "slow," she finished and then walked off to get in her car.

I had no time to defend myself, nor would I try to. My concern was getting Addison to her mother whether these women trusted my driving or not.

Addy was buckled in when I waved the woman off and sat in my car. "*Slow*, mister," she taunted, mocking the women who'd busted my ass since I first arrived in the parking lot.

"Are you making fun of me getting in trouble with Miss Shirley?" I smiled and rechecked her harness straps. "All right. You're good to go. We're taking side roads. I'm not sitting in traffic, and you need to call your mom."

"Am I in trouble?"

"No." I smiled and used the car to call Avery. "I'm the one in trouble."

"Wow," Addy said, as she looked around the car when the phone connected to the audio system while dialing out to Avery's cell.

"When your mom answers, you can just talk in the car and she'll hear you," I informed her. "It works like a speakerphone."

"Jim?" Avery answered her phone. "I'm just now on my way over to Addy's grandparents. I texted you that address too, right?"

"You did and the GPS is bringing us up through the hills. Accidents have the 405 and 5 locked up."

"Thank you so much again. Can I talk to Addy?"

"I'm here, Mom. You can talk through Jim's car. You're in it," she squealed.

"Jim's car?" she asked in confusion. "Is the driver listening too?"

"I'm driving," I said.

"No chauffer?" I heard her laugh. "Well, I have to say I'm proud of you. Freedom calls, eh?"

"Yeah, you won't be saying that when you see my car," I smirked at Addy.

"He has the fastest, coolest car ever, Mom. I want one too."

"I bet he does." Avery's voice changed. "You better not drive that car fast, Jim," she demanded with humor and warning in her voice.

"I have precious cargo, and," I said, looking over at Addy after we turned down another street, "should we tell your mom what the ladies taught me today?"

"Safety first. Children first!" Addy giggled.

"What the hell?" Avery said.

"Yeah, I didn't have a car seat. Miss Shirley almost had a breakdown, but one of the other parents was there at the same time and saved the day."

"I didn't even think about the car seat. Did they give you crap?"

"Bad words, Mommy," Addison scolded Avery.

"Sorry, Addy," she said. "Jim, did they say anything nasty to you about it?"

"They were concerned, as any good person would be when some guy shows up in a sports car and no car seat."

"And knowing you and your car in England…." I could hear the smile in Avery's voice, and it made me smile. "It's probably the most expensive sports car on the market."

"And why would you assume that?"

"I believe I met a man who enjoys cars—preferably Ferraris."

"Well, that one isn't with us today, and last I recall, you almost wrecked my Ferrari."

"Funny," she said, and I could hear her voice calming as we talked.

After Avery and I got off the phone, Addy and I enjoyed my car, grabbing the ground on turns. We weren't flying through the hills; in fact, we were embarrassing the vehicle by taking it slower than usual. The cars behind us were trying to use this route to get out of downtown LA and were likely pissed that my car was moving no faster than the speed limit.

Addy had officially named my car the rollercoaster, and she danced in her car seat to the music on the radio while we drove toward Anaheim to meet up with her mom. I noticed Addy grow quiet when I made the last turn onto the road to her final destination, and her mood changed some.

"You excited?" I asked, seeing Avery standing on the lawn—not in the best of neighborhoods, and I didn't say that because I was some Beverly Hills snob, either. Bars on all houses' windows told me there was trouble around this area. It was clear that, while this might've been a great neighborhood fifty years ago, it'd seen plenty of dark days since.

"I kind of wanna stay with you and mommy," she said.

I brought the car to turn around at the end of the cul-de-sac while some young man stood outside near Avery in a white tank and jeans. His hair was a mess, his arms were sleeved with shitty-looking tattoos, and he hid his eyes behind dark sunglasses. *Jesus Christ, is that Derek?* I thought as Addy looked at the two quietly.

"Next weekend, we can go to the beach, remember?" I said to Addison, hoping to cheer her up some.

I watched the man walk to a lifted—too fucking high—truck and light a cigarette. He eyed my car as I pulled past him and parked in front of the driveway. I couldn't park anywhere else because the truck was taking up the entire curb in front of the house, and all I had was the driveway entrance.

"That's my daddy," Addy said, and this was the first time I noticed the spirited young girl subdued. It concerned me.

"I should like to meet him," was the only answer that rolled off my tongue in response.

Avery was pulling Addy out as soon as I put the car in park. I left it running and stepped out myself after I popped the trunk so I could clear out the car seat. I pulled off my sunglasses. There was no way in hell I was hiding behind sunglasses as this guy looked like he wanted to kick my ass just for being here.

"Nice car," he said. "What the hell, man? That's a 77, isn't it? Shit. Only seventy-seven sold."

"Yes. I'm James," I said, extending my hand out to his.

He shook it but was more concerned with the car.

"Addy, go with Daddy and Papa into the house," Avery ordered after giving her kisses and hugs. "See you in forty-eight hours."

I waved at the older man who exited the house, acknowledging me, yet eyeing his son. I sighed in relief when Addy forgot about the rest of the world and ran into her papa's arms while screaming with excitement to see him. Then they disappeared into the house, and we were faced with Avery's ex.

"So, are you the one who's been fucking my girl?" Derek asked, walking the length of my car and then leaning against the grill of his truck.

"I'm not sure I follow you," I said, feeling more confrontational. This was the shit bag drug addict Avery had to put up with? The guy did look like death. He acted like he was some kind of badass, and I wasn't going to waste a conversation on him.

"Let's go, Jim," Avery said, getting in the car.

She went to close her door as I walked to mine, then I saw where Derek caught hers.

"Get your hands off her door," I said protectively of Avery. There was no way in hell that he was going to intimidate her in front of me. He could confront me all night long and get away with it, but watching an asshole go after a woman? Unacceptable.

"Fuck you," he said to me, then he looked in the car. "Or is that your job tonight, Avery?"

"Your daughter is here to see you. Shouldn't you care more about that?" I said, working to get his stupid ass to direct himself toward me and not Avery.

"So, you get to fuck my girl, pick up my daughter in your fancy car, and now you think you can talk to me however you want? You're a fucking pussy," he slurred.

I glanced into the car and saw Avery's face was in her hands. This loser was high, and Avery wasn't fighting back. This must've been the icing on the cake for her fucked-up day.

"If you don't back the fuck away from my car, I'll drag you away from it myself." Fuck, I had to be cautious. He was high, and I was sober. I couldn't do anything to make this worse on Avery, and reacting to a drug addict that I really wanted to beat down would solve nothing.

"Avery, get out of the goddamn car," Derek said, reaching in for her.

I came around the car and walked over to where Derek was. My sudden move prompted him to step back after he saw me pursuing him. I stood there and towered over this miserable punk while Avery ordered him to get into his house as she dialed out on her phone.

"I said get out of that fucking car, Avery."

"She's not yours to order around," I said sternly.

"Gonna fucking kick my ass?"

That's when the dumbass swung up at me, and I blocked his arm.

God, what I wouldn't give to step behind his leg, and send his ass to the ground.

"Fuck, Derek! Leave him alone and get in the goddamn house," she growled, trying not to alert the entire neighborhood. "He's high," Avery said into her phone. "Get him out of here and call the cops. I don't want him around Addy at all. I will leave with her if you don't fix this right now," she said while Derek danced around me like a buffoon.

"Derek, get up here!"

I jerked my head over in the direction of the stern man's voice. Derek threw his hands up and stomped up toward the front door.

"Are you okay to leave Addy here?" I asked Avery, shocked she would consider it.

"No," she sobbed into her hands after her phone slipped into her lap.

Shit. "One call, and I can have someone here to arrest him, and we'll all be leaving together."

"Let me go talk to his parents, and I'll make that decision. Trust me; he'll waste everyone's time by being passed out by the time the cops show up."

"All right," I answered, seeing that this was definitely not Avery's first shit storm with this guy.

I waited outside, leaning against the passenger side of my car. This was majorly fucked-up bullshit. No one should ever have to worry like this.

I grabbed my phone from my car and dialed my brother.

"Jimmy," Jake answered.

"Hey, how's your schedule right now?"

"Stuck in fucking traffic. Why?"

"If I needed you to get your ass down to Anaheim, how fast could you get here?"

"Anaheim?" Jake answered. "I guess if I made it to an off-ramp and got off this freeway, I bet around thirty to forty minutes? What the fuck are you doing in Anaheim?"

"I might need your help driving Avery. I'm in the Aston Martin and only have two fucking seats. We might need to get Addison out of here. Her dad is jacked up and high on something."

"Holy shit," he said. "I'll try to be there in about thirty minutes, hopefully less."

"Hang on. Avery is coming out now," I said. "We might be good. I'll call you back if I need you to drive this way."

"All right. Let me know what's up when you can, then."

"Fuck all of you, then! I'm out." Derek looked at me as he walked across his father's patchy lawn. "Get this piece of shit out of my way before I run it the fuck over."

"Derek, back the truck up, and just leave, goddamnit. Go sober the fuck up, and if you're not sober tomorrow, I'm getting Addy first thing in the morning." She looked at me after Derek jumped in his truck, backed up, and peeled out.

"Welcome to my life. Nice intro, eh?" she said.

"And Addison?" I asked.

Avery's face was red and stained from tears. "Her grandparents called the cops on him. He won't be back tonight."

"Jesus." I reached for her hand. "Are you okay. Will you be okay?"

"I'm okay now that the front door is locked, Derek is gone, and I can breathe again."

"Where do you want me to take you?"

"Can you just drive for a while? I don't want to go home yet. I just need to drive," she said as she intertwined her fingers with mine. "Your hands, I've missed them."

I brought the back of her hand to my lips. "And they've missed you," I answered. "How about I take you through Laguna Hills, and we'll have dinner in Laguna tonight? Sound good?"

"And if I get a call that Derek's in jail?"

I looked over at her. "Then I'll be profoundly relieved that he's behind bars, and not endangering lives on the road. Who the fuck drives a truck like that and still lives with his parents?"

"A fucking addict who doesn't know what the hell he's doing outside of killing himself?"

"I guess so," I said.

"His friend's house is down that street." She pointed down a frontage road. "He's safely getting his fix and will pass out there."

"He's a jacked-up piece of shit, if you don't mind me saying so."

She laughed and glanced over. "That's putting it lightly."

We got in the car and headed on our way. I needed Avery to tell me more about how she could be okay with Addy staying at that place or anywhere near that guy. I'm sure she had reasons, but I also worried that it was his empty threats that were manipulating her too. Either way, I told her that I would stick by her and help. That's what I planned on doing, but I needed to know more, or I would have great difficulty believing that Addy was safe from her dad tonight—or any night.

CHAPTER TWENTY-ONE

Avery

I had been crying and nearly lost my shit while Jim drove me away from Addy at her grandparents' house. I had to just close my eyes, stay quiet, and breathe through everything that kicked me in the ass up until now. Today had been hell to say the very least. My life was a goddamn tornado, and Jim had just gotten to experience the worst part of it. My emotions were everywhere, and after sitting in jury selection all day, my car overheating, and my daughter being stranded, I had reached my limit.

I couldn't believe my dirt bag of an ex decided to confront Jim, though I should have. Couldn't Derek see that, when Jim stepped out of his car, the man towered over him? I'd seen the biceps Jim sported, and I wasn't surprised when Jim blocked Derek's punch. Jim was a better man than I was a woman in that respect. I saw him exercise self-control that I couldn't imagine any man having after someone tried to throw a punch at them. With Jim's scorched-earth look I'd seen so many times? I would have sworn Jim would follow through and send Derek to the ground. Instead, being the man he is, he opted for the better route—the route that kept me from screaming and cussing out Derek while Jim beat his ass. He walked away and got me safely out of there after I knew the house was locked, Derek was gone, and the cops were on their way to make sure the asshole didn't show back up at the house. What a fucking life I had.

Jim remained quiet while I continued to pull myself together, eyes still closed. I was doing great until I felt the car moving, then slowing, then moving again.

Must be in traffic. It's okay. Just stay calm, Avery. Please, God, just breathe. It's okay. I'm okay. I inwardly reached for meditative and supportive words, feeling a panic attack bubbling up. I couldn't let my mind get the best of me. Not right now. I kept whispering thoughts of reassurance to myself to prevent my heart from racing wildly out of control.

I lost my battle against these emotions of doom I was experiencing in a panicked state of mind. My heart was beating faster than a rabbit's and when I felt the car slowing again, I felt trapped in the vehicle. I opened my eyes to gain my bearings. Bad idea. We were stuck in traffic on the freeway. Fuck. I needed out of this concrete jungle. I felt stuck with no way out, and my anxiety spiked instantly. I fucking hated panic attacks and now I was my own mind's victim.

"Fuck. Fuck. Fuck," I said, leaning over and burying my face in my hands. "Fuck."

"Hey." Jim's hand was on my back. "Avery."

"You have to get me out of here. Please get out of this. The freeway, get off," I said through my hands. I made no sense, but I felt like I was suffocating and couldn't say the right words if I wanted to. "Please, please. Jim, I need off. I need to get out of the car."

"Hang on, sweetheart," he said calmly. "I have to get to the exit. We're jammed up for a second."

I threw my head back, gasping for air, sweating, and trembling. "Please." I was bawling now. "Just let me out here."

Jim hit the accelerator, and my body was pinned to the seat by the G-forces of the car. My eyes reopened to see Jim, speeding past stopped traffic on the shoulder of the road. I held on for dear life.

"This is illegal," I managed.

"So is walking on the side of the freeway," Jim said, then veered off the freeway and maneuvered the vehicle through city streets.

He stopped the car, and I didn't give a shit where we were. I had to run this shit out of my system, or I was going to have a stroke. I was out of the car, taking off like a bat out of hell in my ballet flats, feeling like I couldn't run fast enough.

I wanted to scream it all away. I wanted to take my daughter and disappear, never to be found again—my God, I wanted Derek gone no matter what it took. I'd never felt hatred burning so hot in my veins until now. I pushed myself harder with every stride I took. I saw what looked like a park entrance to my right and then stopped to see if my endorphins had curbed my anxiety.

I bent over, gripping my knees and just focused on good, healthy deep breaths. My heart was still racing, but my breathing was helping me to keep it all leveled out. I felt myself calming down—enough, anyway, to wonder if Jim had just dropped me and took off when he experienced enough of the crazy in my coping mechanisms...and my life in general.

"Forrest Lawn Cemetery?" he questioned in a way that had me look up at him to see if he was teasing about where I'd ended up. "Good as anything, I guess." He looked down at me and half-smiled.

I noticed the man had managed to at least get his suit jacket off and still catch me. I looked over at his brown leather shoes. "I'm sorry I just put you through that," I said. "I had to get it out. I swear I felt like I was going to have a heart attack or stroke in that traffic."

Jim placed his hands on his hips. "How are you feeling now?"

"Like I still have to run this out of my system."

"Well, Griffith Observatory is that way." He pointed down the street where the freeway overpass crossed over. "Beautiful night to observe stars." He shrugged.

"Right."

The sensation of being scared out of my life for no reason came bubbling back up. "Can we keep running?"

"We can run all the way to Bakersfield if that helps you, but are you sure your feet can handle it?" He grinned.

"I'm more worried about the impending stroke than my feet falling off," I tried to tease.

I took off, jogging next to Jim, not needing the crazy-ass full speed run I'd needed from earlier. My crazy, panic run ended with me and Jim at Griffith Park, overlooking the lights of downtown LA.

"Here." Jim took my hand. "Sit with me. Unless you want to keep running?"

"Feeling like we're out of that city and on top of the world is sort of working for me," I said, sitting down, Jim following.

"I won't ask you to talk about it," he said softly.

"My crazy panic attack or the shit that caused it?" I exhaled and rubbed my forehead. "You're a good guy, Jim. A great guy," I said, covering the hand that he'd planted behind him to lean against. "You don't deserve to be around this crap."

"Neither do you," he said.

"Yeah, I did this to myself," I admitted.

"Are you trying to scare me off or something?"

"What?" I looked over at him.

"I am a grown-ass man last time I checked. I don't need you trying to frighten or warn me off from what I know I want."

"Your feet are going to hate you in the morning for this," I changed the subject.

"What makes you think I don't take runs daily in my work shoes?" he countered, and I saw the smile on his face.

"Really?" I said with a soft laugh.

"Yep." He glanced up at the stars. "These things are pretty much my running shoes."

"No shit? Some designer created a pair of men's business shoes that work like running shoes?" I said, finding my smile again.

"For what they cost, I should be able to water ski in the mother fuckers, too. Unfortunately, I can't." He laughed. "Great innovative idea, though. Honestly, my feet are fucked tomorrow. They're not only dress shoes, but they're also brand new and not broken in yet."

"Oh, damn." I cringed. "Jesus, how far back is your car?"

"And the Avery I've fallen for is back." He brought his arm around me, and my adrenaline started crashing with the comfort of letting myself collapse into his side.

"Your car? That thing isn't cheap."

"It's back by the cemetery, most likely on blocks by now. Stripped to nothing, I'm sure." I felt him laugh and rub along on my arm. "What about that poor car of yours?"

"Who the hell knows," I said. "Probably getting diagnosed as dead on arrival at the towing yard."

"Well, shit." Jim sighed, and I could tell he was in a light-hearted mood. "You almost totaled the Ferrari in England, most likely killed your car, and my other car sits back at Forrest Lawn, awaiting its internment."

I nudged him. "Let's get back to your car. I still have no idea why we're over here and not in Laguna. What made you change your mind about going there?" I asked, my mind functioning normally again.

"After we left the house, and while you seemed to be calming yourself down, I had to deal with the anomaly that there were accidents all around us. The 5 freeway was the only one opened up. So, I just figured we take that route, and bring you down through Hollywood Hills instead. Then your eyes reopened, and I believe I had taken the one open route that wasn't agreeing with you."

"Nothing personal. Nothing agrees with me when Derek pulls this shit. I hate him, Jim."

"Is Addison safe with his parents?" he asked.

"Yes," I answered. "I would've put her on my lap and asked you to floor it out of there if I wasn't sure of that. She loves them, and she's also the light of their lives. When Derek is high, he never sees her anyway. They protect her from him when he's like that."

"Then why bring her to him if he doesn't plan on being with his own daughter? It seems as though you both are working things out outside of the courts. I don't understand."

I stiffened and pulled away from him, "You may never understand why, and I might never be able to explain to you why. All I can say is that I can't have the courts fuck me over because of him and put my daughter in the system."

"I assure you that the court would see his records, and see that you are a fit mom to care for her," he said. "I can't in any way see the courts putting Addison in the system like you fear."

"I grew up in the system," I said, knowing he should know about this part of my life too. "With my past as a runaway and a problem child—I feel like I'm getting paid back for all of it. All of the memories of that scare me to death that the courts could possibly rule to take Addy from me and Derek. My past, his current fucked up life—all of it."

"Don't tell me that you're afraid to fight for your daughter."

"It's not like that. I love Derek's family. Her grandparents. They're really good people, and they took me in as their own. They stood by my side and still do when Derek pulls this shit. Sometimes I wonder if it's fucked up to keep this going, though, but Addy loves her papa like she *should* love her dad, and I can't just remove him from her life." I ran my hands through my hair. "I know it sounds so enabling and fucked up, but I'm doing my best. I really am." I felt my voice crack.

"Drug addicts seem to destroy everyone and everything around them while they're intent on killing themselves. It's the most selfish thing in the entire world. My mother did this same shit to my family. My dad, I'm sure, was as torn and distraught as you are currently. No grandparents, as you mentioned, to help my dad or for us to attach to, though."

"It may not make sense to hear it, but we keep Derek's bullshit away from Addy. She just knows her dad sleeps a lot, but fuck, what if the courts ruled that she couldn't see her grandparents anymore because Derek lives with them?"

"I understand you not wanting to upset Addison. Maybe it's not for me to say, but I sensed that she wasn't happy to see Derek. I also did witness her mood instantly shift from wanting to stay with you and me when she saw her grandfather. She was as thrilled to see him as she's acted when she's seen me come out of nowhere." He laughed.

"She's definitely taken to you," I said. "Can you see why, if we try this out—you and me—and it doesn't work, it can mess her up too? You have to be certain I'm worth it. It's not just me, it's Addison too—and the bullshit of my ex acting like he did tonight."

"I understand all of it. What I don't understand, I'm willing to learn and be here to help you in any way I can. Trust me, my brother —who is very interested in meeting you—has already threatened to kick my ass if I fuck this up with you and Addy."

"He thinks you'll fuck it up?" I chuckled. "Nah, I'm sure it will happen from my side of the fence."

"Remember that conversation you heard part of in England before you left me that morning?"

"The conversation I eavesdropped on and walked out on you for—even though you'd done nothing wrong at the time?"

"I disagree. While trying to figure out my feelings about relationships, I lead you on, and I saw the hurt in your eyes. Avery, if I were still confused about being able to commit to a relationship, I wouldn't do it. If you truly allow me in, I'm not just in this with you alone, but with Addison as well."

"So, the magnificent CEO, James Mitchell, is going to try his hand at dating a single mom?"

"He's going to commit himself to ensure he doesn't lose the one good thing that came into his life," he answered. "He's going to do his hardest to make sure Avery and Addison are the happiest two ladies on the planet too."

"Addy will demand the moon, and you better give it to her," I teased with a nudge to his side.

Jim laughed. "I will have to be on my game with her. I will tell you that she's already stealing my heart. I've never met such an outgoing, fun, and confident child. She could probably do my job better than I can."

"She'd run all of your employees and clients right out the door."

"Doubt that. She'd have them eating out of her hands. She's a smart one, like her mother."

"Whatever I did to grab your attention, I'm thankful I did it. I can't believe I have a caring man like you in my life. Sucks that you have to be a damn businessman, or rather a fucking CEO, though. You couldn't just be the man who ran the small business I thought you did. It had to be some global, billion-dollar company, huh?"

"My career sucks?" he asked with a laugh. "I believe I did exceptionally well today in coming to the rescue if I do say so myself."

"About that," I said. "I hope I didn't screw up your meeting or anything else."

"I was finishing up with a client when I got your call, and then I got the hell out of there."

"Sorry that you got the third-degree from the churchy lady."

"You saw the car you rode in, correct?"

I started laughing, trying to imagine what the expressions must have been when Jim rolled up in his badass, wealthy-guy car. "God only knows what those women thought."

"They thought I was a jackass, for starters. Had me practically chanting children's safety first while Addy was mocking them from her car seat."

"You have to watch her. She can be a little spitfire."

"She reminded me of you," he said. "Even if I didn't have the car seat, I don't think they would have won the battle of keeping Addison out of that car."

"They wouldn't have won the battle of keeping her away from *you*." I leaned against him again, "Tell me I'm doing the right thing with this, Jim. Aside from how Addy's treating you, she's not like that with anyone but her Papa. I believe you've charmed my daughter and me."

"Charmed?" He laughed. "I believe that's the other way around, and if all three of us are willing to admit that, I think we are doing the right thing. I want you to know that if anything ever comes up, my phone will always be on to help you and Addy. Don't worry about if you're interrupting work, that's what I have a vice president for. Call me, and I'll help in any way I can."

"That's if you still have a car."

"True." He held me tighter, and I felt his lips on my hair. "Don't worry about the car. It links up to my phone. If someone got near it, it would send me an alert. I have an entire app for the damn thing, and even if I didn't, the car is the least of my concerns. Your sanity and health are my top priority."

"Even now, while your car sits abandoned, staring at the cemetery?"

"Maybe it'll see the ghost you never found in England."

I laughed. "We never did see a ghost, did we?"

"That was my fault. I got carried away in the library where Henry the Eighth's uncle is supposedly lurking. I had other things on my mind."

"Selfish bastard," I teased.

"As I said, I was. I was only thinking of my own needs when I let you walk out of my life that morning. I was selfish and thoughtless." He laughed. "I have no intention of making that mistake again. My only concern now is you and what you want."

"All I want is to feel this," I said, snuggling against him more and looking up at the stars. "Just me, safe in your arms, and losing myself in the stars above us."

"You owe me a foot rub for this, at least." He chuckled, and then gently guided us both to lay back. "Do you know the constellations?"

"No. I don't even know what they look like. Do you?"

"Somewhat. When my dad worked late and my mom forgot she'd locked Jake and me outside, Jake and I would make up images in the stars. It's quite a fun game."

"Okay, then." I nestled into his side and draped my leg over his. "Show me an image up there. I just see the glitter and a bluish-black sky."

That's when I fully relaxed and let Jim's soothing voice calm my nerves completely. I would check on Addy tonight and again in the morning after I woke up. If everything was still good, then she could stay until Sunday. If not, she was coming back with Jim and me.

I didn't know where this night would lead—if I went to Jim's house or he came to mine—but something told me we weren't leaving each other's sides until the executive's elevator doors opened and he disappeared to his office on the top floor on Monday morning.

CHAPTER TWENTY-TWO

Jim

𝒶fter I convinced Avery that my house in the Hollywood Hills could take the place of Griffith's Observatory's lawns, we left for the car. After I showed her multiple goofy characters I discovered in the stars above us, Avery quickly played along. We laughed together like kids would, and I could tell Avery was certainly more relaxed than before.

I smiled when we got in the car and the first thing she mentioned was food. We hit the nearest drive thru for her to grab a couple of burgers, milkshake, and fries, and at that point, it seemed that she had regained her composure completely. She called Addy's grandparents and received confirmation that Derek hadn't returned and was locked out of his parents' home. I sighed in relief along with Avery that Addison was safe from the son of a bitch who had no business around his little girl until he sobered his sorry ass up.

"Holy hell, Jim," Avery said once we drove up the driveway to my place. I pulled the car into my garage, next to the collection of vehicles. "Jesus." She looked at the cars we parked next to. "Is this a damn car museum?"

"At one time it was." I smirked at her. "All of these cars sat in here like they were in one, and for far too long." I took her hand, kissed the soft center of her palm while opening my door, "Until you saved them all." I chuckled and smiled at her.

"What the hell did I do to help these cars?" She laughed and scrunched her face up in humor.

I missed that look. "You got through to me in England," I said. "While I drove my car there, I realized I'd missed the horsepower and being behind the wheel myself."

"Is it why you drove today?" she asked, and I could see confusion spread across her face.

"Today, among other days. Sometimes I am strapped to the laptop and need Blake to drive me around so I can finish up work while on the road."

"Well, well," she said after I took the lead and got out of the car, her following. "Yes, I can definitely say…" She paused with a smile on her face, taking in the luxury of sports cars that surrounded her. "Shit, Jim, you were definitely missing out on life by keeping these beauties parked."

Avery spun back around, and I watched her onyx hair cascade over her shoulder. Damn, she was mesmerizingly beautiful with this smile, this laugh, and the sparkle in her vivid blue eyes. "Well, if little Bunny is dead, I know who I'm going to ask if I need to borrow a car," she said, walking around to where I stood admiring her.

She wrapped her arms around my waist, and I tilted my head down to meet her eyes, "Bunny?" I questioned.

"The name Addy gave my car."

"Ah, the Rabbit," I said, recalling the make and model of her car that definitely could, as she said, have arrived DOA at the towing yard. "Yes, well, you have quite a nice collection to choose from right here." I ran my hand along her cheek, "How are you feeling?" I couldn't begin to describe how I loved having her close like this again.

"After running and then enjoying the views at the observatory— and being relieved that your car wasn't jacked, and then eating?"

"Yes, after all of that." God, I needed to feel her lips against mine.

"Honestly, I'm beat. I am happy to be with you again, though. I can't explain it, but this all just feels…" She paused in thought.

"It feels right," I answered the way I personally felt about us being reunited since losing her in England.

She tilted her head and her eyes shimmered. "It does. Though, I'm still kind of shocked you didn't just drive off and leave me back there. You know, let the crazy panicked woman go and never look back." She smiled, but her eyes remained locked on mine.

I ran a knuckle along her jawline. "After you demanded to be let out of the car on a packed freeway, leaving you in a cemetery didn't seem like a wise decision."

She laughed, and her expression was so light and youthful again, but I could also see how exhausted she was.

"You thought I was going to dig myself a six-foot hole in that cemetery, eh?"

"God only knew what you were going to do." I stepped back and reached down for her hand, "I'm glad you didn't jump into the six-foot abyss of internment, though."

"Holy hell," she said as we entered the glass door that led onto the main floor of the architecturally perfect house. "This is your place? I mean, I guess I shouldn't be surprised, Mr. England Castle."

"It's quite large, I know," I said. "Collin's dad founded an architectural firm. Collin, you may remember, is the neurosurgeon from the documentary piece we watched together. Anyway, they demanded I see this place before it went on the market. Once I was shown the house, I almost couldn't leave it."

She released my hand and walked toward the floor-to-ceiling glass doors that surrounded all three corners of the sprawling living area we were in. She jumped when the glass doors automatically drew back and disappeared before her eyes. It was a unique feature that Brooks Architectural Concepts added in, but I never found it this intriguing until seeing Avery gracefully walk through them. Crazy as it may be, I stood fascinated with her every move.

She strolled down the steps that led toward the infinity pool that was shaped to surround this level of the house. "A pool with palm trees and little islands in it? These views, and…" She ran her hands through her hair, pulling it up as she stared at the views. "My gosh, this view is mind blowing. I've never seen anything like this before in my life."

"I agree, these views are remarkable at night," I said after I followed her out of the house and slid my hands in my pockets. "It's just as impressive during the day as well. You can see the San Gabriel Mountains, Downtown LA, and the Pacific Ocean—even Catalina, on clear days of course."

I smirked when she held her hands out, and millions of city lights greeted her from the poolside view of the house. "This is magical. No wonder you never seem stressed about anything."

"If you want the best views from this place, you'll get those on the lounge area on the rooftop. Unless you want to go for a swim? The water is warm."

She turned and shook her head. "I can't date you." She suddenly became serious. "There's no way I can afford you."

I felt my breath hitch at first, believing she was going to blow me off because of this ostentatious home. In true-to-form Avery fashion, however, I quickly realized that it was her way of teasing me, and probably acknowledging the fact that this was unquestionably too much for a single guy.

"If that's the case," I said while she walked up to me, "I'll simply sell the home and live in a shack."

"Show me the rooftop views, smart guy," she said, taking my hand. "This place is so amazing."

"I think you might find the waterfall that the stairs circle amazing as well." Her bright eyes were so beautiful in reaction to that bit of information. "It's enclosed, but it's still an interesting feature."

"Is there anything you need to tell me?" she said, arching her eyebrow at me. "Are you running a drug cartel on the side or something?"

"I hate to disappoint you if you've already called the DEA." I laughed.

"Just making sure," she said as I led her back into the house. "I've watched a lot of movies and television shows about drug cartels, you know, and they all have homes like this."

"It may come as a disappointment, but I actually busted my ass for this place," I answered with a grin.

"Now that I can believe," she said with a laugh, nudging my side. "Show me around this stunning palace, would you?"

"Every floor has those glass doors, designed to take in the views." I pointed toward the floor-to-ceiling doors that replaced the walls of the home. "The master bedroom is pretty much a floor of its own," I said as she silently observed the unique home while I led her up the stairs. "Addy might enjoy the theater room if you decide the timing is right and wish to bring her here."

"She'll have us both moved in," Avery laughed. "Jesus Christ, I can't bring her here and tell her this is her friend Mitch's home. She'll never leave."

"We could tell her it's a vacation home like you told her about my place on the beach."

"More like a fucking resort carved into a mountain," Avery said as she walked with me onto the rooftop. I used the control panel before walking out to turn on the gas fire pit that was surrounded by lounge furniture. Beyond that was an endless, sprawling view.

"We can sit out here for a while, or we can always go in so you can get some sleep."

"So, is this an official invitation to spend the night with you, Mr. Mitchell?"

I eyed her flirty grin. "I would love for you to stay with me for as long as you wish." I chewed on the inside of my cheek; she looked so tired. "You must be exhausted after the day you've had."

"I just want to see and absorb these views. It's all so beautiful," she said, walking further out on the patio.

"The view isn't going anywhere if you'd rather close your eyes."

"You know what sounds nice?" She walked over, sat on the sofa and turned to me. "Why don't we have a little wine and relax here for a while? Be warned, though. I might fall asleep in your arms."

"I think I can handle carrying you to bed." I grinned. "I'll be back with the wine. Any preference?"

"Surprise me," she said, settling into the cushioned seating.

I walked down to the wine cellar, grateful I could help Avery escape the bullshit of this day. Her ex needed to be behind bars, in my opinion. Neither she nor Addy deserved a scum of the earth shit head like him in their lives.

I loathed drug addicts with every fiber of my being. They were too fucked up and selfish to understand what they were doing to the people who loved them. Avery had dealt with this shit for at least three years that I knew of, and I only knew that because of Addy's age. Thank God she had the strength to leave that self-destructive environment and bust her ass to make it work as a single mom. California was not a cheap place to start over, especially on your own.

All I know is I couldn't be more grateful that in her fight to keep herself freed from that asshole, she found a job at Mitchell and Associates, and by some mystical coincidence, I'd walked out on the floor that day and saw her and Addison.

If I'd never gone to that floor, I would've never seen that she had secretly come back into my life. Was I committed to her? To Addison? After tonight, I could safely say I was. I wasn't letting her out of my life again.

CHAPTER TWENTY-THREE

Avery

The fragrance of masculinity, sandalwood, and decadent leather filled my senses, and I smiled when I recalled I was safely in Jim's house. It was still dark out, and even though I woke somewhat startled that I was not in my own bed, this calmness I felt kept me in a peaceful and restful state of bliss.

The soft, crisp sheets were an experience on their own. The fresh breeze flowing in the room kept everything in my body in this rested state. I turned to curl onto my side, and that's when my eyes popped open. My sleepy bliss was stolen away by reality.

Holy shit. I wasn't awake enough to calculate that I'd made good on my joke about falling asleep on the roof at Jim's place, and he certainly carried me to bed. Now, here I was, eyes open, with the light of the room enhanced by the balcony's garden-lighting. The lighting worked to enhance my view of the man who'd saved me from turmoil in every way yesterday.

I snuggled closer to where he lay flat on his back, and just as I'd fallen asleep in his arms in England, I wrapped my body around him. His right arm came up and pulled me in closer, while his other hand rested on my leg. I loved the few nights we slept wrapped up in each other like this, and I was so thankful we found our way back into each other's arms again. Jim didn't wake, he just held me and like we both admitted…it felt right.

God bless this man's heart. I did remember him carrying me to bed now. I remembered being so sleepy that I stayed in my clothes while he changed into his shirt and shorts—all after I begged him to hold me and never let me go. I guess sleep deprivation made me extra sappy. He was definitely a keeper, though. He'd stuck with me through all of yesterday's insanity, and that deserved some kind of award on its own.

I inhaled his cologne, bringing me back to our wild times in England—that fragrance was intoxicating, there was simply no doubt about that. I couldn't resist kissing his side that I was curled against, and after listening to his rhythmic breathing, I fell directly back to sleep.

My phone's ringing startled me awake. The sun had already risen, and I was alone in the room. I turned to the nightstand and grabbed my phone before it could go to voicemail.

"Avery?" Larry, Derek's dad, said. "Hey, you there?"

"Yeah, what's up?"

"Oh. Hey, hun," he said, and I could hear Addy giggling in the background. "I wanted to let you know that Derek was arrested last night. We're not bailing him out this time."

About goddamn time, I thought, knowing Derek's parents could be my worst enemies at times. "What happened?"

"DUI and tried to resist arrest. He was pretty high. Maybe some time in county jail will help him sober up."

"Yeah," I said, rubbing my forehead and sitting up in bed. "What a fucking jackass. I'm glad you guys aren't bailing him out. He needs to get sober, Larry. He needs rehab."

"Mom and I know that," he said. "We're taking Addy to the zoo today. We don't want her upset that her dad's not here."

"Good." I scrunched my face up in annoyance. "You realize she's more attached to you than him anyway, right?"

"Derek spends time with her," he started to defend him.

"When he takes a nap. Seriously, he needs help."

"We know that," Larry insisted.

Yeah, you know that, but never do a fucking thing about it.

Then I heard Addy in the background. "Papa, let's go to the zoo," she sang the last word while Larry chuckled.

"Go ahead and go. I'll be there tomorrow. I've got to figure out my car situation today," I said. "The damn thing's probably toast."

"Maybe your new job can help you buy a new one?"

"You mean, maybe my new job can cut me an advance, and I can go and hope I can find another one? Addy and I will most likely be finding alternative ways to get to work."

"Yeah, I guess so."

"All right, I need to jump in the shower. Have fun today, and make sure to put on sunscreen."

I got off the phone with Larry, his lack of concern for our automobile predicament not fazing me. Addy and I could easily manage to take the bus or something to get to work until I got paid. I was no stranger to making something work out of nothing.

I slipped out of bed and went on the hunt for Jim. My mood was beyond happy, knowing that Derek was behind bars, and Larry and Annette weren't bailing him out this time. At this moment in time, the stars were aligning in my favor, and I wasn't going to fight it.

I followed the scent of eggs and toast. It smelled too delicious; what was he cooking down here? I sniffed out the location of the kitchen like a starving dog, and I shouldn't have been surprised when I saw it was a chef's dream kitchen.

"I guess I'm never getting breakfast in bed so long as I'm with you," I said, pulling my hair into a ponytail, trying not to be affected by the smack in my face of utter gorgeousness when I first saw Jim.

Jim smirked. He was in here cooking with no shirt on, and his black hair was sexy as fuck—still wet and revealing a natural curl he had. Damn, how long had it been? England felt like forever ago. How could I have forgotten this man had a body of perfection, built with tightly carved muscles that were highlighted by his tanned skin? His biceps, his broad shoulders, his beautiful face with that youthful look I'd noticed when Addison teased him.

I almost wanted to say I loved him after everything yesterday. Since waking up in the middle of the night when he held me close, and now seeing his pleasant expression, showing his beautiful soul on the inside, it was hard to keep my affections to myself.

I had to bring it down a few notches and act more rational. "Derek's locked up," I informed him, following Jim and the two plates he carried out to the poolside table and chairs.

He set the plates down, turned to me, and his expression became serious. "For how long?"

"His parents aren't bailing him out of jail anytime soon," I said as I took the chair he'd pulled out for me. "Thank God."

He kissed my cheek. "Yes, thank God," he said, going back into the kitchen and returning with two coffee mugs. "You still take it black, right?"

"Always," I answered.

"Easy date," he said, setting our coffee mugs down next to his picture-perfect eggs Benedict. "And still the most difficult. I believe I'll never get the breakfast in bed thing down for you."

"Kind of hard to do when your breakfast date can smell food and could very easily sleepwalk to where it's being cooked anyway," I teased.

"Sleepwalking to eat?" He arched that sexy eyebrow at me. "That is a tough one to beat."

"Thanks for bringing me to bed and staying with me last night," I said after cutting into my breakfast and swallowing a bite of food. "I didn't expect to fall asleep out there on you."

I glanced out and looked at the view this morning. This place was like a resort. If only there were a stiff breeze to push out the smog, I knew I could see the ocean from here, but I'd take this view, with or without haze, any morning.

"I was merely being the best host I could be," he said with a smile. "I fucked that job up before, when I sent my young bride packing in England."

I laughed. "You need to stop giving yourself shit over that. I walked because I was getting too attached. I knew better myself."

He dabbed the corners of his mouth with his napkin. "Really? How do you feel about me not wanting you out of my life now? Ever."

I smiled. "Even after a tiny taste of the bullshit of my life yesterday? Derek's actions should have you second guessing this commitment idea of yours."

He did that irresistible smirk. "The only trouble with yesterday was the fact that I couldn't kick Derek's ass myself."

"And if that feeling of not kicking his ass every time he pulls shit like that never goes away?" I looked at his questioning eyes. "If he knows you and I are an item, he'll just get worse. It'll get way worse."

"Well, if I can't kick his ass, then I'll just take a run in my work shoes to work out my frustrations."

"Shit, I forgot about the foot rub I owe you."

"All that matters is that you slept well, you're back in my life, and I suppose the fact that my feet survived your neglecting them," he said with a smirk after taking a sip of his coffee. "I'll promise you this, though: I will ensure Derek remains behind bars one way or the other. He needs to be locked away or in rehab. He needs to fucking disappear."

His expression was severe but mischievous.

"Whoa, yesterday I pinned you for a cartel guy, but maybe I should've gone with mafia don." I laughed. "Fucking disappear, eh?"

"You know what I mean. His ass needs to get help." I watched him do that handsome pucker while he chewed on the inside of his cheek. "Let's just say that if he rejects rehab because he's that big of a dumbass, and he comes after me, that's where he'll do time behind bars. Trust my word on that. He'll eventually fuck up; all addicts like him do." Then he smiled. "Perks of running and owning a successful global business: a team of badass lawyers are at my disposal."

I laughed. "So, no digging holes in Vegas to dispose of the body?"

Jim frowned, but his forehead creased in humor. "Who's the mob boss now?" He sipped his coffee again. "I won't be crossing you any time soon."

"I can't live in some crazy fantasy with you like I did in England." I chewed on my bottom lip.

He nodded.

"I really need to get ready and find out what's going on with my car."

Jim licked his lips and slid his bottom lip between his teeth. "About that," he said, and I saw the tough, business man suddenly look timid.

Confused, I leaned forward. "Do you know something about my car that I don't?"

"I don't want this to come across as presumptuous, but I was hoping that you are okay with me securing another car for you and Addison."

"Securing a car?" I said with a laugh.

He loosened up some. "I called in a favor that Alex owed me. Hopefully, he doesn't fuck it up."

"Are we back to the mob boss shit, and my car is the victim?"

"I figured you could use a new car to get around in, so I had Alex head out to the dealership today."

"You're kidding?"

"No." He smiled. "I managed to discover they made a four-door rollercoaster car, as Addy calls it, since she seemed so impressed by mine yesterday. I also figured it'd help outrun that truck Derek has if he ever tweaks out on you again."

My eyes filled with tears, and for probably the first time in my life, I felt grateful for the help instead of defensive. It wasn't like me to accept charity, but for some reason, it didn't feel like a handout.

I stood up and walked over and hugged him. "How can I ever repay you for this?"

He rose, and I was swallowed up by his warm, muscular chest.

"Allowing me into your life again is all I'll ever need." He stepped back. "I have to be honest; I was terrified that you'd want to kick my ass for taking the liberty of buying the car without consulting you."

"Quite the opposite, really." I smiled up at his brilliant and loving eyes. "I've never had anyone see me going through shit and give a damn. I mean, buying me a car, yeah, that's quite a monumental thing, but I could never be upset about you caring for my daughter and me like this. You are too good to be true. Hopefully, you didn't drop that much on a car, though. I just need something that runs. You could have just helped me fix up Bunny again."

"Damn it," he said. "Do you think Addy will be okay with saying farewell to her car? That poor thing needed to pass on to its great reward."

"Addy might want to kick your ass. That was her car." I laughed at him as he bit the bottom corner of his lip. "But I did kill it."

Jim laughed. "I could easily confirm that fact without a mechanic, I'm sure."

"Change of subject," I said, arms wrapped around his waist. "You smell fresh, delicious, and cleaned up. Do you mind if I take a shower?"

"Absolutely," he said taking my hand. "If you'd like, you can wear one of my shirts…" He paused and eyed me. "Like you did when you walked into my office that night in England."

I laughed. "Sounds fun, but I do need to get ready and run home to get fresh clothes."

"Well, the car issue is settled. It'll be here Monday." He gripped my hand tighter. "To the shower, gorgeous. I also have some extra toiletries that I brought up from the guest bath for you. Toothbrush and shit like that."

"Well, if only you could snap your hospitality fingers like that for some clean clothes, then I'd be good to go."

"I can launder yours while you're showering or soaking in the bath while you're trying to determine what you'd like to do today."

"And if they're not done in time?"

"Then I'll have the privilege of watching you sunbathe naked while I work on sending off some time-sensitive emails this morning."

"Sounds good to me," I said, then covered my mouth when we walked into his bathroom. "You're kidding me, right?"

He hit some buttons on a digital keypad for the shower to turn on, then set the temperature to eighty degrees. "Yeah, this bathroom is a bit overwhelming, but I got over it after my first shower." He turned back and smiled at me. "You have to be going insane wearing those jeans and that shirt by now. This heats up the water or cools it down," he said, bringing the digital keypad to life inside the shower. "Enjoy freshening up."

"Trust me, I will. Thanks," I said, desperately needing to clean up in a nice hot shower.

He walked across the slate floor and over to the large vanity area where glass bowl sinks sat on the counter. No shit. Backlit and everything.

"New toothbrush, hairbrush, and whatever else you need is right here. I'll be outside by the pool if you need me."

I watched him walk out, wondering why everything felt so different now. In England, it was impulsive. It was awesome. It was nothing close to this, this feeling of being more reserved with him and more respectable. It felt as if a relationship had started between us— or we'd just picked up where we'd left off. I loved all of it.

I stepped in the shower and let the waterfall free the last of my frazzled nerves from yesterday's bullshit as I pondered my situation with Jim. It didn't take me long to come to the obvious conclusion: I was falling for him fast. He was an old soul, the type of man they didn't make anymore.

The fact that he'd bought me a new car was overwhelming, but the thing that got me the most about that wasn't about the gift. It was the fact that he cared about me enough to consider I might need one. I didn't need Jim to give me handouts. I'd made it this far on my own without anyone's charity, but to have someone genuinely care without me saying a word—to take notice at all—that was something I'd never experienced before.

I was refreshed when I stepped out of the shower and smelling like a million bucks. I mean, with Jim's fancy shampoos and soaps, it was hard not to. While I brushed out my hair, I figured I'd throw caution to the wind and give Jim my undying gratitude. I wasn't going to lie or hold back. I wanted him. I just hoped this new side of Jim, the more sincere side that I was with now, was as impulsive as he was in England. I was about to find out if he wanted me as much as I needed him.

With this aching desire for more, I walked out naked and shamelessly to the pool. I spied Jim sitting on the lounge furniture that was across the pool and under the shade of palm trees.

I stepped down to the lower area and walked around the pool to where he sat. I felt my heart racing after I knew I was in his view. My smile was wide when I noted his serious expression, twisted lips, and frown as he stared intently at his laptop.

"My clothes ready yet?" I asked. "Hope I'm not interrupting anything important."

"Jesus Christ," I heard him say.

He shut his laptop, set it to the side, and stood. He took off his sunglasses, and his countenance darkened in a way that made my heart fall out of normal rhythm.

I was entirely under his spell now. I felt the charge in the air as he walked toward me, and the energy shot through my body when his knuckles ran over my shoulders. "How the hell could I let you walk out of my life that morning? You're so unbearably beautiful," he said, both hands caressing my jaw and guiding my eyes up to meet his. "I hope to God you walked out here—like this—for more than naked sunbathing or hoping your clothes were ready."

"And if I just wanted to sunbathe nude? I'm sure the neighbors are already calling the cops on you for this," I said, suddenly wondering how secluded this backyard was.

"I have no neighbors that could see this part of my property. The only eyes that are privileged to take in your sexy body are mine," he said, cupping my ass and pulling me against him. "You have no idea the things I want to do to you."

"God, I've missed you touching me," I said. "I've missed you."

I was in his arms before Jim turned toward a queen-sized chaise lounge. He gently laid me on it and climbed up over my body. Jim's eyes went to my lips, then he dipped his head, and his mouth gently tugged on my bottom lip, slowly teasing it, while his strong hands brushed over my hair.

A soft breeze picked up, caressing my body that was heating rapidly to a scorching temperature beneath Jim's muscular chest. I pressed my hands against his back and sighed as he gently kissed along my jawline. I tilted my head up and closed my eyes when his tongue and lips moved under my neck, my chin, and then he softly bit at my bottom lip. I opened my mouth, and his tongue swept in and met mine with desperation. We both groaned in the pleasure of this reunion that I needed more than I could have ever known.

Chills covered every inch of my body that arched into Jim, begging him for more than this kiss that was exciting every female part of me. I felt Jim's hard cock and could only wonder how long he'd allow this kiss to go on.

"Hell," I said, gasping for breath, my head turning toward the view of the skyline while my fingers ran through Jim's soft, wavy hair. His lips found my nipple, and his tongue worked circles around it. I was turning into a crazed woman underneath his slow way of igniting my body and charging it full of so much energy that I could climax here and now. The tip of his tongue gently ran up the center of my chest, my head going back into the lounge pillows he'd laid me against.

Jim's large hands framed each side of my face, his thumbs caressing along my cheeks. His eyes were mesmerizing while mine locked onto them. "I want all of you," he said in a low, firm voice. He touched his lips to mine. "You're mine, gorgeous. You have no idea how many times I've dreamt of being with you again. You also have no idea how close I was to tasting all of you before you left me. I want it all, right here and now," he said with a look that forced a spasm between my legs.

My mouth went instantly dry. "All of me?" I questioned, knowing he might be crossing his own lines.

"Are you comfortable with me wanting to taste you?" he asked while he tempted me by gliding the tip of his tongue around my open lips.

Just feeling this beautiful man's hands and lips on me was enough to ignite my full confidence with him in England. With this look in his eyes, and the way he was hungrily caressing my body with his lips and tongue, I was already falling into a state of ecstasy.

His ravenous eyes made me ache for what I'd never experienced with a man before. "I know I gave you a hard time about not being into oral, but I think you could easily know I've never experienced it."

He pulled back, and his lips pursed in the sexiest way. "I know you haven't," he said. "I understood that when you admitted you'd never came at the hands of a man, but I want you. I want to give this to you, and I want you to come in my mouth."

"Holy shit, you're amazing," I said, my head rocking back when his fingers moved to my pussy. "I want it all, Jim," I said in a soft voice.

"I'm going to fuck you so deep when I'm done making you come over and over in my mouth." His lips devoured mine while my legs fell open as he shifted his body off of mine. "I get the control now, gorgeous. All of it."

I met his challenging and promising gaze with one of my own. "For now," I said, my heavy breathing giving me away. The last thing I saw was the greed in his eyes as his lips and tongue ran a blazing trail of fire down to my abdomen and along the insides of my thighs.

My nerves tried to intervene, and Jim seemed to catch on to my tensing up immediately. His mouth tenderly massaged the insides of my thighs, his fingers moving into my opening while his thumb ran slow circles around my clit.

"Fuck, you're so wet," he said with his mouth against my burning flesh

"Yes. Just like that," I exhaled, relaxing more.

"Jesus, you're so beautiful," he said in a raspy voice.

While Jim's hand worked my pussy, his tongue and mouth seemed to massage every part of my body. He kissed along my hips, belly, my neck, and then he brought his undivided attention to my breasts. His teeth nipped while he sucked and gently pulled on my hardened nipples. I held onto his broad shoulders, bracing my body for what it ached for and knew Jim would give it.

"God, I'm going to come like this," I moaned, aching against his thumb as it worked my clit, his fingers still tenderly pulling on my G-spot.

"You're going to come in my mouth," he said, sliding his fingers out of me and repositioning himself between my legs.

I was so fucking ready to feel his mouth against my burning flesh. Jim's arms went under and wrapped around my legs, and his fingers massaged the inside of my thighs while I felt his warm, firm tongue press onto my clit. I glanced down, and our eyes locked before he closed his, and his mouth closed around my clit, sucking on it. I gripped his hair as I felt the build-up swirling inside me.

Jim's tongue slowly licked the flesh around my clit, and I jerked at the phenomenal sensation it was creating in me. He was licking, sucking, and pulling at my pussy like he had hungered for this moment for much longer than I'd imagined. His groans were unbearable as I arched into him.

"I'm fucking coming," I said in a growl.

Jim's tongue dipped into my opening while his thumb went to my clit, gently pulling this surging orgasm out of me and into his mouth. When I rocked harder into his lips, his tongue probed deeper, he and I both groaning in pleasure as I writhed and rode his perfect mouth in utter ecstasy.

I reached for my nipples, biting my lip, feeling more behind this now that Jim's fingers were back inside of me. "Hell yes, gorgeous. You want more?" he asked, his voice deep, perfect, and urging me on.

"God, yes."

Jim's mouth covered my pussy, and to have him bury his face in my hot entrance, hear his moans, and feel him taking me like he would if his lips were devouring mine in a kiss? It was all too much. His fingers pressed hard against my G-spot, his tongue swirling firmly around my clit, and I was about to lose it again. Damn, was he the best at everything he did?

"Fuck me," I said, my legs tightening after my pussy became sensitive. I had to end the multiple orgasms Jim was pulling out of me before I got dizzy. "I swear I'm going to blackout." I laughed when Jim released my pussy and kissed up my abdomen.

"If my condoms weren't in the house, I'd be fucking you into a blackout state," he said with a smile. "We're doing this all day." His lips went back to my hard nipples. "You taste so good. Your body is mine."

"Getting possessive?" I teased, my breathing finding a normal rhythm.

"Perhaps." He smirked at me. "I'm going to fuck you so deep once I know you're not going to pass out on me."

"No." I smiled at him as he kissed up the center of my chest. I gently gripped his forehead and brought those dazzling green eyes to meet mine. "Now that you've broken Jim's oral sex rules—or should I say you shattered those rules—it's my turn."

"Oh, yeah?" He arched his eyebrow at me.

"Your dick is mine."

"I think if you touched my dick, I'd come right here and now." He chuckled, pulling himself up to lay next to me. "You looked hotter than hell and tasted so fucking delicious. Jesus, I was a fool for not doing this to you sooner."

"My turn." I traced my fingers over his hard V-line muscle.

"I won't last," he said with a sigh that only made me smile.

"This has always been my favorite part of fucking you." I reached into his board shorts to rub along the cock I wanted to taste. "I love your expression when you try to hold back. It's my turn to taste you."

CHAPTER TWENTY-FOUR

Jim

I didn't have a second to take a breath before Avery had my board shorts down and my hard cock was in her hands. Her blue eyes were gleaming with hunger when they locked with mine. With any blow job, I had expected her to instantly take my cock in her mouth, but she didn't. Jesus Christ. She brought her lips and tongue to my balls while she used her hand to work the tip of my dick. I could've exploded with this alone.

Each of my nerves surged in a fiery sensation, pulsating throughout my entire being. Avery's thumb and fingers were slick with my precum as she ran firm circles around the tip of my cock.

"Fuck," I groaned while Avery's mouth enthusiastically licked and sucked on my balls.

"I love your cock," she said in a sultry voice that assured me of the one thing I needed to know—she wanted this as badly as I did. I reached up into the cushion behind me, nearly tearing the thing open when her tongue and lips massaged up my shaft. My hands were pulled into tight fists, clinging to the cushions, when she began teasing my tip. Fuck me to hell. This was taking all I had to hold back.

With one hand cupping and massaging my balls and her other slick hand stroking my shaft, her eyes locked onto mine again. She was so beautiful that I never wanted to break eye contact with her. Her lips and tongue ran circles around my tip, and my aching need to have her finally take me into her mouth was painful at this point.

Her eyes closed, and with a soft moan, her mouth took my throbbing cock entirely. "Fucking hell," I breathlessly said, my eyes rolling back when she took me as deeply as she could. With my balls being worked by her hand and the suction she created with her mouth sliding up and down my cock, I was in ecstasy.

My entire body was in a continual spasm while I groaned in euphoria. Avery's lips moved faster, and her enthusiasm broke through any control I had of holding back.

"I'm going to come," I informed her through clenched teeth.

Her moans told me all I needed to hear. She wanted it, and she wanted it all. I reached down to her hair, my cock deep in her mouth, and that's when I jerked, shooting my cum deep into her mouth. Avery's sigh was the best sound in the fucking world as she continued to swallow every last ounce of cum. Still going, I slowly moved my cock through her lips, listening to her as she swallowed all of me.

Fuck, that was *more* than a blow job. Avery worked my ass over and only proved how ridiculous I was for being so reserved back in England.

"Fucking Christ," I said as my body shuddered with her full lips still wrapped tightly around me. I looked down at her sparkling blue eyes and ran my hands over her hair. "This won't be the last time we ever do this," I said, feeling drunk on the blue-eyed beauty kissing the tip of my cock before she slid up and lay next to me.

Avery tucked herself into my side and rested her head on my shoulder. "You're right on that one," she said, kissing my neck, then draped her leg over mine.

I felt like every last ounce of energy was depleted from me for the moment, and I relished in our closeness instead of fighting for more. I ran my fingertips over her shoulder and kissed the top of her head. "Who's the dipshit now?" I chuckled. "You worked me over in ways I never expected."

She laughed. "You have the sexiest dick ever, so that certainly helped." She glanced up with a daring smile. "And about your *no oral sex* rule, what happened to that little rule of yours?"

I shook my head. "We sort of eliminated that lame rule of mine, wouldn't you say?"

"That's why I have to ask. What exactly made you create such a rule in the first place?"

I gazed out at the small ripples the breeze created in my pool. "It was quite a while ago, in something of a previous life, of course." I smiled at her bright blue eyes.

"Of course." She exhaled with a grin.

"I was pretty much a wild bachelor who took whatever I wanted when it came to women. It bit me in the ass after I had some head case nearly planning our wedding day, buying us a puppy—"

"Shut the fuck up." She laughed. "No, she didn't. Shouldn't it be the guy buying the girl a puppy in the relationship?"

"That's the whole point. It wasn't a relationship. It was a couple of nights together, and the next thing I know, I'm not only being stalked, but I ended up having to change my fucking phone number and deal with *our* puppy." I sighed, "I don't know, after I made it clear—puppy or not—we were *not* in a relationship, she went ape-shit." I cringed at the memory. "She kept going on and on about how I had been leading her on the whole time, and it was all about the oral sex. She went crazy about it. She was asking how I could do such a thing and let her think she meant something to me. It was a whole psychotic episode." I shook my head. "In the end, I lost the puppy."

"Jesus, it's just oral sex." Avery laughed. "In her defense, however, you are very good at it. I might buy a puppy too."

I chuckled. "I didn't think it was a big deal at the time either. Then I thought, maybe men are different, and I wasn't being fair. Not saying all women or men are the same, but—hell, I don't know what I'm trying to say. I just knew that if it was going to complicate the situation for me, it wasn't going to happen again. I don't have time for complications, and I certainly didn't want to have to deal with that shit ever again. If oral made it seem too intimate, then it was easier to keep it to only fucking." I kissed her forehead. "If it makes a difference, the night I got you off after learning a man had never taken care of you properly, it took everything in my power to refrain from just giving into it all. I knew at that time that you were unlike any other woman."

"But that poor green bean I was chomping into scared you off?" She tightened her lips in humor.

I traced her perfect lips with my thumb. "That mildly concerned me," I teased her.

"And yet, I simply treated your dick like it was my favorite dessert and relished in every second of tasting you."

"That's putting it mildly. Best fucking blow job of my life." She reached for where I grew hard again, recalling the constant wave of bliss I was in while she worked my dick over. "Did you have plans today, or can we really just fuck until I have to go back to work on Monday?"

"I do need to get my clothes for work on Monday. The car problem was settled by you first thing this morning, so thanks to you, that's off my list."

I smiled. "I think I'll mandate that you work in my office—no clothes—and that problem will be solved too."

"Hilarious." Her lips twisted adorably. "By the way, are we keeping this a secret? You know, with us working together and all? Should I bring a puppy to work? I'm not sure how you want to handle it."

I smiled at her laugh that I'd missed during our time apart. "Are you asking if we should hide the fact that you're fucking the CEO of the company you work for?"

"That's probably what will circulate through the two goddamn high-rise buildings you own."

"Will that bother you?" I asked, more serious.

"Well, I don't necessarily want to be looked at like your whore," she said.

"Then I simply won't allow those rumors to start."

"Really?" She propped her folded arms across my chest. "How do you plan to stop them? Are you going to send a mass email to everyone in the company?"

"You're my lady," I simply stated. "They'll all learn very quickly that's the case. I don't hide shit. Secrets such as these always lead to rumors like you just mentioned, and I won't give anyone reason to believe a rumor. In one way or the other, they will all learn that Avery Gilbert is mine and mine alone." I paused and kissed the top of her head. "More importantly, I'm entirely yours."

I felt her kiss my side. "This will definitely be interesting. I don't plan on mentioning..."

Avery paused when my phone rang.

"That shit is going to voicemail," I said, ignoring it. "You and I just warmed up for what I've been craving since first seeing you again." I pinched my lips together and closed my eyes when the phone rang again, it stopped, the voicemail alerted, then rang again. "If only we were in the house, I would have abandoned the phone, and we'd be tearing open a condom right about now."

I felt Avery laughing. "You probably should get that, and then I'll gladly roll the condom on for you."

I smiled and sat up after Avery slid off me. I reached for my phone that was ringing again. "Jesus, Jacob," I answered my brother's call, annoyed. "Tell me Ash is having the baby, and that's why you're blowing my phone up like the press is on your ass again."

"Alex has to back out of the convention you two set up for those investors and medical professionals for Saint John's. It looks like you're up to bat, bro."

"The gala in Palm Springs?" I asked, running my hand over my forehead. "Alex didn't call me. What the hell is going on?" My phone beeped the call-waiting tone. "Hang on, Alex is calling in now. I'll handle it. Just get your ass there. It starts tonight."

"I am already down here, dip-fuck," he said as I clicked over to catch Alex.

"Hey, is everything cool?" I asked, knowing my right-hand man didn't back out of anything.

"My mom's in the hospital. I have to fly to Nevada. They think it might have been a stroke. They're still waiting on tests to come back."

"Holy shit. Do you think she'll be okay?"

"Yeah, I think so. I just need to be there. All of us are trying to fly in, and I'm the closest of the kids."

"Yes, of course. Go as soon as you can. Give her my well-wishes. I'll take care of everything with the medical gala."

"Jake's speaking tonight, and Collin will be there tomorrow to present his piece on neuroscience. We have an entire lineup of events for the convention. I emailed and faxed you the entire itinerary a few minutes ago."

"Got it. Is there anything I can do to help outside of this? You're taking the company plane, right?"

I felt horrible for Alex, even though I'd never met his mom nor had ever heard much about her. That didn't matter. It was family, and family had to come before this company, or we'd all lose our minds.

"I'm already on a plane. I'll keep you updated with texts."

"All right, man. Take care of yourself. I'll be here if you need anything."

We hung up, and I tried to gather my senses while Avery sat at my side, rubbing my back supportively.

I looked over at her and gripped the back of my neck. "Are you up for making your first appearance as my lady?" I asked while I contemplated getting her into a gown and on the chopper in less than three hours.

"God dang, is everything okay?"

"My VP is backing out of a significant affair we're having for the company. It's a part of a conference we're holding. He won't be able to attend after learning his mom is in the hospital. I need to take his place and be in Palm Springs tonight and tomorrow night." I bit my lip. "We can pick up and bring Addison if you don't feel comfortable being that far from her. We won't be that far, though, given we'll be using my helicopter for transportation. I can have you brought back swiftly if there's an emergency with Addy."

"Slow down, Jim." She had a look of amusement on her face. "Jesus, I've never seen you so worked up. Yes, Addy will be fine here. When would I be coming back again?"

"Late Sunday night." I cringed at the idea of taking Avery this far away from her daughter. "We can easily bring Addy with us. The hotel is a resort that she'll surely love."

"And I'm sure she'll dig the conference too." Avery laughed. "Let me call Larry and let them know they can keep Addy until Monday. It'll be easier for her to stay with them since we'll be getting back late, and they'll love having her a day longer. So long as Derek's ass is in jail, then I'm not worried about leaving with you if you want me along. I have nothing to wear, though."

"What size are you? Wait, I have an idea," I said while Avery continued to look at me as if I'd completely lost it. I dialed Ash's number. "Hey, kid," I said when my sister-in-law picked up, "your friend that you shop with, does he have any internal connections to that boutique that he always insists you buy your gowns from?"

"The place on Melrose?" Ash questioned.

"Wherever it is. I need a dress for Avery, my girlfriend," I said, winking at Avery. "We have to fly to Palm Springs before Jake has a coronary attack."

"Funny, Jim. I'll call the guys and see if they can get her a gown. They're going to want eye-color, hair color, size, all that shit," she said with a laugh. "And I'm very curious about this girlfriend comment coming from..." She paused. "Wait, Avery? The woman that you met in England? You're taking her?"

"She graciously accepted the invite," I said with a smile.

"Okay, perfect. Let me give the guys a call. They'll have a dress for her in under an hour. They can even come up to the house and handle everything—"

"Why don't you give them directions to the airport where we keep the planes and choppers. I'll have them flown down. They can take care of Avery there. I'm on a time crunch to pull this off."

"You have designers at your disposal; why would you want Clay and Joe involved?"

"They're your friends, and I was quite impressed with how they managed your and Jake's wedding. I know they'll handle Avery's last-minute needs for this event quite well," I said.

"You and your damn heart of gold, Jim. The guys are going to shit when they hear about this. Let me get a hold of them and square it all away. See you when you get to Palm Springs. Oh," she said, her voice an octave higher, "I can't wait to meet Avery."

"Thank God." I smiled. "Once you get acquainted, I'm sure you'll both enjoy making fun of Jake and me in our penguin suits."

CHAPTER TWENTY-FIVE

Avery

*A*fter I'd made arrangements for Addison to stay with Larry and Annette until Monday, it seemed as though a whirlwind of controlled chaos took me and held me from the second Jim and I left his home.

How the man pulled off all of the shit that happened between calling for his driver and managing things with his personal assistants, I would never know. I would also never attempt to understand how this man operated so calmly in the midst of what I would have had to sit and take a month to plan out.

We made a quick stop by my house for me to change and get last-minute travel items. Once I'd thrown my toiletries in a bag, I went to my dresser. Knowing time was of the essence, I tossed in random comfy shorts, tanks, bras, shoes, jeans, and whatever the hell else I could grab to put in my small duffle bag.

Jim was understandably on the phone the entire trip from my house to a private airport. I took this time to get on the phone with

Addy and hear all about her day at the zoo. They were heading to the movies next, and as always, hearing Addy's excitement made me delighted that she was enjoying her weekend. It made me look forward to this trip more, knowing that she was having a blast with her grandparents, which she always did when Derek's stupid ass was out of the picture.

The driver pulled into the private airport and drove the car to where a sweet-ass helicopter was. I watched in awe when a man in a dark suit walked briskly toward Jim's door right as Jim hung up from his call.

"Henry." Jim shook the man's hand, stepping out of the car. "Good to see you. Thanks for handling everything last minute for me," he said, reaching his hand back for me to place mine in.

"Never a problem, Mr. Mitchell," Henry answered while I stepped out of the car. "Will there be anything else aside from what is already on our itinerary?"

"Yes, I do have something else," he said, his hand clutching mine. "I want the security detail to back off a bit. England was too much. I practically had to pay them off to allow me some freedom," he said with a half-laugh. "Other than that, is everything arranged at the hotel, then?"

"Yes, and your suite is reserved where the conference will be taking place," the man answered. "I'll inform and update the men in your security detail about your preferences."

Jim's hand slid across my lower back. "Very good. This is Avery Gilbert," he said, keeping his CEO, authoritative tone. I certainly was at James H. Mitchell's side. "She will be with me throughout the entire trip. Ensure the detail has their eye on her as well," he finished by taking my hand back into his.

"Absolutely, Mr. Mitchell," he answered and smiled at me. "Pleased to make your acquaintance, Miss Gilbert."

I returned his smile, more nervous than anything, but playing along. Jim and I walked toward the helicopter, where Jim's driver had returned from placing our bags. This was beyond surreal. Jim's phone rang, and he took the call as we stepped onto the aircraft.

I'd never been in a helicopter before, so I wasn't sure what to expect, but I definitely didn't expect it to be this massive and luxurious. The smell of leather reminded me of the fragrance in Jim's luxury cars. Four large chairs sat at the front and back of the cabin while the middle area—with hardwood floors—had leather couches lining the windows that stretched along the entire cabin. It was more than high class—this was ludicrous wealth.

Jim guided me to buckle up while continuing to throw out some more instructions about the event we were heading to. I buckled myself in, and followed Jim in chilling out at the back of the helicopter in the two captain-like chairs. This was so fucking badass.

I glanced up to see a monitor that showed the flight patterns on it. The sun was setting, and I don't think this rushed trip could've been planned better. I felt excitement wash over me when I heard the engines come to life, and the shadows of the blades start spinning slowly before they whirled into a blur. The next thrill was when the cabin lights dimmed and an indigo-blue light backlit the area we sat in. The light was muted enough to set off the elegance throughout the helicopter, but it also enhanced my view outside of the windows.

With grace, the chopper gently rose from the ground and hovered for a few seconds before it dipped forward and veered off to the right. I watched the ground below us growing farther away as the helicopter glided through the air, and it was so smooth that I felt nothing but the adrenaline coursing through my body.

We made a few banking turns, and then the ocean was beneath us. The coast was to our left, and the lights flickered off the waves as they rolled into shore now that the sun hid behind the horizon. Jim's hand covered mine, and his thumb tenderly rubbed over the top of it, pulling me out of this extraordinary experience I was enjoying.

"Care to join me for a drink?" he asked, pointing toward the sofa at my right, and facing the windows that gave the view to the coastline. "God, I haven't said two words to you since you accepted this invite. Please forgive me for that; this last-minute shit has had me strapped to the phone since taking over this event."

"I completely understand. What are we drinking?" I asked,

unbuckling and standing up, following him to where he had a bottle of champagne, and then a man walked out with a tray of cheese, crackers, and fruit.

"I'm having a bourbon. You can have this champagne or anything else you'd like."

I eyed the food tray and thought I'd tease him, being that it was my first time talking to him since this whole thing was set into motion. "I might have to back out on dating you again," I said, picking off the tray. "I can't do this lavish lifestyle stuff," I shoved a piece of cheese in my mouth, "at all."

He smiled and laughed. "Unfortunately, I couldn't bring this helicopter through a drive-through window, or I'd have you eating burgers, fries, and a shake instead."

I took the tall glass of bubbly and sipped it. "It's why I can't be your lady, Mr. James H. Mitchell," I said with a dramatic sigh. "I can't eat like a bird. I thought you and I established this a while ago."

Jim took the glass of bourbon he'd poured and sipped. "I will ensure a buffet of food is waiting for you in our rooms when we arrive. The hotel will cater to any and all food cravings you have until you have no other option but to date me because I know how to feed my woman."

I pinched my lips, trying to hold on to teasing Jim, but not able to take my eyes off the glorious coastline view. "Might work," I said, my mind drifting to the beauty of cruising through the air over the ocean. I settled into his side on the couch. "This is remarkable."

"But the food sucks." He kissed my temple. "I'll have to find time to make this right."

I leaned my head against his shoulder. "And how do you plan on doing that?"

"Well, I see it like this: I miserably failed as your host at my place, and now this helicopter food situation almost has you walking out on me again. Let's just say I wasn't finished with you at my house before the SOS call came in. I'm still planning on what we never finished after our little warm up session out by my pool."

"I'd like to see you try to fit in," I leaned up to whisper in his ear, "us fucking."

Jim grinned and kissed my lips. The flavor of the bourbon in his kiss sent a jolt of energy straight between my legs.

"You think I can't find a way to take my lady before, possibly during, and after this charade tonight?"

"I shouldn't challenge you." I laughed, taking another sip of my drink. "I watched you pull this whole thing off like it was nothing." I studied his eyes—sparkling and radiant—before I turned to face him on this sofa. "I have to know. Are you good at hiding stress, or is this shit normal for you?"

"My brother always tries to pick my brain to figure out how I remain calm in complicated or chaotic situations. My only explanation is that I don't allow chaos to govern my mind. I wouldn't be able to maneuver through them if my mind escalated to an unhealthy level of stress. I know it will be handled, and that is the goal I strive for while confronted with things I believe would stress or upset others."

"Wow." I smiled at him. "Makes sense as to why you didn't knock Derek's ass out after he threw a punch at you."

"That was much simpler. I knew if I engaged the man, especially while he was not in his right mind, it would only fuel what I knew he wanted. I chose not to give him any credence whatsoever while trying to upset me." He took another sip of bourbon. "I quickly learned that my weak point with that man is you. Without question, I would fight back, knowing between right and wrong, if he were to attempt to harm you or Addy."

"Well, the prick is in jail." I rubbed his leg. "Don't worry your handsome self about him hurting Addy or me. Just getting away from him helps me."

"Yeah," he said. "And Addy? She's okay with Mom skipping town on her?"

"She doesn't care where Mom is at the moment." I leaned against him. "She's had an awesome day at the zoo and will be ready to crash by seven tonight after the movies. She's having a little party of her own."

Jim chuckled. "Good. She and you both deserve a little fun, don't you think?"

"We'll see how much fun a speaking event can be." I laughed.

"Yeah, you gave me a glimpse of your shit show yesterday, so you get mine tonight and tomorrow." He ran his hand over my arm. "However dull the event might be, I swear to God, you're not leaving Palm Springs without me fucking you senseless while we're there. I've waited far too long for that, and after this afternoon?" He exhaled and licked his lips. "Your ass is mine when I get the first chance. Mark my words on that."

"And now you're working me up."

"Good," he said, reclining against the sofa. "I need you wet and ready for your man when we get in that room." He gently ran his hand over my hair. "Perhaps we can enjoy a hot shower together? It might be the only place where it's private when we first arrive."

"Doubt that. I'm fairly sure that after this helicopter ride, your hotel room will be a house of its own."

CHAPTER TWENTY-SIX

Jim

*A*ll of the itineraries were changed, the venue was amended to accommodate my standing in Alex's place, and any other possible issues that might arise from me taking over at the last minute were settled.

It was always crazy, the shit that had to change to keep people calm when soliciting them to work for or invest in a new company— be it a hospital, or big or small business, or anything, really. The slightest change could create a shit storm, and this whole conference, which was orchestrated to bring in new investors, executive team members, and more medical staff for Saint John's Heart Institute...it all could fall apart with the slightest alteration. Now that we were integrating the neuroscience center, we certainly had no room for error. We needed this to be nothing less than superior.

I felt like the biggest ass ever, having had only a few moments alone with Avery on the helicopter before we landed. My phone began blowing up with bullshit the second we stepped out of the chopper, and I'd been on it since we walked into our presidential suite. That's when Clay and Joe took over in prepping Avery for the night. These guys were practically family since Ash came into our lives, and I enjoyed having them around; however, I couldn't even make the introductions. Thank God Avery took to them immediately and reacted with her usual brightness and enthusiasm.

While I was stuck on my damn phone, it was Clay who took control of the scene and gave me his *what a shame that Jim is such a workaholic* look. I knew Clay well enough and he wasn't a dick about it. This man with his own heart of gold genuinely seemed to feel bad for me, and I never really understood why he did, until I met Avery. That's when I realized it was apparent that I hadn't been living a life outside of my business. Here I was proving I was no different from before because my department heads in public relations, planning, and marketing were not answering their fucking phones.

"Why is Hearken not in attendance?" I asked one of the marketing representatives assigned to this event.

"They backed out last minute," she said timidly. "I can't get a hold of anyone else to help me figure out what's going on, Mr. Mitchell. It's the only reason I called you, I'm so—"

"Text me your contact info on Hearken, and I'll deal with them personally," I said, cutting her off. I didn't have time for excuses or apologies. "We have thirty-two rooms booked for this group. I'm not playing any more games with these people," I said.

Fucking hell, I thought after hanging up, checking Jen's text for the number, and calling out. I swear to God that I was about to lose my shit in this room. Where the fuck were my department heads and my marketing teams that'd handled this before it went sideways? It was one thing to manage my business for all of this, but an entirely different thing to do the jobs of the employees that were hired to handle these issues.

We were on a time crunch, and I had no time to play games and start chewing asses out. It was time to cut the middlemen out and handle things myself.

My frustration eased some when I heard Avery giggling on the other side of the double doors of our suite. Joe and Clay were contagiously laughing along with her—surrounded by the parade of gowns and accessories they brought in—and I heard Ash stop in for a few minutes too. I wanted to be out there with them, and I could have been if my employees were on deck, doing their fucking jobs.

I refocused and sat at the desk, handling this particular medical group that tried to bail out of the conference. It only took twenty minutes on the phone and turning over my company jet to fly them all in tonight to inspire them to be in attendance for Collin's presentation tomorrow. Fucking hell, part of me didn't want this group to have anything to do with this new center for our neuroscience research. They were becoming entitled little bitches through this entire process, and I was having significant doubts about them being around for our opening next year. No one was worth this much trouble.

I leaned back in my desk chair, pinched the bridge of my nose, and forced myself to regroup entirely before getting ready to head over to the exclusive convention location at the resort. This place was to be transformed to create an exquisite and glamorous atmosphere for this event. My teams had better have this prepared as instructed. At this point, I had a feeling I'd be blowing up balloons or vacuuming next.

I glanced over at my ringing phone and eyed it with annoyance when I saw the head of my public relations team calling in. After her call went to voicemail, my head of events planner rang my cell. It only took me getting on the phone—doing their jobs—for them to call me back?

I glared at my phone and instead of answering and listening to excuses, I pulled up my email. I put every department and department head who'd dropped their work in my lap tonight on an email string; this was the only communication they were getting from me tonight.

Alex and I needed to be on the same page with this too. If he let these departments run him over like they just did me, he needed to tighten the reins. No way in hell did I or my vice president deal with this bullshit, especially hours before a massive event that was arranged months ago. I sent out invites for an important meeting on

Monday, and we would all be reminded who got paid to do fucking what. If these employees wished to keep their jobs, then I'd see them then. This was all inexcusable.

I swiveled in my chair when the door opened, and I heard Avery speaking to Joe and Clay as she stood, half-in and half-out of the doorway to this room, wearing silky shorts and a camisole.

"Thank you so much again, you guys," she said in her sexy, scratchy voice that made me observe her with growing lust.

"Tell Jim to take care of his stunning woman tonight," I heard Clay say. "Have fun, girly."

"Tell Jim we said thank you for the VIP treatment," Joe said, always a bit more reserved than his counterpart. "We'll see you tomorrow, Av."

"Sounds great, and I'll tell him," Avery answered with a high-spirited laugh.

"Oh," I heard Clay say, "and tell Jim we're all decided on the pewter dress. He gets no vote."

Avery laughed again. "See you boys later."

The doors closed, and it was just Avery and me now. I watched with desire as she pranced across the room in her tank and no bra, completely unaware of where I sat secretly admiring her.

I rose, knowing I had to change into my suit, but I couldn't go the entire night without being inside her. She was washing her hands in one of the sinks when I walked in and handed her a towel to dry them.

"God help me," I said, looking at her naturally sharp and striking features that had been accentuated by the way her makeup was done. "You look so beautiful."

Avery chewed on her bottom lip while my eyes drank in her beauty. Half of her hair was pulled up and fashioned to complement the artistic skill of her makeup. Her vivid blue eyes held mine captive, and I seriously had to control myself.

"Why thank you," she teased me with a seductive grin, "but it's Clay and Joe's masterpiece you're admiring."

"I'm admiring a woman that I'm so grateful to have in my life."

She turned back to face me. "I met Ash tonight..." She stopped herself then eyed me, it had to be the expression of needing her that she saw on my face. She ran her hand over my hard cock and grinned. "We have an hour, I think, and I'm full from all the food that was brought in the room. You weren't lying about that buffet, were you?"

I laughed, grabbed her ass, and lifted her up to wrap her legs around my waist. "I wasn't lying about my fucking you before this thing, either."

Her hands ran down the center of my chest as I walked over to the mirror and turned her to face it. She smiled daringly at me through the reflection. "I was wondering if you'd failed as my host again."

"Never," I said, wrapping my hands around her waist and pulling her shorts and thong down. My shorts were on the ground after. I pulled a condom out of the toiletry bag I had close by, ripped the fucker open, and rolled it on my hard cock. "In fact, I'm going to hit that spot with my cock, and watch you take me like this through that mirror."

Avery planted her hands on the long granite countertop and wiggled her ass in front of me. "What are you waiting for, hotshot?" she taunted with a smile.

I leaned forward to kiss along her neck while I lined myself up to her wet entrance. "You want it like this? I can't promise I'll be gentle."

"I don't want it gentle," she said as I slid my dick into her hot and tight sex. "Oh, yes," she moaned, her ass arching into me. "God, I've missed you."

I watched her eyes close as I slid further in, knowing her sensitive spot wasn't deep. "Tell me when I'm on it," I said, feeling every last tense nerve from earlier swiftly fleeing, and all that mattered now was bringing my girl to climax. Watching her through the mirror was enhancing the ecstasy of the moment.

"Fuck, you're still so tight." I bent forward and kissed her neck while moving my tip against the inside of her. I wanted to go deep and hard, but her moans as I slid in and out of her like this held back my selfish desires.

"Oh my God," she said as I continued to move my throbbing dick in and out of her. I gripped her hips, using them to position her while I worked her pleasure point. "Fuck," she cried out with her voice that did more things to me than I could explain.

I had one arm on her shoulder, one on her hips, while I worked her sweet spot with my dick. "That's it," I said, my cock massaging her G-spot. "Come on, gorgeous," I said, feeling her pussy constrict around my cock. "Let it go. I'm going to come so deep inside you."

Her eyes were trance-like when they met mine in the mirror. She was so damn sexy. "I'm so close," she said, her hands clenched into fists as I worked her pussy. I attentively watched her lick her lips, mouth open, and her beautiful tits bounced underneath her shirt.

I needed to see all of her. I pulled her top up, Avery's hand coming up to play with her breast while my hand took her other. I was so intently focused on her in this state of bliss that I remained calmer than I could have imagined while helping her climax with my cock.

"You want me to work your clit, gorgeous?" I whispered, my lips licking along her delicious neck.

"I'm going to come just like this," she said in bliss.

She threw herself back against my chest, her entrance clamping down on my cock in a spasm that flipped the switch on my nerves, muting all sensations while I watched her come. Her head shifted to lean up, and my lips captured hers while she moved, coming on my dick. My other hand worked her nipple and I softly twisted it while we kissed through her climax. Her tongue searching and meeting mine in a soft, seductive way.

She pulled away. "I want you in me so fucking deep," she said, eyes glossed over as she returned to her position of giving me her ass again. "Fuck this pussy hard, Jim," she ordered, still breathless.

My hand crossed her chest and held her breast while I positioned myself to bury myself inside her. Her face tightened while I thrust in and out, and her whimpers sent me into ecstasy that second. I pinched and rolled her clit gently as I came inside her.

"Fuck that feels amazing," she panted out. "I've missed this."

Our eyes met in the mirror, both locking while I watched her call out, coming on my dick again. "That's right. You're coming hard, aren't you?"

"Yes. Fuck...yes," she panted out.

I moved slower after I felt us both relaxing into our release and finally having what I'd craved from the moment she left me in England. There were no words, both of us breathing heavily, collapsing forward against the sink.

Coming down off our high, I relished in taking her this way for a few seconds longer. "Fuck, you feel so damn good," I said, feeling my dick rubbing inside her, loving fucking her from behind. I dropped my lips to cover the back of her neck and over the top of her shoulders. "How's that for timing?" I said, easing us out of this position and bringing her to face me.

"Too short, in my opinion," she countered with a kiss to my lips. "You've left me wanting you more now than ever," she teased with a laugh, wrapping her arms around my neck. "I've missed us." She took my face in her hands and pressed her lips softly to mine. "I've missed you. That ended too early."

"The night is young, gorgeous. That was just a taste of what I'm going to do with your little ass later."

"Don't make promises you can't keep, Jimbo." She laughed, forcing my eyes to open wider in humor.

"Jimbo, huh? I see you've not only met Ash tonight, but you've met my brother, Jacob, too." I smirked before disposing the condom.

"If it weren't for your different eye colors and hairdos, you'd be almost identical twins."

"We're told that all the time." I smiled, following her out of the bathroom and into the closet. "I'm guessing he's cool with his presentation tonight?"

"He enjoyed a beer and some food, if that's what you mean. Oh, and he said that he wasn't going anywhere near this room with you on the phone. So that's probably why you didn't see him."

I laughed, half-dressed now, and pulling out my black suit. "My brother, the saint," I said, searching for my burgundy button-down shirt and plucking the freshly-pressed items off their hangers.

Mine and Avery's conversation was cut off as we finished getting dressed for the event. Once my tie was on, and the knot perfected, I put on my cuff-links, socks, shoes, and then I was ready to grab my jacket and get this night started.

"Good God," I said, walking into the sitting area and seeing Avery in her silk, slender gown. "You look ravishing. Your ass is in dangerous trouble tonight. I won't make the entire event seeing you in this dress all night."

"You did mention a before, during, and after fuck, right?"

"And I will make good on that promise. Jesus Christ," I said with a smile. "I believe tonight may be the first test of me being a jealous man."

"Doubt that, Mr. Mitchell."

"Mr. Mitchell is going to have his eye on any asshole who comes around you." I laughed. "Let me call Jake, and then we'll head down." I smiled at the beautiful woman who would be on my arm tonight. "We do have to get out of here, or we're going another round."

"If it helps, I'm going commando, lover-man." She winked, leaving me unable to respond after Jake answered the call.

CHAPTER TWENTY-SEVEN

Avery

$\mathcal{I}$ sat at a reserved table in the front of the venue next to Jim's sister-in-law, Ash, and other executives from Mitchell and Associates. I was in awe from the second we stepped into this hotel conference room. The décor transformed the area to look like we were at some massive convention.

The tone was set with the perfect lighting, a stage, and a large projector screen behind a glass podium. Maybe this was what all resort conference rooms looked like. I had no idea since this was my first time attending anything like this.

We watched a fantastic presentation that was underscored with music that kept you drawn into the history of Mitchell and Associates. It felt as if we were at a badass movie theater. Hell, I already worked for this company, and I'd even gained deeper respect from watching clips of its powerful mission and values on a global level. I almost forgot it was Jim's company until the presentation ended, and the lights came on, illuminating hundreds of eloquently dressed attendees as Jim crossed the stage and walked to the podium.

"Good evening," Jim said with a smile that enhanced his painfully handsome looks. His voice was commanding—everything about him was intriguing to me at the moment.

The room fell silent from its post-presentation chatter the minute Jim's smooth voice greeted the room.

"I'd like to thank all of you for accepting our invitation to join us over the next two days," he said as his eyes scanned the guests. "First of all, I want you to know that you are sitting in this room for a reason. Each one of you were purposefully selected to attend this event based on your value, who you are, and what you stand for. With that said, please know that we've taken every measure possible to ensure that your time is not wasted. Mitchell and Associates understands your time is valuable." He cracked a smile, but his face remained firm and unwavering. "You see, I'm a man who values his time greatly, and I extend the same courtesy to you. Tonight, I am speaking to the most important people I may ever cross paths with. We have exclusive investors, executives from the medical industry, board members from highly accredited universities, and," he grinned, "I believe you all may be asking yourselves this question after our opening presentation: why am I here? This young CEO better not be wasting my time." He smirked when the audience laughed in comical agreement.

I'd listened to him speak in his James Mitchell, CEO voice before but never had watched him in action like this.

"Tonight's portion of our two-day conference will introduce you to why you were each exclusively selected by my company to attend this event. I also know why you accepted our invitation. You've watched the compilation of videos regarding Dr. Jacob Mitchell and Dr. Collin Brooks, both world-renowned surgeons who have proved they are irreplaceable in their talents and work. Saint John's is more than fortunate to have two men who have not only earned awards in multiple areas of their respective fields, but through their work, they've achieved a level of exceptionalism that has garnered global attention."

Jim looked over to where his brother Jake sat, alerting us to the doctor in the room that would be taking the stage after his opening statement.

"So, why are you here, and why has Mitchell and Associates selected this particular group of individuals to present our newest ideas to? The answer is simple. Saint John's new expansions of our heart and neuroscience institutes will not work without you seeing our vision. You see, I am a man who strives to be the best in all I do." He eyed the room with a somber expression. "But in our work, there is no room for anything short of greatness to ensure the success rates of our patients. Even with having two of the best doctors in the world at Saint John's, we need to think bigger, and it's imperative we think better." He gripped the podium with his strong hands, leaned forward, and with a calculated emphasis, he stated, "In doing so, we need to expand with only the best there is in the medical industry." He glanced toward the audience to his left, then out to the center of the crowd as he continued. "We also need investors who are serious about where they invest their money. Earlier today, our exclusive investors in attendance were invited to see the return on this particular investment. Mark my words, even though those numbers looked healthy enough for you, those are conservative estimates. You will see a higher return on this investment, and whether it be proceeds or pride in a worthy cause, it will not return to you void. I guarantee that to you, and this is why." He glanced over to his right, "Dr. Mitchell and Dr. Brooks are only willing to accept interns who graduate at the top of their classes, undergo a grueling interviewing process with them, and have a passion that's evident in their work ethic. This, ladies and gentlemen, is when you will see something unlike any other hospitals have done before. You will have the best in the medical industry working with overachieving medical professionals who are eager to learn and work with these two doctors closely." He glanced around the room. "We plan on taking this to an even higher level, having universities bring in their finest students and create a new course of instruction while students watch live surgeries performed by these two doctors as they explain their procedures while performing them."

I remained silent, watching Jim and Jake exchange smiles that came from nowhere. I grinned at how handsome both men were while they smiled at something all of us could only guess was humorous.

"And with that, I would like to share with you why we must act on this vision. The reason is quite simple. We have deemed it The Bus Test Initiative."

I grinned with the way Jim said it, wondering what the hell he was talking about. Everyone else seemed to follow me in being thrown off when his speech shifted toward some bus test. What the fuck was he talking about?

"Now that I have your attention." He looked over at Ash with a smart-ass grin. "Allow me to explain the Bus Test. Dr. Mitchell's wife is happily pregnant and has cravings at the strangest times. Dr. Mitchell will stop everything to ensure his beautiful wife is cared for, especially in the food department. You see, Mrs. Mitchell might crave something that will undoubtedly lead Dr. Mitchell to cross the road tonight to purchase from a convenience store. If Dr. Mitchell were to step off that curb and a bus were to flatten my poor brother," I could tell Jim was refraining from laughter after looking back at Jake rolling his eyes, "every skill my brother has—everything locked up in his genius mind—would die with him. We would be left wishing we had an opportunity to learn from such an amazing man." Jim looked back at Jake. "Or if Dr. Brooks were to get hit by the same bus on its return route..." He chuckled while Jake shook his head. Jim became serious while the audience laughed. "Listen, it's a silly point, but it's a fact. If we were to lose the knowledge these men have amassed because of a tragic incident, I would consider myself to be a fool never to have embarked on this quest." Jim's eyes roamed over the audience again. "I only ask that you listen closely and seriously consider the worthiness of this investment. We need these men, we need more men like them, and the truth is we only have a—" He paused and looked over to Jake, "How long until the baby arrives?" he questioned with humor in his voice. He looked back to us with a smile that stole my breath away. "Regardless, we have less than nine months to come to an agreement." The room burst into laughter at his wit and charm, and I just fell a few feet deeper for him.

Jim held out his hand to introduce Jake as he walked to the podium. "Please allow me to introduce to you my brother and chief cardiovascular surgeon." He shook Jake's hand. "And someone that I surely hope doesn't get hit by that bus anytime soon. Dr. Jacob Mitchell."

Jake leaned into the mic. "Leave it to my brother to announce my importance as a doctor by sentencing me to death by bus." He looked over at Ash, who laughed along with me. "If it happens, you have this one to thank for it."

As the night went on, I sat in awe of the company I worked for. The event was primarily directed toward their owning Saint John's hospital and ensuring it would be recognized as one of the best hospitals for cardiac and neuro patients, if not the best. I sat through all of the presentations, fully absorbed by them. Who would've thought sitting through something like this would be so informative and intriguing?

If that wasn't enough, Jim had stolen my heart on yet another level. The charismatic businessman had me—and the entire room— connected to every word that came out of his mouth from the moment he approached the podium. I should've known he was this smooth with words, this direct with his approaches, and this passionate about his company.

I'd never met this side of Jim until tonight. I'd been more caught up with the man who ate big macs with me, who role-played as my husband in England, and who took care of me after fleeing his car for the nearest cemetery. The Jim and Mitch who dropped whatever he was doing to pick up my daughter—that was the man I knew more than this one. It sounded ridiculous, but I found myself fascinated with him as a whole now, and the respect I had for him had grown by leaps and bounds.

"The bar is open." I tapped Ash on her shoulder after Jim thanked everyone for their time and closed out the last of the presentations. "Would you care for something non-alcoholic?" I smiled at the beautiful young woman who was married to Jim's younger brother.

Her swollen abdomen complemented her petite figure. They say that women have that beautiful glow while pregnant, and that was apparent on all of Ash's features. Her brown eyes sparkled, her smile was brilliant, and most of all, the young woman had a fun and caring aura that radiated from her. I felt like I'd met a kindred spirit in the small amount of time we'd talked while Joe was doing my hair. I almost felt like I instantly had a wonderful family or group of life-long friends, and I'd only spent a few hours with them.

Ash chuckled and pushed her chair back. "After two hours of sitting, I need to walk or something. I'm dying here." She cracked a smile that easily made anyone who looked at her smile back. "I'll head to the bar with you. After the remarkable presentations tonight, everyone in this room will most likely bombard Jake and Jim now," she said as we stood together. "I definitely think Mitchell and Associates won the crowd over tonight."

"I completely agree. Jake was fantastic; maybe that's why Jim's afraid he might get flattened by a bus tonight." I laughed.

"That was classic," she said with a grin. "Let's hope I don't need him to cross the street for anything I might crave tonight."

"Aside from Jim's goofy analogy, I have to agree with Jim about how important it is that Jake shares his knowledge." I grinned as we stood behind people waiting to approach the bar. "His presentation actually made me feel more comfortable about coronary disease if that's possible."

"Before he and I were an item, he saved my dad's life," Ash said as we made our way to the bar, people moving away after getting their drinks. "Jake really is the best there is, and I'm not biased. I guess I have to agree with Jim's bus-flattening Jake analogy tonight too." She laughed her sweet laugh and took a sip of the ginger ale she requested.

The bar itself was adorned beautifully to match the splendor of the room, complete with a crystal counter that was backlit with a magenta glow. This entire event was as fancy as it got.

"How long have you and Jake been together?" I asked, interested in the adorable couple's relationship.

She grinned when I sipped the martini I ordered. "Well, honestly, when we first met, I thought I was only having a one-night stand with some sexy guy named Mitch. That was the name he gave me anyway, and it turns out that alias he used that night is poor Jim's nickname." She rolled her eyes and laughed, "I think he does that shit to intentionally piss off his brother sometimes."

"Mitch? My daughter is fascinated with Mitch as her good friend." I laughed and rolled my eyes. "Jim met her and tried to help her gain some trust with him by saying that people call him Jim or Mitch. Mitch stuck with Addy."

"Oh shit." Ash laughed. "Well, hopefully, if Jake meets your daughter, he won't die laughing when he hears her calling him Mitch."

"So, how did Mitch become Jake?" I asked.

"By saving my dad's life." I could see her eyes glow with passion. "He nearly died, and who would've thought that my one-night-stand was the surgeon who would save him from his heart attack that night. It took some time—mainly time for me to get over myself—and Jake and I realized we just couldn't push away the attraction we had for each other."

"I love that. What a special story," I said.

"It's pretty crazy, though. It all happened so hard and so fast. It took me a while to understand I was in love with the man. It's sort of hard to accept that word, you know? For me, anyway."

I looked out into the crowd and saw Jim standing with his brother and a group of men. Earlier I thought I was gawking and obsessing over this new side of him, but could it be that Ash was onto something I wasn't daring to admit to myself?

"It is," I answered. "It can be such an overused word, I think. It's the commitment, the pull toward someone, and you just can't resist it even if you tried."

"Yes," she said, and as we were getting through the small talk, she was cut off by a man to my right.

"Dirty martini?" I heard a low, humorous voice, a little too close to my ear, say.

I pulled my eyes from Ash's narrowed ones and turned to face the robust man with blond hair, sporting a suit that most likely cost a few pretty pennies.

"And I'm about to order another," I said. "Are you here with the medical groups?"

"One might say that." His grin broadened. The man was pretty damn fine looking, a neatly trimmed mustache and beard—yet I instantly didn't like him.

"I'm not asking what one might say, I'm asking what you say," I said. I hated it when men in bar situations tried to play coy. "You're either with the group, or you're crashing this place for free booze," I said, looking at his gin.

He smirked. "Maybe there was a stunning woman I caught a glimpse of, and I decided to crash it for her instead."

"Are you hitting on me?" I must've had the most bewildered look on my face because I couldn't believe something so ridiculous was happening at such a stylish event.

"Going to report me, blue eyes?" he said, his dark brown eyes locking onto mine as he sat on the stool next to the one I took moments ago.

"I might. You probably shouldn't hit on the girl who's with the man who could have you thrown out."

I saw one of the men who'd been assigned as security detail to Ash and me take notice of what was happening. He was dressed sharply in an all-black suit, and he had one of those curly plastic earpieces that people in the secret service wear.

"Is this gentleman giving you a problem?" the man asked as he approached and stood protectively by Ash and me. "He can and will be removed if that's the case."

I glanced around to see that Jim's eyes were locked on where Ash and I sat. I'd like to say this was that jealousy thing in him that he was talking about earlier, but his dark gaze—the scorched-earth look— was telling me he wasn't a fan of the random dude in a suit who was talking to me. I smiled at him, letting him know it was all good at the bar. He nodded, did some lethal eyebrow arch toward the man at my right, and I could tell he was doing his best to remain in conversation with the group that surrounded him.

"I'm fine," I smiled at the secret bodyguard, and then to Ash's playful grin. "I'll handle the trash in here. I'm sure you get paid to handle the real men."

The man nodded and backed off.

I turned back to the idiot that I could instantly tell Jim didn't like, and I was sure it wasn't because the douchebag was flirting with me. "Looks like your ass is hitting on the wrong girl," I said, hoping to move him on.

He smiled and leaned against the bar counter. "Trash, huh?" He covered his heart. "This Tom Ford suit tells a different story."

"Tom Ford, Henry Ford, who really gives a shit? And the suit may tell a different story to you, but," I took a sip of my new martini, "I'm pretty sure what's underneath it is trash."

"You've got a sharp tongue, don't you? That's pretty fucking hot."

"What the hell do you want?" I said, now that the curse words were commencing.

"I just want to see what James Mitchell's little charm is all about. You've got to know that's what you are, right? Just something to show off."

I rolled my eyes. "I'll take that as a compliment." I smiled and looked back to see if Ash was cool with me continuing to interact with this dick. She smirked, arched her eyebrow at me, and I turned back to the douche.

"A compliment? To be some executive's playmate for the weekend?"

"You have no idea." I decided to role-play this bitch out of my presence. "No idea," I playfully grinned at him, "how much I'm enjoying being his playmate."

He tightened his lips and eyed me. "Where did he pick you from?"

"Pick me from? Let's pretend that it doesn't sound like I'm a contestant on a game show for a second, or that I live in a cabbage patch. Does it matter?" I responded, swirling around the olive in my martini glass. "Who the hell are you, and why do you give a damn who's on Jim's arm tonight?"

"Perhaps that's for me to know, and you and that cutie carrying Jake's kid to find out."

"A man of mystery?" Ash asked from behind me.

"Oh, he's definitely got me intrigued," I said, staring at him. "I want to know more about being James Mitchell's playmate and what others think about that."

"You have heard of the circle he plays in," the man said, seemingly pissed but not leaving. "He and his boys are the Billionaires' Club, only fucking girls who don't reach into their pockets for handouts."

I nearly choked on the sip I was taking from my martini glass. "Holy shit." I glanced at Ash, laughing, "Jim's in a club? This is news." I feigned being amazed, while trying not to laugh at this dip shit who was trying to make Jim look like an asshole.

She pursed her lips and became serious. "Yeah. Sorry that I didn't let you in on that one. It's very exclusive." She chuckled. "Sadly, Jake was kicked out of it after he hooked up with my poor ass."

"Is that so?" I questioned her with a smile and turned back to the douchebag. "Well, now I feel like shit for being here with him."

"You should," he said. "He's using you."

"Using me?" I questioned. "I hate to burst your bubble, but I'm not worried about that part. It's just that I don't measure up to these exclusive Billionaires' Club standards I've just learned about. I have a feeling that now—since you've managed to crack this case wide open —he might get his ass kicked right out of it." I looked over to see Jim was still in conversation, face dark and unreadable. "I'm broke as fuck. So, please tell me, have I ruined the man's billionaire reputation by being here with him?"

"James Mitchell would never date outside of money," he answered.

"Someone said that about a certain doctor as well," Jim's brother, Jake, said as he walked up to the man and looked over at Ash. "However, some woman took the heart doctor to school with her free spirit and charms unlike he'd ever seen."

"Indeed?" Ash said as the douche and I watched Ash and Jake interact. "Charms, huh? I heard she was dabbling in the dark arts so she could take the good doctor down with her."

Jake gripped the dick's shoulder, and I smiled when he virtually jumped out of his skin at the gesture. "Far from that," Jake said. "She was the only one, you see," he looked at the man who stared darkly at him, "who could tame the wild side of the doctor. So they say." He sighed. "I believe it's what they say, anyway?"

Ash nodded seriously. "Well, it's universally known that she trapped him by getting pregnant. She was a college dropout, and you know those ones will do anything."

"Tell me about it." Jake's blue eyes seemed to twinkle as he stared past me, his hand shaken off from the jerk, "And the horror when he found out about that on their honeymoon as well." Jake sighed, "She took him for more than just his heart. Fucking amazing heart surgeon falls for her and loses his rightful throne in this Billionaires' Club that he helped co-found."

"Billionaires today just can't catch a break," I chimed in. "You think Jim will get kicked out when they find out he's with some chick who drives a beat-up 1980 VW Rabbit?"

Jake smirked. "Last I recall, she's a single mom also. I even heard he already bought her and her kid a pretty badass car, so that's something."

He looked at the dick who'd managed to stick around this entire time for some unknown reason. If the asshole left now, it was apparent he'd have to hold his head in shame, and from what I could discern, this guy wasn't here for that, and he was most definitely too prideful to walk at this point.

"This is a joke." The man stared darkly at Jake.

"Does it look like I'm joking?" Jake became more serious. "What the hell are you doing here, Mason?"

"It's Mr. Forrest to you, doc," he countered, and all the lame-ass bantering ended. "And I'm here because I'm sick of your brother's company sliding in and taking every business under the sun."

"Perhaps that's because Jim is a goddamn genius, and you're too slow and unable to keep up with his talent." Jake stepped back and eyed the man. "And now here you are hitting on his girl? Big fucking mistake to piss off this particular CEO."

"Yeah?" The man rose from the barstool, trying to meet Jake's height. "What the hell is your big brother going to do to me?"

"You're in a bidding war for that." Jake waved his hand in the air. "What was it? Who the fuck knows." He sighed. "All I know is winning that account over Mitchell and Associates would take the Forrest Group and bring them the business they need so as not to close-up shop. You need that deal. Even I know that, and I'm not running my family's business."

"Jim is nowhere near securing that deal," he countered. "No fucking way."

"Then why is your sorry ass here in this room?" I asked, more interested in this dick bag who was here, spying on his competition. "Then you decide to come at me because I'm here with Jim? Give me a break. Is this how you wealthy assholes work? Spy on the competition when you get intimidated? Jim's speech was pretty badass, so I know that must've stung a little." I smiled at his reddening face. "Now, here we are. You're trying to make him look like a sleaze to the girl he walked in with. God, I wasn't wrong when I referred to you as trash in a suit."

"You're a little mouthy cunt," he said.

"Now, now," Jake said. "That's no way to talk to a lady, is it, Mason Forrest? Fuck, man, did your parents hate you or something? *Mason Forrest*...Shit." He looked over at Ash. "Make sure we pair up first and last names with the little one so he doesn't end up sounding like a goddamn idiot when he grows up like this guy."

"Fuck you, doc," he snapped.

"Mr. Forrest?" Jim's voice cut through the bullshit, and I could tell this was going to end and end quickly now that we had a CEO-tone slicing through the air. "Is there a reason you're in attendance tonight?"

"You need to back off our deals, James," he spat.

Jim's hand took mine while Jake walked over to Ash, and stood behind us. "I asked why you're here?" Jim insisted. "I'm unsure as to why the vice president of Forrest Group is at my convention. You'll explain here and now why you chose to walk in on something that is none of your company's business."

"Mitchell and Associates better back the fuck off our medical groups," he demanded.

"We're not on them, Forrest," Jim said. "They chose to show up tonight, and while you were over here acting like some kind of viper with my lady, I was closing and securing handwritten signatures of all the executives and investors that are insisting on funding and joining Saint John's new medical center. Gotta learn how to do the job, man." Jim's voice lightened some. "The days of playing games with a man's woman to piss off the competition are over. You see, I play chess with my business tactics. You're playing checkers."

"Did you merge with Brooks?"

"You're fucking joking, right?" I heard Jake say from behind me.

"I'm not. I want to know. Did Collin turn that company over to his best friend's brother?"

"If you follow the stock market," Jim said sternly, "which I'm suddenly questioning if you even know how to watch the damn thing, you'd have your answer to that question." Jim's face grew severe. "Unless I call for a personal meeting with you, I don't ever want to see you sniffing out my company and its business again. You and I will never have another conversation unless it's when I'm buying your company out, and I'm quite certain that, if you keep up these childish games, it will be very soon."

The man said nothing, only glared at Jim, and then stormed out of the enormous banquet hall. Jim looked at me, "Did that asshole say anything bothersome to you?" he asked, looking like he was still in CEO battle mode. "Avery?"

I smiled at him. "You must've completely forgotten who the girl is that you're wearing on your arm tonight." I sighed and looked over to Jake and Ash. "Though he did mention that Ash was the reason Jake got kicked out of the Billionaires' Club, and I'm going to hit you straight, Mr. Mitchell," I said looking back at Jim. "Dating a broke single mom? That shit's going to destroy you in that elite circle."

Jim frowned and looked over at Jake's smile. "For fuck's sake," he said in a low voice, "that buffoon brought that up to Avery?"

"Gave her all the criteria and everything." Ash chuckled. "We're all betting you're out next, Jim."

Jim shook his head and rolled his eyes. "I swear to God that when old man Forrest turns over that company to that idiot, that company will fall."

"And you'll be there to catch it?" Jake smirked.

"Nope," Jim said, the lights dimming and the music picking up to fill the dance floor. "I'll let it fall and acquire all of the failing businesses under its umbrella. All because he has no idea the meaning of busting your ass to keep a company going and growing. Lately, I've found myself exhausted with entitled assholes. Forrest showed his value in coming here tonight. What a singularly stupid fucking idiot."

"All right, it's mingle time." Jake eyed Jim.

"The event is now in your hands." Jim smirked. "I need a goddamn drink and not in the company of the guests." He glanced at Ash. "You know you're not forced to deal with all this nonsense."

"Jake and I will handle the room." Ash smiled at us. "Go grab your drink; we'll manage the rest from here."

"Why do you always give into him?" Jake looked at Ash with a funny smile.

"Because you're forever dumping stuff on Jim." She laughed. "I think Jim and Avery could use the break after rushing down here to take Alex's place."

"Thanks, Ash." Jim smiled at her. "How about you, Avery?"

"I just know I'm starved," I said, prompting Jim to laugh, then he saw the daring expression on my face. "I was told I'd have some food before, during, and after this fine event. I'm thinking that while dancing is commencing, we could step out for a few minutes."

"Better get this one back to the hotel room and feed her, Jimbo." Jake laughed and shook his head. "Ash and I are going to mingle while you two are *eating*," he arched a knowing eyebrow at me. "Make that shit quick. Regardless of what my beautiful wife says we're doing, I'm certainly not fielding all of the BS questions for my brother." He winked, and then he and Ash drifted into the crowd.

Jim didn't hesitate to take my hand and lead me out of the large hall. We walked briskly to our room, no words spoken, and the man who'd towered over the douche walked with a purpose that made my insides swirl with excitement. I glanced up at his expression, and I knew this interlude might turn into something I wasn't expecting from him but would never forget.

We barely made it into the hotel room, the door forced closed by his strong hand, and I was now up in his arms, and his lips on mine in a way they had never been before. I was trying to keep up with his urgent and devouring kiss, but my adrenaline spiked. Fuck, I was so taken by him.

His tongue was forceful, and his groans sent shivers down my spine. "You remember me telling you that you're mine?" he said in that commanding James voice.

"Yes." I bit my bottom lip, the territorial look in his eyes was so fucking hot that I could hardly think. "Are you about to claim what's yours?" I tried to tease him as he placed me on my feet, and his hungry lips found my neck.

I ran my hands through his perfectly styled hair as his mouth skimmed lightly over my shoulder, following his soft but firm hands as they steadied me standing in front of him.

"I'm going to do more than that, gorgeous," he said, dark eyes locking intently onto mine while he stepped back, slid off his suit coat, and draped it over a chair.

I watched him with a desire of my own as he removed his tie. "Holy shit, I thought the mirror sex was pretty hot…" My thoughts and voice were cut off when Jim walked back over to me and I was lost in this gorgeous man's fiery look of passion.

His emerald irises searched into my damn soul. "You looked so stunning tonight," he said as goosebumps covered my sides where his fingertips gently caressed my skin as he eased my dress off me. "Having you back in my life like this, being back together again…" He paused, tracing his knuckles down both of my bare sides. "It's like we never were apart."

"I feel the same," I answered reaching up and unbuttoning his shirt. "I want to pick up where we left off in England."

Even after our fallout in England and knowing I'd probably never see Jim again—much less getting back together—I felt a draw to him unlike anything I could explain. I felt so comfortable, secure, and complete with him. Jesus Christ, I did love this man. I'd already fallen in love with him in England and didn't know it until this moment.

My head dropped back as Jim's hands cupped my ass, and his starved mouth covered my nipple, hardening the moment his teeth gently captured it. God how I loved his teeth and mouth on me like this. I could sense the hunger and urgency in him every time he brought his mouth to taste my body. He made me feel so beautiful, which no man in my life had ever done before.

I was fucking spinning and couldn't keep up with this new aggressive, yet gentle side of the man I just recognized I was unreservedly in love with. There was no doubt about that now. I loved the Jim and the James side of him. I was going to be in serious fucking trouble if I lost him after I embraced these emotions wholeheartedly. There was simply no replacing him.

"I want you in more ways than you know," he said as he lifted me into his arms and carried me into the bedroom of our suite.

I worked to slow the wild man down, his eyes still dark with a desire that sent shivers through me and between my legs. "How do you want me?" I asked, after Jim was completely naked and he pressed my body firmly against his.

He was hard and I needed him inside my body that was aching for him. I took the lead in stepping back, pulling back the covers, and crawling onto the bed. My heart was racing with anticipation when I felt Jim's warm body move next to me and his breath caress my cheek.

"You have to know that I'm utterly in love with you by now," he said as I turned to lay on my back. "I want more with us, Avery. I hope to God you feel the same as I do?"

His voice was different. It was sincere and suggestive in a way that made me wonder if there was more to his words. "What are you saying?" I asked, my heart pounding under his gaze as his hand massaged the inside of my leg. "Because I know what I want, and that is to never be without you again."

"I'm telling you that you're the only one my heart has ever loved. I don't want anything to ever come between us again, including that fucking piece of latex. Tell me you're using any method of birth control," he said. "I want to give you something I've never given any woman. Mostly, I have to know if you would even want me like I want you now. When I say you're mine, this is partly how I desire to show that to you."

My heart nearly stopped. "Jim," I said, reaching for his face, "if this is because of that asshole, don't do something you might regret."

"I couldn't care less about that clown," he said. "Being up there tonight, speaking," he kissed my side as his hands roamed over my stomach, "seeing you..." He stopped and looked up at me. "That's when I realized that I was more than in love with you. I can't imagine my life anymore without you in it, Avery. Having you in attendance tonight was the most incredible part of this entire thing. You supporting me. Fuck, your goddamn smile? I could hardly think."

I licked my lips and smiled at his eyes returning to mine. "Didn't seem like that from where I sat. All I saw was a man who knew what he wanted, charmed the room with more than his looks and expensive suits, and I saw your passion for your company in just the way you spoke. All of it. It was intriguing for me to finally experience this side of you."

"My passion for the company is earnest, and nothing has ever replaced or matched that, and, until tonight, I never believed anything would. Then my eyes fell on the one person that has helped me find life again, life outside of all the bullshit that suffocates me at times. I never understood everyone's pity for my being married to it until you pulled me out of the pit I'd fallen into. I wasn't living, I was running a goddamn business and using that to help others have better lives while putting mine on hold." He took my hand and brought it to his lips. "You have reminded me that my happiness was lost, and I now see that. I saw it tonight more than ever."

"Jesus, Jim," I said, my heart sort of breaking for the man. "Was it all that bad?"

"You have no idea." He smirked, his lips caressing my jawline now. "I won't lose the best thing that's ever happened to me, Avery. Even Addison and her sweet, fiery spirit, it's more than I deserve, but I'm not shying away from stating that I want it. I want it all, gorgeous."

I smiled at him. "Shit just got real with us, then?"

"It was real before." He kissed along my abdomen. "It's just more solid now." His eyes drifted up to mine while his lips massaged along my hip. "Unbreakable. When I say you're mine, I mean that sincerely, and I want to take you and me to a level where I've never been before in my life."

"I've never been here," I answered. "I couldn't imagine what it is you're referring to now?"

His body covered mine. "You and me, gorgeous, forever. No matter what may happen with your ex, anything—I want you wholly."

I felt tears welling up in my eyes. I'd never had anyone—damn it, *anyone*—feel this way about me. What the hell did I do to bring this compassionate and loving man to beg me for a solid relationship?

"Avery," he said while he cradled me in his arms, his hands drying my tears. "Talk to me. Did I take this all too far and too fast on you?"

"No," I reassured him with a kiss to his lips and then smiled at him. "Jim, you have to know that I…" I sighed, pulling back the tears that I didn't expect to surface. "How do I say this? My life has been nothing but shit, and I'm not even close to exaggerating."

"It's all in the past," he said. "I'm here now and never letting you go. It's you and me now. If anyone wants to waltz in and try to fucking bring tears to your eyes over anything, I won't tolerate it. I will protect you and Addy from all of your ex's bullshit. Anything you ask, I'm here for you."

I swallowed hard. "Is this even real?" I softly laughed. "What did I do to make a life of horrors turn into this dream come true with a man like you?"

"I feel the same as you do." He smiled. "I had my own hell that I'd built for myself before you, and your sexy little ass pulled me out of it," he said, nuzzling my neck and rolling my body to mold into where he laid next to me on his side. "I love you, Avery…I fucking more than love you."

I bit and tugged at his bottom lip. "All in and forever, eh? You're taking on Addy and me and never letting go?"

"I'd make one phone call, and both of you will be calling my home yours as well," he said. "Or we take it slow with Addison. I'll let you lead the way with what's best for her."

"Why don't we start with the fact that I am on birth control." I eyed him, "I've never had unprotected sex before."

"Nor have I," he said, more serious again. "Though, I must know, does that mean that you adopted Addison?" he teased.

"Broken condom. What are the odds, right? I trust nothing but the pill after that—and because of that scare, me being too drunk to be smart enough to *not* screw Derek for the hell of it, I had my ass tested for everything." I shrunk down some. "I'm telling you, you might not want to commit. Addison is here because I was too drunk to think, had sex with an addict I'd just broken up with, and the condom broke. Still interested?"

"Sometimes beautiful things come from bad," he said. "Finally, a first for both of us."

"A first?" I questioned.

"No condom. I want you, and I don't want the damn thing blocking any further sensations I'm aching to feel while having sex with you anymore."

"I don't want to kill the moment, but can we save the awesome sex experience for after this gala thing? I figured this was a quickie, and we'd be back down there before your brother killed you?"

Jim dismissed everything I said by kissing along my throat and reaching his hand down toward my hot pussy.

"Jim," I said, breathless as he ran his fingers over my clit, igniting my nerves. "Jake and Ash."

"Jacob is set to give the final farewell. Collin flew in early." His lips more concerned with my body as he continued to massage it with his lips. "I'm no longer needed. I was merely here for the opening and to secure signatures from our significant guests. We can either do this or go dance." He looked up at me. "Right now, the bar is open, and the dance floor filled. Your choice."

I looked at him and smiled. "So, Jake was just—"

"Being Jacob." He smiled. "I'm done for the night with anything having to do with my company. It's all you now, as it should be."

"Are we crazy for being all-in so fast? I mean, it is fast, right?" I said, part of me thinking it was something I had to say to get it out in the air. It didn't feel fast in my heart, but I needed to know we were on the same page.

"When things are meant to be, it just works. And this—you and me —it works. We just had to wait for the correct timing and for our paths to cross finally."

I looked at him and smiled. "I love you, James Mitchell."

That was all that he needed, and Jim and I were well on our way to stamping this commitment in stone. He was right with his philosophy about our paths finally crossing and the timing of it all. I knew I would have never appreciated this man as I did now if I had met him before Derek, or even a year ago, when I was so defensive towards people that I was officially the world's biggest bitch.

It was strangely perfect timing for the man I felt a connection with and who my daughter loved instantly. Talk about stars aligning. Things like this didn't happen unless fate was smiling down on you, and that's why I wasn't fighting him or this. I was all in.

CHAPTER TWENTY-EIGHT

Jim

I laid Avery on her back, needing to see her vibrant blue eyes that had shone beyond the beauty of the extravagant room where the gala was held. Her smile helped assure me that she was as confident as I was, creating a closeness I'd never shared with any woman before, and she was so fucking beautiful that I couldn't resist not being inside her a second longer.

"Fuck, Jim." She writhed beneath my hands, her voice making that moan that I loved so much. "Please," she begged as I continued to maneuver my dripping wet cock along her belly while relishing in the taste of her soft and full breast. "I need more."

Her fingers slid through my hair, gripping it, and her legs fell slack. I ran my hands up her arms, bring them to rest in the pillows above her head.

"Can you come for me, gorgeous?" I asked, bringing one of my hands down and sliding two fingers between the seam of her heated entrance. "You're so tight. I want you to come in my hand," I said, massaging her pleasure spot.

Avery bit down on the corner of her lip and called out while I felt her pussy in a spasm around my fingers. "That's it, Jim." She moaned my name, her body moving beautifully flexed in a spasm that made me work to hold back coming then and there. She was so hypnotically sexy when she came. "Jim," she muttered my name while she rode my hand in pleasure.

"I love hearing you call my name like that," I said, breathless myself, feeling how hot and wet she was.

Avery smiled, her eyes still closed. "I need more, Jim, now," she begged in a voice that called directly to my aching cock.

I forced all of my eagerness into a deep and aggressive kiss while I lined my cock up to her warm pussy. *Fuck me to hell,* I thought as I slowly pushed my unsheathed cock into her tight entrance. She was so wet, so hot, and this was so goddamn surreal that it halted my breath while I moved in and out, my cock feeling the warmth of a woman for the first time in my life. I'd been scared to consider this, but it was her—it was the woman who managed to breathe life back into me that made this the best fucking moment of my life.

Avery's hands pulled out of mine, and her fingertips dug into my back as I moved slowly—to save myself from instantly exploding in her—while adjusting to this sensation of her warm juices surrounding my cock.

"Fuck." I kissed along her cheek. "You're so warm, tight, and fuck, Avery, this is so goddamn amazing," I said, finding a rhythm that I could hang on to.

Avery moaned the deeper I went, accepting me fully with her legs open and knees resting on the bed. I could only imagine how sexy she looked right now, her hips pulling off the bed, and her head buried back into her pillows. She was all mine, and I could easily see she was just as taken by this as I was. Her nails dug dipper into my back the farther I slid into her.

"You're so fucking huge," she croaked out. "It feels so good. Damn." She licked her lips. "This feels so fucking good."

My cock was almost buried fully when I reached her deep spot, and her fingers went to my hair as they always did when I thrust my sensitive tip into this spot. "Harder? Tell me what you want and how you want me, gorgeous," I said, knowing I was now in full control of holding myself back.

"Slower. God, I love you. Right there," She moaned.

My forehead went to her chest, feeling her pussy clamping down on me. "Shit, gorgeous, you..." I was silenced when her pussy clenched around my cock tighter than before.

"I'm going to come again..." she trailed off, her hands pressing against my back.

"Come on me, gorgeous," I pled, bringing my head up and needing to watch her. "Open your eyes. I want to see you come." Her eyes reopened and shimmered in their blue and spellbinding color. "Come on, Avery. Let it go. I need to feel all of it."

I reached down and massaged her clit, knowing it would send my lady over the edge.

Avery's breath halted, and that's when I matched her in cursing while feeling her juices around my cock more than before. I felt the pulsating spasm of her hard orgasm, pulling the cum out of me in that second.

She turned her head and I had to see those beautiful eyes while I came in her. "Look at me, gorgeous," I said, pumping harder. "I need to see your eyes," I begged, while I brought my hand up and gripped the low headboard behind her.

Her eyes returned to mine. "God, this feels so good," she said, coming down, "I want all of your cum inside me," she said, her teeth capturing my chin and then pulling at my bottom lip. "Harder," she begged, her mouth sucking and pulling gently along my neck.

My fingers dug into the headboard. The feeling was more than I could take. Avery's body was molded and buried beneath mine as I fucked her pussy harder and deeper than I'd ever done. I was too lost in sensations of euphoria to be gentle with her and couldn't stop now unless she begged me.

"Holy fuck," I growled, holding the headboard with both hands and fully burying all of myself into her. My release moved hard and in a spasm that shot violently through me, forcing another groan of pleasure out of me. "Goddamn, I love this," I said, hearing and feeling that both of us were unraveling together.

"Oh my God." She arched into me. "Ag...again," she half-laughed and moaned while her teeth and mouth went to my neck. That enhanced my expanded feelings of ecstasy of this moment. "Can you feel me coming on your dick?" she asked in her raspy voice of pleasure that I loved.

My cock was sensitive and felt more than I imagined possible. "Yes," I said, staying buried in her, but carefully shifting my body to meet her lips.

Our mouths collided and our tongues fluttered against the other to taste every ounce of each other's kiss. Avery's response was hard, aggressive, and it felt so perfect. All of it. With Avery taking all of me this intimately, and my cock having nothing to shield it from the only woman I ever wanted to have again—I felt more from our connection than I believed I would have. I loved her and there was nothing stopping me or straying my mind from that now.

My movements slowed. "I could fall asleep inside you like this," I teased, kissing her nose and rolling to my back, bringing her with me. "This is the most amazing fucking feeling in the universe."

"No shit." Her teeth captured my chin playfully—a mannerism she always seemed to be fond of doing. "I almost bit the hell out of your neck, though," she said, laying her head on my chest.

I cupped both of her perfect ass cheeks in my hand, not letting my cock lose its favorite place in the world just yet. "A hickey would have gotten me out of tomorrow's conference."

"I'll remember that if we decide to keep at this all night."

"You feel so amazing right now." I ran my hands through her hair that we managed to destroy from its previously perfect style and now was cascading down my side. "All of this." I leaned my head up and kissed the top of her head. "Fucking unreal."

"It was, hands down, the best sex I've ever had."

Her hands grazed up my sides in a way that killed every part of this moment in less than a heartbeat. "Fuck. Shit. Don't." I squirmed.

"What?" Avery said, her eyes devious and playful while my cock, unfortunately, fell out of the one place it could live for eternity. "Are you ticklish, Mr. Mitchell?"

I smiled. I was entirely at the mercy of this playful woman with wild eyes. "I'm just sensitive," I lied.

"The hell you are." She ran her hands up my sides in that damn way again, and it made my body jolt. I tightened my lips and closed my eyes. I was so fucked now. I saw it in her eyes the minute she was tuned in to my ultimate weak spot. "Well, well, well," she said in her playful voice. "Looks like I've got the big bad CEO at my mercy."

I gently maneuvered her hands away from my side and rolled her onto her back, she and I both laughing at how this had destroyed the aftermath of fantastic sex. "I've been at your mercy since seeing these gorgeous blue eyes and your perfect smile when we met on that plane, Avery Gilbert."

She smiled. "I still have no idea how that incident stays with you. I was so livid pissed about that last-minute phone call from my sister, and your sorry ass got to hear all about it—the entire flight."

"I loved every second of it. Your cussing and making the other first-class passengers uncomfortable was priceless. You, raising your voice, so I could fully grasp how shitty it was that you had to put up with whatever it was you were going on about was pretty adorable also." I smiled, recalling how bold and captivating she was—how different it felt to be in a strong woman's presence who didn't give a fuck about what I or anyone else thought.

"Was I that obnoxious?"

"I was certain—and still am—that they put you on the no-fly list." I chuckled. "Looks like you'll be taking the private jet from here on out."

She rolled me off of her. "Shut the hell up." She leaned on her side, and I followed, facing her. "I kept it down, especially when I cussed."

"Really?" I teased. "Because there was a couple—"

"No." She arched an eyebrow at me. "Those people didn't count. That lady was a bitch, and you know it."

I laughed, "Why was she a bitch? Because she thought she should have the cabin to herself and the child seated in front of her quietly playing games was not to share first class with her?"

"Yes, exactly. That little boy wore his headphones, played his games, and then slept most of the way."

"People like that woman are always in first class. They are quite annoying with their unnecessary attitudes."

"Are they wealthy, and they just look down their noses at the rest of us?"

"Not necessarily." I pursed my lips and tucked her hair behind her ear. "It's usually the ones who went in debt for a first-class ticket who act like they own the plane."

"I think it has less to do with money and more to do with manners. Maybe it's just me." Avery sighed. "I'm glad she was uncomfortable with me up there. It's worth taking a boat across the pond since I'm on the no-fly list now."

I laughed. "As fun as that might seem, when you and Addy are able to join me on trips to London, we're probably going to be flying on my plane."

"You have a goddamn plane on top of everything else?"

"As I mentioned to that joker earlier, you have to actually work and work hard to be where you want to be. I didn't take handouts; that man does. I took a company over that my dad busted his ass to build. I worked my ass off in school to graduate at the top of my class, and my dad made me start at the bottom of Mitchell and Associates and work up from there. I earned that chair after he passed, and it made it easier to assume the monumental role I took on after that. No one respects the trust-fund brat who steps into Daddy's shoes straight from prep school. I wasn't about to be one of those guys. My father wouldn't allow any of his sons to be one of those guys, and that was well known in anyone's company we kept. So, with all that said, I earned that airplane too." I smiled at her. "It's what I also find so admirable in you. I see that you have Addison first—not looking for handouts—and you're busting your ass and letting nothing stop you from achieving a living for yourself."

"Wrong about the handouts, though, buddy." She playfully poked my chest. "You just ruined all of that by buying me a car. Since I have a car that I can actually depend on now, I can definitely live a little better, knowing I'll make it from point A to point B."

I grinned. "You don't feel as though you earned something like the car I purchased for you?"

"That's a tough question. Sometimes I feel like the shit in my life happens because I sort of deserve it. I mean, I don't take any bullshit sitting down, but I seem to get my face rubbed into the ground no matter how many times I get back up to fight back. It got exhausting at times when I was always fighting for myself. The ultimate bitch, I think people would say." She laughed. "But it all changed when I had my baby girl. Yes, life still seemed to want a piece of me at every turn, but I have more determination than ever. I have Addy to fight for now too, and I guess that makes it easier to get back up." Her face became solemn. "Now, I feel like I've gotten a break—a break from the shitty hand life dealt me." Her eyes looked soulfully into mine.

"And what was that?"

"Simple. You." She shrugged. "I've never met anyone in my life who gave even half a damn about me as you do. Who knows, maybe the plane crashed on my way to London, your dreamy face was the last thing I saw, and this is all my slice of heaven. Here I thought I lived a life that would surely send my ass straight to hell." She laughed.

"Straight to hell, eh?" I ran my hand along the beautiful curve of her body, from her shoulders, down her sides, and over her hips. "What happened when you were growing up? You said you were afraid of Addison going into the system should you fight for full custody of her."

Her eyes diverted from mine, and she frowned. "I don't think anyone would believe it. I was shocked that Derek's parents believed it, but they knew my foster mom after my sister hung out with one of their friends for a while. When I came back home, they already knew my story, so I didn't have to share it."

I continued to run my hand along her side. "Avery, I'm not any of them. I'm the man who cares for you more than you know. Tell me what happened."

"Well, I'm no saint," she said.

"All children are products of their parents' behaviors," I said, trying to lighten her up some. Her expression had me concerned. "However, you mentioned that you ran away from home, so was there no parental figure in your life?"

"My mom died when I was five," she said softly. "I guess she had that shit coming. She brought all kinds of men into the house." Avery's eyes filled with tears.

"They didn't fucking touch you, did they?" I instantly grew furious out of protective instinct.

"No." She shook her head. "My mom took them into another room. At the time, I didn't like the noises she made. It scared me. As you can imagine, she was using her body to pay the bills."

I watched Avery shiver, and I almost did the same as I imagined my beautiful woman as a sweet, five-year-old girl, having to deal with that horror. "Oh my God," I said softly. "They pulled you out of that shit hole then?"

"No." She laughed in disgust. "I found my mom unconscious on the floor. The child in me couldn't understand why her mom wasn't talking or waking up. I dialed 911—probably the only thing my mom had ever taught me to do, if anything were to happen—and that's when things changed." She exhaled. "I found out later that my mom had overdosed."

"That's when they put you in the care of a foster family?" *Holy fucking shit, and here I thought Jacob and I had it bad growing up.* "I never found my mother dead on the ground. I just was aware that she was bringing men home to fuck and feed her addiction behind my dad's back—that's nothing like finding your mom gone at five years old."

"My foster family at the time was worse than living at home with my mom, bringing guys in for money. Those mother fuckers starved all of us children. They locked the cabinets and fridge, and at the time, no one came to check out the living arrangements. I just remember always being so goddamn hungry all the time."

I tightened my lips. "And with the way my girl loves to eat, I can definitely see you fleeing the house."

Avery didn't laugh. I'd thrown her back in time, and I could tell she was reliving this nightmare. "The psychiatrist said that is probably the reason why I feel like I'm hungry all the time. Dr. Maxwell said that after I brought it up as a joke, but it makes sense, I guess. Anyway, after running away at ten years old and getting caught, the law dealt with those people and shut them down. That's when I moved in with my grandma. Unfortunately, she couldn't get past the death of her daughter after five years, and so she took her own life. Maybe it was seeing me that made her do it? I have no idea. Sometimes, when I think about it, it feels like it was my fault. I have no idea, except to state what I always say when shit goes south—my fucking life and luck it would have happened after I moved in."

"Avery, are you fucking kidding me?" I asked, totally floored by this revelation. "Your grandmother took you in, then fucking killed herself?"

"It was all bad," she said. "I didn't grow up on the right side of the tracks, so the saying goes. I survived it all, though. I'm here. I have Addy, and I'm happy." She ran her hand along my cheek. "Even before you, I found a way to be happy. I'm sure I have issues—in fact, I *know* I have fucking issues from all of that shit. It's why I ran away from Jill's and lived in Santa Cruz. At thirteen years old, I was a hellion. Anyone who was trying to lay down rules for my own good, I would flip them off, and so finally, I took off on Jill. It's why Britney is the way she is with me too. I fucked Jill over, and Brit knew it. I lived outside of life's reach for hurting me. That's how it felt anyway, but the truth is that all it did was destroy me. I tried to clean my shit up, and then there was Derek. And you're pretty much up to speed on that now."

"I think you're one of the most profound and strongest women I've ever met. I've never known anyone to deal with so much tragedy and come out the other side. To go through that nightmare—" I stopped and smiled. "Yes, I'm reading between the lines here as you don't need to divulge details to me for me to grab onto the point. However, if you ever want to talk about this—any of this—I'm here. Always."

"I know. I guess I should have spoken up about my past a while ago."

"I understand childhood trauma isn't something people bring up on a first date. You have no reason to feel obligated to have done so sooner. I can only imagine the strength it takes to talk about it at all, so please know that I'm glad you told me now," I said, bringing my lips to hers. "I will do everything in my power to make sure you and Addy are happy and well taken care of. I swear to God, if there's anything I can do, I'll do it. If the house is too fucking big and you want to move into a nice neighborhood with children playing around? I'll buy us a place that will suit us three together."

"You weren't messing around when we went down this road tonight, were you?"

"No," I said. "It might not be a marriage proposal, but it's everything like that and more. When the time is right—for you and Addy—to trust me, you'll be my missus."

"Might want to hold off on the suburbs, champ. At the rate you're going, we'll be married tomorrow night."

"Here at the gala?"

She smirked. "It's probably the nicest décor in a room I've ever seen. Who needs wedding planners when you have it all set and ready?"

"Guests all including doctors, board members, investors, and executives?"

"Why not?" She laughed. "Someone's gotta show up for the wedding of the century."

"You, Avery," I brought her into my arms, "are seriously too much. And don't think I didn't pay attention to the neighborhood you currently live in. If anything, I'll buy you the house in the suburbs right now, and I'll move in when you're ready to bring me into your life like that."

"What if Addy and I don't want you to move in?"

I laughed. "Well, that will suck really fucking bad because I would very much like to come home to both of you one day."

"Call me a spoiled little bitch," she poked my ribcage, "but I'd rather live in your resort in the Hills. In the city but still high above it. Rooftop sex?"

"Rooftop sex?" I arched an eyebrow at her, and suddenly my dick wanted to enter the conversation. "You can move in tomorrow night after we land. Your car is being delivered there anyway."

"Let's go slow for Addison."

"Let me find you a better neighborhood, then, or I'm sleeping on your fucking couch."

"No," Avery said in this commanding, yet charming voice. "Derek has no idea we live there. He's our only threat, and that's when he's high. Other than that, Addy and I are safe. I love that you care, but I don't need to be taken care of like that. In this department, I need us to move a bit slower."

"I know you are perfectly capable of taking care of yourself and Addy. Okay, fine," I sighed and conceded. "For now, though."

"For now," she simply stated. "I know we're trying to play a heavy commitment game, but trust me on this, okay?"

"Avery, I won't hurt you. I promise you that."

"I know," she said, but I saw the sadness in her eyes, sadness as if I'd already hurt her but had no idea what I'd done.

"Hey," she pushed up and sat on her knees, "I'm jumping in the shower. Wanna join me?"

"You don't even have to ask." I sat up, pulled her into my chest, and kissed her lips. "I already want you again. It's just about how I'm going to take your sweet little ass this time around."

She laughed, kissing my nose. "You love to run the show in this department, so you have to share the little sexual interludes, Mr. Mitchell."

"You realize I hate hearing that come out of your mouth, right?"

She laughed with that sweet, scratchy, sexy laugh. "Well, you are Mr. Mitchell, the fucking CEO of the company I work for."

"We have to find you another job," I said, rolling my eyes. "To everyone I have to be an asshole, I'm Mr. Mitchell. To you, I'm Jim. I love hearing you say my name like you do. No nicknames, no professional work titles—I'm Jim to you. The Jim that enjoyed every minute of having you with me in England and having you back in my arms again."

"Oh shit." She covered her smile. "Ash told me about Jake using Mitch as his alias when he screwed her before they knew each other. Their one-night stand?"

"That shithead used the name the guys call me sometimes. He used it every time he messed around and screwed women over. And guess who was getting eyes on them out at the bar when the name Mitch was called? My sorry ass."

"You're kidding."

"Nope." I bit the inside of my cheek. "I almost got decked by some prick whose girl cheated on him with my brother."

"Are there any chicks still hunting for this player named Mitch?"

"I haven't been looked at oddly, nor have we gone to any of those bars recently."

"I think it's funny as hell if I'm honest." Avery got up, and now my eyes were on her perfect ass, "Are you coming, Mitch?" She stopped and laughed, looking back at me as I followed her, unamused.

"You just realized you killed the moment for me, right?"

She laughed while I went to turn on the shower. "I killed the moment for myself."

"No shit." I laughed at her. "What do you say we ease Addy out of the Mitch name?"

"She loves her friend Mitch."

"Perhaps one day, I'll be more than a friend then." I smiled.

Avery grabbed my cock, and I jumped in shock as she started pumping my dick in her hand. "It might be a long night for you and me, Jim."

"That wouldn't bother me at all."

We stepped into the shower and my inward hope of seeing Avery's lips wrapped around my cock happened. One thing was for sure: this woman and I would not be leaving each other's sides any time soon.

I knew that, as much as I wanted her one-hundred-percent, I needed to take things slowly and carefully, and I needed Avery to take the lead with Addy. I was deeply devoted to Avery, yes, and even though I felt that sure of this, the reality was that we needed much more time. We hadn't been together long, but I knew—without a shadow of a doubt—there was no one else in the world that I'd rather be with. I knew it from the first time I saw her and became more than intrigued with her. Call it love at first sight, call it hopeless romanticism, call it crazy, but I knew this was worth everything. More than all of this though, the heart and innocence of a child was involved, and Addison's well-being had to be considered over my desire to beg for both of them to be in my life forever. Avery was a single mom who knew how to manage this better than I. This would be the first time I released the control over anything I wanted to pursue. If I truly loved Avery, I would respect her wishes in how we approached our relationship with Addison involved as well.

CHAPTER TWENTY-NINE

Avery

*O*ur second day in Palm Springs went as smoothly as the first. Collin did an incredible job with his presentation. Jim expounded upon what Collin had to say by speaking again, standing there in a dark suit with a new glow on his face. The crease in his forehead and his brilliant smile captivated the group, and it wasn't long before the people were responding with lively excitement. All-in-all, Jim and Collin had enchanted the room, making everyone seem to enjoy this day and the reason they were here even more.

I was on Jim's arm most of the time, and it was euphoric in its own way. No nasty looks from people I understood were in the upper class of elites. There were only casual conversations and a lot of fun.

I would have thought that Collin—the gorgeous neurosurgeon—would've been far too young for his position, and the same went for Jake. By the looks of them, you'd think they were young and naïve doctors, but the men were brilliant. Captivatingly intelligent. Thank

God for that too, apparently, because if they weren't, this conference would have been a waste of time.

The night we flew home was as mesmerizing as the helicopter flight in. This time, however, Jim surprised me with burgers, fries, and a shake. He said he believed I would appreciate that more than roses or jewelry in gratitude for joining him to Palm Springs, and he wasn't wrong. He knew the way to my heart was through my stomach, and that was enough for me.

By the time we got to his place, and after our commitment of love declarations to each other the first night in Palm Springs, I thought Jim and I reached a mutual understanding that he didn't have to thank me for anything. I loved being with him, and now I was having to pull it together while getting ready on Monday morning for work, knowing we'd both be going our separate ways.

This was going to be my last morning here at his home. I had to think about Addison in all of this. I had to make sure Jim and I were solid like he said we were. We needed much more time together before I made any dramatic changes with Addison.

A lot of this stemmed from my own trust issues, not of Jim, but myself. Derek seemed to be great in the beginning too. I was blinded by a lot of things when I thought I was in love with him. The way I felt about Jim was more than anything I'd ever felt for Derek, though. That was a fact. Maybe that had me a little frightened too. I don't know. I just had a gut feeling we needed to try our hardest to take our relationship slow.

I was single—but a single mom. If I was hurt, Addison did feel it. No matter how hard I tried to hide it from her. She was already dealing with a fuck-up for a dad, and the last thing she needed was her mom prancing around, acting spontaneous and free-spirited. Stability and security didn't come free in my experience, and that was for fucking sure. I hated feeling this way because all I wanted was to be with Jim, but I had to be cautious. I knew how the world worked, and it didn't change overnight just because I did.

"Yeah," Jim said as soon as I finished sliding my lipstick over my lips, "your new position is in my office." He smirked. I had no idea how long he'd been leaning in the door frame, looking handsome in his three-piece suit.

"Firing your personal assistant?" I teased.

Jim stood up straight from leaning against the doorway. "You wouldn't be half wrong about that, but Summer had nothing to with dropping nearly the entire event in my lap last minute. It'll be my events planning team who will hate the hell out of me today when I'm done with them. Them and the two PAs who have been assigned to this for months."

"Jesus Christ. I'm not going anywhere near your office today." I laughed, packing up my makeup. "I didn't think anything was wrong." I shrugged as I cleaned off his bathroom countertop from any makeup residue I may have left behind. "It was all badass."

"The reason I couldn't even introduce you to Joe and Clay, and the reasons for another company *not* showing up at all yesterday, was all their responsibility. Apparently, they were having cocktails by the pool while my goddamn phone was being blown up."

I walked up to the tall man whose face was hardened now, pissed for reasons he hid well from me. "Shall we fuck before you head to work?" I thought I'd tease him and knock the look off his face with my proposal.

It worked. I was taken by one of Jim's arms, that lighthearted expression was back, and his lips were on mine. He pulled away and brought my free hand to his hard cock. "That gets to stay with me while I wait it out all week until we're together again." His eyes were pleading, "There's no way—"

"Jim." I smiled, scooting past him and trying to get to my bags I'd packed up. "We discussed going to the beach with everyone this weekend. Addison hasn't even seen the new car that her friend Mitch bought her. Let's start with that. Sleepovers, however." I started laughing as he grabbed me from behind, and I spun around in his arms. I put my palm up against his hard chest and arched an eyebrow at his beautiful expression. "They have to wait."

"Then I have to have you now. Perhaps during your lunch?"

"You are one very naughty CEO," I said, walking into the room and zipping my makeup bag into my duffle. "You have to wait."

"After you get off work, then?"

I smirked at him. "With those cameras in your office? Yeah, I'll pass."

"Shit." He chuckled. "I can't win, can I?"

"I take lunch out in the courtyard garden area at noon with Alyssa and Amir. If you'd like to join us, you can."

"I have a meeting then," he said. "It's one that I can't move."

"And I'm on the clock. I have a set schedule," I said, putting my hands on his waist. "This is going to suck, isn't it?"

Jim took me in his arms. "More than anything. It won't be as bad as losing you in England, but after the weekend we've shared, yes. You have no idea how much I'm dreading coming home to an empty house. I want to see you and watch Addy play in that pool or something."

"I know." I stood on my toes and kissed his lips. "Addy deserves you and me having more time together as we did in Palm Springs. I might need to start farting or something. We have to get more familiar for her sake."

Jim's face tightened in humor. "If you love to fart so much," he kissed my forehead, "then you and Collin will be the best of friends."

I laughed. "He does have a fun and witty side for a neurosurgeon, doesn't he? Not that I know many neurosurgeons, but he's a one-eighty of what I'd expect from one."

"You have no idea with that man. Put him and my brother in the same room with a few beers, and the comedy show rages on all night."

"A night like that sounds like fun."

"We'll do that on Saturday night, after the day on the beach. You and Addy are still going on vacation and staying at my beach house, correct?"

"Yes," I conceded. "The first sleepover."

"Okay." He sighed, then his phone beeped, he checked it, and smiled at me. "Someone's new ride is here. Let's go handle the pink slips, or we're both going to be late for work."

When I walked out to Jim's driveway, I was looking for a regular car, not this badass, four-door, black Aston Martin. I quietly followed everything the man and Jim were saying. The damn thing was at the top of its game after Aston Martin decided to make a four-door vehicle that would sweep the market in luxury sports cars. I glanced back a few times to see how it matched Jim's car, what he said Addy'd referred to as the roller coaster car.

I signed the dotted line, my hand shaking at the fact that Jim was gifting me this car. I was utterly speechless. I'd never had a pink slip to my name—ever. Now, here I was, standing in front of a car that I didn't quite match. Shit, this thing was going to get ripped off at my apartment complex. Maybe Jim and I would have to move in together. We pretty much adopted a child with this thing, and I instantly didn't want a scratch on it or anyone fucking with it. Mostly because it was a beautiful gift from Jim.

While Jim finished up with the man, I peered into the car. I smiled, seeing a custom car seat for Addy in the back. Jesus Christ, this was too much.

"Thank you, Mr. Mitchell," I heard the man say.

"Have a good day," Jim said, and the man was gone in a dealership car that'd followed him to Jim's place.

"Think Addy will be impressed?" he asked, while I looked at him in awe. "And perhaps you could try it out while giving me a ride to work?"

"How is it that you think of everything?" I asked with a smile. "How in the living hell did you manage to get a car that matched yours?"

"Alex is my car guy, the go-to man, so to speak," he said with a broad grin. "He mentioned it after I asked if there was anything out there like my Aston Martin. It turns out there was."

"Well, partner," I was holding back tears of gratitude and overwhelming joy, although my cracking voice was giving that away, "this is quite a step up from the car I had. Tell Alex I said thank you, and you?" I shook my head and swallowed back more tears. "God, thank you." I hugged him and was molded into his body, smelling his delicious cologne. "Thank you, Jim, so very much for this. For taking care of us."

He pulled away, and his lips brushed gently over mine. "Always. I'm just hoping that you don't kill this one," he teased, easing me out of the explosive ugly cry of gratitude.

"I'm not a crappy driver. You saw me driving in England. Big difference."

"Well, my darling," he said, walking to the passenger side with his briefcase and putting my duffle bag in the backseat as the garage closed, "let's see if you're a lead foot out here the same as you were in England."

He kissed my cheek as I sat in the most luxurious leather seat—more like a cockpit. The steering wheel even felt glorious.

I took a deep breath and looked at him. "I don't think I can handle this kind of extravagance." I started laughing. "What if Addy spills something in it?"

"Or gets French fry grease on the seats?" He smirked, adjusting the seat back to fit his long legs. "Then it will be the perfect family car, I would say. Right now, it's new and needs something spilled in it."

"My ass." I eased the car back and then turned the beautiful baby to purr down the road. "This car begs you to floor it. Listen to this motor," I said, hearing the throaty growl of the sports car.

"If you fucking kill yourself in this because of that lead foot of yours."

"Chill out," I said, easing through his driveway and wishing we were near an open highway. "At least this will be comfortable in traffic," I said, wiggling my body in the comfortable seat.

"We're taking back roads, gorgeous," he said, pulling up the business address on the GPS. "I'm never on the freeway unless I have to be."

"Through the hills, then?" I smirked at him.

"Just keep us on the road, please."

"Hey, if we bite it because I let the car get away from me, the workers you're going to rip into today will be that much happier," I teased.

"Fuck," Jim gasped when I stepped on it, finally letting the car loose. "Avery, swear to God if you—"

"Quiet, darling," I said, using our fake marriage pet names from England. "I'm trying to focus. I don't need your bickering nonsense as a distraction."

Jim laughed. "We need to do something—like a new driving test or what the fuck ever. You like speed way too much for comfort."

"I love fast things." I glanced over at his serious yet humored expression. "And huge cocks."

Jim closed his eyes and smiled. "Drive the damn car, darling," he said, pulling out his phone after it started ringing. "Just get us there alive."

CHAPTER THIRTY

Jim

I sat in my office, perusing a spreadsheet and crunching numbers on a company based in London that I wasn't convinced Mitchell and Associates should acquire. The decision could easily be made without flying out to the London headquarters, but this one wasn't looking robust enough for me.

The market was saturated with these particular pet products, but perhaps Party Pets could raise more awareness toward organic food being brought in for animals. We'd certainly have to change the name and relaunch the company, which would be easily done; however, the owners' proposal gave me the feeling that company names would be more of a struggle than reaching an agreement on company shares and money issues.

I leaned back in my chair when Summer announced herself, and with my best friend right behind her. I smirked and shook my head when Alex's flirty eyes held hers for a second too long.

"Mr. Mitchell, I've called for the heads of HR to conference room

D for the meeting with public relations and the team leaders you requested from the Palm Springs event. It's in fifteen minutes."

"Thank you, Summer," I said. "I think we're all set."

"The head of marketing has also set up the video you requested for the meeting as well."

"Excellent."

Summer left, and Alex sat across my desk. I swiveled my chair back and forth, studying my friend and giving him a look that told him that he was playing with fire regarding Summer.

"What the hell is that look?" he asked with a smile. "My mother is fine, by the way."

"I know," I answered with a smile. "You assured me of that on Saturday. You should've stayed longer, though. That's your mom, for God's sake."

"A mom I hardly knew," he answered. "Or do you forget the part where she walked out on us when I was three?"

"Yeah, yeah, I know." I smiled and leaned forward on my desk, crossing my arms, "How is it most men seem to have daddy issues, but somehow we have issues with our moms screwing us over?" I shook my head. "I'm glad she's well. You're a good man to forgive her for her trespasses. I, however, am never going to fare well in that department. Seeing that addict piece of shit that Avery was with, all it does is fuel my hatred for those selfish mother fuckers."

"So the rumors are true?" Alex chuckled. "James Mitchell's got a sweet spot for the hot woman with blue eyes in marketing."

"I figured all of it would start circulating through the circles and eventually into the company after I brought her to the medical gala this weekend. She was fucking awesome there too." I smiled, recalling how I loved having Avery there with me this weekend. "Even Forrest, who waltzed in like the bottom feeder he is, tried his hand with her, and she took him down before Jake showed up to handle him. I was in the middle of securing three goddamn companies for us, and all I had was—"

"Jesus, man," Alex cut me off. "You're a smitten fool, Mitch." He started laughing then looked at the clock. "Hey, we only have five minutes for you to spit it out."

I pursed my lips and shook my head. "The rumors are true. That's all I can say." I grinned. "But those rumors are likely not as dangerous as the ones that will start on the top two floors of this building if you and Summer don't keep your personal affairs outside of work. Avery's different, and you know that. Summer came from Brakken and Brothers, our only real fucking competition, and her sister still works there. You can't take chances with my office assistant, and yet here you are, lighting the rumor mill on fire yourself. You're both being too obvious."

"Too obvious?" He pulled out a note and waved it in the air. "How about this shit for too obvious, brother?" he said, waving what I saw was the note that I had sent with Avery's lunch delivery today. "Hey, Gorgeous," he cleared his throat, mimicking some deep voice that sounded nothing like mine—I hoped, "lunch is on me. I figured this would agree more than the flowers you deserve." He arched an eyebrow and my unamused expression, *"Forever yours, J."*

"How did that make it into your hands?" I asked, wondering if I'd caused Avery any trouble with my note. She did text me thank you for the fish tacos I'd had delivered.

"Well, in Avery's words or mine?" he asked.

"How did a personal fucking note for Avery end up in my VP's hands?" I asked, slightly annoyed.

"You aren't going to believe me, but I'll tell you anyway," Alex started. "It looked like a third-grade lunch cafeteria when Summer and I walked through the garden courtyard after lunch. Avery was trying to grab this from some dude's hand like he was playing keep-away from her after he found Willy Wonka's golden ticket. I stepped in and took the note from the idiot before Avery threw him to the ground for acting like a dip shit. She was fine after that. She knew I'd handle it."

"Who was this person?" I asked. "Did Avery do anything that would cause HR to throw this in her face?"

"No, she didn't do anything wrong," Alex said. "In fact, HR stepped in after I heard him call her a cunt, and his ass was leaving early today. He's been fired because of this and subsequent complaints. It turns out, Tyler Matthews, some asshole supervisor in my acquisitions department, has had a few women come forward with grievances since this happened. Avery and your cute little love notes blew his bullshit wide open."

"What the fuck?" I said, more concerned. "This shit is going to hit the news. What the hell has he done, and for how long? Son of damn bitch, man."

"I'm handling it," Alex said. "Calm the fuck down, or you will fire everyone in that meeting. They're already nervous that you're going to drop the hammer."

"What complaints have the other women come forward with? Why didn't I know about this when it happened?"

"Because HR and I, the *Vice President* of Mitchell and Associates, did our jobs, and did them efficiently. It's being handled appropriately."

I settled down some. "Fuck, man," I answered. "You know I hate shit like this in our business."

"Well, it's in every business with tens of thousands of employees from the US to London. It's why we have a special HR team. If I couldn't handle it, I would have called you. Just be glad you and your sappy shit helped to free up women from this bag of dicks harassing them."

"Sexually?" I cringed.

"Verbally," he answered. "And he's fired. If anything, we'll put out a public statement and start backing a movement for employees to have a platform to speak out against their hotheaded managers."

"I'd like to see that happen. Managers take advantage of their positions too easily. I've seen management-level pricks lording themselves over employees too often. It's fucked up."

"Since that's all out of the way," he slid the note over to me, "you can give this back to Avery." He stood up. "And now that you're in full-blown dick-mode, we can go deal with the groups that dropped the ball this weekend."

I left the bullshit of this guy, Tyler Matthews, in Alex's hands. I didn't have time for it, and quite honestly, Alex ran this company arm-in-arm with me. I had nothing to flare up over, but it was disturbing to know that there were those in my company who had verbally abused others.

EVERYONE BUT ALEX and I sat at the boardroom table, the lights dimmed, watching a ridiculous 1980s instructional video. The cold air blew on my neck where I stood at the back of the room, arms crossed and watching each employee who'd pissed me off this weekend. They sat like mannequins, watching this stupid thing. It was seriously some kind of show that came out of a business education class in middle school.

"Why the fuck are we watching this goddamn nightmare?" Alex leaned over and whispered into my ear.

"You'll see," I said after the video ended, and the lights slowly brightened.

I walked to the front of the room and stood at the head of the table in front of the fourteen people who'd had a part in fucking up Palm Springs.

"I believe I can read all of your minds at the moment," I said, eying the group of young and old men and women trying to maintain their composure. "Why in the world," I said dramatically, "would Mr. Mitchell waste our precious time with such a mundane and highly obtuse video. Am I correct?"

The group stared at me.

I smiled. "It's a simple question. If you enjoyed the video, by all means, take it home as a gift from me to you. If you found it to be a waste of your time," I held onto that word, "then you'll easily understand how I felt when I was doing *all* of your jobs this weekend." I grew more solemn, ensuring I eyed each individual. "We all are tasked with a job in this company. Each one of you at this table is accountable for that job. However, apparently I failed to get the entire team's memo that we clocked out on one of the largest conferences of the year."

"Mr. Mitchell," Gary, one of my PR heads, spoke up, "we had no idea about half of what happened, or that Jen was sending all the calls to you."

I narrowed my eyes at the man. "I *so* wish I loved hearing excuses. It would make my life so much easier. Unfortunately for you all, I despise them. I like solutions, Mr. Maldonado. So instead of trying to excuse the fact that none of you knew that multiple groups were bailing out on us last minute, leaving me all but vacuuming the banquet hall for the event, I want solutions for why it won't happen again. Why my time won't be wasted again," I pointed at the screen behind me, "as I just wasted thirty minutes of your precious time. Solutions," I said, eying him and then the rest of the room. "Do I need to bring in the solutions department to educate you all? You, one of my most-trusted groups of associates, who Alex and I depend on greatly for hosting these events?"

"No, sir," some said.

My God, I sounded just like my father. I hated having to rip into my teams, but I couldn't let any of this slide. No fucking way. I might've sounded like my father, but they had behaved like children. Give them an inch, and they'll take a mile? Truer words have never been spoken.

"Now, we have an expo coming up in six months," I said. "I have to be able to depend on all of you up until the last piece of trash is picked up off the floor. The expo will yield one of our highest investment opportunities yet. The media will be there, and many journalists as well. This event cannot fall on my or Alex's shoulders when things start falling apart. All of you are getting paid nicely to do your jobs. Please remember that when putting this event, and any other event, together and seeing it through until the end. I will never field calls like that again. Does it all make sense on how it was pretty unfair for you all to throw this last-minute stuff in my lap while I'm trying to do my job?"

"Absolutely, sir."

"That being said, what you *did* organize was phenomenal. Everything ran flawlessly. I expected no less, and you didn't disappoint. You're all creative geniuses, and I appreciate every one of you. I would hate for any negativity to cloud my appreciation for your great talent. That is all, and you may return to work."

I met Alex in the corner, a tactic we used in pointedly avoiding any kiss-asses after we had to bring it in to remind employees of their jobs and how they have to stay on top of shit. "I need to speak with Avery," I said to him.

"Then call her to your office. Why are you telling me?"

"Just go escort her up here, please. I thought of something with that pet company in London. I'm going through the proposals. I need to start it now, though, because I have a feeling they'll hate that I don't like their company name."

Alex laughed and waved his hand over as if he were making a rainbow. "Party Pets!" he exclaimed. "Taking your pet to a party in healthy ways."

I rolled my eyes at him, the room now empty. "That's why that damn name needs to go. The catchphrases would be ridiculous and distract from what this company could do for animal health and well-being."

"I'll go get your girl," he said. "Handle your shit. It's Kinder's tonight, right?"

"Every Monday." I smiled. "For now, anyway. If Avery and I finally move in the direction I want, then I'll be passing on eating out. Unless, of course, you'd all like to change the venue to McDonald's with her and Addison."

"I can see Jake and Collin now, fighting for the happy meals."

"Get the hell out of here." I smiled and was prepping myself to apologize to Avery for any inconvenience that the lunch letter might have caused her.

CHAPTER THIRTY-ONE

Avery

The week went faster than I'd imagined it would, and Friday was finally here. Addy and I were packed up for our vacation on the coast. We'd be staying at Jim's beach house tonight and coming back on Sunday night. It was the perfect getaway.

Little by little, we'd break her in like this; at least that was my plan. Jim was buried with a deal he was working on for his London office, and the only communication we'd had all week was through texts. When we tried to talk on the phone, he was always getting interrupted by calls that he couldn't miss.

Around lunchtime every day, he would text me and tell me he wished he could join me and the others, which was a better alternative than sending a note after the last debacle. In the evenings after Addy was asleep, a text would buzz through from him telling me that he missed me and that London had just woken up—which, to me, meant that he was going to work with the London office while I fell sound asleep.

It was pretty cute, and I could tell he was trying to keep what we had in Palm Springs going, but I wasn't a complete idiot either. The man ran a fucking empire—I saw that with my own eyes at the gala. I missed him, but I worked and had a life too. Thankfully, I had Addy to fill the time when my mind would wander toward wanting desperately to see him again.

Luckily for me, I didn't feel lonely. I had a routine and didn't necessarily stop until Friday anyway. Weekends with Addy were spent like this weekend would be, doing fun things like going to the beach, the zoo, movies, or the park. Weekends without her consisted of going out with the girls when I could, but seeing my friends was few and far between on its own lately.

I'd not seen my sister in longer than usual, and I had a feeling that when we reconnected, she was going to shit a brick when she found out how things were going with Jim. I could guarantee that she'd throw up a million red flags in my face too. She would warn me off of dating the man for every reason under the sun. I guess I'd given her the right to do so since everything she'd ever witnessed from me was reckless and impulsive. This time, however, for the first time in my life, I was with a man who made me feel far from reckless.

I was the one who was forcing myself not to do what I really wanted, which was to spend every night at his house and move into that badass place, but I refused that for the sake of Addy. One might say I actually was learning from past mistakes and finally growing out of doing things impulsively.

It was ten in the morning, and I was intently going through the mundane tasks of my morning routine by answering calls and setting appointments for approval of the managers on my floor. The managers I'd only seen the day Jim had shown up.

"Momma." I jerked when I heard Addison's playful voice. "Mom!"

I swiveled on my chair, pulled off my headpiece, and my heart nearly stopped when Addy's bright blue eyes met mine with a brilliant smile. Her hand was locked into Jim's, who stood smiling at me. His green eyes were dazzling, and my heart forgot how much I loved and missed the man wearing the same mischievous grin as my daughter.

"Good morning, Mr. Mitchell," Amir said, my eyes meeting his wide ones. I smiled, seemingly starstruck by the man myself.

"And to you as well, sir," Jim said.

"That's Amir, Mitch," Addy said, running the floor like she owned the place, not Jim.

"Hey, Addy," Amir said. He'd gotten to know her pretty well during the lunch breaks when I would steal her from the daycare to join us. "Will you be having lunch with us today? I brought too much hummus again, and I think I'm going to need your help to finish it."

"I might be," she answered him.

Jim and I probably looked like two complete idiots by now. Both lost in each other's eyes. Addy and Amir were the only ones on the floor who said a word. I think time just slowed for me, though, because Jim couldn't stand on this floor and lose that CEO composure.

"We're here to ask a huge request of you," Jim said after nodding to my manager, Stefanie, and another dude I'd only seen once before— both with looks of utter shock on their faces. The room slowly grew into whispers and murmurs, but my daughter was still the loudest, forcing Jim to hold back a smile.

"Go ahead." I folded my arms and leaned back into my chair, wondering if Addy broke loose and found Jim in his office, and he was here to bring back my lost child to me. "You both look like you're up to something."

"We need to get beach stuff, Mom," Addy said with her usual sass.

"Really?" I looked up at Jim. "Right now? I figured we had everything we needed."

The entire company knew about Jim and me, and I'm sure there was plenty of gossip outside of my friends—Amir and Alyssa—but I didn't give a damn. So long as Jim didn't mind it, I'd dealt with worse shit before than rumors about fucking the boss, but this was the first time everyone on my floor saw it with their own eyes. I had a feeling Jim was working this in his own way. Maybe gossip had floated across his desk, and he came down to clear it up. Who the hell knew.

"Not quite," Jim said. "Would you mind me stealing away Addison to have her sized for a wetsuit and a life vest?"

"The water is cooling," I said, looking at Addy's vibrant smile. "She doesn't—"

"Nonsense," Jim said. "We're off to the beach this weekend to enjoy every ounce of it, M*om*." He winked down at Addy as she looked up at him, hoping I'd give in, and he'd convince me of this. "If you don't mind, it will be easier for me to take your car with her seat in it than call for Blake—"

I pulled my keys out of my purse and smiled at him, "Here. Please don't let her con you into getting extra things."

Jim grinned. "I've got this. We'll be back in time for lunch."

"McDonald's!" Addison nearly screeched.

"Addy. Shh," I tried to calm her down. "Now, give me a hug," I said. Addison did her choke hug of excitement while my eyes never left Jim's.

I'd give anything to feel his lips on mine again. *Tonight!* I reminded myself.

"We'll get you a wetting suit too, Mom," she said, looking at Jim.

"I'd love one, but I'm chilling in the sun." I looked at Jim. "It's been a long week for Mommy."

"It's been a fun week. We have a new car, Mom."

"Yes." I smiled at her and Jim. "We certainly do, and I want to think about that the entire time my eyes are closed, and I'm soaking up the sun."

"Can I speak with you for just a moment?" Jim asked.

I could see that Jim needed to have a quick conversation without Addison being present, but I could also tell he struggled with letting her hand go.

"Hey, baby," I said. "Why don't you sit in Mommy's chair, and if my phone rings, have Amir get it for me, okay?"

"We can answer calls together, little mama," Amir said.

"She doesn't touch the phone, Amir." I eyed him.

"We've got this," he said, smiling at Addy as she climbed into my chair.

I turned back to Jim, expecting to follow Mr. Three-Piece-Suit out of the cubicle area. Wrong. Jim took my hand, intertwined our fingers, and the sea of people who were moving around on the floor parted for us. We walked toward the executive elevators without a word, and I was confused as to why I was leaving my kid at my desk.

Once in the elevator, Jim pressed the doors to close then stopped the thing. I looked at him with a confused smile. "You taking me to your office, Mr. Mitchell?"

"This is the only elevator without cameras in it," he said. "It's been extremely tempting not to request you meet me in it so I could fuck you senseless. Goddamn, I've missed the hell out of you."

He brought me in for a tight hug, and his cologne swept me out of my right mind right then and there. "I'd take that," I teased his skin with my teeth.

"Jesus." He sighed, and then rose and looked into my eyes. "I had to just have a moment alone with you. I'm sorry that I've been so busy this week."

"Week is over, handsome," I said, straightening the perfect knot of his red tie. "Seriously, don't let Addison scam you into buying the entire store or wherever you two are going. Wait," I said, his lips ready to devour mine, and I fucking stopped it with a mom-girlfriend moment. "How in the hell did you make time for taking her shopping today? This morning?"

He rose back up, his hands holding my sides while leaning back against the elevator wall, "It's partly the reason I've been gone all week. That London deal is kicking my ass, but we finally closed it at four this morning. On top of that, I pushed my Friday meetings out and canceled the ones I knew would go over. That's another thing," he said. "I'm going to have to give you the address to the place in Malibu. I'm calling ahead to have the security let you into the place. I planned on being out of here at five with you so we could drive down together; however, I have to meet with an investor at five. I'll be done no later than seven, and the freeways will be cleared up then, so I'll be at the house at eight, possibly earlier."

"You trust us in what I'm imagining is one hell of a house in Malibu?"

He grinned. "I've had pool toys delivered, and the hired help is stocking food, and they have taken care of setting up the pool for Addy. I think you're going to understand what I want to see for my own eyes."

"And that is?"

"Seeing her smiling and swimming in the pool. I haven't forgotten how adorable she was in that video you showed me in England," he said. "Those pools are used for my exercise only, and would love to see her face when she splashes the hell out of the pool area."

"The things I take for granted," I said with a laugh. "You know it drives me insane when she acts like a maniac in the pool and disrupts everyone trying to enjoy our pool at the apartment, right?"

"That's exactly what I look forward to." He pulled me in. "Now, if I don't kiss you, I'm going to fuck you here and now or something."

"Something tells me you'd do both."

He smiled. "It wouldn't be fair to you."

"How so?"

"Your boss didn't seem to realize I was making plans to take you and Addy away, so you'd have to stay back and work while I left, utterly satisfied, and got to go shopping."

I pulled his tie and brought his laughing and gorgeous lips down onto mine. The kiss was just as hungry as I'd imagined it would be. The worst part was that we should have found a way to make a quickie happen, but we both knew everyone who wanted to check—and some asshole likely did—would know the elevator never lit up, showing it hadn't gone anywhere. They probably already thought that we were fucking in here anyway—we should have just gone for it.

"You made it all worse, you know?" I said, pulling out of our kiss.

"I can handle the office," Jim said, his voice returning to CEO-James mode.

"I'm not talking about that," I said, feeling my flushing cheeks as the doors of the elevator opened and let us onto my floor again.

He smirked at me and pulled his phone out. As he typed, I looked for Addy, who was in some great conversation with Amir and Alyssa.

My phone buzzed as Addison ran to Jim. "I'll see you tonight. Addy will be bringing lunch back for you two." He winked, and after I kissed my daughter, they left like a king would with his little princess. It was a pretty beautiful sight.

My phone buzzed its second alert. I picked it up.

Jim: *It might seem like I made it worse, but trust me, it'll be worth it tonight.*

BUZZ AGAIN.

Jim: *I've missed you*

I smiled at the texts.

Avery: *Yeah. About tonight. Addy will be in the house, remember?*

Jim: *We're in the car now. Can't text and drive. I'll cover your mouth. I had a room made up for her. Will she sleep alone?*

I covered my smile. Should I let him wonder? He did get me all worked up and piping hot for more in that elevator while he took off.

Avery: *Yes, but it's a new place. She'll be very excited and not able to sleep, no matter how cool the room is. Sorry. You're out of luck, buddy.*

Jim: *Might have to wear her out in the pool then. We're leaving now.*

Time for Jim to experience life as a parent, especially with a child who went full-steam ahead in new, exciting environments. Jack shit was happening tonight unless I set an alarm for three in the morning.

I smiled, trying to imagine how this would play out with our first night together under one roof. I missed the hell out of him.

"Hey, sister," Amir said with a laugh. "You going to survive? You haven't seen him all week, and then he comes down looking like a hot piece. You have to be dying."

"I'll manage," I said, trying not to agree with him too eagerly.

"Well, he certainly looked like a goddamn snack, if I do say so myself," Alyssa said with a laugh. "Never thought he could get better looking than his airbrushed, front-page magazine covers. You lucky girl. That man is all yours."

"What?" I laughed this stupid, nervous-excited laugh I didn't realize I was capable of making.

"Oh, please," Amir said. "The entire office saw that look on his face. Come to think of it." Amir looked at Alyssa. "The three times I've seen Mr. Mitchell on the floor, he's always looked like a dick—a gorgeous dick, but a dick nonetheless. Now he's just—he's totally chill."

My office phone rang, and I answered it.

"Avery?" It was Larry. "Did I finally get the right extension?"

"Yes, Larry, you did. It's Avery. What's up?"

"Addison left her backpack and her stuffed puppy here. Mom just found it."

"Shit," I said, relieved. "It's been hell this week without pup. I had to lie and tell her he must've found a lonely little girl who needed to snuggle with him. It was working, but staying at the beach house tonight might've been a nightmare without her little comfort pup."

He laughed. "Well, we've got it, hun."

"Addy and I will swing by and get it tonight."

"I can meet you."

"It's not a problem. Jim's getting off late anyway. It works out fine. Besides, Addy loves riding in her new car."

"No kidding?" he said. "Okay. We'll see you tonight, then."

I TEXTED Jim and told him that I had to head to Larry and Annette's before driving to his place, and with traffic, the drive from downtown

LA to Anaheim and then back to Malibu was going to be a massive bitch. It was a damn good thing we loved this car because we'd be arriving at Jim's place about the same freaking time as he would be.

We'd finally made it to Larry and Annette's at six-thirty. Traffic was a bear, but this car kept Addy content with her videos, and I could relax forever in the comfort of the seat.

When we walked up to the door, the screen door flung open, and my heart nearly stopped. "Addy, go say hi to papa," I said in the calmest voice I could manage. "And close the door." Once the door shut, I turned around and glared at Derek as he walked toward my car. "What the fuck are you doing out of jail?"

Pissed was not even a word I could use to express the rage I felt.

"Believe it or not, Avery, people sober up," he said. He didn't seem high, but who knew. "Nice car. Did that douchebag let you borrow one of his trust-fund toys?"

"None of your business." I felt my entire body shaking. My life had been so carefree for a whole week. It was like I'd let my guard down, and now, reality hit me like a Mack truck. "A week in jail doesn't sober up someone who's as sick as you. You need rehab. You need to do it for Addy."

"Does your rich boy-toy know you're just as bad?"

"What the hell are you talking about?"

He waved his hand at the car, "Rich assholes like him—James Mitchell—they don't fuck with hood rats. So, either he's got you a supplier, and you're using again, or—"

"You are out of your fucking mind, and here I thought you weren't high. You're on something, just not fully tweaked yet."

"Did you tell him who he's dating, Avery?" Derek lit a cigarette, inhaled deeply, and pointed at me with his cigarette between his fingers, "You could make the front page of the news with your past, fucking with a CEO like him. You act like I'm so horrible, but you were always the worst, and that doesn't change."

"Shut the fuck up. My past is in the fucking past. Quit trying to fuck with my mind. I hate you so much."

"I'm just saying. If you're falling for this asshole, you'll probably fall flat on your face. That guy is so far out of your trashy league that you don't even have a clue, do you? You just like pretending you aren't some glorified whore."

"You can go straight to hell," I said. "Addy and I are leaving. I'll think about whether or not she comes here next weekend. I'm done bringing her around her dad, who is constantly high as fuck. She deserves better. Why don't you stop worrying about me and start getting the help you need so that you can see your daughter again, huh? What a novel idea."

"That man and all his fucking lawyers can't help you get the custody you think you deserve. We've both done jail time, and what will the judge think about that along with everything else you've ever done? They'll take her from you too, and it will be all your fault."

"I did one fucking night in jail seven years ago."

"Tell that to the custody lawyers. You'll bring my daughter next weekend. You fuck it up, and I'm taking you to court. We both know my parents will get Addy."

"Fuck you, you mother fucker! *Fuck you!*" I screamed. I was so furious that I could hardly see. I stormed into the house, my nerves tightening with every passing second. "Addy, let's go," I said in a stern voice that my daughter didn't deserve.

"Mommy, are you okay?" she asked. "You're crying. Daddy made you cry?"

Goddammit, I was fucking crying. I took a deep breath and smiled, "I'm fine, kid. Do you want to go and get some McDonald's?"

"Yes," she squealed and gave everyone hugs and kisses goodbye except for Derek. She walked past her dad and smiled at him. "Hey, daddy."

"Does dad get a hug?" He knelt, and I watched the scene in disgust.

Jim knelt to bring himself to her level with so much kindness and adoration, and it was the most precious sight. But this? A drug addict, asking his daughter to hug him goodbye after being a complete fucking dick to her mom? The man disgusted me more and more, and I didn't even need Jim in my life to realize that.

I barely made it through McDonald's with Addy. I was a wreck and holding it all in as best I could. Derek had brought out my biggest fear again, the custody fight for Addison. Jim questioned why I didn't fight for her, and this was precisely why. Because even though I didn't see myself as the drug addict that I was eight years ago, Derek treated me like I'd never changed. He made me start to believe that this stain could never be wiped out of my life. Never removed.

When my mind started veering in the direction of breaking it all off with Jim, believing Derek was right that I could somehow ruin the man's image and life if anyone dug up my past, I knew I needed to go home and regroup for the night. Addy was already asleep in the car anyway. It was eight o'clock, and we could just go to bed and head down to the beach early in the morning.

I wasn't going to spiral, believing the master manipulator and his bullshit just yet. I wasn't giving up on myself. I deserved better. I deserved to be with a man who loved me. I deserved to be with Jim, whether or not he was wealthy. Derek would never see past the wealth part, but I did. I didn't fall in love with James H. Mitchell. I fell in love with the kindest, most loving man. A man who gave a damn about me: I fell in love with Jim.

CHAPTER THIRTY-TWO

Avery

I was up at three in the damn morning and wishing I was in Malibu. I'd let Derek get to me yesterday, but I woke up with one thing in mind: My life had reached an ultimate turning point, and I was moving forward with it. I was fearless and content to accept myself, my past, and the fact that history had helped me to learn from those mistakes so I could raise my daughter to be happy no matter what. So, I wasn't going to let the demons of my past scare me from going after what I wanted. They'd never frightened me before, so why would I allow them to stop me from having what I wanted most now, which was Jim and happiness for Addy and me.

Jim didn't hassle me about staying the night at my place. I could tell he'd reached the end of his day as well when I called him to let him know about Derek, and that I needed to head home to cool off. The fact that Addy was already asleep made it an easy decision anyway. If I'd have driven to Malibu, she would have ended up taking a nice, long car nap in time to play in the pool until midnight, and I wasn't having that under the best of circumstances. We both agreed that if I were comfortable waking up early and taking Addy to watch the guys surf in the morning, it was just as convenient for us to stay at my place.

We were finally packed, in our swimsuits, and flying up the interstate to Malibu to meet up with the group. I was excited to do this. Even during my bad days, when I went surfing, I felt like I was truly living, being out in the ocean. Was I surfing this morning with the guys today? Hell no. I hadn't been on the board in years, and I wasn't in the mood to drink half the ocean and have the other half up in my sinuses. Today was a relax in the sun day, even though we were heading down so early.

I'd surfed Santa Cruz waters, but never this far south, so I didn't know much about where the best spots were. When I talked to Jim this morning, I figured out that the guys were sacrificing their usual surf spots for Addy. They didn't have to do that on her account, though. She loved jumping shallow waves and building sandcastles, and she probably could've done that at any beach, but it was a sweet gesture.

We followed the GPS and pulled in where a badass CJ7 Jeep was parked next to a classic 1970s Bronco. Both tops were off, and I could tell that the surfers were here. I smiled at the idea of how cool it would be to ride in either one of those restored vehicles. Next to those were two sleek sports cars.

Yep, this is the right beach.

Addy and I walked out past a nice restaurant that had an outdoor bar where you could drink, but still be safely and legally on the beach, protected by the restaurant's outdoor seating. Next were all the cabanas—we had definitely upgraded from our usual beaches. I glanced through the cabanas, guessing that if Jim and all his friends were out here, the guys most likely already had one reserved.

I was wrong. Ash walked over to us from a nicely set-up area. Surfboards were lying out in front of canopies, keeping us closer to the shorelines. Beach blankets were laid out carefully, and there were chairs that I could sit on and fall asleep in if I wanted to.

"Hey, you," Ash said from under a floppy, white hat with oversized sunglasses, looking stylish with her pregnant belly in her swimsuit and beach coverup. "The guys are already out there screwing off. You just missed Collin's wipeout." She chuckled and looked at Addy. "Hey, sweetie. I'm Ash. You look like you're all ready for a day at the beach."

"I am. I'm Addy. Can I surf too?" She pointed out to a man in a wet suit who just took a wave.

Ash laughed and looked at me. "That's Jake. He's my husband. At the rate he's going, you're going to watch him bite it, and then you might not want to do it. How about some smaller waves?" She looked at me, wondering if she'd overstepped her bounds.

I smiled. "We'll see, Addy. Let's just relax and watch the guys for now. You can take those cool beach toys that I know you conned Jim into buying you and play with them."

"We didn't buy toys, Mom," she said.

"That was Jake and me," Ash smiled, and looked at Addy. "We thought you'd love to bury Jake in the sand."

Addy giggled her tired laugh. "I'll bury him to his neck," she said, making Ash laugh.

"Then I'll help you give him a mermaid tail. Do you like mermaids?"

"I love mermaids and unicorns." Addy started to perk up.

"Then we'll make Jake a mermaid when he comes in and is too tired to care," she said, leading the way to the cabana area they'd set up.

"So, do the guys own this part of the beach or something? This is insanely awesome," I said, sitting in a lounge chair next to Ash.

"They definitely act as though they own it," she said with a laugh. "We're rarely here, so this is a nice change. Maybe if we're all not wiped out this afternoon, you guys can come to take a look at my gallery. I have some neat mermaid paintings." She shrugged. "Jake pulled off some miracle, and with the lighting in there, it looks super cool. It blew my mind, and I painted the damn—" she covered her mouth, Addy sitting in front of us, but still ignoring us. "Oops. I'm sorry, *dang* things." She shook her head. "It might be fun for Addy to pick out a picture."

"You all are too good to her and me."

"It's nice to have the company of a woman I can relate to. The guys are all great, but having a woman around who's not prattling on about superficial stuff all the time is a breath of fresh air."

"That bad, huh?" I smiled.

"I'm just glad you're here," she answered as she reached for a thermos. "We brought coffee. Do you want some?"

"Yes, please. I take it black, thanks," I said, reaching for the cup she handed me. "So, are they all single?"

"Alex is messing around with a girl named Summer. She's come around once or twice, but being that she's Jim's secretary, they're trying to play it low key. She seems sweet, but she hardly talks, so I don't really know. I'm not one to judge people prematurely, but she seems more interested in the superficial side of Alex. That could just be a bit of immaturity. Who knows. As long as he's happy." She eyed the men out there, catching waves, "Collin is hit and miss. He brought one woman around, but she acted like she was being tortured by having to hang out with people who were beneath her. Jake and Jim instantly didn't like her. She seemed like maybe she was more suited to date a prince or something. Honestly, I don't blame any of the women. These guys aren't exactly serious. Maybe someday," she finished with a shrug.

"I get what you mean," I said, knowing Ash was probably holding back so she wouldn't sound like a beauty-parlor gossip. Some people made it hard to have something nice to say about them, and I got the feeling these guys attracted a lot of those types. It was hard to attract meaningful people if you acted like a goof, though. Ash was right about that.

"Then," Ash hung onto that word while I sipped my coffee, "I never thought I'd see Jim loosen up the way he has since being around you." She pointed out to where Jim surfed, disappearing into a wave that curved beautifully. "That is something no one thought we'd be seeing today. Jake said last night that if Jim got on the board today, he thinks you're sticking around forever. He's never seen Jim living it up this much. It all started since he came back from England." She smiled at me as I watched intently to see if Jim could stay ahead of the wave, he popped out and then did my favorite part of surfing, carving the board back and jumping the white, dominating the wave.

Nice one! I thought, feeling my legs aching to be out in the water and on a board again.

"I gave him a pretty hard time in England." I smiled at her. "The poor guy lived on that phone. It didn't take much to realize he was married to his work. We drove through the gorgeous English countryside, and he missed it all because he was staring at his phone. I felt bad for the guy. He had all these remarkable things, but I didn't see him enjoying any of it."

Ash laughed. "Did you know who he was?"

"I had no clue," I said with a smile, pulling my hood over my head, chilled by the cool morning breeze. "We role-played this ridiculous act of being husband and wife like crazy people. It was pretty hilarious."

"Role played?" She looked at me in confusion.

"I have no idea how it started, but we faked a fight, and then the crazy BS started flying. We faked it so much at one spot that we had to go eat somewhere else."

Ash laughed. "You're good for him." She looked at Addy. "And so is she."

"I'm still trying to wake up from it all."

She giggled. "I felt the same with Jake too." She relaxed under the blanket she'd draped over her. "That's why it's nice having you around. You're down to earth. The other women who come around seem to act like they're owed it all. I don't know. It just creates a tense environment when we're all together. This is nice, though." She smiled. "It makes me more and more excited for when our little one is here."

"When are you due?"

"November," she said. "I can't wait."

"It's the best. Holding and seeing your baby for the first time." I looked at Addy, "Then watching them grow into their little personalities. It's the biggest trip."

"There goes Jim again." Ash chuckled. "He's schooling those guys. They all made bets that Jim would hear his phone from shore and stop after one wave if he got out there at all."

"That's a good one." I laughed and then leaned on my elbows to watch my man surf, "When's the last time he's surfed?"

"Jake said they grew up out here, surfed almost every day. Jim was a natural, but once he took over the company, he never went out anymore. I know Jake is loving this. All of them out there."

WE SPENT the morning watching the guys catch waves, and I loved every second of their mini pro-surfer competition. The waves were breaking much bigger than I expected, but fall and winter brought big swells to the Southern California coastline.

It didn't take long for Jim to paddle in and Addy to pop up and run out to meet him. He held his board with one arm, trotting through the knee-deep water, and smoothing back his onyx black, wet hair. I knew I had the cheesiest grin on my face, watching him with lust.

Then my expression changed from lust to covering my mouth as I watched the sweetest thing this mom could ever dream up for her daughter and herself. Jim made it to the sand and was hurrying to where Addy was pointing and squealing at him. It looked as though she wanted in that water so bad, but it wasn't the water she wanted, it was the man who'd scooped her up in his free arm and met her with as much happiness and eagerness as she'd met him. I leaned forward and folded my arms over my lap, watching this beautiful moment play and wishing I'd recorded it on my phone to watch over and over again.

Jim managed to maneuver her to his side while hanging onto his board, and then our eyes met. I smiled at him, Addy pointing at his board as he walked up the soft, dry sand toward us. He set down the board, and let my crazed daughter, who was now obsessed with it, examine it.

"Careful, Addy," I said. "You can snap that thing in two. No getting on it."

"I'm just petting it, Mom," she said, not looking back as Ash and I laughed.

Jim's smile was beaming and his eyes bright as he approached me, sitting in my chair. He unzipped the top portion of his wetsuit, and before I could admire his tanned abs, his lips were quickly pressing hard against mine.

His wet cheek met mine. "You look beautiful," he whispered, "and tonight is ours." He brushed his lips across my cheek and sat in the chair to Ash's right.

"Here, trade me," Ash said, starting to stand.

"Relax, little sister," Jim said, positioning his chair to face Addy and us two ladies. "I'm fine. Besides, the best views are right where I'm at."

I smiled along with Ash, but Ash's attention was drawn out where Jake had just caught a wave.

"You looked pretty fantastic out there," I said. "I didn't pin you as a man who surfed."

He glanced out to where Jake disappeared into a barrel. The waves were badass. I was feeling a yearning to get out there—too bad I didn't take Jim up on the wetsuit situation yesterday.

"Well." He shrugged, grabbing a bottle of water. "I figured I'd lost it after all these years, but the guys all bet against me, so I felt inclined to prove them wrong."

"You did amazing, Jim," Ash said. "Jake's gotta pay up. He's the one who started the whole bet."

"Of all the people, Jakey knows that when my own brother places wagers against me, I'm going to beat him." He laughed, eyes dazzling when they met mine again. "Even if I kill myself."

I couldn't focus. I wanted to be in his arms. I wished I'd just gone to his house last night. I glanced out at the ocean after Addy lost interest in Jim's shortboard and went back to digging for treasures in the sand.

"Those waves are incredible."

"Then get on the board," Jim said.

"Funny." I looked over at him. "Tempting to take that on in a bikini, but not tempting enough."

"Good thing that I asked Ash to borrow one of her wetsuits after an adorable little girl told me she wanted to surf like Mommy."

"What?" I frowned. "She's only heard stories."

Jim laughed. "You have a wetsuit waiting for you. Get back on the board, Mom."

"Yeah, Mommy," Addy said.

"You two are starting to work dangerously against me," I said.

"Go have a little fun. Where'd you surf?" Ash asked.

"Santa Cruz." I smiled, wondering if I should do this. More surfers were out, and I wasn't in the mood to deal with assholes.

"Hey," Jim said, standing up and walking over a badass wetsuit, "get into this thing. The guys will make sure no one drops in on you out there."

My lips twisted as I studied the wetsuit.

"Av," Jim said, snapping my attention to him. No one shortened my name like this except my sister. I suddenly loved that coming out of his mouth. "What happened to the girl who taught me how to live life? Will she sit on the beach and miss the last of these perfect waves?"

"I have a kid." I smirked at him.

"Addy's on my watch now," he said. "I promised I'd build sandcastles with her anyway. Go live a little."

"Fine," I said, Jim sparking up the adventurous side of me. "She doesn't go into the water."

"I'll make sure she doesn't bribe Jim." Ash laughed. "We've got Addy. Go have some fun."

CHAPTER THIRTY-THREE

Avery

I squeezed into the wetsuit and took out a board that was a little longer than Jim's. Hopefully, Collin didn't have a special attachment to the one I initially thought was Jim's other board. If I jacked it up, it was on my dumbass for thinking I still had it when it came to surfing.

I paddled out and duck-dived a wave that curled over me. It was a good sign that at least that part came back to me naturally. Then I was out past the breaks and paddling to where I saw Jim's brother, waving while the three guys sat on their boards, catching a break.

"And she comes out to make us all look like fools?" Collin—the one I'd met for a few minutes at the medical conference—said. "Good to see you again, Avery."

"You too," I said, pulling myself up to straddle the board and watch the ocean currents. "They're breaking nicely. I never thought Malibu got this kind of action."

"You'd be surprised," Jake said as everyone kept their eyes on the currents. "It was that storm over the Pacific that went south this week. We're pretty much on the last of the good tidings that it brought the coastline." He smiled at me. "You know I lost a bet over you today?"

"What, that I wouldn't show?" I asked, hands in the water, keeping the board in place.

"No, that my brother wouldn't get his ass back up on the board."

"He looked badass out here." I smiled.

"Yeah, it's nice to have him out again," Jake said, then splashed water over at Alex. "Your two dumbasses left the therapeutics of the water for far too long."

Alex nodded in my direction. "We've got this one to thank," he said with a laugh. "I swear to God, you've changed my best friend entirely."

I shook my head. "I'm glad he's enjoying life. Guess he and that phone finally broke up."

"Not just that." Alex grinned over at Jake and me. "Remember how he was going to rip into that entire team on Monday for fucking up Palm Springs?"

"Did he fire them?" Collin laughed.

"He showed a fucking thirty-minute cartoon instructional video about doing your job and doing it right."

"Shut the fuck up." Jake laughed and arched an eyebrow at me. "Avery Gilbert, saving jobs and CEOs' overworked lives."

I laughed and looked at Alex in disbelief. "You're kidding, right?"

"Nope. I expected an hour of Jim chewing asses out, and if anyone dared to speak up? Fired. All that shit. Instead, he brings in all of them and then makes everyone watch that stupid thing."

"What did he tell them afterward?" Collin asked while laughing.

"That he hoped it wasted their time as much as they wasted his time when he was doing their jobs on Saturday. Then he chewed into them a bit but ended it on some sweet note about appreciating everything they do. It was pretty good, tactic-wise, but it wasn't typical Jim."

"Well, then." I laughed. "Maybe I'll make a few friends at the office from the upper floors."

Alex smirked. "Nah." He shook his head. "The only friends you need on those floors—the only two who are worth a damn—are Jimmy and me."

"All right, enough bullshitting. We're wasting Avery's waves," Jake said. "Are you waiting on it to die down some?"

"Just trying to pick the one that's not going to kill me. It's been ten years."

"Ten years is nothing," Collin said. "You've got this. Pick your wave, and we'll watch for anyone trying to drop in on you."

"All right," I said, watching the sets that were rolling in.

I laid on the board and started paddling with the water rolling nicely with me. The wave was setting up, and as it began to crest, I forced everything from my arms and was half-thrilled and half-surprised when I hopped directly onto my feet. The shorter the board, the more the work, so I had to be quick to get my feet settled and balanced as I dropped down onto the wave. The drop was a good six feet, and my stomach felt it.

I lost focus with the excitement of getting up on the board for the first time in years and getting it right. The curl was on my ass now, and I was about to get rolled. *Fuck!* I bailed before I got buried, diving off the board and going with the undercurrent.

I popped up as soon as another wave broke right behind the one that almost kicked my ass. I started aggressively paddling out, knowing I was in what I called the fucked zone and instantly ducked another breaking wave. Thank God I was a runner because otherwise, there's no way in hell I would've had the stamina for this.

"Almost!" Jake called out. "Going for more?"

I smiled, sitting on the board. "This feels like reuniting with an old friend. Can't leave her just yet."

Collin laughed. "Flex would marry you here and now after saying that shit."

"Flex?"

"Our Tahitian surfer buddy. The dude is badass. He surfs all over the world."

"Got it," I said. "Yeah, don't fuck with the Polynesian surfers. They are seriously one with the water."

"Speaking of which..." Alex looked back. "Setting up well again for you. Better take it before Jakey or Coll start getting greedy."

"Good point," I said.

I turned, feeling the exhilarating sensation of the board being pushed by the water. This one was more aggressive, and I had to kick up my paddling with the current a notch. Once I found the break, I popped up—faster this time—dropped down, and focused on enjoying the ride this time instead of the fact that I could get up. I leaned back some and carved the water—nice fucking board—and rode next to the wall as the wave curled over me. The familiar sound it made—like banging on a hollow pipe—surrounded me. Now, it was time to stay ahead of the water that was on my ass. I put more pressure on my front foot, crouched down, and sped up the board. It felt like such a rush, needing to beat the powerful water that was crashing in on itself behind me.

Come on, I thought, crouching more, knowing I was inches ahead of where the water was crashing. Now, it was just me and the wave I chose. Nothing else mattered but beating this. I was only zeroed in on outrunning the tunnel. Once I made it through, I instinctively threw both hands in the air, and before I ended up sinking in the whitewash, I cut back on the shoulder of the wave and dropped down, paddling out some and kissing the board.

"Fucking hell!" I heard one of the guys say as I paddled over to them.

Jake met me with a high five, and I grinned. "Wow, guess that makes two of us who still have it after all these years," I said, looking for Addy on the shore. I smiled when I saw her holding onto Jim's hand and jumping up and down. "So sweet that he had her watch me," I said, mainly to myself.

"You killed that," Collin said. "Are you taking another?"

I brushed water over my forehead and face. "I'm not conditioned to sit out and surf all day. Just needed to beat the hell out of a wave and feel victorious for a second."

"You looked great," Jake said. "Tell Ash I'm riding one more then I'll be in behind you."

. . .

THAT AFTERNOON we were all relaxed and sat around talking about random shit. Addy stole Jim away from me more than once, obsessed with her sandcastles and digging for treasures that she and Jim were using great imaginations to find.

While they were occupied, it gave me time to get to know Ash more, and it didn't take long to feel like we connected really well on a friendship level. She told me about the struggle of losing her mom to cancer, almost losing her dad, and how Jake was pretty much her saving grace. Their story was beautiful, and I could definitely relate to her about finding herself—virtually overnight—in a relationship with a gazillionaire. Neither of us came from a champagne and caviar background, so it was nice to bond over that.

I didn't go into great detail about my life history. God only knew that my past wasn't something I liked to drop on people, and that was more to save them from feeling uncomfortable. Most people didn't know how to react, and I didn't want the pity anyway. I only gave the highlight reels of how I was a runaway after being stuck in a shitty foster home, rebelled outrageously, and practically lived in the ocean for years in Santa Cruz. Even if I didn't think it was a depressing subject, the truth was that I wasn't very comfortable opening up to people. I guess that's what happens after being on your own for so long. Maybe it was out of fear of judgment, or perhaps it was self-protection to avoid talking about the trauma of it all, but either way, that was all I was comfortable sharing for now.

As I listened to Ash talk about her mother, my heart went out to her. Ash had had a close relationship with her mother, and she gave up college and all of her young-adult prospects to take care of her while she was dying. I always imagined there was a special place in heaven for people who sacrificed so much to care for other people. That kind of sacrifice wasn't something I'd ever experienced—certainly not from my mother—so I couldn't relate to Ash's experiences in that way, but listening to her story gave me a look into what kind of person she was. I knew instantly that people like her were rare, and it didn't surprise me one bit that Jim's brother didn't want to let her go. After hearing her story and the story of how Jake and Ash got together, watching them interact reaffirmed to me that love truly could conquer all.

I smiled at how corny that phrase could sound. I'd heard it a million times, but I never believed it. Not until now. Not until I felt myself growing wildly in love with this man who treated my daughter as if she were his own. I desperately wanted to hang onto this forever, but I had to remain as level-headed as I could, and thank God for Jim's patience in that. It proved to me that the man cared for me, and Addy, on a level that I might never understand.

"Collin," I heard Alex say as I lay on the lounge chair, eyes closed and soaking up the sun. "What's up with you today?"

"What's that?" Collin said, close to where I was laying on my stomach, in and out of sleep since Jim was with Addy, and he insisted I relax while they help Ash bury Jacob.

"You're quiet today, and you hardly surfed. You okay?"

"Meh, it's nothing," he answered. "Still dealing with the bullshit of the company. That woman who took it over is like the devil in fucking stilettos. Evil as hell."

I heard Alex laugh. "She's *hot* as hell." I leaned up on my elbows as the guys talked, watching the surf roll in. "Maybe that's the problem. Jim and I met with her more than once. She's a businesswoman. It's to be expected."

I looked over at Collin, who was wearing his trendy shades and staring at Alex. "A businesswoman who treats me like a fucking dumbass because I'm not stepping into my dad's shoes. She can go to hell, and she's lucky I haven't used Jim's headhunters to replace her."

Alex's eyes drifted toward mine, and he smiled. "Collin lost his dad pretty recently. His dad ran a similar company to Jim's. In fact, Collin's dad helped Jim deal with the loss of his father, Howard, and he helped Jim takeover Mitchell and Associates as CEO. He was a no-bullshit kind of guy." He looked at Collin, who was smiling at the commotion of the others as they buried Jake in the sand. "Which is why he set her as his VP. I think you just have a little ego problem with her, or is there more to your story with Tate?"

"Yeah, no." Collin dismissed the question.

I could tell the guys were holding back, and it cracked me up. They didn't know me, so the breaks were on.

"Shit," Alex said, looking out to where Jim was, and I startled as Jake busted out of his sand burial grounds and acted like a monster coming for Addy. "Hey, Mitch."

Jim's smile and laugh were contagious as Addy ran to him for protection, and he caught her from the sand monster, Jake. "What's up?" Jim said as Jake and Ash walked out to the shore.

"Check out the bar. It looks like more sea scum washed up on shore."

Jim's eyebrows pulled together behind the silver frames of his aviators, forcing me to look into the mob of people at the oceanside bar.

"Hey, Avery," I heard Jim say, his voice lighter than expected.

"Momma! Mom, mom," Addison said in my face now that I had turned and sat up.

"What, kiddo?" I said, accepting her puckered lips for a kiss. "You having fun?"

"So much fun," she said, balling her hands into fists. Then the look came as soon as the tall man's shadow showed up. "Guess what, Momma. Guess what I know?"

"Addy," Jim said in some funny voice I'd never heard him use before. "She might not like it."

"Like what? What are you two up to?"

Addy leaned toward my ear and whispered, "Jim likes you, Momma."

"He's going to be my friend too?" I dropped my legs over the edge of the lounge chair, where Jim sat next to me. "Hey, I thought he was Mitch?" I laughed, looking at Jim.

"Turns out, I'm Jim. Jim's cooler because he surfs," Jim said as he ran his hand over my warm back, my insides tingling with the few times I'd been touched by him today.

"How'd we manage that one?" I asked as Addy left me and walked over to where Collin was now at her service, pulling a juice box from the ice chest for her. Addy had four gorgeous men at her service all day, and it was only two in the afternoon.

"Jake started the rumor, and it took off."

I laughed and was shocked when Jim's lips captured mine, his hand cupping my side, bringing me against his warm, firm body. "I love you," he whispered, and it sent a shiver down my spine. "So much."

He finished with a discreet kiss to my forehead. I looked into the dark frames of his sunglasses through mine. "Me too. You've been unbelievable today with Addy. All of you have been."

"She's a spark of energy that we all needed after this long week. I have a question, though," he said, and he looked at me as if he were scared out of his mind.

"I'll answer it if you tell me what the hell is at the bar. I was going to head up with Ash and see if they had some ice cream or nachos or something."

Jim eyed the bar. "Some chick I hooked up with a while ago. Everyone hated her. I was too stupid to see why. She leeched on and was one of the ones who joined forces and tried to ruin Jake's life." He smirked at me. "Like Alex said, sea scum. She's probably trolling the area for some poor soul who can't see through her Chanel sunglasses." He grinned. "My wallet's over there. Take it and get whatever you want. They have awesome margaritas if you want to pair that up with your nachos."

"That sounds refreshing."

"Hell," Jake said, walking towards the cooler, cracking open a bottle of water, "it's always five o'clock somewhere."

"What was your question before?"

"What do you think about me putting on Addy's wetsuit and life vest and letting her ride the board some?"

"You're not taking her out deep, are you?"

He rolled his bottom lip into his teeth. "Would you get pissed if I coerced the guys to follow me out after she's played on it some and learned to balance on her knees, and we rode that longboard in together?"

"You're out of your fucking head."

"The rip currents aren't bad," he said like he was a kid himself.

I looked out at the water. He was right. The currents were mellow, and the waves were breaking long and nicely for a simple ride in. If he had the guys out there with him, I knew they'd spot him with Addy. The longboard had more surface and was much easier to stay on because of that. I glanced around, seeing that the lifeguards were on deck as well, which was good. She had a life jacket and would be surrounded by four experienced surfers and lifeguards too.

"How about this," I started, "why don't you clear it with the lifeguards in the tower? They see the breaks farther out. If they think it's okay for you to act like some Hawaiian, bringing his kid out to surf on the same board as him, then I'll be okay with the idea. Everyone has to be out there, though."

"You want to join us?" he asked.

"I'll stand on the shore with my phone set to 911 in case it all goes south."

"All right." Jim kissed my temple. "Oh, and yes, Addy asked me if I had a crush on you."

"Your answer?" I laughed.

"I said that I had the biggest crush ever."

"You both are too much." I kissed the warm skin of his shoulder. "I need to spray Addy down with more sunscreen and put it on her face."

"I'll get the wetsuits."

"After you talk to the lifeguards." I smiled at him.

AFTER EVERYTHING HAD BEEN CLEARED with the lifeguards, the four men walked out to the water with Addy—her personal bodyguards—and Ash and I walked up through the gated area where you could drink on the beach.

I ordered the loaded nachos and a margarita and got Ash her ginger ale, leaving Jim's wallet back at the beach site. Excellent of him to offer, but I had to pay for something.

"Is this a pregnancy craving?" I asked with a grin, handing her the drink.

She sipped it and smiled. "I guess so. I've found myself loving it lately. We have a whole ice chest full of it, so I don't know why I ordered one."

I held my plastic cup up to hers. "It just wouldn't taste the same if you brought the drink to the bar."

I glanced out at the ocean and laughed, seeing Jim pulling Addy around on the massive-ass longboard that was brought out. "Damn, that thing is huge."

Ash chuckled. "I learned on that," she said. "Then, apparently, I became a natural and played on it all day."

"How'd you like it?"

"You were right about missing an old friend by being out there with the water. I only had a day out and had the time of my life. Something about the force of the water pushing that board? It's awesome." I watched her run her hand over her stomach. "But this little treasure decided to butt in and slow it all down."

"Wait until you first meet that little treasure," I said with a smile, looking out at Addy. "You'll wonder how you ever lived without your child all these years."

"Excuse me? Is that you, Ashley Taylor?" I heard a woman ask.

I turned and almost jumped when I saw large glasses, a big as fuck sun hat, and bright red lipstick. Her dark lenses hid her eyes, and I couldn't help but wonder what her makeup looked like under the shades. Her sheer, leopard print cover-up was over a black swimsuit with a matching leopard print belt. I couldn't stop staring—this was more than I'd ever seen on a beach before. Her long, porcelain legs were held up by strappy stilettos. Talk about extra. This woman was doing the most.

What the fucking hell, I thought, leaning back so Ash could have a conversation with this lady.

"It's Ashley *Mitchell* now, Lillian," Ash said politely, but with some irritation in her voice too. "Shocked to see you out today."

"Yeah," she said, her dark, bug-eye glasses looking in my direction. "Who's your friend?" She leaned against the bar while I took another sip of my margarita, "Or should I ask it differently, who's Jim's new friend?"

"Oh, for fuck's sake," I said in a low voice, not in the mood for some rich snob to mess up the beautiful day I was having. "I'm Avery."

I turned back to look at Jim, and Addy was following all his rules as I'd instructed her to do.

"Someone has quite the mouth," she said, trying to get into my peripheral.

"What do you want, Lillian? I can't imagine why you have the nerve to speak to me at all after what you pulled," Ash said.

"Well." She cleared her throat. "I noticed Jim with that child. I had no idea he had a child."

I pinched my lips and was so annoyed with this woman's fake as fuck snob tone that I was ready to abandon my nachos at this point.

"That child is mine, lady," I said, intently focused on Jim and Addy. "Anything else?"

"Unbelievable," she said. "I just—I didn't know—"

"There's a lot of things you don't know, Lillian," Ash said. "Like when to stay the hell out of people's business."

"I'm just wondering now if that child is the reason Jim broke it off with me."

I pulled off my sunglasses and looked at the woman with disbelief. "Are you serious? I just met you, and I can point out a few reasons why he might've broken it off with you that have nothing to do with my child, the first of which is the fact that you're at the beach, dressed up like you're about to step onto a runway for fashion week," I said, reaching my limits when I probably shouldn't have been. This woman was annoying as fuck. "God, lady, what do you want?" I asked her directly.

"You heard my question!"

"And you heard Avery's response. Since Avery doesn't know you as I do—my super sweet ex-boss—" Ash's voice dripped with sarcasm and irritation, "the fact that you're a shady snake who reveled in the destruction of his brother's life and career doesn't exactly shoot you up on the marriage proposal list. Get a clue, and stop living in the past."

"And speaking of putting things in the past," I stood and Ash followed, and I grabbed my nachos. "Have a good one."

"She's a heartless bitch," Ash said as we walked away, leaving the woman standing there speechless.

"How fucking weird do you have to be to be her? Jim must've been super desperate to have that woman around."

Ash laughed. "I think I speak for everyone when I say that Jim befriending her was a massive mistake. There's something about her and even Jake's crazy ex before me. They give the lovely women who have money a bad reputation."

"Well, if Jim was in that no gold-diggers allowed club, he was certainly blind to how fake that broad is." I laughed.

Ash and I sat on the edge of the lounge chairs, and I almost dropped my nachos when the men were lying on their boards and paddling out.

"Good God, I'm going to have a heart attack," I said.

"No kidding. Hold on, little Addy," Ash said as we both watched them paddle out to deeper waters.

I glanced over to both lifeguard towers, the guards leaning on the rail of their tower, eyes concealed behind sunglasses but watching the guys. The water was moving and breaking so smoothly that I chilled out a bit. Jim had this. I watched him surf earlier, and Addy was perfectly positioned on the front of the longboard. Her hands gripped each side, and she sat perfectly still, butt molded against her ankles.

I looked out farther to where the guys were spotting Jim for the wave to take so that Jim could focus on Addy. *Fucking hell.* This was the coolest thing in the world, but scarier than shit.

The waves are breaking nicely. Clean breaks, Avery. Fucking breathe. I set my nachos to the side and stood. Ash walked down to the shoreline, where kids were playing like normal children on boogie boards, but not my kid. My kid was out with an even bigger kid about to fucking surf.

I watched intently, seeing Jake's hand go up. They were taking this set. Jim started paddling well with the push of the wave, and Addy's smile was brighter than I'd ever seen it. Her body was secure on the board while the wave started to crest. A two-foot wave, I think. It wasn't a significant drop. Just a wave to get Jim up on the board and steer it in while the water pushed him in. It broke into the foam, pushing the board after Jim got up. Addy stayed down while they both surfed the wave in together.

I clapped and cheered from the shore, proud that Addy didn't let my cheering them on distract her. She was in her own world, surfing with Jim. It was so damn beautiful. They'd survived. Addy was one with the board, hunched on her knees, and I could tell Jim had to have researched this shit to make sure he got Addy out surfing.

"Damn it! I didn't even record this."

"Got it for ya," Ash said. "Look at the guys," she laughed, holding her phone up and getting this on video.

"This is the sweetest thing in the world," I said, watching Jake, Alex, and Collin, diving off their boards and screwing off with the small waves.

"You did it!" I held my hands up and did a little happy dance for Addy while Jim jumped off the board and ruffled her hair.

"Again?" He held his hand out for permission.

I gave him the thumbs up. They had this. Addy was responsible, and following the rules, so I could trust this now. Jesus Christ.

The four guys came in, telling Addy's fish stories for her. My child was stealing everyone's hearts today. I watched in humor as Jim and Addy took the waves as best buddies would.

It went on like this for about twenty minutes until I heard a commotion coming from behind.

"Avery!" I heard Derek's voice growl.

"What the hell?" I said, my heart beating so fast I thought I might pass out. "Derek?" I asked, seeing him storm onto the beach like a lunatic. "How the fuck did you know where to find me?"

"Cell phone tracker, bitch. Addy has the phone I bought her. I don't need to wonder where my daughter is when she's out with you."

"Hey," I heard Jake say, "why don't you take your shit back home, man?" He walked in front of me, guarding me against Derek.

My first instinct was to fight Derek angrily, but the humiliation of him coming here like this—in front of Jim and his friends and family —made me freeze up. I couldn't fucking believe he'd planted a phone in Addy's backpack to track us down. I wanted to scream at him and freak the fuck out, but I crumbled. Addy was going to see all of this too. My full-blown dysfunctional life was on blast, and nothing good was going to come from what was about to happen.

"Get the fuck out of my way," Derek said. "Why is that mother fucker in the water with my daughter? Fuck you, Avery!"

"You're high," I heard Collin say. I helplessly sank into my chair as Jim came to shore right when hell was beginning to break loose.

The next thing I knew, the guys were holding off my high as could be, train-wreck of an ex while the lifeguards and the beach patrol couldn't get here fast enough.

"Fuck you!" Derek said as I held Addy, and tears streamed down my face. "Addy, you're fucking coming with me. Right now!" he barked, then looked at Jim.

I held my hands over Addy's, not able to fucking think while I watched this disaster take place in front of God and everybody. I prayed that the beach patrol or the goddamn lifeguards would just haul his ass away. I held Addy tightly, and for the first time in my life, I sobbed while holding my daughter. Oh my God, I couldn't pull it together if I tried.

Derek was a fucking nightmare who would never leave us alone. Never. He wasn't a human being. He was a lunatic whose brain was fueled by drugs, and he was screaming and trying to engage Jim in a fight—and all while other families and their kids watched with fear for what might happen next.

I couldn't hide any of it from Addison. Me breaking down, her dad acting like a crazed maniac, I couldn't hide any of it. It didn't take but a few seconds for Addy to start crying.

"Come here, baby," I said, and then I pulled her in and held my little girl as tightly as I could, trying to shield her from watching the disaster unfold.

CHAPTER THIRTY-FOUR

Jim

I couldn't get Addy and me out of the water fast enough when I saw the commotion on the shore. I couldn't fucking believe that Derek had found Avery, at the beach of all places. Addy had buried her face in my neck after she screamed, watching her dad acting like a messed-up madman.

Addison ran to her mom for protection after I'd set her down on the sand. There was no time to console either one of them, just a mutual nod from Ash to let me know she'd care for the two while I tried to shut down this situation that was beginning to draw a crowd.

"Fuck you," Derek said after Collin and Alex darted off to grab the beach patrol before this lunatic hurt himself or someone else. "Fucking my girl, trying to kill my fucking kid," he spat while I stepped over to him.

"You need to calm down," I said, in the firmest voice I could, given how pissed I was. I looked at Jake. "Don't touch him." I knew this loser was looking for a fight, and what better place than in front of people with all their cell phones, capturing the entire thing?

"Just try to fucking touch me," Derek challenged, and then the dip shit stepped forward and took a swing at where I stood.

I reflexively blocked it with my elbow, hearing the crack when Derek's fist made contact. The prick dropped while the fucking audience instinctively gasped. I leaned over and extended my hand. "Get the hell up," I said in a growl.

"You broke my hand, asshole."

"*You* broke your own hand on his elbow," Jake said with restraint. I could tell my brother was holding back like never before. We both knew the consequences of reacting to a dirtbag like Derek.

AFTER LAW ENFORCEMENT SHOWED UP, beach patrol took reports, two lifeguards on quads and one lifeguard truck rolled up, and then the show was over, for now. That little mother fucker was heading to jail in the back of the patrol car, and I had no idea how Avery and Addy were doing.

"How the fuck did that son of a bitch find us here?" I barked to Jake in a low voice, leaving the scene after pressing charges and giving my statement.

I left Jake and knelt in front of where Avery was sobbing in her hands. "Hey, sweetheart," I said softly, Addison leaving Ash's arms and clinging onto me. "Look at me, Avery."

Her eyes were swollen from crying. The fucker finally broke her into a position where she wasn't fighting back. I even had his daughter clinging onto me for security.

"Let's get you two out of here," I said. "They cleared the area. Give me the keys to your car."

Avery sniffed. "I'm so sorry." She looked at me, then reached for Addison. "Baby, I'm so sorry you saw that."

"Mommy, Daddy scared me."

"I know, honey," she said, holding her tight.

While Avery consoled Addison, I worked to get us the hell out of here.

"Jake, I need someone to drive my Bronco back to my place," I said. "Can you guys get the boards and all of this packed up? We'll just meet up there."

"I've got the Bronco," Collin said. "I rode here with Jake and Ash this morning." He glanced around, and everyone was more solemn with the fact that my two girls were fucking traumatized by a selfish and high as fuck bastard who'd tracked them down.

"We'll see you at the house."

"Beach house?" Alex said.

"Right." I nodded.

I was direct, and my only focus was on Avery and Addy. I peeled off my wetsuit while Avery peeled Addy out of hers and put on her cover-up. I hoisted Addison into my arms, and while Jake handed me my wallet, Ash gave Avery her bag.

"We've got this." Ash smiled. "It's going to be okay."

I nodded and smiled at my sister and then took Avery's hand in my free one. Once we were in the car, I tried to tease Addy while locking her into her car seat, but it was painfully obvious that she was not in the mood for fun and games. She was rattled. I couldn't believe anyone could do that to their child, especially this sweet little girl.

I set my phone to connect to Avery's car, knowing shit could go any direction once I got moving down the highway.

"I'm scared of vacation," Addy said as I saw the tears streaming down Avery's cheeks again.

I reached for Avery's hand while exiting the parking lot. "It's over now, sweetheart. We're going to my house on the beach now, just as we planned," I said, seeing tears welling up in her frightened eyes.

"No," Addy said in a whimper, her eyes spilling out tears as she covered her tiny face. "I don't want the beach."

"Okay," I rubbed Avery's arm. I needed her with me right now. I didn't want either of them to be alone. "Why don't we—"

"Just take us home," Avery said, trying to breathe it out.

"Why don't I take you to my place in the Hills instead? It seemed to help you the last time?"

"That's fine," she said.

I glanced back, and Addy was staring blankly out of the window, sniveling. I had no idea how to console her. All I wanted was to find that mother fucker and beat the shit out of him for hurting these two sweet girls. The two most important people in my fucking life.

I called out for my phone to dial Jacob.

"Jake," I said when he answered, "change of plans. We're heading to my place in the Hills." I looked at Avery. "You guys can do whatever."

"It's okay if they come. I'd actually like the company," Avery managed to my surprise.

"All right. Let everyone know we're meeting up at my place. Swing through a drive-through and load up on burgers and shakes," I said, going for what I believed was comfort food.

"You're asking a cardiovascular doctor to—"

"Jacob, please," I cut him off. "You know what I'm asking you to do. Grab the happy meals too. Ash?" I said, knowing I was in earshot of her.

"Yeah, Jim," she said. "We're switching out cars at the house, and we'll handle the food."

"Thanks."

After the call ended and we were cruising through my shortcut from Malibu up through to the Hills, I saw that Addy was sound asleep, and Avery's head was resting against the headrest.

"I went ahead and pressed charges," I said in a soft voice. "You won't be seeing him for a while after he violated the terms of his probation," I said, reaching for her hand as her leg bounced nervously where she sat.

"You didn't need to do that," she said solemnly.

What the fuck? The hell I didn't, I thought. Her response hit me sideways, but I wasn't willing to argue back at this point. That asshole needed to be behind bars or in a rehab center before ever being in the presence of the child again after his behavior today.

"You sure you're okay with everyone at the house? It can be just us three," I said, feeling her turn her hand up to intertwine her fingers with mine.

"I'm fine with it." She shook her head. "Good God. What must they think of your girlfriend now?" She laughed in disgust.

"What I think." I smiled, glancing to my left, changing lanes and getting the horsepower out of this car that I fucking needed right now.

"And what do you think?" Her humor was nonexistent and for a good reason.

"The guys and I would love to kick his ass," I kept my voice low, so as not to wake Addison, who slept with a frown on her face. "Simple as that."

"It's my fault." Avery shook her head. "I swear, fuck," she said, looking out her window.

"What's your fault? You didn't tell him where you were going, did you?" I asked, partially wondering since she didn't seem happy that I'd pressed charges against the fucker.

"Fuck no," she said numbly. "Never. He…" Her voice cracked, and I brought the back of her hand that I held to my lips.

"How did he know where to find you?"

"He put a new phone with a tracker on it in Addy's backpack. All I did was take out pup, her stuffed animal, last night. I guess I should've gone through the thing."

"Jesus," I said, gripping her hand tighter. "This is not your fault. That guy has serious issues. There's no way anyone would anticipate a fucked-up tactic like that." I glanced over at her tears, "Hey, it's over. He's back where he needs to be. We were all pretty much ready to pack it up anyway. Take a breath, sweetheart. We'll get home, and Jake and Ash will bring in the food to put a smile back on my woman's face."

"Sounds good." She sighed.

"So, no running to the cemetery then?" I teased, thanking God that she was settled down and out of that same zone she was in the night we left Addy when Derek had pulled his shit in front of me.

"I can't believe Addy saw all of that. She's never seen him pull something like this. I've always sheltered her from it."

"We'll make sure she's okay. If we're all swimming in the pool with her, we'll make it fun tonight."

WE ROLLED into the place before anyone else. Addy was still sound asleep, and unfortunately, I had no room set up for her in this damn house. I had Avery follow me to one of the rooms on the first floor, Addy drooling adorably with creases in her cheeks from sleeping so hard on the ride up to the house.

"Do you think she'll be okay in here?" I asked. "I have the glass doors on all floors open for whenever she wakes up. That way, we'll be able to hear her."

"She's fine," Avery said, brushing the hair from Addy's forehead and offering her a small and raggedy, gray stuffed animal.

Must be pup, I thought with a smile of adoration.

I heard Jake come in and left Addy and Avery in the bottom room. It was the one closest to the open glass door, where I'd had the security company set the motion sensors for anything that would walk out to the pool area.

"Pool's closed? You're such a fucking asshole sometimes." My brother nudged me and grinned, testing the waters in his own way. "How are the girls?" he asked as I grabbed bags of food from Ash.

"What the hell, man?" I shook my head while Ash laughed along with me. "Did you buy out the entire restaurant?"

"Jake acts like I've never asked for a McDonald's cheeseburger before," Ash said with a wink to her husband.

"No tomatoes, I know." He smirked at her.

"Oh my God," I heard Avery say, her voice light with humor. "First of all, McDonald's doesn't put tomatoes on their cheeseburgers unless you ask for them, and second, what army are we feeding with all this food?"

Ash shook her head. "I tried to order, but Jake wanted to prove he was a fast-food champion or something. Poor girl taking his order probably quit her job tonight after that."

I looked at Ash's humored expression as she leaned into Avery at her side and hugged her. "You wear the pants in that relationship," I teased. "How the hell did you allow this dip shit to ruin some girl's day?"

"She was laughing too hard." Jake arched an eyebrow. "I tried to get assistance, but some gorgeous brunette in my car was laughing so damn hard she couldn't help, which made it all worse."

Avery started laughing as we set all the food on my counters.

"How unacceptable," Ash said, countering Jake, going to my fridge and pulling out a beer for himself, me, and Avery.

Jake grabbed the ginger ale I had on hand for whenever the two showed up, and he handed it to Ash while Avery came to my side. I could feel all her energy had been drained, so I held her close after twisting the cap off her beer and handing it to her.

Jake took a sip of his beer. "The experience could have been so enticing, yet here we are." He held out his hands to what easily looked like twenty fucking bags of food. "The poor girl is most likely still frazzled."

I looked at Avery's gleaming eyes as we watched Jake and Ash play out their excuses for ordering everything on the menu. "Well, I can say this: my little girl is going to wake up and think she's in heaven when she sees all of these happy meals."

"Thank God." Jake smiled at Avery. "I ordered different types of each meal to make sure she got the toy she wanted."

I almost choked on the drink of beer I had just taken. "Jacob Allan Mitchell, fuck me to hell."

Jake's eyes zeroed in on me. "James Howard Mitchell, you will go to hell if you ever drop my middle name in conversation again. Who the hell are you, *Dad?*"

"I tried to tell him that there were only three toys and that you could actually request them." Ash laughed again.

"Did you, now?" Jake walked over to Ash. "The only way I'm going to stop this laughing of yours is by kissing your little lips."

"You're a heart surgeon, right?" Avery said, amused by their interaction.

Ash lost it again, and Jake couldn't answer before Collin and Alex walked in.

"What in God's name?" Collin said, eying my kitchen island that was lined with bags of food. "So the cardiologist wants to kill all of us tonight, then? Trying to experiment on us?"

"I was thinking the same. You missed his lame-ass excuses for ordering all this shit," I said.

"Guess so." Alex pulled a burger out of the bag and started in. "I'm not complaining. I'm starving."

I was watching Avery more than anything as Collin started going through all the bags. "Avery, what's on the menu tonight? In Palm Springs, it was nearly everything at the table." He glanced back and smiled. "Seems like Jake caught on when I told him Jim's girl could throw it down better than he does."

Avery shook her head and stepped forward. "I'm glad my appetite can enhance conversations," she said, pulling out a burger.

"Hey," Collin said, leaning back against the counter, "when your best friend is a doctor, and all you do is share reports of that?"

"All fucking night," Jake said, bringing his arm around Ash. "Then we talk about crazy shit like my brother dating a woman who could eat an entire buffalo."

"Buffalo? Jesus Christ." I laughed. "Avery and I are heading up to the top. Addy is asleep. Grab your dinner—compliments of Jake—and we'll hang up there and let Addison sleep."

"The outdoor fridge stocked up there, brother?" Collin asked.

"Yep," I said as Avery moved toward Ash, who asked how she and Addy were doing. "Let's head up. I have the motion alarms on to the pool in case Addison wakes while we're up there."

"Nice. Sound the fucking sirens when the poor kid wakes up in some strange place," Alex said, trailing everyone with me.

"Avery," I said before we headed up. "Do you want to change?"

Even I wanted to get the fucking salt off me.

Avery, looking gorgeous in her crochet, cover-up dress, stopped and laughed, "Yeah, actually I do."

"Go get cleaned up. Jake and I jumped in a quick shower before heading up. It helped give us both a second wind," Ash said. "We'll watch out for Addy. Take your time."

I followed Avery into the bathroom and turned on the water. "You don't mind if I join you, do you?"

"If you didn't, I would think you were kicking my ass to the curb after everything."

"That shit storm wasn't your fault. You need to get that out of your head," I said, helping her out of her swimsuit. "I imagined us seeing each other in a position like this." I ran my hand over her ass after she turned and pulled the Velcro open on my board shorts and dropped them.

"Like what?" she taunted, and my Avery was back without reservation.

"Well, for starters, I wouldn't have sand in my ass. Let's get in the shower." I kissed her lips gently, "Allow me to clean this salt and sand off, and then, I'll be washing you up."

Avery was in before me and turned back to me with a few pumps of my cleanser. "How about I help get the sand out?"

I jumped when her hands moved under my balls and up my ass. I reached for the wall. "I have to admit," I cringed, "there is nothing sexual about this for me." I bit my bottom lip while Avery laughed.

"How so?" she asked, kissing my side.

"It feels like you're rubbing sandpaper on my balls and up my crack." I laughed when her eyes met mine.

Avery's head fell back in laughter. "Oh shit," she said, her hands wrapping around my waist. "I'm so sorry. You should have rinsed off first."

I chuckled and walked over to the area where I could get this damn sand off my body and appreciate my woman's hands all over me. I'd waited all fucking week for her, to touch her, to see her eyes in euphoria—I wasn't sure that would happen in this shower with everyone here and my concern about Addy waking up in a strange house. The door was locked, of course, and once again, I was following Avery's lead, but it still had me a little unsettled.

The shower wouldn't be about me. It would be about bringing Avery whatever she wanted—anything—that's all I wanted, to see Avery's eyes, glistening while she climaxed. Her hands, gripping my hair and begging me for whatever she wanted. It's all I'd longed for all damn week. Maybe this would be an excellent start for removing Derek's bullshit from our day. Hopefully, anyway. I could tell this shit was still sitting with her, and I wanted nothing more than to take it all away.

CHAPTER THIRTY-FIVE

Avery

*A*ddy was still sound asleep when Jim and I got out of the shower that had lasted for too long. This man had done everything right from the start of the day up until now. That shower was exactly what I'd been longing for since he and I were in the elevator.

The water rained down on both of us, and it fueled me to beg him for more than what he'd already offered. His lust and desperation drove him to pick me up and place my back against the steamy shower walls. His face was perfect as the shower ran over both of us like rain, and his eyes were swirling with more desire than I'd ever seen from him. Feeling his large cock pry into my sex threw my heart out of rhythm, and then he was thrusting, wild and deep. My forearms rested on his shoulders while my forehead leaned against his, his teeth softly nipping against my cheek.

That's when this miracle of me coming without any assistance from my clit rushed in fast, making the sensation of my orgasm feel like I'd warmed up for this raging ball of energy that was barreling down and exploding around the large cock that filled me up. I called out his name as the orgasm pressed on. My head was against the shower as Jim kept pumping harder and harder. Jim kissed my neck, and then I felt goosebumps cover his shoulders as he grunted with his release that must have felt as intense as mine.

That was confirmed after we were dressed in lounge clothes, and his lips captured mine one more time before leaving the room. I was fully satiated and probably should've started using this with Jim for my new way of getting my tightened nerves unwound.

I tried not to beat myself up for taking this time to enjoy myself when I knew Addy could wake up, but Ash had promised to keep watch and make sure Addy was okay while I was in the shower. I knew I needed to relax and stop feeling guilty at every turn when it came to Addy also. I had to start focusing on making sure I was mentally healthy and okay if I wanted Addy to follow in suit.

I sank against Jim's side as we all sat around the gas-lit fire pit on Jim's comfortable outdoor couches. I found myself lost in the view. This was glorious, and at this rate, Addison was well on her way to sleeping through the night.

"She's lost in the view," I heard a humored voice say.

I snapped back to see Jake with Ash on the sofa to mine and Jim's right. Jake sat in conversation with Collin, who sat across from Jim and me, and both of them fiddled with their beer bottles, having some conversation about their hospital. Alex had his feet kicked up on the sofa to my left, taking a drink of his beer, and I was brought back to reality and the fact that I'd been zoned out.

"I'm sorry. This day has seriously kicked my ass," I said as Jim rubbed my arm.

"Nothing to apologize for, gorgeous," Jim said, sipping his beer.

"You want another?" Alex nodded toward my warm, half-drunk beer bottle.

"I'm good. I probably shouldn't have had this after the bullshit with Derek today," I said, catching everyone's attention. "I'm so sorry that asshole showed up like that. So humiliating. I don't even know what to say."

Collin grinned from across me, taking a drink. "If you want to say anything at all, say that we can go kick his ass if he ever gets out of jail and fucks with you or your daughter like that again."

"Funny," I said.

"This is the shit you have to put up with?" Jake asked sympathetically.

"It's a nightmare, to say the least," I said, looking at Jim's somewhat peaceful expression.

"He's a fucking roach who never goes the hell away or leaves Avery alone. Always with the aggression and harassment," Jim added. "He was locked up last week, and then today, we're greeted with his high on life personality at the beach. I guess some people don't know when to quit."

"No shit," I said. "It's like the bastard has a get out of jail free card. He tracked us down by slipping a phone in Addy's backpack. Who does that?"

"Forgive me if I'm overstepping here," Collin interjected. "How in the hell do you not have a restraining order against his ass by now?"

"Long story." I shrugged. "I try to fight my hardest for Addy, but I always seem to lose that battle. I know it would be the same in court. I just do my best to keep Addy protected from it all," I said and felt Jim's posture stiffen as he sat up some.

I know Jim wanted me to fight Derek in court. Now that he was growing attached to Addy, I had a feeling that he and I were going to butt heads on this topic. Unfortunately, I wasn't strolling around with the cleanest of records. Derek knew he had shit on me, and that's why he always threw it in my face. It was a battle I was scared as fuck to fight.

"How do you think Addy will do?" Ash asked. "Has she ever seen him act out like he did today?"

"Never," I said, feeling a knot form in the pit of my stomach. "I keep it all from her. I have no idea what she'll be like when she wakes up. For her to beg to leave her vacation—" I felt tears again, knowing my baby girl had been fucking traumatized by her father. "It will sit with her."

"Well." Ash smiled at me as Jim leaned forward and rested his elbows on his knees, looking at his sister-in-law. "She is young, but she's got strength in her spirit—strength like her mom. Don't be hard on yourself. If I can suggest anything, it would be for you to let her talk about it and be honest with her if she has questions. Children don't need the gory details, especially children her age, but it's also not your responsibility to cover for him. You can be honest with her without laying down all of his misdeeds."

Ash was onto something. I'd always made excuses for Derek for the sake of making Addy think everything was okay. "You might be right about that. She saw the real side of her dad today. The side we hide from her. Maybe she needs to know he's sick."

Jim's eyes were on me now. What the fuck was going through his mind?

"That's a good starting point," Jim finally said in a softer tone than I would've expected from his expression.

"Then get that guy some help," Alex said. "If you're not going to fight for custody for whatever reasons, do some sort of intervention or something like that."

Jake laughed. "I'll toast to that!" He raised his beer as Collin clinked his bottle against it with a laugh.

"Who is going to sit around the living room and guilt-trip that little shit? You?" Alex rolled his eyes.

Jake chuckled. "I'll come up with some sad fucking story about how he and I could have been such great friends."

"The master manipulator taking out an addict manipulator?" Alex laughed.

"That would turn into a bad Jerry Springer episode like what happened today at the beach," I said, feeling myself getting pissed all over again.

"Speaking of disgruntled people," Jim said, leaning back. "I had a nurse file a complaint against your ass."

I looked at the two doctors whose faces grew serious pretty quickly.

"Who now?" Jake asked and took a large gulp of his beer. "I'm getting so fucking sick and tired of this shit."

"It's against Collin," Jim said. "Please, God, tell me you're not fucking around in that damn hospital."

"What? That shit is so far in the past—like internship days. Who the fuck had something to say about me? Everyone knows I'm the cool one. When did this shit happen?"

"Eight in the evening, I got the email. Cindy Blackwell feels as though your language is uncouth and bedside manner entirely irresponsible."

"Cindy Blackwell?" Jake laughed. "Sweet Jesus, that woman will be the death of you. She's as bad as that old bat, Nurse Jackie. Get her off his ward, Jim. I've run into her during my rounds a few times. She's fucking toxic, man."

"She sits with nurses and makes up stories and gossip. Do you know what the bottom line is, Jim? She despises how young I am. That's it. She doesn't give a fuck about my success rates, or the fact that I'm a goddamn prodigy. She can say whatever she wants, but I'm fucking fantastic at what I do, despite people like her who are continually finding something negative to say. You don't get to fuck around and make it to where I am, being able to do what I can. Negative-ass hag. She acts like she's a fucking prison warden. I'm sick of this shit."

Holy shit. This just escalated. Collin had always seemed so relaxed, but it was apparent that this woman had struck a chord with him.

"Chill out." Alex laughed. "She's already being dealt with."

Collin picked up a closed beer and tossed it to Jim. "You're an asshole. You know that?"

"Making us sweat for your amusement." Jake shook his head. "You do realize we run on zero sleep, right?"

Jim chuckled. "I couldn't resist. You two get worked up so easily. It's highly enjoyable to watch."

"You can say that again," Alex said.

Ash and I sat and watched the men bantering with smiles on our faces. These guys had such good energy. We all sat around until about eleven, and when it was time for everyone to leave, Jim took the extra bags of too much food and forced everyone out of the door with them.

We stood and held each other in silence after the house grew quiet before I checked on Addy. She stirred, and then her head popped up. She instantly started crying, and I just held her.

"Addy, baby," I said softly. "We're at Jim's house high up in the hills. He has lots of happy meals for you to choose from."

Addy started to wake up more and then looked at me. "Daddy hurt Jim."

"Daddy hurt himself today." I pulled back. "Addy, look at me," I said, her face somber. "Were you scared today?"

"Yes," she said, rubbing her eyes. "Daddy was so mad."

"I know. Daddy was mad because I have a crush on Jim."

Addy looked over my shoulder and then at me. "But why?"

"It's confusing, isn't it?"

"Yes," she said.

"Daddy will be going away for a while. I think he needs some help to be a happy daddy, don't you?"

"Yes."

"Then we will make sure he gets happy and know he is at a place that might make him learn that he did a bad thing today," I said, hoping I was saying the right things and not making anything worse.

"Yes. Papa will be mad."

"Papa will be mad," I agreed.

"I'm hungry."

JIM SEEMED satisfied now that Addison was eating and content. I had no idea if my conversation with her helped or not. Hopefully, it worked to give her mind a little peace.

We all were invited into Jim's oversized bed after Addy and Jim reunited and told their fun stories from surfing together. A scene I would never let leave my mind. A man whose heart was where a dad's heart should be. It was heavenly to see, and my heart swelled with love for him.

Jim lay next to me, and we both smiled over at Addy, who lay on the other side of me, watching the flatscreen on the wall in his room. I was growing tired, and the shows Jim bought for Addy to live stream would keep her up until tomorrow if we didn't turn them off.

"Addy, let's get under the covers and try to sleep. We'll play in the pool tomorrow."

"I'll even have some more toys brought in for you," Jim said.

"Okay," she said, and then the lights dimmed.

As I tried to doze off, Addy started getting restless.

"Addy," I said, "try to sleep."

Bad idea, keeping her knocked out since five and expecting her to go back to sleep in a new place.

"I'm trying hard, Mommy."

"Do you need to sleep in your own bed?" I asked, knowing Addy wasn't used to sharing a bed, and this whole situation could be keeping her awake.

"I'm a little scared," she said meekly.

"I'm not turning those shows back on," I said.

"Jim." Addy sat up and turned to him. "Can you read me a story like my papa does?"

Whoa! This is new. No one took the place of her papa, reading her stories before bed.

Jim smiled at her. "I'm afraid I don't have any books with me unless you brought some?"

"Use your 'magination." She chuckled. "Like in the car. You told me about the little girl who was tough on the farm, remember, silly?"

"Of course. All right," Jim said, looking at me for help.

I lay flat on my back, my head propped up by pillows, shrugged, and smiled. *You're on your own,* I mouthed to him as Addy laid down again. Jim propped himself up on his elbow, looking at Addy on the other side of me as she waited eagerly for his story.

"So, that little youngster," Jim smiled at Addy, who started giggling, "she decided to take that nice farmer and his wife up on their offer."

"Those silly boys, right? She's gonna win," Addy said.

God only knew what story Jim was telling, but she was on the same page as he was, so I wouldn't dare interrupt to ask questions. I was intrigued by their interaction. Jim was positively a different person at this moment. He sat up, telling her the story, and she looked at him as if I didn't even exist between them. It was like they were instantly in their own world.

"Well, she can't just go in and win. She's got to think really smart," he said. "Those boys, you see, they love poking fun at—" he stopped, looking thoughtfully at Addy. "What was her name again?"

"It's your story, you know."

"Right, I most certainly do. Little Sally. She was oh so sick and tired of the boys poking fun at her. So, instead of poking fun back at them, she decided she would be smart when they all helped Mr. Jones, the farmer. Mrs. Jones, however, promised delicious muffins for all of the children."

"Oh no." Addy ducked and hung onto the last word. "Sally's going to want to eat the muffins now!"

"She sure does want a muffin," Jim played back. "But she needs to work hard for that muffin, and she knows it. She can't be tempted or the little boys that like to poke fun," Jim arched his eyebrow at Addy, "they'll plant the seeds in their rows, and little Sally won't plant anything at all."

"No. Sally has to work. She's planting seeds, Jim. She is, right?"

"Of course, she is." Jim grew serious. "Now, she plugged her nose so she couldn't smell those delicious muffins coming from Mrs. Jones's kitchen. I think Mrs. Jones was sneaky, trying to see who would leave the rows they promised to plant to come for her muffins."

"Then, they wouldn't work," Addy said.

"Maybe, maybe not?" Jim said. "Sally focused on her row, one long line in a mound to where she could take her little hand to shovel and scoop her seeds in. She looked over at those boys, and they were a little way ahead of her."

"It's because she smelled those darn muffins," Addy said.

"That's right, but," Jim eyed her, "she was determined to plant her seeds and think of nothing but her reward at the end. So, she planted three seeds in a hole at a time, just like Mr. Jones had instructed. In fact, she was actually having some fun now. She was not thinking about anything except what it would be like when her seeds grew into sprouts, and that special day Mr. Jones had promised in the beginning when she could come back and help him pick the corn that she helped grow."

"And eat it!"

"And eat it." Jim smirked at me as I watched them with adoration. "Anyway," he grew serious again, "while she was focused, suddenly, her piggy tail was pulled," he said, reaching over me and pulling on one of Addy's piggy tails that I'd put in her hair after her bath.

Addy giggled and hid her hair from his hand. "Those rotten boys did that," she said in a low voice to match Jim's.

"Well, one surely did, and Sally stood up, forgetting about planting seeds when she got upset that he'd pulled her hair. 'Don't do that, Jake!' she said to the boy."

"Jake?" Addy asked. "Like your brother? That Jake?"

Jim chuckled. "Just like him. Being a bit ornery, but always having fun. Now, then, Jake took a bite of his delicious muffin, and instead of wanting the muffin, Sally looked over at his row. He didn't finish planting. 'You are supposed to finish first, mister,' she said to him. Jake looked at Sally and said, 'I'm done. I have my muffin. I'm going home.'"

"Well, that's not fair."

"Not fair to Mr. Jones, nope," Jim said. "So, now Sally ignored that Jake was going home and even that he'd pulled on her piggy tail. Instead, she worked harder and even faster now."

"Oh, wow," Addy said.

"When suddenly," Jim's eyes opened wide, "she was pushed down in the dirt."

"No, no, no! Not fair, Jim," Addy said, ordering Jim in the right direction of the story.

"Well, it didn't hurt Sally. It was just a little nudge, is all," he said. "So, she looked over, and there was silly old Collin. He was smiling and eating a muffin."

"Ugh, Collin!" Addy said with exasperation. "Collin, like our surfing friend, right?"

"Pretty close," Jim laughed, his eyes mischievous. "So, Sally looked at Collin's row. 'You didn't finish your work,' she said. 'You can't eat that.'" Jim mimicked the cutest voice for Sally. "'Oh, Sally, we want to play. Come play with us.'"

"She has to work." Addy was catching on to Jim's story, and if this interaction could've filled my heart with any more joy, it would've burst wide open.

"That's right. So, Sally got up, brushed off her little overalls, and let Collin run off with Jake to go and play. Now, she was working really hard, was almost done, and then there was Alex."

"Oh, no, Jim. Not Alex from the surfing too. He's so nice."

"Yeah, he's nice, but that didn't stop him from eating a muffin before he was finished working. He decided to eat that muffin while Sally ignored him. Then Sally finally finished, and when she got up, Alex laughed that she was last, and he followed her into the house when she went to get her muffin. When she walked in, she looked all around, but there were no muffins anywhere to be found."

"What?" Addy gasped.

"Yep, you heard me right," Jim sighed. "It felt like all her hard work —no cheating like those rascals had—had got her nothing. No food. Nothing. Not that warm, buttery muffin she'd been smelling, and her stomach wanted so badly now."

"This is such a sad story, Jim."

"It's not over yet. Do you think Sally would give up so easily?" Jim asked.

"No." Addy became more intrigued.

"That's right. Sally kept looking, and then Mrs. Jones walked out with a basket filled—almost overflowing—with muffins. All kinds of different flavors too."

"Oh, wow," Addy said.

"Then Mrs. Jones said, 'Thank you, little Miss Sally. You worked hard to help Mr. Jones and me today. You didn't give up even when the sun was warm, and the muffins smelled yummy. This is for you to take home to eat for you and your family,'" Jim said in a funny, old woman's voice.

"What did Alex say? He was there too," Addy reminded him, her eyelids getting heavy as she struggled to stay with the story.

"Alex was not happy that he learned a tough lesson that day. He knew that he didn't work as hard as Sally had, and even though Alex got a muffin, he wasn't rewarded for his full day's work. So, he got to watch Sally achieve a goal and go home happy with a full basket of food. Sally was so happy when she figured out that she may have been a bit slow, but she never gave up. She got her piggy tail pulled, and she'd gotten pushed down, and, of course, she had little Alex, laughing at her and watching to see how it would all end for her, but both of those little ones learned their lessons that day. Work hard, get up, and keep going, no matter what happens, and there will be a reward at the end."

Before Jim had reached the end of his thought, Addy was breathing heavily. I made sure the blankets were tucked around her securely, and then I lay on my back and brought my hand to Jim's cheek.

"I think she crashed once she knew little Sally was taking home the bacon in your life-lesson story for children," I whispered.

Jim leaned over and kissed my lips. "Muffins," he corrected me. "And, yes, all she needed was a little happily ever after with food, of course. Now, she's out like a light."

"This story will stick with her, you know. So, Jake, Alex, and Collin will love you for making them the rascals in your silly story."

Jim laughed and ran his hand over my hair. "Will she sleep well in here tonight? I'd hate to move her."

"I think she might have the best sleep in her life," I said. "You really are the best man. I love you and love that you, obviously, aren't a rascal like the others, eh?"

Jim smirked. "I never made it into the story. I was back at home working with the mules."

I covered my laugh. "You're such a nut." I rubbed his chest, "I love this. I love us."

"Me too, more than you know," he said.

"I am so tired."

"Do I need to tell you a story too?" He chuckled, and I could see his eyes were tired.

"You just did. The happily ever after part with food is all I needed to hear."

Jim snuggled around me, and as we fell asleep, I couldn't stop thanking God that Addy and I had found someone so remarkable.

CHAPTER THIRTY-SIX

Avery

I woke up to an empty bed, wondering where Addy and Jim were. I was sure that if Addy'd had a rough morning, still thinking about her dad, then Jim would have woken me up. Addy slept soundly last night, and even though I should have been knocked the hell out, I slept with one eye open, my mind still trying to settle down.

I heard giggling coming from downstairs, so I got up, pulled down my tank, and readjusted my comfy shorts. I walked out onto Jim's luxurious balcony and looked down at the pool. It was more like a fucking patio out here than a balcony. It was arranged with large pots with palms in them, another fire pit, expensive outdoor furniture, and beautiful rugs to tie it all together. This view went on for eternity, and it was magnificent. I redirected my attention when I heard Addy squeal, but I saw no waves in the infinity pool below.

Where the hell are they? What time is it? I thought, happy and fulfilled with this gorgeous new day. I was leaving the garbage of yesterday's hell in the past and not letting it ruin this.

I walked downstairs and into the kitchen to see Addy, sitting on the counter and stirring what looked to be green pancake mix while Jim was cooking at her side.

"Mommy!" Addy wiggled her legs. "We making green eggs, look!"

"Green eggs and ham, eh?" I laughed and kissed her forehead before I wrapped my arms around Jim as he intently worked his stovetop like a master of culinary. "Good morning, handsome."

He leaned his head over, and I gave him a peck on his cheek.

"Ew, mom, that's gross." She giggled, stirring her green scrambled eggs. "Green eggs and ham!" she teased at Jim.

"I will not eat them, Jim I am!" he said with a laugh.

"Jim said this is so gross," she said in her adorable little Shirley Temple voice. "You will eat them. Yes, you will." She was so animated and happy that I couldn't help but smile.

"The coffee's fresh, Av," he said, pointing tongs in the direction of his coffee mugs and French press.

I poured myself a cup and leaned against the counter, watching the two. "I have to say, I like it when you call me that."

Jim smirked. "I like it when you call me Jim," he said with a sexy wink.

"Yes. His name is Jim now, Mom," Addy confirmed.

"Got it. And Jim I am is not eating his own food?"

"The only green things Jim eats are vegetables," he said, sliding the ham off the griddle and onto a plate.

"Now, *that's* gross," Addy said.

"That's healthy, little missy," Jim teased, taking the bowl of scrambled green eggs from her. "Even my doctor says so."

"Doctors, ugh." Addy dramatically sighed as she watched Jim cooking her eggs.

"Oh," I said, sipping more coffee. "You don't like doctors?"

"They boring, Momma," Addy answered me.

Jim smirked. "You know my brother is a doctor, and my friend is one too."

"No way, mister," she said in a playful voice.

"Yes way," he said, looking at her. "And Jake and Collin might cry when they find out that you think they are boring."

"Oh." Addy cringed, crinkling her nose. "They're my friends," she said thoughtfully.

"They are fun," I added with a smile. "And they are doctors. They save lives, Addy."

"Okay." She sighed. "But I'm not eating veggies. I don't care how much they love me," she said, her eyebrows raised to emphasize how serious she was about the subject.

"What if Collin and Jake say you should so you can grow big and strong?" I asked while Jim held back his laughter.

"And get big muscles like Jim's?" she asked.

Addy was stating the obvious. The guy was wearing a T-shirt, and the poor shirt sleeves struggled not to burst against his massive biceps. How much did this man workout, and how did he find the time? He might've had some good genetics, but to get this, he had to have been working overtime. At least that's what I guessed. Who was I kidding? I didn't give a shit how he got it. It was lovely to enjoy it.

"Yep," Jim said, spooning the green scrambled eggs onto a platter. "I have to eat my veggies, so," he turned to her and gripped her calf, to which she squealed, "I can get big strong legs," he poked her nose, "smell food better," and he squeezed her while pulling her off the counter, "and pick up little ones like you."

Addy ran over to me, and I hugged her while Jim went into his zone and started plating dishes. His consisted of ham and fruit, and after I gave him a nod of being okay to eat my green eggs, he served up mine and Addison's on his white, square plates.

"Jim, you have to try them. You have to try green eggs," Addison said, her little hands holding onto the counter, watching him.

He took all three plates, balancing one in the bend of his arm, "I will not eat them here," Jim said, setting my plate at the table, facing the view and pool, "I will not eat them there," he said, setting Addy's plate in front of her, "I simply will not eat them anywhere."

Jim sat as I poured Addy orange juice from the carafe on the table, and she took the glass. "You are ruining the story, Jim," she said, sipping her juice. "He does eat them in the end." She poked her fork into her fluffy green eggs. "And he loves them." She took a bite and then moaned and gave Jim a thumbs up and a brisk nod.

I looked at Jim as he teased Addy by forking a piece of cantaloupe and eating it.

"You don't like the eggs because they're green?" I asked.

He swallowed and shook his head. "Nope," he said in the playful tone he'd used with Addison.

"Jim's crazy. Green eggs are my new favorite," Addison said.

I took a bite. This guy could fucking cook. The eggs were seasoned deliciously, were fluffy, and could melt in your mouth.

"These are so good," I said. "Are you roleplaying Addy's favorite book or just suddenly not eating eggs?"

"I prefer them over-easy." He leaned over and snuck a kiss after I licked my lips. "With eggs, I'm quite picky."

"Well, the book shows green eggs, over easy, not scrambled, so you cheated." I smiled at him.

He smirked. "Shh."

THAT MORNING, we toured Jim's house, Addy leading the way as I explained that it was another cool vacation home that Jim had brought us to. She was attaching quickly and already not wanting to leave. She had no idea how badly I wanted to stay here forever too, but I kept reminding myself that Jim and I were taking it slow. At least I thought we were.

That afternoon, we played in the water, Jim throwing Addy over his shoulders and teaching her diving maneuvers. Now Addy's new favorite thing to do was dive in the water and swim to Jim's arms. Their laughs, the random kisses I got when they both approached me on my floating lounge—I could die right here and now, this was the most content I'd ever felt. It was as though we were the last three people on earth.

Addy chose to lay next to Jim in the shade when we got out of the water, and I laid down on a lounge chair watching as Addy fell fast asleep. Jim and Addy were stretched out on one of Jim's outdoor queen-sized chaise lounges. I was so relaxed that I closed my eyes and let the warm sun soothe my entire body and soul. This was paradise.

After about thirty minutes or so of closing my eyes, I reopened them to peek over at Jim. His eyes were hidden behind his dark aviator sunglasses, and his lips were twisted into a look of concentration while he stared intently at his laptop.

"Hard at work, I see?" I playfully nudged his side with my toe.

He grinned. "Just handling this last issue so I can enjoy my girls and turn it all off as I should have before," he said while I eased myself off my chair and squeezed onto his and Addy's lounge where he was propped up on huge pillows.

"This has been such an awesome afternoon," I said. "Makes the horrors of yesterday go away. How was Addy when she woke up this morning?" I asked as he shut the laptop and tossed it off like it didn't cost the four-thousand bucks that little logo made it worth. "I didn't even hear either of you get up." I smiled at him.

He brought his arm around me. "I sort of had to switch some gears —mental ones, with her," he said, kissing my temple, "but all is well now, I think."

"What do you mean? Why didn't you wake me up?" I asked.

"There was no reason to wake you up. I just—I don't know. Addy said she wished I was her real dad," he said carefully.

"Oh, shit," I said. "Well, I don't blame her. I actually like that she wants that."

"You have no idea how much I loved hearing it, but I also know what's going on with her real dad," he said. "It's got to be very confusing for her."

"I know." I sighed.

"What did you do with that phone he planted? Is it still with you?" he asked, his voice growing serious.

"I threw the damn thing in the first trash can I could find at the beach. That mother fucker can go find it on his own if he wants it back."

"Why won't you get full custody of her?" he asked. "I mean—"

"You know the reasons. I already told you." I didn't like where this conversation was headed, and yet, I felt like I knew this was coming.

"You did tell me your reasons, I just don't think I understand them," he said.

I pulled away from him, feeling defensive. "I'm not risking her being taken away. I won't do it."

Jim's lips tightened, and he shook his head. "How the hell did he even get out of jail?"

"His parents most likely gave in like the suckers they are, too worried about him being in jail, and bailed him out."

"Unreal." He shook his head in disgust. "And the phone? I'm fairly sure the idiot's credit is shot."

"His parents probably got it for Addy. They worry."

"Come on, Avery." He leaned up. "This is not fucking healthy for you."

"My daughter being as happy as I can make her is what's healthy for me." I was starting to reel. Why did this have to come up now after the peaceful day we were having?

"You think yesterday fulfilled that dream of her happiness?" he said in a quiet voice.

I instantly started to flare up at him. "Of course not!" I snapped. "But ripping her away from her grandparents isn't going to make her feel any better. You have no idea. If I get full custody of Addy, she'll never see them again."

"How the fuck so?" Jim was getting pissed, but his voice stayed steady and low. "Avery, how do you not see that she can't be around that dick again until he gets help?"

"She loves her papa and grandma, and he lives with them. If I get full custody, they don't ever see her because that's his residence."

"Why haven't they kicked his ass out? How old is he?" he asked.

"Thirty-five," I answered. "Still living at home."

"My brother is fucking Chief of Cardiology at thirty-five. I'm two years older than Derek, and I run a successful business after busting my ass to get there. And this piece of shit lives at home?" His eyebrows rose while I stared at him, livid-pissed he was going off on me about Derek's bullshit as if I hadn't lived with it every single day for years. "He fucking lives at home with a nice truck. Then he bullies your ass around like he did yesterday, can't give two fucks about the way it traumatizes his daughter. It makes no sense to me. None."

That last part was Jim in that CEO tone I'd heard him use when he started commanding shit. I was furious, and I didn't know exactly why. Was I angry at Jim for making it sound like I didn't have my daughter's well-being in mind, or was I mad at myself because he had witnessed enough to draw that conclusion?

"You don't fucking understand," I said, trying to keep it together.

He shook his head, and I could tell he was not happy with that answer. "No, Avery, I don't fucking understand. I imagine that after yesterday you would want nothing more than to ensure he never comes around you or that precious little girl again."

"I can't take—"

"I get it," he said, getting up. "One thing I despise is excuses. I am not programmed to accept them, I guess. Jesus Christ, I can't even handle them from my team members, let alone when it comes to the two people I care for most and the one person who can do something about it, but she won't."

"This is my child and my life. I'm doing the best I can with it," I shot back angrily, following him away from where Addy was asleep. My defense mechanisms were in full swing. How dare he or anyone say anything to me about caring for my child? "You don't know how much she loves Larry and Annette."

"Then her grandparents need to stop bringing that fuck-up around the granddaughter who loves them so much," he said, hands in his pockets and staring past me. "It's all fucked up, Avery, I know that. I know how hard this must be for you. Addicts like him mess everything up. I see where this dick is fucking over you and Addy, and I'm telling you, you are the only one who can end it."

I crossed my arms. "I'm doing everything I can, Jim." My voice cracked as I tried desperately to hold back my anger and my tears. "I think I've been doing it well, too, since way before you came around. Addy and I are happy. Derek does this shit, and then it just goes away."

"Av," his voice lowered with pity, "you have to see through this bullshit somehow. If not for you and the two breakdowns I've witnessed that scumbag force you into, then for your daughter. I need to know you're going to take the help I promised you in Palm Springs to get that fucker out of your life." He ran a hand through his hair when the door chime audibly alerted him on the outdoor intercom, and Jake's voice came through, announcing that he and Ash were here with more pool toys.

The problem with what Jim expected of me was that I wasn't brave enough to use the lawyers he would hire to help me gain custody of my daughter. Jim didn't know the details of my dark history. My jail time, me being a user, and that being the reason why I ended up with Derek in the first place. How could I ever expect someone like Jim to understand?

CHAPTER THIRTY-SEVEN

Jim

I might have overstepped my bounds in my conversation with Avery by the pool that morning, but I couldn't help it. I loved her and Addy too, and so this Derek asshole ignited a rage within me that was hard to explain. He brought out feelings inside me that only one other person had—my mother. Living with an addict was detrimental to my brother and me in so many ways, and the last thing I wanted was for Addy to have even a sliver of the childhood I'd experienced.

The more I thought about Avery and Addy's situation, the more unanswered questions were brought to my mind. Would my mother have cheated on my dad if she weren't using drugs? Would she have given half a damn about her two little boys if she weren't a selfish addict? Would it have all been so different if she weren't so consumed with her self-destructive habits?

It didn't matter now. I couldn't change the past, but I could help shift Avery and Addy's future.

· · ·

AVERY and I sat at a quiet corner booth in a diner, not having said much since our disagreement from earlier. She and Ash had dropped off Addy at that church to practice singing for her Christmas program earlier in the afternoon, so Avery and I hadn't had a chance to finish our conversation. If I was honest, I wasn't sure what else to say, and from Avery's lack of engagement on the topic, I assumed she felt the same way.

"Jim," Avery interrupted my thoughts, "are you still with me?"

"Sorry. There's a lot of shit on my mind," I answered truthfully.

"Well, we have about twenty minutes before I have to leave to pick up Addy from her singing practice." She grabbed the check off the table and smiled at me. "This one is on me."

"No, no. You don't have to do that," I insisted as Avery stood up.

"I know I don't. Be right back," she said with a wink as she walked up to the register.

I placed my elbows on the table, folded my hands together, and watched her handle the transaction. She was such a strong, capable woman, and maybe that was why I couldn't fucking understand why she was cowering in this aspect of her life when it mattered the most. Why would she be so intimidated by such a small, insignificant, manipulative man?

I had no control over Avery's decisions, and I definitely couldn't understand them, but I wasn't the type of person who was capable of backing down, especially when it came to something important to me. Avery was an attentive and doting mother, making her behavior when it came to this toxic man utterly baffling.

Why not pluck the weed out from its root and be done with it? Why not set custody in stone and demand he gets help? Why all of the enabling? There was no excuse for his behavior, in my opinion. No amount of guilt, or whatever the fuck Avery was dealing with, would make me bring that child around that man if it were up to me. I don't give a shit if Addy's grandparents were Santa and Mrs. Claus, there's no fucking way I would want her in that environment with an unstable drug addict.

I took one last drink of my iced tea and stood with a forced smile. I had to clear my head. I was on the brink of having to fly to London for work, and I didn't want to leave my girls like this.

We walked to our cars, which were parked next to each other in the back of the gated parking lot. I leaned against mine, wishing we'd had more quality time together. I despised the tension between us.

Avery studied me after I pulled on my sunglasses, and she crossed her arms. "You're pissed off at me, aren't you?" she questioned with a snarky grin.

"Not pissed, gorgeous." I reached for her hand and pulled her to where I reclined against the passenger side of my car.

I went to kiss her, but she covered my mouth before it reached her lips. She giggled, and it instantly lightened the mood. Maybe this potential of having to fly to London was partly to blame for my attitude.

"Yes," she said as I kissed the palm of her soft hand, "you're pissed. You hardly said a word at dinner."

"I'm sorry if my temperament made you uncomfortable. I never want to make you feel that way, no matter what is on my mind."

She smiled, leaning against me, her arms stretched over each of my shoulders. "It's okay."

I missed her perfume, her kiss, her ass—where my hands instantly went. I missed her so much and couldn't lose her. Fuck that miserable prick for being a thorn in my side, and me not being able to do a damn thing about it.

I ran my hands up her back, feeling her warm skin through her light shirt. "I'm having a pretty hard time not throwing you into the backseat of your car and fucking you here and now," I teased, tickling her neck with my tongue and lips now.

"That doesn't sound half bad to me." She ran her fingers through my hair. "But I could only imagine what it would look like when we got caught doing that."

I smiled against her flesh. "And with a car seat in the back, no less."

I brought my face back to meet her brilliant blue eyes. "At least they wouldn't question we'd be needing another one in nine months?"

Avery shook her head, "You're impossible."

I chewed on my bottom lip. "You've seen me on my phone and doing emails since this morning. It's because my London offices are trying to send me into an early grave, and now I'm dealing with something."

"Spit it out," she said.

"I know this coming weekend is supposed to be our weekend together, given you're having Addy stay with her grandparents, but I may have to fly to London on Friday. I'm trying to bust this shit out with every resource I have available, but I don't know if I'll be able to get out of this one so easily."

She smiled. "I can survive a weekend without you."

"I may be there through the entire week after," I said. "It all depends on the hotel chain we're working with. I'm certain if I don't meet face-to-face with the owner, wining and dining and shit like that, we'll lose the damn deal."

"Hey, now. Will you be finding another wife to help you pass the time?" She arched her eyebrow at me.

I laughed. "I'll be staying in the city, and the first chance I get, I'm flying home," I said.

Avery's cell phone alarm went off. "That's my timer. I had a feeling I'd get caught up with you and forget to pick my little Christmas angel up from practice."

I stood and brought her in, holding her tightly against me. "I love you."

"Well, if you can manage," she said, "meet me for lunch tomorrow."

"I'm stacked in, gorgeous," I said. "Trust me, I'm doing everything I can to get out of flying to London."

"I know I gave you shit for being chained to work, but I do get it. I am still here, and Addy will still be here. Women have their men traveling for work all the time. Don't start slacking on your job just because you're dating some crazy hot chick with dazzling eyes, Mr. Mitchell."

"You have it all nailed down, don't you?"

"I'm at peace with it. In fact, I wouldn't be shocked if your elite, sexy ass had to take your private jet to Dubai for some business conference too." She laughed, and then after a small kiss, she turned to get into her driver's seat. "Despite the low points, I had a fantastic weekend, Jim. Thank you so much for everything. Addy loved it, and so did I."

"I love making my ladies happy," I said, relieved we ended our weekend on a high note.

I waved her off after she blew me a kiss and then floored it in the open parking lot, most likely just to taunt me with the reminder of her lead foot.

AFTER A PAINSTAKING WEEK of non-stop work, Thursday night was when I knew I had to fucking fly to London for sure. This deal had me by the balls in the worst way. It didn't matter that I'd busted my ass all week—missing out on so many opportunities to see Avery—this trip couldn't be avoided.

Friday morning, I called Avery to give her the news. It was bad enough that I'd sacrificed so many lunches and dinners that we could've shared all week, now that was all for nothing.

"I'm getting ready for work," she said. "I'm guessing this is the call that we're not seeing each other this weekend?"

"Yes. I'm so sorry. I tried everything, really," I said as I buckled into the leather captain's chair on the company's jet. "Next weekend, perhaps we can try out the beach thing again?"

"You might need drysuits instead of wetsuits this time. It's going to be chilly next weekend since we are heading into fall."

"Those are the best waves," I said with a smile.

"Yeah, Addy isn't going near those."

"What if Addy and I watched her badass mom enjoy them instead?"

"Are you already at the airport? Damn, you're leaving early. You must've been up since three in the morning." She laughed into the phone. "Oh, hold up, that's Larry calling me," she said before clicking over.

I watched the tarmac as the plane backed out, Alex sitting across from me, finishing up whatever call he was on before we took off. I did not want to leave, but I knew I'd be more focused once we were in the air, and Alex and I would start going through numbers and marketing pitches for the chain we were busting our asses to secure.

"Jim," she said in a softer voice when she resumed our call, "are you still there?"

"Yeah, we're slowing backing out, everything good?"

"Listen," her voice became stern, "I'm never going to hide shit like this from you, but don't lose it when I tell you I've got this and can handle it, okay?"

I rubbed my forehead. "Go on," I said, knowing this was about Derek and praying with all that I was that she was about to tell me she was keeping Addy this weekend if that fucker was out again.

"Derek's at the house. He's out. I'm fucking pissed about it too, but Larry and Annette said they'd be the first to call the cops on his ass if he so much as touches anything to get high around Addy."

I swallowed the lump in my throat and forced the rage into my balled-up fists. "I won't even ask how he was released," I said as calmly as I could. "You feel comfortable with Addison around him after he scared the fuck out of her last weekend?"

"I'm leaving this up to Addy. If she doesn't want to go, then she stays with me."

"Jesus, Avery, she's a three-year-old child," I said, beside myself that Avery was handling this situation in this way. It was as though the beach incident had never fucking happened. "You have to make this decision for her," I pleaded. "Avery?"

"I know how to deal with my daughter and Derek, goddammit. Please don't do this again. Addy will tell me if she doesn't want to go."

"Okay," I said, my jaw so tight I felt a spasm in both cheeks. "You have Jake and Ash's numbers, right? I'll even have Collin text his number to you."

"Slow down," she said. "I don't need you trying to protect me from

London. I'm sorry you've seen this dick bring me to my limits, and I'm sorry you've even had to meet him, but this isn't new for me. I'll be fine."

"You'll be fine, and so will Addison when he's out of your life. He's a loose cannon. How can you trust her around that asshole?"

"Because I've dealt with this for three fucking years, Jim," she said. "And, yes, I have Jake and Ash's numbers. Ash invited me over this weekend."

"That'll be fun for you two," I said, completely at a loss for words.

Did I need to shut up and find my place? Should I keep pressuring Avery, expecting a different result when she had so obviously made up her mind and didn't want to hear my point of view? What the fuck was I supposed to do? I was trying to give her my best advice from the eyes of someone who wasn't twisted up in this toxic situation, but she didn't want to hear it.

"Hey, I've got to go. The plane is on the runway. I'll try to call when we land."

"Okay. Be safe. We both love you."

Jesus, stab me in my fucking tortured heart.

"And you," I managed, and after ending the call, I threw my cell against the leather sofa across from me like a pissed-off teenager.

"My God," Alex said. "You've been in dick-mode all week, and now the cell phone is on the receiving end of your bullshit? What the hell is going on with you?"

"That piece of shit is out of jail, and Avery's still going to take Addison to his parents' place tonight." I leaned back, the G-forces of the plane pinning me into my seat.

"Are you joking?" Alex said. "She needs to bury that little bastard with your lawyers. Do you think she might be bothered by you hiring the lawyers, not her?"

"No," I shook my head and stared at him with an expression that probably looked as pathetic as I felt. "She's fucking scared of him. That fucker has her right where he wants her, and she doesn't see it."

"Damn," Alex said. "How is it that the addicts manage to take down everyone with them?"

"A question for the interventionist that I'm confident the family will never ask for. How can no one see that this fuck up is either going to end up dead or taking them all down with him?" I ticked each of my fingers against my thumb one-by-one, staring out the window at the clouds we were climbing into. "I don't fucking know where my place is in all of this."

"All you can do is support her. Hang in there, no matter how shitty it gets. She'll eventually see it, but you have to let it play out. I know it's hard, standing by while a child is involved, but you know how messy families can be. It's never black and white."

"I worry for that little girl more than I have a right to, I guess."

"Avery's a mom. They have better intuitions than guys." He smiled. "She's also tough as fucking nails. I fear for that dickhead if he fucks with that little girl and scares her again."

"She is leaving it up to the three-year-old to decide whether or not she wants to be around her dad."

"Avery isn't stupid. I know you're frustrated by her decision making, but it is indeed her decision to make. Children's instincts are good too, you know? If Addy doesn't want to see that fuck-head, then you have nothing to worry about." He smiled and reclined in his chair, "Speaking of children's instincts, my God, you'd think she was yours and Avery's daughter, not the other dude's."

I stood while the plane started to level out. "I'm getting a bourbon before we open these computers. What are you having?"

"I'm determined to drink all of the special scotch Jakey-boy had stocked on the plane before he flies again."

"That is a trip I do not wish to be a part of." I laughed.

I knew I should stay in my lane and let Avery handle the Derek situation the best she knew how, but I had so many feelings about everything, and none of them were good. I could only hope I stayed busy enough in London not to drive myself crazy.

CHAPTER THIRTY-EIGHT

Jim

The week in London was nothing compared to the three weeks that followed it. Avery and I had stayed in better contact than the week before I left for the UK; however, we were in this stalled-out zone, one could say, with her ex. He hadn't been off the rails entirely since that day at the beach, but I wasn't a fool to think he was clean and sober. People with addictions like his didn't walk away from daily use without rehab. No fucking way.

Was I still irritated that Avery wasn't pursuing his ass in courts? Fuck yes. It was making me miserable, seeing her acting like someone who was backed into a corner. What was bothering me most was the feeling that this dirtbag was a heartbeat away from another bender, it was only a matter of time.

Avery and I had a friction point in our relationship because of him, and it was driving me insane that we couldn't see eye-to-eye on this issue. She seemed closed-off to hearing my advice, and I was not going to lose her over this asshole, so I was pushing it all down.

The two weekends I'd spent with Addy and Avery since Derek's beach blow-out episode were the highlights to the past month. I was officially in over my head with stories of *Sally and the Three Little Rascals*, and Addy wasn't letting these made-up characters leave anytime soon.

Avery gave me the okay to renovate one of my rooms for Addy to use when they stayed the night, so the previous Saturday, we had a shopping experience, to say the least. Since Avery and Ash had become a lot closer in the last month, Clay and Joe even came along, making it an all hands on deck situation. Addy was as adorable as ever, gripping my hand as she put the master of design, Clay, in his place while picking out her favorite color for everything—purple. I laughed as I looked around and realized that all of these grown adults had bent over backward, doing whatever this little girl wanted, and she ate it up that whole day.

Now, here we were, dropping off Addy with her grandparents for the weekend again. I'd been dreading this all week long. Avery had asked me earlier in the week if I would like to come along to meet Larry and Annette in the hopes that it might ease my mind about Addy staying here. I appreciated Avery's gesture, knowing her heart was in the right place, and I hoped I could make some kind of sense out of Avery's rationale after meeting them.

"Hey, daydreamer, are you coming?" Avery asked, letting Addy out of her car seat in the back of my two-door Bentley while I sat in the driver's seat, zoned out.

"Just thinking about tonight, Av," I said, getting out of the car, peeling off my suit jacket, and draping it over my seat.

Avery's hand grabbed mine as Larry let us into the house, and we walked into the quaint but nicely-arranged living room. Larry closed the door and followed us in, greeting me and shaking my hand. "I'm Larry," he said. "It's nice to finally meet the man who papa's little peep talks about all the time." He chuckled.

"She's the best," I managed, studying the casually-dressed man. His clean goatee and graying hair made him look well put together, and made me question why in the fucking world he hadn't kicked his adult addict kid out of the house yet. "It's nice to meet you. I'm Jim."

"Have a seat," Larry said.

I sat on the other end of the sofa from Larry, noticing his television was turned to some boxing documentary.

"Hey, there," a woman said as she popped her head into the room from around the corner. She smiled, but it was painfully evident that she was worn down. She was either overworked or just fucking done with life. "I'm Anne."

I heard Addison and Avery in the back of the small house, Avery seemingly getting Addison in the bath.

"Avery, I can give her a bath," Anne said, walking down a hall that was lined with family pictures from across the decades.

"Don't worry about it," I heard Avery say. "Go back to baking whatever you're spoiling Addy with tonight."

"You ever see this guy fight before?" Larry asked, pointing at his television after tossing some peanuts into his mouth and casually leaning back on the sofa.

I crossed my ankle over my knee and loosened my stiff position. "No," I said, studying the black and white highlight reel of two boxers.

"That's Sugar Ray Robinson," he said with a knowing laugh.

"He's a bit before my time, I guess," I answered. Boxing had never been a sport I'd regularly watched, so I had nothing to contribute to this conversation.

"Do you realize this guy fought over two hundred and fifteen times?" he asked with a laugh. "With only two losses and one draw."

"Holy cow," I said, refraining from cursing. "Are you kidding me?" I was no expert, but that sounded like a hell of a record.

"When this guy turned pro in 1940, he was eighty-five and zero with sixty-nine knockouts."

"Dang, man," I said.

"He was only nineteen years old." Larry laughed again, casually having more peanuts. "This guy knocked out more people before he was nineteen years old than most fighters in their whole career."

"That's pretty incredible. What was his professional record?"

He looked at me, and his forehead creased in humor. "A hundred twenty-eight—one and two," he prattled off. "The guy actually retired in two weight classes, then came out of retirement and took another damn title," he said with a laugh.

I was settling in some with the man and understanding why Addy enjoyed his company. He was more likable than I'd imagined. I could see why Addy's relationship with her grandparents was so crucial to Avery—especially since she didn't have much in the way of a family on her own. Unfortunately, it didn't take long before I saw a shadow making its way down the hall. Derek stepped into the living room, gave me a nod, and took the recliner situated next to his dad.

"Best fighter right there," Derek said, reclining and eying the television. "What's up, Jim?" he asked. "Nice suit. I've got some expensive ones like that too."

Larry was silent as he looked over at Derek. "You just now waking up?" he asked. "What time you get in last night, bud?"

Fucking bud? I thought, growing more irritated every second, seeing this idiot wearing his hoodie and sagging jeans.

"Late, but I was at Rick's place."

"Rick?" Larry asked. "Is that the guy who owns that dealership?"

Derek eyed me, smiled, then looked at his dad. "Yep," he said. "They got some badass trucks that came in this week."

"No kidding," Larry said dismissively.

Unlike Derek's father, I wasn't dismissing shit at this point. The fucker had been out all goddamn night and was just now waking up? Rick, my ass. Derek's bullshit may have manipulated this family, but where he'd lost Larry's attention, he'd gained mine.

"Yeah, they're pretty legit, like the truck I got."

"What's the name of the dealership?" I questioned, knowing my company had acquired a few in Anaheim years ago, seeing their potential in this location.

"Rendell's," Derek said, our eyes locking. "Why?" he asked, settling into his chair like the dick he was. "You interested in trading in your million-dollar Aston Martin for a nice truck?"

"I don't think so," I answered. "Rick Rendell. I've met that man," I said as Larry looked back and forth between Derek and me as the tension in the room grew.

"Old man Rendell, you mean?" Derek asked.

"No, we acquired that dealership and another a few years back. Interesting that you know Rick," I said. What I wanted to say was that I knew Rick had a family, and the multiple times we'd met over dinners, this man never once struck me as the type to hang out with the piece of shit that was now trying to stare my ass down.

"Well, that's my boy," Derek said.

"Nice," I responded, and then Avery walked out with Addison, running to her papa first and then me—not to the prick who started to argue with Avery about what time we got there even though he was asleep when we did.

"You ready to have fun with your papa this weekend?" I asked Addy.

"Lots of fun."

"Get over here and come say hi to your daddy," Derek said, leaning forward in his recliner.

"Hey, Dad," Addy said, then looked at me. "Bye, Jim."

I watched how the once-calm atmosphere of the room became more and more toxic after Derek had entered it. Avery was going over last-minute details about picking Addy up on Sunday while Addison walked to her papa, who focused on her, her stuffed pup, and a book she brought with her.

I stood, knowing we were about to leave, and once farewells were given, Avery and I walked out, leaving Addy in the care of her grandpa. Her dad, however, apparently couldn't give a shit about his daughter being there since he felt the urge to follow Avery and me out to my car.

"What are you doing, Derek? Go back inside," Avery ordered him while I pointedly ignore him.

"You know my boy, eh?" Derek said, lighting a cigarette.

"I know enough," I answered, opening Avery's door for her and making sure Derek didn't feel inclined to charge the car and start ordering her around again.

"Enough? What the fuck does that mean?" he asked, taking a drag from his cigarette. "You trying to make my dad question me about being out all night?"

"I was just wondering if you were talking about the same person who owned the business I acquired a few years back," I said, walking toward my side of the car.

"You don't know dick."

This mother fucker had no idea how thin the thread was that was keeping me together.

"If that's what you want to assume, then I'll allow that," I said, holding back.

"Oh, you'll allow it?" he mocked.

"Let's just go, Jim," Avery snapped.

I sat in the car, disturbed that this unstable mother fucker was going back into that house with Addy, pissed off that I was leaving with Avery. Fuck this whole situation. I fired up the car and looked at her while Derek wandered around the back of the house.

"That jerkoff is too angry for us to leave Addy here, Avery," I said in a low voice.

"Jim, drive the damn car. If you haven't caught on to the fact that he hates you yet, I don't know what will help you figure out why he's pissed."

I clamped my mouth shut and drove the fuck out of there.

"YOU HAVEN'T SPOKEN since we left Larry and Annette's," Avery said a few blocks from my house.

"Sorry. I'm just struggling with all of this, Avery," I finally said as I pulled in. She nodded as she unbuckled, and we both entered the house, kicking off our shoes by the front door, and I threw my suit coat over the back of a chair while she set her bag down.

After I'd poured myself a bourbon and Avery had poured herself a glass of wine, we sat on my sofa.

"Jim." She ran her hand over the vest I still wore. "Tonight was weird. I'm sorry about that."

"Don't be sorry, Av," I said, kissing her head. "Jesus, I don't know what to ask you to be at this point."

She sat up. "What does that mean?"

"Larry," I said, looking at her sharp eyes, feeling her defense mechanisms coming up around her. "He's a nice man. Although, when Derek came out—after just fucking waking up from his long night out —he only mildly questioned him and then ignored it. It was almost like he didn't want to start shit with him."

"No one wants to engage Derek's bullshit," Avery said.

"It's not right, Avery," I said, leaning my elbows on my knees, holding my glass of bourbon with both hands. "How can any of you not see this?" I looked back at her. "I know you're not afraid of that little shit, so why—fucking tell me here and now—why won't you protect your daughter from him?"

"Fucking hell, Jim." She sighed. "You knew this was the bullshit side of my life when you signed up for it, and now—fuck. You're trying to—"

"Help you?" I interrupted. "How is it that I'm the bad guy in this situation?"

"I never said that, did I?"

"You're defending this dirtbag by not allowing me to help you. You get so fucking angry every time I ask why you won't fight for custody of Addy. How is it that I'm not okay with leaving her anywhere near that house with that fucker, and you are?"

"Because I know Larry and Annette," Avery said. "I know they won't let my daughter get hurt no matter how badly Derek behaves."

"Behaves? That's the fucking word for what he does now?"

"Wrong choice of words. Jesus Christ," she said and rubbed her forehead. "I can't do this." She stood up. "I can't fucking do this with you, Jim."

"Damn it." I stood and brought her into my arms, and then lifted her chin, bringing her eyes to meet mine, "I don't want to do this either. I want to help, but I have no idea where my place is in any of this anymore."

"I don't need you trying to step in and control this. This is how it's been for a long time. Larry loves Addy as much as you, Jim. She's the light in the darkness that Derek puts him and Annette through. You have to know he won't let anything happen to her. I know this because I know them."

I couldn't pretend to understand why Avery was so sure about Derek's parents. It all seemed so dysfunctional.

I sighed and pulled her in and held her tightly. "I hate this," I said. "It brings up shitty memories of my mom's addiction, and Jake and me being left with that woman. Maybe I feel that is what's happening to Addison when we drop her off anywhere around that prick."

Avery's tense muscles loosened, and she returned my hug. "I'm sorry you have to deal with any of this."

"Stop fucking apologizing," I said. "You have to stop apologizing for something you can fix."

"I know," she conceded.

The rest of our night was not what I'd imagined it would be. It seemed that we'd been heading this direction since the beach incident. I couldn't fix anything or help anyone. I had no say in this, and every time I opened my mouth, all I did was push Avery away. For the first time in my life, I was fucking stumped.

THE WEEKEND IRONED itself out in its own way. Avery seemed always to wake up happier and healthier than the day before. I opted to shut my fucking mouth about the whole thing so we could enjoy each other before heading back to work and having to squeeze in time together during the workweek. We enjoyed a full day on Sunday, Clay coming over and putting the final touches on the transformed room that I couldn't wait for Addy to see. Now, it was Monday again, and time for another hectic week.

"Hey," Alex said, nodding back at Summer dismissively.

"Everything okay?" I asked, eyeing the papers Alex held.

Alex pinched his lips and looked past me and out my windows as he sat across from my desk.

"Alex," I said, "did you and Summer finally call it quits?"

What the hell is his problem?

Alex rubbed his forehead, then cleared his throat. "This was my responsibility, and I was going to handle it."

"Am I firing *you* today?" I smirked.

"Funny," he said. "Jim—"

"Save the drama and suspense, dude. What the fuck is wrong with you?"

"Here are the reports from the investigation that's been ongoing since that lady in the preschool gave Avery and Addy shit," he said, holding a stack of papers.

"I've been getting reports for the last month when they started in on investigations in all departments. What are those papers?"

"The ones we have to terminate immediately. They never passed background checks, but they were hired anyway. The investigators were looking into it, and they pointed out that we need to tighten up the system we're using or use a new process. We have to fire around eighteen people today because of this fucking mistake," he said.

"Being that it was our mistake—in one way or another, we misled these employees—we'll send them with a severance package," I said. "I don't want the reputation for throwing people out on the street."

"That's not the issue."

"Okay, so what, then?"

Fuck, he didn't look well.

"Avery—your Avery—was one of them."

"What? Why? Because of something stupid? Maybe we ought to look into these cases, then. I don't want people fired over nonsense."

Alex leaned forward and slid the papers that he'd been holding across my desk. I felt the blood leave my face when I read Avery's report. All this time, I'd been made to feel like the bad guy. Maybe I was willfully blind. All I knew was that the reality of the situation was something I wasn't prepared to see.

CHAPTER THIRTY-NINE

Avery

I had just finished my lunch and sat at my desk when Stefanie walked up with her usual, solemn *Avery fucked up* look. I swiveled in my chair to face her, just about to hit send on a text to Jim, saying that I'd missed him at lunch today. I'd actually thought for a second that he was going to show up since this was the first time he hadn't sent out a buffet of food for me to enjoy in his absence. The poor man was probably hung up with something, and I couldn't blame him at all for getting distracted.

"Mr. Mitchell has requested that you meet with him in his office," she said. "I believe you know your way to the executive elevators."

I eyed Alyssa's smile and refrained from the one I was about to display. "Yes," I answered. "I'll be back soon."

"Get it, girl," Amir whispered, Jim being the constant topic of conversation between all three of us at lunch. I never blamed them for their curiosity. I'd want to know more about the elusive man who ran the company if I were lunch pals with his girlfriend too.

I rode the elevator up to the top floors, the elevator that reminded me of Jim and me nearly going for it, and I got an exciting swirl in my stomach, knowing I was going to see him. Who the hell knew what he was up to, but I wasn't going to complain. Maybe this was a new effort to see each other during the workweek? Perhaps he was going to make good on his funny little promises of wanting to fuck me in his office after he uninstalled the cameras in them?

"I'm here for Mr. Mitchell," I said to Summer, Jim's secretary and Alex's girl. She was intently typing before she looked up at me and then stood.

"Follow me," she said.

I trailed her into Jim's office as she announced me, and then she quickly rushed past me again, closing the door behind her.

I almost said a joke about her leaving like something was on fire, but as soon as I locked eyes with Jim, sitting behind his imposing desk, his icy glare sent a shiver of fear down my spine.

"Jim?" I questioned.

"Avery," he answered, his voice low and emotionless.

"What's going on?" I asked.

"Since the debacle of the preschool situation, I had the company perform background investigations on all departments," he started.

Oh, no. Not this. Oh, my God. My heart was pounding so hard that I was surprised I could still hear him speaking.

"The reports of those employees who did not pass the background checks made it to my desk today," he finished.

I felt my stomach drop. I'd never thought that I had anything to hide from this man—and never did so intentionally, per se—but the shame that flooded through me at what I knew he'd seen was paralyzing me.

"I suppose I'm here because of that."

"Yes," Jim said, coldly. "Among learning why you're not eligible to work at this company," he sat back in his chair, "I've also discovered why I've looked like the asshole in our relationship for this entire last month."

"What the fuck does that mean?" I snapped back.

"It means that after discovering the reasons you failed background, I also found out that you've withheld pretty serious information from me. Information that leads me to believe these are the reasons you are so defensive of your ex and completely argumentative when I've asked you on numerous occasions to open up and explain why you feared taking him to court." He cocked his head to the side, "I guess I was the fool in this relationship this whole time."

"You..." I paused, my defenses shooting up around me, and my heart pounding with rage at his accusatory demeanor. "Jim, you were never the fool," I tried not to shout. "That shit is in my past. I should have—"

"Past or not, Avery, you brought it to the present, and you keep it with you. You won't fight for your daughter because of this?" He glanced down at the paper that I knew revealed my messed up past to him: the felony DUIs, possession of controlled substances, and God knew what else between all of the charges that had actually stuck and the ones that'd been thrown out or expunged over the years. It was all the horrible shit that'd stained my life, and that I had moved on from years ago, and it was sitting on his desk. "You made me out to be the sucker in all of this, knowing these were the reasons you won't protect your daughter from that man. You listened to me go on and on about my mother for months, and you never said a word."

"I have my own reasons for that. It was never your place to tell me how to take care of my daughter in the first place."

"I won't listen to you, standing there and trying to spin this into being my fault. You have proven that you have no respect for me whatsoever, despite everything I've done to be there for you. I don't know how many times I asked you why you cower to that son of a bitch, and you never trusted me enough to tell me the whole truth about your past. Complete, fucking addict behavior, hiding everything from people who care about you."

"Fuck you! Don't you dare try to use the mistakes I've made against me," I barked, his dark expressions not shaking me. "And you demand my respect? You're not my fucking husband. You were my boyfriend."

"It doesn't matter, does it? Not anymore, anyway. I can't trust someone who is willing to lie by omission straight to my face multiple times. Even when I opened up to you, stating I would never lose you and would fight for you, you knew—the entire time—that you had no intention of ever doing anything, and you didn't say a word. I've been driving myself crazy for over a fucking month, walking on eggshells around you, holding back everything I had to say so as not to upset you or interfere with your parenting decisions. Little did I know why you were making such horrible, co-dependent, and enabling ones. You're so fucking willing to hide in your secrets that you put your daughter through this? It's fucking sick, Avery."

"Walking on eggshells? Fucking please. I won't listen to this shit from you. You were born with a silver fucking spoon in your mouth. You don't understand what it's like to have nothing and no one and still somehow manage to straighten yourself out, pick up the pieces, and keep going."

"I understand enough to know you'll never do the right thing for your daughter," he said in a voice so lethal that if I were standing next to him, I would've slapped him across his face.

"I'm going to pack up my shit and be out of your company and out of your life. I'll leave the keys to your goddamn charity car at my desk."

"The car is yours," he said. "I don't want the thing."

"I'm sorry you feel this way about everything, but I couldn't tell you. I wasn't ready," I managed. As much as the defensive part of me felt that I didn't owe him any explanations, something inside me knew this was all wrong.

"You would never be ready. If you couldn't be ready for your daughter, what makes me think there would have ever come a day that you trusted me enough to tell me the truth? To tell me everything. Instead, you allowed me to beg and argue with you about it constantly. It's not in my character to take a step back, but I did so because I loved you, and look at how that gets reciprocated. It's been a lie since the beginning, in my opinion. I will not be with someone who hides things from me, especially when they should've known I was there to help."

His words were searing through me, and I was so fucking angry I could've thrown the chair across the room as he spoke. Inside, I felt like there was a demon, hearing a priest speaking Latin in an exorcism. Jim was right to be so angry with me, but my fucking defense mechanisms wouldn't allow me to back down.

I should've spoken up and told him that things weren't as they seemed, and I didn't consciously do anything deceptive, or that I loved him more than I'd ever loved anyone, and I would do whatever it took to earn his trust back. But I couldn't say it. I couldn't say anything that would've been redemptive. The demon inside me didn't want to, and the part of me that loved him didn't feel like I deserved it. What did I care, anyway? This wouldn't be the first time someone abandoned me when shit got hard. Stand in line with your disappointment, Mr. Fucking Mitchell.

"Well, I didn't need your help," I said. "I don't need anyone's fucking help to raise my daughter. I've done it this long without you."

"Do what you need to do," he said. His tone was dismissive, his posture stiff, and it was evident that I was his worst enemy—that was written all over his face.

"Is that your paper or mine?" I asked, ready to walk out of this place and Jim's life without batting an eye.

"The copy is yours if you want it. I don't care to ever look at it again. Do what you will with your life; you have it all figured out, right?"

"Goodbye," I said, spinning around and walking out the door, feeling absolutely nothing—total numbness.

There was nothing left to say. This ended the way everything else in my life did—horribly. The real fool in this situation was me because, for a while now, I'd believed this life was something real. What an idiot I'd been to think anyone on the outside could understand my life.

CHAPTER FORTY

Avery

$\mathcal{I}$t had been a month since I'd heard from or seen Jim. Luckily, I managed to find a decent-paying job as a receptionist at a dentist's office in Anaheim, and since I'd opted for a month-to-month contract with the apartment I'd rented near Jim's office, it wasn't a problem to move out and rent a new place—a much smaller studio apartment—not too far from my new job.

Addy wasn't thrilled about leaving her preschool or moving away from Jim, but she adjusted quickly and was excited to be able to see her papa more often. Larry and Annette were both retired, so it was convenient for them to watch Addy on the three days a week that she didn't attend her preschool.

Many times, Addy had questioned not seeing Jim after we moved. Being a three-year-old, I didn't want to saddle her with the details, so I explained that since we moved, Jim lived too far away, and that was why we didn't get to see him. Luckily, her papa was there—as he always was when my life seemed to crumble—so he filled the gap, thank God.

Even though I cut off all contact with Jim, I was still in regular contact with Ash. We chatted about how her pregnancy was going and how busy her gallery had been lately, and we had the inevitable conversation about Jim and me.

Ash wasn't judgmental of any aspect of my situation—from my past issues all the way up to Derek. I told her what Britney had said to me after the breakup—and what seemed to be one-hundred percent accurate—Jim or no Jim, I needed to deal with my Derek issues.

The way I saw it was the way it always had been—Derek was the root of every problem in my life or any other life that he touched with his addict bullshit. I was made out to be the bad guy in Jim's eyes because of that piece of shit. Larry and Annette had been turned into horrible enablers because of their son's manipulative personality. It was fucked up all the way around, and the source of all the chaos was always fucking Derek.

Ash listened to everything I had to say, and she convinced me to go to an Alcoholics Anonymous meeting to hear stories from people who'd lived through similar situations and managed to get sober. I knew that a lot of my defensiveness came from a place of knowing I wasn't able to share my experiences with anyone who could relate. Perhaps this might change that. All I knew was that it couldn't hurt to see.

I PULLED my hair into a ponytail and fastened my hoop earrings before I headed down the outdoor steps of my apartment to where Ash waited for me in her car. I walked by my Aston Martin and couldn't help but laugh at how fucking stupid it looked here, entirely out of place. It was a stark reminder of the image of mine and Jim's relationship. What a fucking joke.

"Hey, Ash," I said, sliding into the passenger's seat of a brand-new Mercedes, happier to see her glowing and pregnant self than I thought I'd be.

"Hey, you. It feels like it's been forever, right?" she chirped. "You hungry?" She grinned, remembering well how I loved food more than anything.

"I already stuffed myself before I got ready. Didn't want to risk there not being any snacks." I laughed. "Look at you. It's almost baby time, huh?"

"I should probably say how glorious it is to be pregnant, but I'm ready to have this little man out of me."

"I feel you on that," I said as we left the apartment complex and headed toward the freeway. "You should've let me drive. Jesus. I'm sorry I didn't think of how uncomfortable this stage of pregnancy is."

She arched an eyebrow at me. "Hence the reason Jake insisted on buying me this car. I swear, I don't adjust to such expensive things very easily. Don't get me wrong, I appreciate it wholeheartedly, but good grief with that man sometimes."

I laughed. "So, have you two picked out a name yet?"

"We're still officially undecided." she shrugged. "Although I think we are going to go with John." She looked over her shoulder and accelerated onto the freeway to merge into the second lane. "That was Collin's dad's name. He passed away not too long ago, and he was like a father to Jacob and Jim. He was there for both of the guys when they lost Howard." She smiled at me. "In case you somehow manage to run into Collin, don't tell him. Jake wants to surprise him and Jim. He can be such a big goofball sometimes."

"I don't think I'll be running into Collin any time soon, so don't worry. That's such a sweet thing to do, naming your son after him," I said, and then I took notice of how slow we were driving. "I thought this place was about twenty minutes away," I said, wondering why the hell we were driving so slowly. "Are you getting off somewhere?"

"Oh, my God. Not you too," Ash said with a laugh. "Jake despises how slowly I drive on the freeway. I think I'm perfectly safe, don't you?"

I chewed on my lip. "Well, I know I drive a little too fast, so maybe I'm not the one to judge you, but if we have a ways to go on the freeway?" I scanned around, looking over my shoulder and at her.

Her hands were at ten and two, and she cracked me up with how she looked driving. It was like this was her first time out, and I was the driving instructor who was going to determine whether or not she was getting her license.

"We're fine here."

"Next time I am driving," I teased. "So, your stepmom, Carmen, suggested this meeting? How do you think it's going to go down? I'm feeling kind of nervous."

"Carmen told me that one of her nursing friends started going to AA after getting out of a relationship with an addict. She had major codependency issues and some addictive behaviors of her own, so she ended up at a meeting because she didn't have anyone else to talk to who could understand what she was going through. After seeing the bullshit Derek pulled on you at the beach and then hearing your story, I couldn't help but think of this."

"Well, I'm glad you suggested it because I don't think I would've ever thought about it."

"Let's see what it's about," she said encouragingly. "You never know when wisdom is going to decide to smack you upside the head."

ASH COULDN'T HAVE STEERED me in a better direction with the suggestion of AA, and she and I started to come to these meetings every Friday night. I felt terrible that she was continuing to drive all the way here to do this with me, but Addy got to see her on a few occasions, and my little girl loved that.

Coming to these meetings was oddly comforting to me. It made me feel a lot less alone in the world. People had it so much worse than me, more than I would've never imagined, and I was reminded of that tonight when Sharon spoke.

I felt my stomach drop like I was on a roller coaster and tears well up in my eyes. She was speaking directly to my hardened heart and soul with her realization that even though she'd stopped using, she was still sick. Sick because of the addict. Sick because she was always making excuses to enable her husband and not leave. Her codependency and enabling resulted in her children becoming addicts also, something that she'd thought she worked so hard to prevent. Her entire life had been one, long, miserable fight.

I was in tears when she finished speaking, realizing that I was sick like she was. I'd stopped abusing drugs many years ago, but I never stopped hiding and making excuses. I didn't see it before, but my choices made me as much of an enabler to Derek as his parents were.

"You doing okay, Av?" Ash asked as we got into her car. She could see I'd been crying since we listened to Sharon's story, and I could only imagine what was going through her head.

I smiled through my tears. "I think I had a breakthrough," I said with a certain amount of surprise in my voice. "It's only the beginning, I know, but I get it now. At least I think I do."

"Sharon's story was heartbreaking," she said, rubbing my arm. "May I ask what part of her story got through to you? I saw your entire demeanor change when she was speaking."

"Week after week, I've listened to these people share their stories. My whole life, I've felt like I was dealt the shittiest hand possible, and since we've been coming here, part of me feels like I've softened up a bit, knowing that there's always someone who has it worse." I tried to organize my thoughts as they flooded into my mind. It was like a dam of information had burst.

"Don't get me wrong. I take no pleasure in hearing the horrible things these people have had to endure."

"You don't even need to say that. I know you don't," Ash said.

"It's just that—well, I've been using the pain of my past as a barrier, I think. I know that sounds strange." I shook my head, thinking that I probably sounded like a rambling idiot. "It's not easy for me to admit this, but I think that I've probably spent my entire life being the victim. God, I fucking hate that word—victim. If I'm honest about it, I've used that word as a justification for me not to share my life with people. It's the dark cloud that follows me everywhere, but it's there because I let it be there." I rested my head against the headrest. "I lost Jim because of it. I was too fucking stubborn to open up all the way. I hid my dirty, dark secrets, allowing Derek to get away with whatever he wanted. My enabling cost me the most important relationship I've ever had."

I started sobbing, and Ash leaned over and rubbed my back as I cried into my hands, the gravity of my actions slamming down onto me like a ton of bricks. It wasn't just about Jim. It was about my entire life. I'd always blamed my upbringing and young adult life for being the reason why my life always seemed to turn out wrong, not realizing that I was feeding it. I'd been self-sabotaging for as long as I could remember, and now, it felt like everything was coming into focus so suddenly that it made my head spin.

I finally took a deep breath and sat back in my seat. "I need to eat or something."

Ash laughed as she pointed at a Denny's across the street. "Breakfast for dinner is always a good idea."

AFTER FILLING myself up on pancakes and sausage, we sat at our table, and I fidgeted with my coffee cup quietly.

"You know, when Sharon was talking, my heart broke for why she finally gave up, hoping it would make up for the past of everything that went bad."

"I know," I said, curious as to what had struck a chord with Ash.

"After my dad had his heart attack, I did a pretty quick downward spiral. I was an absolute mess, thinking about losing him after I'd lost my mother. Jake tried to help in the beginning, but I instantly snapped at him and pushed him away. I was so frightened of losing everyone that I subconsciously tried to push them away. It sounds so ridiculous, right?" She took a sip of her milkshake and shrugged her shoulders. "My point is that we are all such complex individuals, and I think there is so much going on under the surface, driving us to do things without us realizing it. The fact that you can see where you've used the victim role as a crutch—knowingly or not—is crucial because now you can try to control it instead of letting it control you. It's all about choices and taking back your power. You drive your life. Your life doesn't drive you."

I grinned. "I like that—taking back my power. I feel like a weight has been lifted. When Sharon said it was forgiveness that helped her take her life back, that the things that'd happened to her weren't her fault, that really hit home."

Ash reached across the table for my hand. "Avery, have you felt that what happened to you since you were a little girl was your fault?"

"My mom overdosing and screwing men? I mean, why would you do that if you loved your child and wanted them around? My grandma killed herself after I moved in. Was it because I reminded her of her daughter? Or was it just the burden of having to take care of me? Either way, she killed herself all the same. And then, of course, there were all the foster parents. We were burdens to them, and they never let us forget it in more ways than one. They just wanted the money." I rubbed my hand over the back of my neck as I spoke, knowing that talking about it would only help me find a place for my feelings. "No one ever told me any of those things weren't my fault, so I guess it never occurred to me that maybe they weren't. By the time I stopped running away and found a good family who cared about me, I was too far down the rabbit hole for any of it to mean anything to me." I placed my elbows on the table and gripped my forehead, "I guess the weight of that made me feel kind of worthless. Maybe it's easy to keep making fucked-up choices when your self-worth is non-existent. That's why I ended up hooking up with Derek against everyone's advice. After getting pregnant and all that, I just felt like I'd made my bed and now it was time to lie in it. I realize now, that couldn't have been farther from reality. It seems so clear to me at this moment."

Ash and I just stared at each other and laughed with my newfound realization. I knew I had a very long road ahead of me, but at least I understood now.

"What are you going to do now?" she asked, stealing the thought from my head.

"Derek is the most toxic thing in my life," I answered her as I sank back against the booth. "In Addison's life. I have to get him out of it just like Jim was saying all along." I shook my head, loving that man for trying so hard and wishing I had been smart enough to listen to him. "I have to find a way to sell my car," I said. "I have no idea where to start, but I'm going for it. I've had an irrational fear—planted by Derek—that the court system would take Addison from me if I ever went after him. He says I'm no better than he is in the court's eyes, but I don't believe that. I can't believe that if for no other reason than the fact that my record is old and his is fresh and still racking up charges regularly."

"You have no reason to be afraid that she'll be taken from you. None. I can't believe he made you think you were no better than he is after everything he's done," she said sympathetically. "I wish I'd picked up on this earlier."

"I wouldn't have listened," I answered her truthfully. "It's why I walked out on Jim and never looked back. He tried helping. I shut him out for it."

"Out of curiosity, why are you selling the car?"

"That car has to be worth a lot of money," I said. "I can get a retainer on a lawyer and another regular car to get Addy and me around. In his own way," I smiled, hoping one day Jim would one day know that he did help me, "Jim helped pay for the lawyers."

"You're going for it, then?" She smiled.

"My sponsor, Javier, told me about lawyers who help people in my position."

"Call Javier tonight, then, and if there's anything Jake and I can do to support you or help in any way, you know we'll be there."

"Would you mind asking Jake if he knows anyone who can help me sell a luxury vehicle? I'd really appreciate that help."

She smiled. "Done. And if you can't find another, trust me, Jake's as much a car enthusiast as Jim is. We have a Range Rover that we never drive. Why don't we trade the cars out? Jake will sell yours for you, and you can use ours until you find something else." She eyed me. "You're going hard and fast. You need to be sure you're ready for this."

"I know what I need the most, and that's to get that addict away from my daughter. If he doesn't want help, he can destroy his life, not hers."

"Let's get out of here," Ash said with a smile, grabbing the ticket. "Dinner's on me, sweetie."

THE NEXT MONTH went by slowly and roughly, but it was steady. By the time I got the money to retain a lawyer and begin the custody battle for Addy, Derek had rolled his truck in the canyons and was in critical condition for over a week. I never went to see him in the hospital. I only got reports from Larry and Annette. I was still throwing everything I had into getting custody of Addy, and I was determined to win this case no matter what.

The week after Derek was released, I went over to his house to talk to him about custody, but I didn't want to go alone, so I asked Javier to go with me, needing the support from my sponsor, and he was more than happy to come along.

Addy played in the backyard with her papa while I got real with Derek.

"You won't see her again until the court custody battle is over," I said. "I'm done having her around someone who is constantly putting her safety in danger, Derek. That will never happen again."

"No, I get it," he said.

"You need help, Derek," Javier said gently. "There is a program, but you have to be willing to commit yourself and leave it all behind."

"Leave it all behind?" Derek laughed. "What does that mean? I'm clean now."

"A brush with death will sober you up, but you have way too many triggers and enablers here." Look at me, giving addiction advice. Who would've seen that one coming? "You'll learn more if you really want to get sober. You have to do it for you, though, not for anyone else."

"What about us, the family you and I started?"

"We lost that a long time ago," I said. "You have to remove that idea from your mind. We can never be a family, Derek," I said firmly. "I'm not in love with you. I never really was. Your feelings for me aren't love either. They're codependent. You have to make this decision for yourself, but I will get custody of our daughter, no matter what."

Never in my life would I have imagined Derek agreeing to this, but I think he'd hit his bottom, and he knew that he couldn't continue in this way. He gave me full legal and physical custody of Addy, and he agreed to pack up his things and head to a ninety-day recovery program in Florida.

I was finally free of all the chaos that I'd helped create in my life. I would continue my healing and keep taking things day by day, but my black cloud had dissipated, and I was determined to let the sun keep shining down on me.

CHAPTER FORTY-ONE

Jim

I strummed my fingers on my desk, studying numbers on my computer screen. We had to make changes for sure. I wasn't going to grow this business by taking on anyone and everyone who wanted an opportunity these days. In my board meeting this afternoon, I hope that I'd gotten that message across to everyone in my acquisitions team, who'd been headhunting like we were trying to buy up every last business on the entire globe.

"Jimmy," I heard Collin's voice call out when Summer announced him into my office.

I glanced up, needing to give my eyes a break from the list of businesses I was going to send to Alex. I needed a fresh set of eyes and more information before I decided whether or not we needed to pull back on investing.

"How's the brain surgeon this fine afternoon?" I asked, leaning back in my chair and happily greeting the man who sat across from me.

"Better than your sorry ass." He crossed his leg over the other and reclined back. "How long have you been staring at that computer?"

"I think you know the answer to that. Alex most likely wants to kick my ass, though." I chuckled, resting my chin on my fist.

"Well, I'm only here to ensure this damn documentary for the neuroscience wing at Saint John's is finally in my past, but if he wants to kick your ass, I might stay to watch that," he joked. "What's going on with you?"

"We lost a deal to fucking Brakken a week or so ago, and ever since, it's had me thinking that we need to slow down. We're turning into fucking sharks, feeding on chum in the water these days. I'm not going to lose my grip on this company by expanding too hard and too fast."

"And so, he's doing hard cutbacks." Alex walked into the room, holding papers in his hand. I knew he was here to argue about what I'd emailed him. "What the hell is this, man?"

"That was faster than I imagined." I grinned at him as he sat next to Collin across from my desk.

Collin laughed. "Here we go!"

"We're not dropping anyone, but cutbacks, yes," I said to Alex, ignoring Collin. "We're just trimming the fat."

"This is because you lost to Brakken, isn't it?"

"Partially, but I couldn't have won that battle no matter how hard I tried. We need to take a step back some." I nodded at the spreadsheet he held in his hand from the data I'd sent him, "Those businesses are not developing as well as we thought they would. We'll be throwing money away soon enough."

"Kicking some businesses out of the nest and letting them learn to fly on their own, eh?" Collin chimed in.

Alex glanced up from the paper and looked at me, "Some of these poor little birdies won't figure it out before they hit bottom."

"I'm not that big of an asshole, despite what most might believe, Alex," I said. "I'm not dropping anyone. We'll cut back, and either they'll work harder to increase growth, or they can find a new company that is more suited to help them."

"I get it." Alex nodded in agreement. "Some of these have lost buyers' interest, and some are flat out bad with reviews."

"The hotel chain with multiple bed bug complaints?" I sighed. "I'm not dying on that hill. This is why we need to either be more invested or pull back completely. We can only help so much. They need to be willing to do the rest."

"It's pretty much five o'clock," Collin said. "I left the office early to ensure my shit was done and over." He glanced over at the spreadsheets Alex held. "Unless I'm on your little blacklist and have to learn to fly on my own."

"You're good. When we go to launch, I have a feeling this will be the best introduction to medical science since Jake's heart institute."

"Having cameras in the room while he instructs on his surgeries—it's Jakey's dream come true."

I smiled at Collin's remark. "If we can get you to do the same, I have a feeling Saint John's will officially be on the map."

"Slow down, cowboy. I thought you were taking things slow." Collin laughed, standing up and walking over to my office fridge and pulling out a bottle of water. "Speaking of which, now that we have your complete attention, you realize that if you back out on Saturday, Jake's going to wipe the floor with your ass, right?"

"Fuck," I said, rubbing my forehead. "I had planned to go through more—"

"A man who despises excuses," Alex leaned back in his chair across from me, "is about to drop one on his poor brother. It's the only thing Jake wants to get out of his way before little junior gets here in two weeks."

"Hasn't he considered the fact that our lame-ass bike ride up to Big Sur is potentially dangerous for a soon-to-be father?"

"Oh, hell," Collin said, taking another drink of his bottled water. "You know?" He looked over at Alex. "I'm confident Jake hasn't considered the death rates of taking his street bike up the coast with his brother and friends."

"I'm serious," I said. "We did that shit before Jake was about to have a kid. I'm pretty sure Ash would like to—"

"Save it, Jim," Alex said. "Don't go into the dangers of taking out our street bikes. I think we should focus more on the dangers of you being glued to work and hardly even going out with us at all for over a month now. Jesus."

"Yeah," I said, not daring to allow the topic of Avery to come up. Everyone had left it alone, and that's exactly how I wanted it. "What time and where are we meeting up?"

"Jake's house at six in the morning tomorrow." Collin stood. "I'll see you there. I feel like I haven't slept in weeks with all these lined-up surgeries and neurology consultations. It seems like I've been busier this month than I was during my entire residency."

"You look like hell." I smiled as I stood and started to pack my shit into my bag. "I just didn't want to insult you after you drove all this way to make sure I wasn't lying when I texted that your documentary was good."

"I don't trust texts." He smirked. "A chick tried to dump me over a text, and when I went to see her, she said she didn't mean it."

"What the hell?" Alex laughed.

"Dead serious," Collin said, turning to leave. "I told her that maybe she didn't mean it then, but I meant it now. Anyway, I'm out," he said, waving and leaving my office the way he'd waltzed in.

Cool as a cucumber. That was Collin.

"See ya, Coll," I said, knowing my friend was probably exhausted from work. I felt bad that he had to drive here to confirm that he was good to go with his part on the new wing of the hospital. My work was hard, but I wasn't saving and changing lives the way Collin was.

"You enjoy the guys tomorrow." Alex sighed as he stood. "I've got to meet Collin's worst enemy."

I frowned. "You're kidding. Tell me you're making the mistake of hooking up with her, or otherwise I'm going to assume it's because she's a bitch who's overstepped her bounds with my VP."

"It was my idea, dip shit," he said. "Since you and Avery split, I haven't had time for jack-shit outside of this place. I have to go over the final numbers for the quarter with her. It's not that big of a deal. I just didn't want to drop it on Collin after he showed up tonight, looking tired as fuck."

"Now, I'm definitely sucked into this bike ride." I scratched my forehead.

"What are best friends for?" He laughed, then left my office.

I had been running hard, and so was almost everyone else around me these days. I knew precisely why Collin had driven up here, too. These guys hadn't seen me as much because I'd been buried in work, and I knew what they were thinking—it was because of Avery.

Sadly, throwing myself into work was the best healing remedy for the pain in my chest. I was so madly in love with that woman. I still couldn't imagine myself without her, but I couldn't imagine myself with a woman like her either. Fucking lies and secrets? It's all our relationship added up to be, and that was what cut me the deepest. If Avery had loved me as she said she did, I wouldn't have been left in the dark with her past.

Maybe a fast and adrenaline-filled ride up the coast on my street bike would do me good.

WE TOOK off from Jake's house bright and early, and the love for being on the bike, especially riding it up the coast, was coursing through me. There was something about controlling all this horsepower, bringing it and me through the turns, laying it over hard, and finding the apex to where I pulled smoothly out of the turns. It was fucking magical and made me return to my carefree days when I did this all the time with my brother, Collin, and Alex.

Pacific Coast Highway wound through the side of the cliffs above the ocean, and with the tight curves and the sea below us, it was my favorite place to be on the bike, especially on this particular ride farther north to Big Sur.

After arriving and having lunch at our favorite diner—all of us still acting like adrenaline junkies from the ride up the coast—we walked across the street and sat at a bench near a vista point, seeing the waves crash below us.

"Damn," Collin said, leaning his elbows back to the table behind him and stretching out his legs, "it's almost like you can appreciate the ocean more from this vantage point."

"What, you'd rather be up here with waves violently rushing the shore instead of checking out the ladies on the shoreline?" I asked, sitting on the table and using the seat to prop up my feet. "You must've lost your mind somewhere back there."

Jake sat on the far corner of the long picnic bench, sitting and leaning against the table with his legs stretched out and crossed. Being on a bike for hours made one's body beg to stretch out after all that crouching.

My brother shook his head and pulled off his square aviator glasses. "You are kidding, right?" he asked me. "You do know what time of the year this is, don't you?"

Collin laughed while I stared out at the ocean. "Right. My God, November came out of nowhere," I said.

"You're going to miss the birth of your nephew if you don't get your head out of that company and come up for some air," Jake said. "It's fucking ridiculous. What is that place to you now, a hellish cocoon that you hide in since you and Avery called it quits?"

"Assume what you want about that, Jacob," I said. "I knew your sorry ass would bring it up eventually, and how I'm the dick in the equation."

"What the hell is wrong with you?" Jake stood up. "This isn't about Avery, Jim. It's about my fucking brother. Before her, you were a control-freak workaholic." He walked toward where he faced me, both of us escalating in our irritation. "And after her, you're right back to the grind, huh?"

"You have no idea—"

"Right!" Jake snapped, cutting me off. "Let me guess. I have no fucking idea what it takes to run the goddamn company," he mocked me in some fucked-up tone. "No, *Dad*, I don't. I don't want to fucking know, either. What I do know is that when you were with that woman, the whole damn place didn't fall apart, did it? It still fucking ran like the well-oiled machine it is."

"Why are you bringing this shit up?" I asked, pissed-off, and ready to blow up.

"Because we finally had you back. Fuck, we actually had you back better than we ever had you before, and now it's this shit again."

"Say what you want, Jake," I answered. "Leave Avery out of it."

"You're the one who showed me—through Avery—that you could have a relationship outside of that fucking place. Now it's over, and you're buried in it again."

"You'll never understand."

"You know what, fuck you, Jimmy," he said, angrier than I'd ever seen my brother. "I can't ever have a normal conversation with you. After all these years, you still use this fucking bullshit CEO tone with me? Fuck that. I don't work for you. I want my goddamn brother, for fuck's sake. I want my kid to have his uncle. You're so buried in that place that I'm pretty fucking sure you'll just have your secretary send cards."

"Oh, calm down, Jake. Jesus Christ," I said. "You make no sense."

"Maybe not to you," he answered.

"All right," Collin interrupted. "Fucking enough between you two." He exhaled while Jake threw his hands up and walked away in frustration.

"Fuck," I said, annoyed with my brother, watching as he walked down the coastline from where we were, calming down. "Is he that wound up that I'm working again?" I leaned my elbows on my knees. "If I'd known Avery and our breakup would turn my brother against me, I would've never gone down that road in the first place."

"It's not that," Collin said, turning some to face me. "What happened between you and Avery, exactly? Was she hiding shit from you? Did you even give her a chance to speak her side of the story of her background check? I haven't been able to get past that: Jim and Avery split over a background check."

"It's more complicated than that. She made me look like a jackass for an entire month, shutting me down when I'd question why she wouldn't take her ex to court. Poor Addy." I exhaled, feeling the anger over the idea of it all again. "That little girl has no one to protect her from her loser of a father. I fucking hate addicts, and Avery was in his corner the entire time." I glanced over at Collin. "All because she was just like him. It would've been nice if that part of her life had come up in conversation."

"Would you have kicked her ass to the curb if it had?"

"Her charges were so fucking long ago, and she's clearly pulled herself out of living that kind of life." I ran my hand through my hair and looked out at the ocean. "I would have never broken it off over her past, Collin," I said. "It wasn't about that, not entirely, anyway. It was mainly the fact that she was still enabling this bullshit because of her past. I know all too well how fucked up it is to enable an addict like that, much less bringing an innocent kid around that shit and making excuses for doing so as if you aren't hiding from your secrets. It fucking reminds me of our mom. Jake wants to stomp off like that after I've done nothing but carry the weight of what that woman did to us? I shielded him from everything, and then I took Dad's seat in the company, so Jake didn't feel the pressure. He has no idea how much I love his stupid ass, and I hate that work might do exactly what he said, and I end up having some weird, distant relationship with my nephew."

"You do let that place swallow you up. Jake's right about that. You also know you can run that company and still be present like you were when you were with Avery," Collin said. "Listen, we've grown up together, and I know for a fact that you still struggle with hating your mom for what she did to you."

"Don't sit here and tell me I shouldn't hate that bitch," I said.

"Your hatred for the woman is being projected." His voice was low and sympathetic. "No room for error," he said with a smile. "It's the rule Jacob and I live by as surgeons. We have to, or we lose a patient. You, however, live by that rule harder than anyone I've ever seen in my life. It's all stemming from the bullshit you're carrying with you because of what your mom did. You project all your shit onto something else. You can't hold down a goddamn relationship—even when it's a fucking stupid mistake like you made with Julia or Lillian, mostly a good one like you had with Avery."

"No room for error?" I softened up some. "Well, in Julia or Lillian's cases—"

"Those women were the epitome of the word error." He laughed. "I'm not shitting you, though. You have deep-seated issues, and they're fucking with you big time."

"Even if I agreed that you might be correct that I don't give anyone a chance—perhaps, in Avery's case, specifically. I don't know. It was like as soon as I found everything out, all I saw was my mom, someone who was okay to put her child in danger to cover her secrets. It's just—I don't know. It's a lot."

"That's when therapy comes in, my man," Collin said. "I work arm-in-arm with therapists, and I know they can help you get all this scarred-up shit out of your system. You need to talk to someone, though. You have to let go of this hatred for your mom."

"And if I can't?" I asked him, knowing he was right, even though I wished I could tell him he was full of shit. There was no denying what he was saying was accurate. "Then what?"

"You lose Avery for good, even after she was brave enough to get help and try to fix herself," Jacob said.

"What are you talking about?" I asked, pulling off my sunglasses and looking at him as he approached. "She went to rehab? Was she using?"

"This is what I'm fucking talking about," Collin stood and stretched. "Look at you, jumping to accusations." He snapped his fingers. "And just like that, too."

"She didn't go to rehab, you dick," Jake answered. "She and Ash have gotten pretty close since you broke up. Carmen had a friend in nursing who went through a similar situation as Avery did, so she started going to AA meetings to be surrounded by people with similar experiences who could show their support and encourage her. They've been going to meetings every Friday for weeks, and Ash said that Avery's done some intense work on herself as a result. She even decided to sell that Aston Martin to pay for lawyers so she can get custody of Addison. Say what you will, but she's taking care of herself and doing the work that needs to be done, and she's doing it for herself, which is more than I can say for most people in her situation."

My lips were suddenly dry. It never even crossed my mind that she would change anything, let alone face her problems and fight to do what's right. I'd slammed the door on her and our relationship the second I saw that report. I'd lumped her into my mom's category and threw away the key. Collin's revelation to me that I projected my issues onto others was slapping me in the face at this very moment.

"Wow." I looked at Collin. "You were fucking right, both of you. I guess Mom took away my ability to believe people can be redeemed, huh?" I was half-joking, but if I was honest, part of me felt like I might spontaneously cry, and I think the guys could tell.

"That's why you need therapy," Jake said thoughtfully.

"That's what you gotta fix, Jimmy," Collin said. "I've got some friends that you can reach out to. You just need to learn to let the fucking hate go, man."

"Once you get some help, maybe you won't blow up your next relationship," Jake said with a shrug.

"Well," I smiled at both Collin and Jake. "Glad this bike ride turned into a Jim therapy session for us."

"You're lucky you have Collin." Jake smiled. "I couldn't give a fuck before he started talking sense into your stubborn ass."

"Let's go before I decide to throw you over the cliff as my therapy," I said.

"Let's do it," Collin agreed.

I KNEW the work that I needed to do wasn't going to be easy, but I needed to let go of the resentment I held toward my mother. She'd made horrible decisions, but she didn't control my life anymore. As much as I hated her for what she'd done to my father, brother, and me, I needed to forgive her. Forgiving someone who never bothered to apologize is not the easiest thing to do, but I knew I was doing it for me, not her.

My therapist told me to write a letter to my mother, and when I was done, light it on fire and let my feelings go with my words. I didn't feel some kind of a weight being lifted from my shoulders or anything by doing the deed, but I can say with certainty that I felt lighter somehow.

I guess it was put to the test when I came to the hospital for the birth of my nephew, and I saw Avery in passing. I didn't see the addict, the liar, or the one who'd hurt me by keeping her secrets from me. I saw a woman whose face and bright blue eyes had always spoken to my soul. She looked healthier and happier than I'd ever seen her, and even though she was no longer mine, knowing she was in a good place made me feel extremely content.

I wanted to stop her and talk, but what would have come of that if I had? Would we have tried this thing again? I knew she was working on herself, and I didn't want to get in the way of that. More than that, I knew I still had a lot of work to do on myself. I was still a fucking workaholic, and those issues almost had my therapist ready to put me in a straitjacket.

I had a long road to travel, unraveling years of issues, and there's no way I'd bring Avery or Addy back into my life until I figured out how to live it better without needing Avery to be the one to help. This was all on me, and for the first time in my life, I was the one working on fixing myself.

CHAPTER FORTY-TWO

Avery

*W*ho would have imagined how freeing and marvelous life could be when leaving one's guilt and burdens of their past in the damn past. It wasn't an easy road, but what helped was staying in contact with Javier and Ash during the rough times.

Once I started down the road to forgiveness, dismantling my defenses wasn't always easy. At times, I found myself feeling alone and even a bit depressed. As strange as it sounded, I'd grown used to the chaos, and sometimes it felt like I didn't know what to do with myself without it. That was my dysfunction. I hadn't been addicted to drugs for a long time, but I had been addicted to the chaos and the fight to survive. Now, things were different, and I was learning how to enjoy the peace that my second chance had gifted me.

Derek had completed his ninety-day rehab, but against the advice of his counselors, he decided to move back home to his parents' house instead of staying in Florida and moving into a sober living facility. His relapse followed shortly after he arrived in Southern California.

When Derek had initially gone to Florida, Javier had encouraged Larry and Annette to attend counseling for families of addicts, to learn how to stop their cycle of co-dependency and enabling, but they chose not to participate. After Derek's relapse, however, they changed their tune. Derek had his sponsors, and they managed to persuade him to go back to Florida and stay there, and they convinced Larry and Annette to get the help that they needed too. Derek was addicted to drugs, and they were addicted to Derek. It was a horrible cycle, and it needed to be broken.

Addy and I were moving through life, one happy meal at a time. Her uplifted spirits and constant story-telling kept me going through the tough times as well. She was the reason we spent nearly every other weekend with Jake and Ash. I still couldn't believe that handsome little son of theirs. Little John had big blue eyes, a head full of dark, black hair, and he was already crawling at six months old.

The day that sweet little chubby cherub was born was the first time I saw Jim again. We shared a glance and a smile, and that was it. We left and continued going our separate ways. I wouldn't lie and say I felt nothing, or that I was okay with him walking away. Letting him go again without so much as a conversation was the hardest damn thing I'd done since getting on this new road to recovery.

As much as I wanted to regret what had happened between us— me, losing the best thing that'd ever happened to me—I wouldn't. I couldn't regret what I'd done, and I wouldn't make any excuses for it. If it'd never happened, I would have never realized that I needed help. I would have never sought help and started working on myself. So as much as I could've wallowed in self-pity or cast blame, I wouldn't.

He was the best thing that'd ever happened to me for many reasons, but mainly for leading me to find the road of self-love. I knew now that it was impossible to love someone without genuinely loving yourself first, and he'd given me that gift. For the first time in my life, I could honestly say that I loved myself, and that was worth more to me than anything.

The other gift he'd given me was Ash. I was sitting next to Collin in the backseat of Jake's Range Rover, heading with Jake and Ash to the yacht to celebrate her birthday. We were close to the port where the boat was docked, waiting for us to board. Springtime on the ocean? I knew this was going to be exciting. Ash's dad and stepmom were caring for the kids at Jake and Ash's beach house so the grown-ups could enjoy this three-day event.

"Jacob Mitchell." Ash reached over and gripped his arm as he turned into the parking area, and I saw their massive-ass boat, lit up like fucking Christmas. "Why the hell does the boat look like Jim has been hosting clients on it?"

Jake took her hand and kissed the back of it. "They're your clients, angel," he said. "Now, we mustn't be rude to everyone who has come to celebrate April fourteenth—the very day the world was blessed when you entered it."

"Good God," Collin said, eyeing me with a smirk. "You two should just keep this damn yacht excursion to yourselves. Spare us the sappy BS, Jakey."

"I'm sure you and Avery are so devastated that your single butts might run into a lovely single man or woman too," he teased with a wink through the rearview mirror."

"Damn it," I said as Jake parked the car. "My secret is out now. I'm not here to celebrate Ash's big day. I was only showing up for dudes and booze."

"Same here," Collin said. "Well, the booze part, anyway. These guys aren't my type." He laughed.

"Well, you two might be spending it that way." Ash looked back at us, "If Jake invited my gallery clients, I might not even see him tonight."

"Oh, you'll see me, even if I have to steal away the birthday girl. All right, kids. Let's get it started," he said, and that's when I was swept up into a tornado of bliss and craziness.

THE YACHT WAS luxurious beyond my wildest dreams. The party crew and catering were out of this world, and I ate more than my share. After moving through crowds of people and meeting Ash's clients, I was ready to give myself a break and have a martini. It was empty at the bar area, everyone hanging out in their own crowds, enjoying the music, the dancing, and the enchanting atmosphere after the boat took off a couple of hours ago, cruising through the bay.

Even at the bar, situated under the overhead deck, the cool breeze blew through and kissed at my face. I loved the salty air, and this martini was adding to my relaxation.

"Excuse me, ma'am?" I popped the olive in my mouth after cracking some lame joke to the bartender, and I turned to the man at my left.

"Sir?" I said, seeing Jim's brilliant green eyes, spellbound by his presence.

"Does your husband approve of you, sitting here at the bar all by yourself?"

I eyed him as he sipped his bourbon. His expression was light and happy. I thought I'd never see that look again.

"Why would my husband disapprove?" I asked, playing along like I would've when we were in England. I hadn't seen him in so long that I didn't know if we were still the same people anymore, but I wanted to talk with him—laugh with him—more than anything.

"Well, you're dressed as if you're here and single." He nodded to where everyone was dancing and enjoying the night out to sea. "And there's plenty of men out there, eyeing you in this stunning dress you're wearing."

I looked in the direction he looked, and then my eyes met his playful ones. "Interesting. To answer your question, though, I'm not quite sure what my husband would think." I shrugged, "I haven't seen him in many, many months."

"Months?" Jim's eyes widened as he sat next to me at the bar. "What the hell happened? Long-distance relationship?"

"It all started on our honeymoon." I waved the bartender over and ordered another martini. "We got all caught up in this Henry the Eighth and Anne Boleyn love story, stayed at an amazing castle, and who would've thought we'd turn into the pair—the modern-day version, of course."

"I see you still have your head, so maybe you're trying to say that he's the one who got his head cut off?"

"Alas, no," I sighed. "Anne Boleyn had a few secrets that she chose not to divulge to her beloved Henry—you know, past misdeeds. It turns out that Anne and I had that in common, and we were too stupid to speak up."

He eyed me. "I do recall that king was extremely hurt, and his rage —perhaps his madness of insecurities and his own personal demons led him to do the worst thing possible to his wife. Could it be possible that your husband did the same?"

"I'm not sure—just as Anne wasn't sure what the hell was going on in Henry's mind when he had her executed."

"Do you believe the queen was innocent?"

"I believe the queen had no other choice in her mind than to keep things from Henry. Unlike that queen, however, I didn't have people plotting to get my head lopped off."

He smirked. "This is a sad story. Does it also have a sad ending? I mean, for you and your husband that you haven't seen for months?"

"Not necessarily." I took a sip of my martini. "I don't know about my husband, but like Anne being stuck up in that tower, I sort of went through my own darkness when I learned how very wrong I was to my husband. I wanted to continue to hate everyone and everything for it all going to hell, but it took losing my husband to gain my knowledge that he'd been right about a lot of things. I was just too blind to see it."

Jim's face grew serious. "I believe this is the part where you can no longer compare yourself to Anne Boleyn and the mad king who had her killed."

"No?" I said, curious and smiling at him.

"Well, perhaps your husband was mad like that king, dealing with his own shit, but he got the hell over it, and it took him seeing his beautiful wife again to help him realize he had to have her back in his life. The mad king never changed." He smirked. "This is where your story should have a better ending, I would assume."

I felt my heart beating as it always had when I was at a loss for words with Jim, this beautiful face, and his mesmerizing eyes. "I would hope that, since I still have my head, it does end happily."

His forehead creased while he laughed. "I've missed the hell out of you. I'm not here to ask you to take me back, but I have to have you in my life again."

"If you're not here to ask me back into your life, sir," I reached for his hand that held his bourbon, and he turned his hand up to hold mine, "then why in the hell are you here?"

Jim pulled me gently against him. "Jesus, I don't know where to start, but I think I need to start by telling you that I am so sorry. Whether or not you can ever forgive me for the things I've done and said, I want you to know that I love you, Avery."

I framed his face with my hands, gently kissed his soft lips, and I smiled into his searching eyes. "I forgave you a long time ago, and more than that, I forgave myself for everything that caused me to hurt you."

"You have no idea how happy it makes me to hear you say that," he softly said. "I am just at a loss for words. You look more beautiful than ever."

"If it helps you find some words, I'll say this: I never stopped loving you. Ever."

CHAPTER FORTY-THREE

Jim

*A*lex and I had been caught in a last-minute meeting, leaving us the last two to board the yacht before the thing set sail with more guests than I'd imagined Jake would have invited. These were Ash's friends and beloved clients, though. My sister-in-law was as passionate about her clients as Jake was with his heart patients, so I shouldn't have been surprised by the turnout, but I was stunned when I finally spotted Avery.

As I stood in conversation with Jake, Ash, Collin, and Alex, my eyes drifted over to Avery—the most beautiful woman on the entire boat. She stood out in her blue, strapless, and form-fitting dress, and I could only imagine how her blue eyes sparkled under the light where she stood, talking to Clay and Joe. I could see how much happier she seemed all the way from here. She glowed radiantly, and I had to resist the urge to run over to her and scoop her into my arms. I wanted to wait for the perfect time before I approached her, and then, like a gift from heaven, she went to the bar—alone. It was a *do or die* moment for me.

I knew Avery was the woman I wanted to spend the rest of my life with, but how did she feel about me after our last conversation? I had so many questions, and as soon as I spoke to her, it was like we'd never skipped a beat. I didn't know if I would ever be lucky enough to hear her tell me she loved me again, and when she did, she answered my prayers.

I stole her away to a more private area of Jake's yacht, and we sat away from the noise. Jake and Ash smiled and nodded in approval when I looked to them to make sure they wouldn't bust my ass for leaving and taking Ash's friend with me as the night rolled on.

"So, that's what I've been up to since you last saw me and how I've dealt with all of those crippling issues," she said.

I was so entranced by the way her blue eyes twinkled as she told me her story, her beautiful smile and her scratchy voice were so sexy they had me silenced throughout most of our conversation.

"You look so much happier," I said, then I smiled and brought her hand to my lips from across the small table. "I can't even think." I laughed.

"You look happier too." She used her free hand to trace her fingers across my forehead, "Your usual frown line is gone." She chuckled.

"Believe it or not, I had my own shit to work out. Leave it to my brother and Collin to tell me I needed counseling."

"No, really?" She pulled back and crossed her arms, staring at me with her adorable questioning look. "Working too much? Yeah, probably trying to break you up with that damn phone you dumped me for, I'm sure." She laughed, and all I could do was smile and look at her like some fucking idiot.

"Actually, that's partially true." I smirked. "I'd reignited the old flame of being married to my work after we split up." I sighed and looked deeply into her eyes. "It turns out that I brought a lot of hatred into my life and kept it there due to my mom's addictions. Letting that all go—plus no longer hiding in work, and feeling like I had to fix anything and everything—it was the hardest thing I've ever done. It definitely took some time in therapy to get me to forgive that woman."

"Holy shit," she said. "I would have never imagined."

"You and me both. However, it was why I was such an unapproachable dick to you when I found out about the background check. I'm so sorry for the way I handled all of that."

"Don't be." She smiled. "It's all in the past. I let it go a long time ago."

"I can tell," I pinched my lips together, "because I truly don't deserve this second chance with you."

"Yes, you do. We both deserve what we want most in life. I say that assuming I am what you want most in life," she said playfully.

"You have no idea how accurate those words are." I stood. "Would —Do you..." I stopped talking and ran my hands through my hair. "Fuck, I can't think straight."

She rose and wrapped her arms around my waist. "Jim, it's still me. Stop being so damn nervous."

"What do you think about a change of scenery? I have a room to myself," I said, holding her. "Perhaps you'd like to join me in the spa on the balcony in my suite?"

"There's a fucking spa on your balcony?" she asked with wide eyes. "I would have to see this to believe it." She stood up on her toes, and her lips met my chin, sending an electric charge through me.

"Not kidding. Jake went all out on this goddamn boat," I said.

I texted Jake, letting him know that Avery and I were going to call it a night, and I had a request sent to the galley to deliver food to my quarters—it was still my Avery, right? She was probably starving.

"All the food you could possibly want will be delivered shortly," I said, looking back at her, trailing me down the spiral staircase. "Better than flowers, right?"

"Damn right," she said with a laugh.

When we got into my room, Avery and I laughed when we spotted her duffle on my bed.

"Jake thinks of it all, doesn't he?" I said.

"I would've never guessed, but I am also willing to bet that after all these months, Ash and Jake have had some good pillow talk about us. They probably knew this was inevitable," she said. "I've missed you." She was so sincere that it stopped my thought process —again.

"Let's make the most of this three-day boating experience, shall we?" I said. "Through those doors, you can change into your swimsuit, and meet me out in the spa."

She chewed on her bottom lip, then took her bag back in the large bathroom area.

Once we were out in the spa that overlooked the bay, Avery sat in front of me, leaning her head against my chest and rubbing her hands along my legs.

"This is the most beautiful scene, sitting in a Jacuzzi on a massive yacht, gazing at the lights on the shoreline. Fuck, this is the most amazing experience of my life."

"And here I thought taking you to a castle was," I teased, finally loosening the fuck up. I'd been acting as though it was the first time we'd ever met.

"Well." She turned her face up to bring her lips to where I could kiss them. "We didn't have the buffet there like we have here."

I ran my hand over her belly. "I never believed I'd hold you again. I fantasized more than once about finding you and bringing you back into my life."

"We're meeting again at the perfect time, I think," she said.

Then she was the one who fulfilled my aching need to touch her again. Her hand came over mine, guiding it down into her bikini. "Are you sure you want—"

"I want what I've been fantasizing about since losing you," she said, her voice low as she slipped off her bikini bottoms. "That night you first made me come. Remember it?" she asked while her head rested further under my neck. "You think you can match that?"

"I can do much more than match that, gorgeous," I said, taking the strings of her top, untying them, and kissing the back of her neck and over her shoulders. Damn, her moans—I fucking missed her moans more than I knew. "You're mine, Avery."

"Prove it," she said while I covered her hardened nipple with my hand and used my other to gently massage her clit.

I loved every part of this, Avery's ass pushing against my hard cock while I dipped my fingers into the warm pussy I longed to bury myself inside of again.

"Fuck, Jim, right there," she said. Avery loved it slow when I massaged this area, putting pressure at a certain point. I knew that once I brought my thumb into play and ran it in circles over her clit, I would have the woman coming in my hand. That was the only thing I wanted.

"Oh, sweet Jesus," she groaned, her fingers digging into my legs like they did the first time we'd done this. "God, it's been too long."

"I need to see your eyes, gorgeous. I need to see you come." She turned her head, and those glossy blue eyes were mine again. "Fuck, yes," I said, caught up in this with her. "Let it go, Av." My voice was low and breathless as I watched her ride out the orgasm. She dug her nails into my legs, and her lips reached to mine, our tongues and mouths fighting aggressively for the reunion they longed for.

After Avery came slowly down, my fingers slipped out of her, and I held her, tasting her delicious kiss. I was in pain for her—for more.

"I need all of you." I pulled away, and Avery turned her body to face mine. "Now," I said, her lips and teeth running along my neck and chest.

We were out of the spa, and I was laying Avery on my bed. We were both wet, but I didn't care. I had a feeling this night was going to roll on until morning.

Her legs parted for me while I stared at her beautiful pussy. "Fuck me, Jim," she said. "Deep."

I was out of my shorts before she could say another word. "I can't promise I'll be gentle," I warned.

"I don't want you to be," she said as I lined my cock up to her slick sex and began thrusting myself hard and deep into her. My elbows were firmly planted on each side of her head, and her hands covered my ass while I felt her warm, tight, and clenching pussy, pulling and accepting me with every thrust I used to bury myself deep into her.

"Oh, my God." Avery dug her fingers into my lower back. Fuck, I loved to feel her do this. "Like that, Jim. Right there." Her breath caught when my tip ran deep into her, "I love you," she called out, and I held myself still, knowing her sounds and her tightening around my cock meant my girl was coming.

I had this obsession of seeing her expressions when she climaxed, her face tightening, and then her biting her bottom lip while I felt her pulsating sex in a spasm around my cock.

That was all it took, and then I came so fucking hard. Every last sensation of losing her, needing her, wanting this, and never believing I would have it again was all leaving me while I filled her with my cum.

"You're mine," she said, running her hands up my back while I rested my forehead against hers and grinned. "Next time, I'm riding you."

Imagining that, watching her full breasts, bouncing for my viewing pleasure, made me wish I could instantly recover. I thrust myself into her. "I look forward to your magical ways of getting my dick back in the game, then," I said, then kissed her lips. "I fucking love you with all my heart, gorgeous. How about we do this all night?"

"Why not three days? They won't miss us, will they?"

I slid myself out of her and brought her naked body to lie on mine. "Part of me believes this whole birthday party was more of a ruse to get us out to sea together for three days." I laughed and swept her hair out of her face. "If you're up for three days of this, you know I'm not arguing. We've got a lot of time to make up for."

AVERY and I did exactly that, made up for not seeing each other in far too long. One thing was certain: I had my girl back now, that's all that mattered.

After the yacht docked in port, we followed Jake and Ash to their beach house to pick up Addy from Mark and Carmen, and I was positively the happiest man alive, knowing I had Avery back and I was about to reunite with the sweetest baby girl on the planet.

"Promise me you won't be as nervous with Addy as you were with me?" Avery teased as we flew up the clear freeway, following my speed-demon brother.

"I'm finally getting both of my girls back. You can't imagine how happy I am." I kissed her hand. "So she thinks that you both just moved away from me?"

"Yes," Avery said. "She just turned four, so you'll hear all about that too. That and I'm sure your little Susie stories will have to come back too."

"It's Sally, and don't forget about the rascals," I corrected her with a smile. "What if—I mean, if Addy does as well seeing me again as you imagine, do you think we're moving it too fast if I moved you both in this week? I'm ready, Avery. I want you both forever, and I mean that."

"We're finally ready," she said. "I think between the sex, food, and our private therapeutic sessions on the yacht, I know I'm never letting you out of my life or sight again."

"Same here," I said, feeling more confident about this decision I'd wanted to act on for too long, even when we weren't ready. It might've seemed absurd to the outside world, but this was my woman, and I would be a fool if I let her go again, even if it was only to a different house. "We've been apart long enough."

When we got to the beach house, my nephew and Addy were playing in the gated room. I must have looked like a rude asshole to Carm and Mark, but I wanted to see Addy and John more than anything. Jake scooped up my nephew after the little guy gave me a kiss, and then Addy's eyes met mine, and her smile could've lit up a baseball stadium. God, I missed this little girl. That smile was the prelude to her hugging me tighter than ever before, and I picked her up and held her in my arms.

"I thought I'd never see you again, Jim," she said. "Mom sold my car, too."

I smiled. Her info-dump was as adorable as she was. "We'll have to go find another one, won't we?" I said, Addy looking at her mom with the sass I missed so much.

"Yes! And a new house. Mom and I sleep in the same bed, but I don't like it when I can't stretch out good. She always says I steal the covers, but I don't know what she's talking about."

"Can't stretch out good means she can't lay like a starfish," Avery said with a laugh.

"What if I told you I never wanted to lose you or your mom again?" I looked at Avery, and she nodded. "What if I told you I want you to live in my house in a new room?"

"A new room? Like the one I picked the decorations for before we moved away?" she asked, her eyes wide.

"Exactly like that," I said. "Just the way you wanted it."

She choked my neck and squealed with excitement. "I love it!"

"And more Sally stories too?" I probably sounded like a damn fool, but I missed this little girl as much as I'd missed her mother.

"And those darn little rascals," she said with a crinkled-up nose.

"Yes." I laughed. "I think we're all set, then. You're moving to your new house, and we'll never have to miss each other again." She pulled back and nodded. "Deal?"

"You got it, mister."

THAT'S when I knew life would change forever. All I knew is that Avery, Addy, and I needed each other. They were my family. I had my life now—and it was finally complete. This was my final step in living the life I'd promised myself I would have after letting that demon of my past rule it for far too long. Those demons were gone, and they were replaced with my two beautiful souls of saving grace.

CHAPTER FORTY-FOUR

Avery

*I*t had been five months since Jim and I had reunited on Jake's yacht. One might have expected that reconnecting so quickly would have brought about some significant issues after so much time apart. Hell, if I were a betting woman, I would've put money on it. However, this was Jim, and he was different. Everything was different. He'd fallen out of my dreams, and after I'd worked out my issues, I was able to fully appreciate the gift that God had given Addy and me.

Jim had guided me in fulfilling my new passion for helping people who'd gone through similar life experiences as me, and he helped me to revamp and expand a women's shelter and support center in Los Angeles. My heart was burdened to share my story and to help encourage others and give hope to those who'd been suffering silently with trauma. I was living proof that there was always hope. We all had a choice to change our lives and live it on our own terms. I needed others to know how necessary it is to forgive yourself, even when it's the hardest thing in the world to do. Nothing brought me greater happiness than helping others come to those realizations.

On top of coming home every day to the most handsome and loving man in existence, and the wildest, sweetest daughter, I was living such a fulfilled life. I could never ask for anything more.

Addy was back in preschool at Mitchell and Associates, which made it easy for me to pick her up after work, but my favorite was when Jim would surprise me by showing up with Addy at the women's center for our McDonald's date night. The man's generosity and love had me constantly on the verge of bursting with pride for the beautiful family we had become. It was meant to be—we were meant to be this family.

"You realize you two have to pack some time today, right?" Jim said while he sat on the lounge chair next to where Addy and I played in the pool.

"We get to fly high!" Addy squealed, floating over to the steps of the pool and climbing out.

Jim tossed his laptop into the cushions next to him as Addy darted in his direction, soaking wet.

"Hey!" He snatched her by the waist and threw her over his shoulder. "You are going to injure yourself greatly and spend your entire vacation in a hospital, little missy."

"Addy," I said, my heart racing while I stepped out of the pool, "you're about to lose your pool privileges for a week if you don't stop running while you're wet. You know the rules."

"Sorry, momma," she said as Jim pulled my wet daughter to his side, and she clung to him like a little monkey. "Sorry, Jim."

"Apology accepted," he grinned.

I pulled Addy from his arms and set her feet on the ground. "Listen up, kiddo," I said, eying her and Jim, "you're way too spoiled, you know? Jim forgives you too easily when you're in trouble." I smirked at him when he bit his bottom lip, "You're going to go into your room and start picking out some warm clothes for our trip. Got it?"

"Yes, momma," she sulked and turned back to Jim for some support.

Jim quickly brought his attention to the sky, ignoring my daughter as she tried to tempt him to help her out of being scolded.

Addy went into the house with her new pal, Frances, Jim's housemaid. I swear, if it weren't for Frances, I'd lose half these battles of wills with Jim and Addy. The big, bad CEO was the world's greatest softy when it came to Addison.

Jim and I laughed when Frances started in on Addison, and Addy took the older woman's hand, listening quietly as she imparted her words of wisdom to back me up on Addy being safe at the pool.

That night after Addy was sound asleep in her room, Jim and I wound down our evening on the top deck of our home. I sat up from where I leaned against his shoulder and placed my wine glass on the table.

"Okay," I said, seeing Jim close his laptop and slouch against the sofa, "all of the work stuff finalized?"

"I'm sorry I've been neglecting you today." He ran his hands through his hair, "Since having you and Addy back in my life, bringing work home like this is the worst feeling ever."

I ran my hand over his leg, "You're lucky that I can enjoy the breathtaking views from up here when you're working on your laptop at ten at night." I smiled while he pinched the bridge of his nose and shook his head.

"Trust me, this will end. September can be a nightmare for me at times."

"I'm not worried about it," I said, scooting closer to him and running my fingertips through his hair.

Jim leaned closer to me, and I kissed his forehead. "Thank God for that."

"There's something you and I should talk about," I said. My tone made Jim sit up straight, and his eyes met mine with concern. "This spoiling stuff with Addy, we have to tone it down a little. It's starting to concern me."

"What exactly has you concerned?" he questioned. "Me giving in to her so easily?"

"Well, you're a pushover with her, that's for sure," I laughed. "I know there's gotta be one in the parental role who has to be the mean one—the grown-up." I arched an eyebrow at his lightened expression. "We both know that's me, but you're good with rules and mandating she follows them too."

He pulled me onto his lap, and I straddled him. "Then what has my beautiful lady so concerned? She's still the same child I adored from the first moment I met her."

"I just don't want her to live in a complete fantasy. I need her to learn that everything she has now, living here and in all this luxury, it doesn't come free. She needs to start to understand that you worked hard for it. I don't want too much to come so freely to her. Does that make sense?"

He licked his lips, "I will always work to make you and Addy both the happiest women on the planet, yes. I will have you know that I let her in on how I run the business that provides for us, and so, she's getting a good look at how to run a business like a true executive."

"Oh, really?" I smoothed my hands over his shoulders. "How exactly did you do that?"

"I had her help me in my office the other day."

"What the hell?" I laughed, imagining *that*. "What happened? Why didn't you tell me?"

"It was nothing. They were concerned about Addy's sneezing and running nose at the preschool. Didn't want to pass around a potential cold."

"Shit. Her allergies were bad last month, and I forgot to give her allergy meds. Was this when you texted me, asking which ones to buy for her?"

"Correct," he answered. "I knew it was allergies when they called me about her runny nose, so I walked down and asked if she'd like to work with me for the day while I sent for her allergy relief."

"That's the day you left work early and took her to go get ice cream, right?"

"It was easy enough to have Alex handle the meeting I had scheduled, and I could just work from the house."

"You took her to get ice cream." I arched an eyebrow at him.

"Of course, I did." He smiled. "My sweet gal's allergy meds hadn't kicked in yet." He chewed on his bottom lip.

"You're doing a fine job of derailing my initial concern about her becoming too spoiled and not understanding how hard you worked for the beautiful home she has, amongst everything else. I want her to appreciate it all."

"Very well, then." He cleared his throat and feigned being serious. "*Before* we left to get ice cream, I had about an hour's worth of work to finalize. So, I put her to work as the CEO's best assistant."

"Right, and I'm sure your secretary and Alex both enjoyed having a kid up there, bossing everyone around."

"Addy was an excellent help to us. I had her walking out a few portfolios to Summer. We played a few pranks on Alex too." He gave me that funny, handsome look whenever he was defending him and Addy. "We pranked him only because it's Alex, and, hell, it was fun." He shrugged and smiled.

"Pranks?" I sighed and laughed at his innocent expression.

"It kept her busy. The best was the paper airplane we made together," he laughed. "It was actually important numbers on a term sheet I had printed out for him. I would have naturally walked that down to him in a portfolio, but watching Addy go through the perfect movements of gliding that sucker into his office was priceless. I'll have to have Summer text you the video she took of it."

I started laughing, "You two are trouble."

"Only when mom's not there to bust us," he ran his hands up my thighs while bringing his lips to meet mine. "Other than that, Mitchell and Associates' vice president delighted in the paper airplane idea—until he unfolded the plane and saw the request for changes on the term sheet. I knew that would piss him off. He hates it when companies send shit back to us, requesting more addendums before signing."

"Even though I'm glad you found a fun way to deliver shitty news to Alex," I framed Jim's face with my hands, "you and Addy can't be trusted sometimes. This story helps the point I'm trying to make."

"What's your point, Av?" he looked at me in confusion.

"So, I've been thinking about this since we started planning this trip. Please don't get pissed off, but I'm a bit concerned about us taking your company's jet to England," I said.

"Do you believe it will crash?" he looked at me with more confusion. "That thing is a 787 Boeing. It's designed as nicely as Jake's yacht. Beds, rooms, everything is on that aircraft. More food than you and Addy could ask for as well." He laughed. "Addison wouldn't even know how long she was on the nonstop flight to—"

I silenced him by pressing my lips against his. "There," I ran my thumb across his bottom lip. "Now, let me finish. This is what I'm talking about—a private airplane. I've flown on your helicopters and one of the company jets already. They're beyond luxurious. I'm wondering if, for this trip, maybe we can book a *regular* flight for the three of us. Like, you know, one I would've normally taken if I were bringing her out there myself." I hoped I was making sense.

I knew Addy was only four, but I wanted her to appreciate the life we'd been blessed with. I wanted her to know that *real life* didn't come so easily, and most people would never know the luxury we had access to. Jim was a brilliant businessman who'd worked his ass off to get where he was. Addy needed to have her feet planted on the ground so she didn't lose herself in having things that most kids her age could only dream of. If it weren't for Jim, she wouldn't have anything close to what she had now. I needed to make sure she appreciated all of it and never took it for granted.

Jim studied me while I was silent. "Do you believe our lifestyle will turn her into a spoiled and unruly child?"

"It's not the lifestyle—I mean," I stopped myself and ran my hand over my forehead. "I don't know how to put this. I just want a hint of normalcy for her."

"That's perfectly understandable. Let's go for it with a commercial flight, then." Jim pulled out his phone and looked at me, "I'll see if we can get a last-minute flight out. First-class tickets will be more difficult to…" he paused and eyed me, chewing on my lip. "You want us in coach, don't you? The way we would fly if we were not wealthy, correct?"

"Would it be okay? You said work is finalized except for a few things at your London headquarters when we first get in, and so you won't need the company plane for business stuff."

I couldn't discern the look on his face. Was I being ridiculous?

"It'll work fine." He smiled and then started typing on his phone.

Close to five minutes later, he chuckled and smiled at me. "We're booked out on the first flight in the morning."

My phone rang, and I looked and saw Ash was calling.

"Hey," I said, answering the call.

"You ready for the big trip tomorrow? I thought I'd throw in a quick goodbye. Sorry that it's so late."

"I'm excited. We're leaving first thing tomorrow morning now."

"First thing?" she said. "Hang on, here's Jake. You're on speakerphone. My kid's out of bed again."

"How are the lovebirds faring?" Jake asked.

"Jim's excited to be flying commercial tomorrow," I said, smiling at Jim, who was sitting patiently while I put his brother on speakerphone. "He's right here."

"You're flying her out commercial?" he laughed. "And here I thought you were the charming prince."

"In fact, I am. Instead of the luxury jet—or first class, for that matter—I'm riding with my ladies at the back of the plane."

"You're joking, right? You understand your long-ass legs won't fit in coach, correct?"

"Hey, we're on a mission to show Addy that not everything is luxurious," Jim insisted.

Jake's laughter was making Jim laugh and making me feel like shit. "Fuck," I said, "I didn't think about you being cramped up on the plane."

"Damn, I hope you got a layover or three before flying out of the states." Jake said with another laugh.

"Nonstop," Jim said. "I'll survive it. It's a small sacrifice to make sure my girls are well taken care of."

"You'd better hope you got an aisle seat, brother. Avery?" Jake called out.

"Right here."

"Video this shit for me, please?"

AFTER THE LONG TRIP, and seeing Jim do his best to seek comfort at the back of the plane, it was evident to me that I should've thought about the man's height before I started throwing around ideas. We were definitely going to fly back to the States in the company jet since Alex was flying to London in it the next day.

Now, we were at the castle where Jim and I shared a lot of *firsts*. Addy loved the place more than I believed a child her age would. We explored the halls, played silly *haunted castle* games—Jim being the ghost and hiding all over to scare us. It was four days of picnics, walks, and us three being a family.

The day had finally come when Jim had the stablemen arrive at the house, and his horses were brought up to his massive barn—a mansion for horses. I noted seven horses were saddled, and I laughed when I looked at Jim, carrying Addy down in the adorable riding outfit we bought for her in London.

"You get to pick the one you want to ride," Jim said.

"Wait," I gripped his arm. "You promised you were riding with her, and she was sitting in front of you."

"I did, Mom," he answered. "I'm just letting her pick her favorite."

"We'll be lucky if I can remember how to ride from my teenage years," I said, feeling a bit nervous.

"Lose that attitude," Jim laughed. "Those horses are the most well-trained, best-behaved animals around; however, they'll feed off any fear you have, and you'll regret it later."

"You're right."

It took us a while, but we were now on our way. We rode at a slow pace through the massive amount of acreage at this place, and I basked in the contentment I felt, enjoying this peaceful ride through such beautiful terrain. I felt like we were the only three people in all of England. Once Jim saw that I was comfortable on my horse, we picked up our pace. As we trotted through the lush fields, I glanced over at Jim and Addy, and the sight alone made my heart smile with joy at the way they rode his horse together. Jim rode like a true equestrian, all while Addy beamed with pride as she sat safely in front of him.

We rode for about an hour when I noticed that we'd circled back to where Jim and I had sat under a walnut tree, overlooking the hills that rolled on forever, the first time we were here together. He dismounted, helped Addy down, and then I felt his hands on my hips as he guided me off my horse.

"You see," Jim started, taking Addy's hand while I held onto his arm, "your mom once wished she had time-traveling binoculars." He smirked at me and pointed toward the vast hills of England's stunning countryside.

"But why?" Addy asked him. "That's silly."

"Some might think so, but I thought it was a fantastic idea," Jim said while he led us to the tree, and I smiled at the memory. "You see, your mother wished she could see back in time so she would witness the history of this beautiful land."

"The history?" Addy's face scrunched up in question. "Why, though?"

"Because mommy loves the history of England," I said in an excited voice. "There are so many things that could have happened out there. With my time traveling glasses, I could've seen when kings and queens rode horses like we did today. Wouldn't something like that be pretty cool?"

"That would be," she said with a look that made it clear she was humoring me.

"But that's not all," Jim added. "If you could put on those glasses, you could see your mom sitting next to me at this tree. It's where I realized she was the most delightful woman I'd ever met," Jim said with a smile. "I wished I could marry her then and there."

I looked at Jim in confusion. This was a beautiful side of the story I never got.

Jim looked at me, "We were both chasing ghosts back then, in our own ways, of course. So, asking you to marry me then—well, that just wasn't the right time." He walked over to me and took my hand in his, "But being here now is different. I had to sort out so many things to be able to appreciate the woman who had stolen my heart in a way no other woman could," he said. "Perhaps we had to go through the fire in order to purify our love for each other?"

I grinned, "That's one way of putting it."

Jim's solemn expression didn't waver, "Avery Gilbert, you have fascinated me from the first moment I laid eyes on you, and you have changed my life in ways I didn't know possible. I love you so deeply, and even more so than the first moment that I knew I wanted you in my life forever."

I reached for my throat, almost about to choke on the lump that was suddenly there. Was he really doing this?

"You bring me peace that I can't explain. You breathed life into me from the moment you sat next to me on that plane. You've given me everything and asked for nothing except for my love," he said. "Before you, I was on autopilot, going through the motions of life but never truly living it. I can't go on another day without you understanding that you and Addy are the best part of my life, the part of my life that was missing. I humbly ask you to trust me and know that I will always love and protect you, and I promise to devote my life wholly to you and Addy above all things. Will you please bestow upon me the highest honor I'll ever achieve by becoming my wife?"

"Oh, God," I said, tears pooling in my eyes. "Oh, my God."

He pulled out a blue box and opened it. "If you'll have me, then I hope you'll enjoy this ring, one that I believe a king from long ago would've given the queen he loved so dearly."

"Without sending her to that tower, of course?" I laughed, cried, and then hugged him so tightly that I couldn't speak.

"I think we both served our time in that tower when we were apart for far too long," he said as I felt him laugh, and then I pulled back to lose myself in his shimmering eyes.

"Yes, of course, yes," I said as Jim brushed the tears from my cheeks. "But are you sure? Marriage might make—"

"What? Might make me the happiest and most complete man on

the planet?" Jim said and then silenced me with a small kiss. "I love you, Avery. There's no doubt in my mind."

I watched as Jim turned and knelt as he had the first time he'd met Addy, bringing himself to her level. Addy was smiling, but I could tell she was confused. "You are my best girl and the one I have the most fun with," he brushed his finger over her nose. "I can't marry your mom unless I ask something pretty big of you as well."

"How big?" Addy said.

"Huge." His eyes widened as he dramatized his answer. "Remember that one morning when you and I made green eggs and ham?"

"Yes," she crinkled up her nose and laughed.

He took her hands into his, "Do you remember what you told me you wished for me to be for you that morning?"

Her lips twisted in thought, and my ugly cry was in full effect. Was Jim asking Addy for her approval too?

"For you to be my real daddy," she said. "When I say my prayers at night, I always ask for it to come true one day. Do you think it can?"

"I think it can." Jim smiled. "In fact, that was the *huge* question I was going to ask. I wanted to know if you would still like me to be your daddy."

Addy's reaction was priceless as she hugged Jim, and then I heard her crying. I walked over to where Jim had her swallowed her up in his arms.

"Addison," I said, rubbing her back.

She looked at me through teary eyes and smiled, my own tears streaming down my face as I wiped hers away. "These are happy tears, yes?" I asked her.

"Jim loves us both so much," she informed me, hugging me tightly. "We can finally be a *real* family now. He asked, and we have to say yes, mommy. He's the best daddy ever."

"He certainly is," I said to her, then looked at Jim as he smiled brilliantly.

"I have something special for you too, Addy," he said, pulling out another blue box. "It's a charm on a necklace. Its symbol means that

I'll be your daddy forever. I'll always protect you, care for you, and love you more than you can ever know."

"Oh, my goodness," she smiled at Jim. "Can I wear it forever too?"

Jim grinned. "I truly hope you do," he said, putting the necklace on her and smiling. "Forever."

I watched as Addy held the charm out that Jim had clasped around her neck.

"That's the infinity symbol," I said, still kneeling next to Jim. "It means that Jim will love you longer than forever. That his love will never end."

"Yes, and now you'll always know that I'll love you as my very own daughter for all of our *forevers* together. I'm just not sure if you said *yes* or not?"

I watched Jim's forehead crinkle in humor.

"Yes! Forever you, me, and mommy." She hugged him again.

"Thank God, they all said yes!" I heard Collin's voice and then turned to see the entire gang was here—the reason for the other saddled horses. "Sorry, but I figured I'd be fighting that damn horse for the rest of the night if Jim didn't get his words out."

Ash was running toward me, and we collided in a tight embrace. "That was the most precious thing I've ever witnessed." She sniffed and stepped back, "I videoed the entire thing, but started crying after you said yes, then Jake rescued the video, so forgive my sobbing sounds."

"She handed me the phone, so it's probably really going to suck for Jim to watch after mine and Collin's commentary." Jake laughed. "I think it'll add to the moment nicely for you, though. Ash had no other option than to hand me the phone after she lost it completely once Jimmy proposed to Addy next." Jake smiled and hugged me. "Welcome to the family, kid," he said, then went toward where Ash was embracing Addy.

"You sure you want in on a *binding contract* with this guy?" Alex smirked at me as Jim approached, and Addy was already showing her beautiful necklace to Ash, Jake, and Collin, proudly telling them that Jim was her dad now.

"The binding contract will be signed." I laughed, hugging Jim's best friend, then leaned into Jim as he brought his arm around me. "The real question is, can all of you take us?"

"We accepted you both a long time ago," Jake said as he rejoined us with a wink. "Hey Addy," he said, reaching for her, "let's get out of here and let mom and dad look through their time-traveling glasses together. My horse is faster than Jim's, anyway."

"Yeah, he's sorta my dad now, Jake."

Jake chuckled. "Well, then, that makes me your uncle, and I expect to hear *Uncle Jake* come out of that mouth next time."

THEY ALL RODE OFF TOGETHER, leaving Jim and me alone to soak up this treasured moment. We sat down next to the tree. "God, I love you," I said, tearing up again. "I'm at a loss for words."

Jim brought his arm around me as we reclined against the tree. "So, I planned that we'd take off for that little hotel we stayed at before. Then, after a night alone, perhaps you and Ash will start in with the wedding arrangements."

"It doesn't need to be anything fancy." I laughed.

"Fantastic," he kissed my temple. "Then, when we're back in the States, we'll head to the first courthouse we see. The next monumental question I want you to consider heavily is solely up to you and what you believe is best for Addy."

"What is it? My mind is still stuck on your amazing proposal."

"Well, I was thinking," he said, "you know how you got full custody of Addy after Derek got locked up again?"

"Kind of hard to forget when your kid's dad flunks out of rehab for the third time and then goes on a crime spree before getting sent to prison for the foreseeable future, don't you think?" I said with a half-laugh. I wished I could say things were going differently for Derek, and he was now the father he should've been, but the truth was that he was better off in prison, and that was precisely where he'd landed himself.

"I think we all saw it coming from day one with that guy," he said.

"That's sort of what has me thinking. With me being surrounded by lawyers daily, I tend to overthink things sometimes, and I worry about things. What happens to Addy if something were to happen to you?"

"Jesus," I thought, almost in a panic. "I'd never thought of anything like that before."

"Well, I say all of this because I want you to know that I would gladly adopt Addison after we're married."

I shot up and looked at Jim as if he were high or something. "That is asking a lot of you. I mean a lot."

"Truthfully, I'd want it no other way. It doesn't change the way I love her or plan to care for her for the rest of her life, though, but it's asking you to trust me as her legal parent. Maybe it's a heavy thing to consider. I just want you to know that I'm all in, one-thousand percent."

"You're the best thing to ever happen to both of us," I answered, turning to face him. "I trust that we *will* be together forever."

He pulled me into his arms. "Then it's all settled." He kissed my nose, "You will soon be Mrs. Avery Mitchell, and our little wild child will be known to all as Addison Mitchell. Has a damn good ring to it, doesn't it?"

I straddled him. "What do you say we get these horses back to the house, say goodbye for the night, get in that car, and blast up to that castle?"

Jim arched his eyebrow at me, "I think I should drive this time."

"That's the thing about marriage, *darling*," I used the term we used when we were fake-married on our last trip, "what's yours is mine now."

Jim chuckled and nipped at my lips. "Are you sure you want that pain-in-the-ass company? That's the downside of this marriage, you know. I get a sweet little girl as my daughter, and my gift to you is that damn company." He laughed. "Still want everything that's mine?"

"I want the good times, the hard times, and the *until death do we part* times. I want you, and that's all that matters."

"God, I love you more than words, gorgeous," he said. "I'm inclined to fulfill a wedding night wish out here and right now."

"Anybody around?"

"If they were," he smirked as we lay back on the grass, "I think we'd scare them off."

"Then hurry up and kiss me." I laughed, and that's when Jim and I took advantage of the gang taking off so we could celebrate this event alone.

I WOULD NEVER ALLOW myself to forget this moment—this day, that would change our lives forever. The way Jim's face was lit up with happiness the entire time. Dreams couldn't get better than what I had with this man. My life was fulfilled before this unexpected proposal to my daughter and me. Who would have imagined that, after everything I'd been through in my crazy life, I'd be so utterly blessed to have this man as my husband, and more importantly, the new, *real* father to my daughter?

My life was abundantly full. Did I deserve it? Before I got help, I would have said *no,* but now that I was healthy in my heart and mind, my answer was yes. I deserved this happiness, my daughter deserved this family, and we were *just* getting started.

DR. BROOKS: FIRST CHAPTER

BILLIONAIRES' CLUB BOOK THREE

Dr. Brooks

Collin

Medical conferences usually intrigued me, but this one kicked my ass. Thank God it was finally over. This thing was as dull as they got. The only presentations that seemed to shed new light on the medical science industry were the lectures Jake and I had delivered. Everyone else's talks and presentations made it feel like we were back in freaking high school when the substitute teachers determined we'd watch videos from the 1970s in science class.

I guess the most irritating part of this conference was the fact that my best friend, Jake, Chief Cardiovascular Surgeon, and I were the only presenters who seemed to have done our goddamn jobs to share our research. Contrary to what I'd been bored to fucking tears by since this started three days ago, mine and Jake's presentations were current, not some rewind of known case studies from forty years ago.

Thank God I was born with the gift of unwavering patience, or I'd have left this final lecture of the day. I was at my limit, and I needed a drink. Tonight, Jake and I would attend the after-party event, something we'd passed on the previous nights. Maybe one reason no one was complaining about the boring lectures was that they'd all probably been nursing hangovers since they got here—one of many reasons not to hold business functions in Las Vegas.

Vegas came to life at night. I knew that, and I'd lived that on numerous weekend trips before. This trip, however, I stayed off of the strip and stayed safely at my hotel's pool. Granted, it was the biggest party pool oasis I'd ever seen before in my fucking life, but it was still less trouble than I was used to. The pool was lit up to create the ambiance of the nightlife, transporting and treating guests to an enchanting evening in a tropical paradise. Acres of water, palms, and any other treat you'd expect to find while vacationing in your own tropical world were present. What wasn't present was the gin I needed in my hand right about now. That's when I spotted Jake, sitting at a spot that was designed to impress our sizeable medical group and further this experience by bringing us into an enchanting Tahitian resort.

I stepped up to where Jake was already seated on a barstool. "Hey, sexy, looking for a date tonight?" I gripped my best friend's shoulder as I slid onto a stool next to him. "I'll have a Bombay Sapphire, on the rocks." I motioned to the bartender who'd moved my direction.

"I don't date pretentious assholes who drink gin," Jake said with a laugh while drinking his scotch. "Jesus, man." He rubbed his forehead and looked over at me. "Am I ever glad this shit storm finally blew the fuck out of here."

I took a large gulp of my favorite liquor and let the drink bring my mind back to life again. "Yeah, Obstetrics 101 was my favorite course."

"Obstetrics 101." Jake rose his glass to me. "That's certainly one way of looking at these fucked-up lectures."

"Well, this whole conference is easily compared to the nightmare of our college years. What the fuck was this damn thing for anyway? Hell if I know anymore."

Jake laughed. "My guess is a lesson to teach each medical

professional about what others do for a living." Jake leaned his elbows on the polished wooden bar. "So, OB 101, eh? Did you learn how to deliver a baby today?"

I laughed, slowly unwinding with each sip of gin. "Yes, and it's a good thing I did." I brought the rim of my glass to my lips. "So, when you knock up Ash for a second time, she can use me as her midwife, and I can help deliver your next child in your bathtub."

Jake smiled. "The only in-home delivery you'll be doing for Ash is when she calls for Chinese takeout." He sighed. "Shit, this area is larger than I thought. Three fucking pools, waterfalls, palm trees?" He frowned. "Where are we, Tahiti?"

"I was actually looking for the exit to the beach when I walked out here," I said. "Though it's still not tempting enough to keep me here until morning."

That's when my eye caught the image of a vivacious and attractive young woman. She strolled out with a group of individuals, her beaming smile and the liveliness in her step instantly caught my attention, but it wasn't a minute before she disappeared through the crowd that surrounded the multiple pools.

I had no business letting my mind go in that direction with a woman while at a medical conference after-party, but I couldn't help but be taken aback when I saw her.

"Excuse me, gentlemen?" I was the first to look back and find a tall, hot blonde with bright red lips and a barely-there bikini, heading up a pack of what I quickly concluded were single women.

It didn't matter how fucking hot they were. Jake and I had drawn a hard line in the sand when it came to fucking around with women at medical conferences. That had nearly cost us everything while we were interns.

"Yes," I said, keeping the flirting at bay and smiling to be polite.

"We're from the Institute of Science medical internship," red lips started, "and we're looking to enjoy the night after this long conference. Do either of you mind if we join you?"

Jake's eyes met mine in warning, and this week had been such a disaster that I figured I might as well spice it up a little. My happily-married best friend was so in love with Ash that I didn't think he even noticed hot chicks anymore. His wild days were in the past, and so it was up to me to shake things up a little. The bastard had put me through hell enough times, and so I enjoyed repaying the favor now and then.

"Join us?" I answered the blonde. I eyed her red bikini and red stilettos, and I figured that if there were a Poolside Vegas Barbie doll, it would've looked exactly like this woman. I had to give her credit, though. She'd matched up her outfit—if you could call it that—to her lipstick. "You must be complimented on how you've coordinated all this red." I waved my hand toward her while the group of girls behind her giggled. "You'd make those hot chicks on Baywatch a tad bit jealous. I assume that was what you were aiming for?"

She laughed while Jake pointedly ignored the trap of women I'd been lured into. "Red is my favorite color," she said. "So, you guys are okay with us hanging?"

"Son of a bitch." I ran my hand through my hair. "I'm sorry. I almost forgot, and now I have to break your heart. You see, I'm married."

Jake looked at me while I slid my left hand discreetly to him, and he quickly picked up on my need to borrow his wedding ring so I could get out of this. These were interns—young, hot, and trouble. Being best friends since childhood, Jake and I read each other as twins would. Though, he had no idea what I was really up to, which made this situation that much more enjoyable.

I slid his ring on while using the distraction of ordering another gin. What the hell, did they water the liquor down at this place? Cheap-ass medical group most likely asked to have it served up that way.

"I didn't see a wedding ring on your hand," the shorter redhead in the bunch said. "Nice one."

"Oh, it's there, it just doesn't stand out so easily. Must be the onyx color of the band, but it's right here." I wiggled the fingers of my left hand and elbowed Jake. "If you want a hot and single doctor, this is your man right here."

"You're fucking joking, right?" Jake grumbled in a whisper.

It didn't matter how quietly Jake responded. These girls were tuned in and hanging on to every word.

"Well." I smirked at Jake, "I would be fucking joking if you weren't the best man at my wedding."

Jake turned back to the women, and his eyes widened when he took in Barbie and the whole Vegas gang. "Wow, you must like the color red..." he stopped himself, and I smiled. "Sorry. I thought my friend was fucking with you until now. You really did match up your lipstick to that bikini."

"You're awfully blunt," she snapped.

"It's why he's single," I chimed in. "You see, he's most likely already determining which one of you he's going to take back to his room and fuck before he sends you on a walk of shame." I met Jake's humored eyes. "You know I'm one hundred percent accurate on that one."

"There are plenty of women to back that up," he stated factually.

I looked back at the woman in red. "Does that lipstick rub off?" I pinched my lips while her face that twisted up into the pissed-off look we'd pulled out of her by acting like dicks.

Jake held his hands up in innocence. "Hey, I'm just the single asshole." Jake gripped my shoulder. "It's Mr. Forever Guy who loves to cheat on his wife while we're out..." He eyed me as if to show he'd just kicked the ball back into my court. "If you're into the brilliance of a sexy brain surgeon," he gulped his scotch, "this is your boy right here."

"Then why would he wear a wedding ring?"

"It's kinky," I said. "I think chicks dig being home wreckers. Now, I'm curious as to how you'll look with those red lips and no matching bikini."

"Right," Jake feigned curiosity. "Like, would it all work without the matchy-matchy?" He shrugged.

"Exactly." I took a sip of gin, "Do the lips complement the bikini?"

"Does the bikini complement the lips?"

"Heels no heels?" I answered him.

"Maybe I do want to find out for myself too. You up for sharing after you find out?"

I held in my laughter. "I'm shocked you're considering sloppy seconds this time." I looked at Jake, both of us being dumbasses like we were known to be when we weren't interested.

"You deserve first dibs. This conference was harder on you than it was me."

"Truer words have never been spoken. I'll text you when we're done." I glanced back to be confronted with deadly looks. "You still up for it, Barbie?"

"Let's get out of here, Kimmy," another girl said, but my attention was instantly diverted from the women on the prowl.

"They always say the hot ones are pricks." I think it was Barbie who said that. I didn't know or care. I was locked in on the gorgeous woman from earlier. I was fully absorbed as I watched her dance, swaying her hips fluidly in a flawless salsa style of dancing.

"Yeah," I said in a dismissive tone while I glanced around Jake to keep my eye on the sexy woman. I gripped Jake's shoulder. "Who the fuck is that on the dance floor?"

"The entertainment?" he answered, looking past the bar where we sat and out to the dance floor. "The hell if I know."

"I'm about to go find out."

Jake grabbed my arm. "Bad idea," he said. "She was in one of my seminars. She's off-limits."

"The hell she is," I said.

"Coll." Jake looked at me as if I were crazy. "What the fuck are you doing? And give me my ring back, you jackass."

I absently gave him the ring. "Remember when we learned salsa years ago?" I smiled at him. "I'm about to cash in on that shit."

"That was a long ass time ago and in Florida, not Vegas." He sipped his drink. "It was also to get those two Cuban princesses in their thong swimsuits to dance with us and—"

"And into our beds," I finished his sentence. "Well, it looks like that was for the greater good because I'm about to put those skills to work."

"You still think you have those moves?"

I nodded. "I'm about to find out if all that money in lessons paid off."

"You're a horny idiot. Pull your shit together, and remember where the fuck we are. A medical conference shindig. Jesus, read the goddamn room or something."

"That's precisely what I'm doing," I said, watching every flawless dance step while she showed off her perfectly round ass in a fun and exuberant way.

Unlike everyone else who was out here, either dressed to impress or wearing bikinis that matched their stilettos, she was dressed simply and casually.

Jesus H. Christ, I was smitten as fuck by this woman. She wore a plain white tank that enhanced the glow of her naturally tanned skin. Her super short, cut-off denim shorts were frayed at the hem, highlighting the strong muscles of her gorgeous legs. Her tight ass moved and played along to the rhythm of the music that the live band played, making me believe we were actually in Florida. Florida, Vegas, heaven—I didn't even know where I was anymore. I just knew where I wasn't—out there on the dance floor, joining this woman.

Her smile was effervescent, and even though I couldn't hear her laugh, I could tell it was something I had to be close to. This wasn't about me wanting to fuck some hot chick I'd spotted who was shaking her ass out on the dance floor. This woman had fucking bewitched me with the way her hips moved to the music and the animated and cheerful way she lit up this whole place.

I stayed back and admired her from a distance, but I wanted more. No way in hell could I sit here and hide behind my rules of never pursuing someone in the medical field—not with this woman.

The more I watched her, the more I needed to be in her presence. I couldn't explain any of my behavior or the way I felt. All I knew was I was wasting time sitting here and debating right versus reason.

All sense left my mind, and Jake's warnings and reminders about staying away from females in our line of work—gone. All that was on my mind was cutting into her dance, pulling her against me by the small of her back, and guiding her in a more challenging dance—and into my arms from there.

"Fuck it. Just go get it." Jake laughed. "You're already consumed by this woman. Don't say I didn't warn your stupid ass."

I walked toward the crowd she'd drawn in, easing myself to the side and slipping out to where she teased the musicians by following the music—her movements fluid and sexy as hell.

I watched her feet, her style, focusing on her skill instead of that beautiful smile that I knew would trip my ass up. If I was going to interrupt her entertaining the group, I had to fall in perfectly. If she were the natural talent I was witnessing, she'd easily follow my lead.

As if it were meant to be, I stepped in behind her slowly-swaying hips and took the hand she held in the air and clasped it into mine. She reacted like someone who was expecting a dance partner, and she allowed me to clutch her hip with my other hand and spin her back to me. I dipped her for the hell of it, and that's when her golden-brown eyes met mine.

I pulled her up in one fluid motion, her hands molding into mine as if they were created to be held by them alone. She arched her eyebrow, her lashes emphasizing the chestnut irises I wanted to drown in.

"May I ask who you are, sir?" she asked, moving her hips, complementing each step I took to guide her in our dance that became more intimate with each movement.

"Your future husband." I grinned, spinning her away from me.

Her long, flowing hair breezed through the air while I spun her back, and I took her other hand, turning her back to mold against me.

"You're confident." She laughed as I twirled her out and dipped her to add to our little routine while bringing her to face me in our dance again.

"Goddamn, you're beautiful," I said, almost missing a step as I let her eyes and that bright expression of hers that had lured me out here take me as her victim.

"I could say the same about you," she said as we continued to move our dance into a more daring—after dark—routine.

"And what would you say about me?" I asked when I pulled her in close.

"I have no idea who you are."

"Collin," I gave her my real name.

"You dance well, Collin," she said, her lips full. My God, this woman's spark of delightful energy radiated from her. "Where'd you learn to dance like this?"

"Doesn't matter," I said, pulling my face down to her neck. She smelled like paradise. It was coconut, and some floral scent mixed together, assaulting my senses in the best of ways. "All that matters is that I'm out here with you."

She laughed again, and I never wanted this dance to end. Did someone slip me a love potion? What was going on with me? Who the hell was this woman?

After the dance was over, she thanked me, then tried to escape my grips. "I believe I owe you a drink?" I bit my bottom lip, watching her smooth her hair back into a ponytail.

"I believe you do." Her forehead creased in humor. "So," she said as I held her hand and guided her through the crowd as the music changed behind us to allow for more dancing, "are you a doctor or an intern?"

I grinned. "What do you think?"

"I don't think doctors are as handsome as you." She giggled and nudged my arm as if we were reunited friends from a past life. "And I also don't think doctors dance as well as you."

We arrived at the bar where Jake was in conversation with two older gentlemen and two younger women. He halted his conversation and eyed me and the woman I'd snatched up from the dance floor.

"You think I'm an intern then?" I asked. "What are you having?"

"Water for now," she said, sitting on the stool next to where Jake sat. "Hey, Mario," she smiled at the bartender.

"You looked great out there, Elena," he said. "It's going to suck around here after you leave tonight."

"I believe I have a question for you," I said, taking the stool to her left, Jake now fully facing the bar, listening in on us.

"Well, then, ask away, dance partner," she said, holding up her bottle of water. "Thanks," she said with a wink to the gentleman behind the bar.

"Seems like Mario knows you well enough." I kept my eyes locked on her. "Are you part of the medical group or the entertainment?"

Jake laughed. "Mario and I both think that she was doing well out there alone before your sneaky ass joined her."

She turned and smiled at Jake. "Well, if it isn't the famed Dr. Jacob Mitchell," she said with a laugh that could probably cure a lot of diseases in our industry.

"In the flesh. I see you've met my best friend and intern, Collin."

She turned back to me, and her expression was a dead giveaway that she read Jake's face well enough to know he was bullshitting her.

"Wait." She delivered the sexiest and most dynamic expression I'd seen from her yet. "You both are the two steamy and sexy docs from Saint John's, correct?"

"Don't tell me you know who I am from when the media followed my sorry ass around, documenting the lamest bullshit ever?" Jake said.

She giggled and tipped back her bottled water. My dick was joining in on the party now. Her full lips could've been viewed in so many better ways than wrapped around that water bottle.

"I didn't see that part." She laughed. "I felt for you when my dad told me what'd happened when your life was exploited." She shook her head. "But no, I just watched you in that docuseries. You were fantastic in your presentation here too. It makes me wish I looked more into becoming a heart surgeon now." She laughed then looked at me, "And *you*, Dr. Collin Brooks, the youngest neurosurgeon with a level of boldness and genius skill that is unmatched, yet you still find the time to be an arrogant asshole, or so your predecessor says." Her eyebrows shot up in humor while she and Jake laughed together. "Are the rumors circling this conference about you accurate?"

I arched my eyebrow at the sexy way she teased me. "Perhaps. It looks like Dr. Alvarez's parting words were sent in the invitations to everyone here at the conference. Not a very nice predecessor."

"Is that so?" She hit me with a toying look. "What exactly were Dr. Alvarez's parting words to you?"

"Well, as he gladly passed the torch to me in taking his place on our ward, his final words were mostly that I was the only arrogant asshole he trusted to stand in his place as neuro chief."

A laugh erupted from her in the most delightful way. "Seems like you've already met my dad, then? He's Dr. Alvarez."

That's when Jake nearly choked on his scotch, using the back of his hand to cover the fact he'd sucked the alcohol down the wrong pipe.

"Your dad?" I questioned in disbelief. This should have ended my fascination instantly, but instead, I couldn't give a shit who she was related to. I'd somehow mentally staked some claim on her and wasn't losing her over anything now.

"According to your introduction to me on the dance floor, he's your future father-in-law. I do hope you both get along. Life will suck if I have to pick between my beloved father and you, Dr. Brooks."

I grinned and ordered a beer. The gin had handled my nerves from earlier, and now, all I wanted now was to nurse the beer and enjoy the company of the woman who made every cell in my body come alive.

"Dr. Alvarez was quite the brilliant neurosurgeon. We were sad to see him retire. And you?" I questioned. "You never thoroughly answered my question."

"And which question was that?" she asked.

"Yeah, I think all questions are nailed into your coffin by now," Jake warned with a smile.

Damn, it was so intriguing how she blended in with Jake and me as if we were all old friends.

"You think my dad will kick his ass for hitting on me, Dr. Mitchell?" she asked Jake while studying me.

"I think Alvarez will definitely kick his ass," Jake said with a laugh.

"So the question is," she said, ordering a beer herself, "am I worth that ass-kicking?"

"Yes, and you're smartly avoiding my main question," I said, taking another sip of my beer. "What exactly is it that you do, and where the hell have you been all my life?"

Jake's eyes widened while he shook his head. "I'm going to need water and a Heineken, Mario," he called out to the bartender and then looked at me. "This is going to be a long, entertaining night."

Jake knew I'd already destroyed all our guidelines for playing it safe in this industry. Now here I was, pursuing our former Chief Neurosurgeon's daughter. Miguel could easily kick my ass even in his sixties. Was it worth it? To see this smile and be around the boisterous energy of this woman for the rest of my life, you're goddamn right it was worth it.

"Hmm, where have I been all your life?" she said with a devious laugh. "Well, I've been in Florida, busting my ass so I can work at Saint John's. Looks like you and I might be getting married after all, Dr. Brooks. Well, professionally, anyway," she teased.

I licked my lips after taking another sip of beer. "How so?"

"I'm working in Saint John's neuro ward and will have my own office outside of the hospital as well. Quite the dream that I worked very hard to achieve."

"What will you be doing exactly? Surgery? Research?" Jake asked, but I already knew.

She never pulled her eyes from mine. "I'll be the new—"

"Neuropsychologist," I finished her sentence.

"That's right, Doc," she teased me with those luscious lips.

"You're moving into my office building," I said, studying her. "And yes," I arched an eyebrow, taking another sip of my beer, "you and I will be joined at the hip mostly. I'm the one who requested a neuropsychologist to work closely with me, my patients, and even in some of my surgeries. I didn't know they'd already hired someone? I was supposed to have the final say in who took the new position."

"Looks like we both got screwed this week, missing my brother's board meetings," Jake said, shifting to face us both and leaning against the bar. "Looks like you and your new wife have a lot to iron out, and forgive me if I say that it looks like the honeymoon is over for both of you." Jake took a sip of his beer and smiled knowingly at me.

That's when I watched a tiny ounce of vulnerability flash across her face. "Holy crap." She softly giggled, pink coloring her cheeks, and her hypnotic eyes shifted the night's gears into another pace. She held her hand out to me. "Allow me to introduce myself formally. I'm Dr. Elena Alvarez," she said as I accepted her handshake. "Lovely to meet you, Dr. Brooks. I can already say I like your style."

"And I can safely say, welcome to Saint John's. Whether I hired you or not, those issues are irrelevant after meeting the woman who will make my job much more entertaining."

"Quite a compliment," she said. "I think we'll enjoy each other's company. I absolutely adore working with arrogant asses."

"Is that so?" I smiled.

"It is." She reached for her beer. "I love putting them in their place."

"Then, it's a match made in heaven." Jake raised his beer. "Though, I have to ask you, Dr. Elena Alvarez, do you think you'll enjoy working around this guy?" Jake chimed in, and I could tell my best friend was enjoying the collision course of career death I was on now.

"The question is, will he enjoy working around me?"

"As I mentioned when I met you on the dance floor, you'll be my wife—work partners or not."

I had no idea how to stop this when everything in my body was screaming that I should run this woman off to the closest wedding chapel and have fake Elvis marry us. It was insane. I never believed in any of that love at first sight bullshit. Ever. That was all crazy talk for sappy romantics and hippies who collected crystals—and yet here I was, staring this woman in the eyes and knowing I'd make good on the promise that I'd marry her—or at least ensure she was mine.

Was her dad going to kick my ass? Yes. He knew me all too well. Could my medical license be on the line? No. At least I didn't think so. There was no way I was going to let any of that get in the way. With the way she was flirting with me, and the way she treated Jake as if we were the three musketeers reunited, I knew this was somehow meant to be. She would be mine, and I would ensure that her gorgeous smile brightened more and more as each day passed with her in my life.

Thank God she had three weeks before her assignment began. I'd just taken two weeks of much-needed vacation for the first time in three years at Saint John's. So, get ready. All it took was seeing her on the dance floor to know that my days of playing women were over.

This was going to be the biggest mistake of my life or the best thing that ever happened to me.

Click here to grab your copy of Dr. Brooks on Amazon today

BILLIONAIRES' CLUB SERIES

Dr. Mitchell: Book One in the Billionaires' Club Series. "Jake's Story"

Billionaires like him have a type. And it's *not* me...

I'm not the kind of girl who has one-night stands.

Except...I did.

What can I say? After a few drinks with a gorgeous man who made me feel *alive* for the first time since losing my mom, I was powerless to say no.

And I didn't regret it. Not one minute of our hot, mind-melting night together.

But he wasn't a *forever* kind of guy. So I walked away. I wasn't supposed to ever see him again.

Then I did.

Turns out my sexy one-night stand is Dr. Jacob Mitchell—and he's the cardiothoracic surgeon who just saved my dad's life.

Click here to grab your copy of Dr. Mitchell and read all about Jake and Ash's story today.

Dr. Brooks: Billionaires Club Book 3

We shared the love of a lifetime. Too bad I don't remember any of it.

Pieces of my life were ripped away without warning. My career, my control, my sense of self...it's gone.

So are my memories of *him*.

I now know him as the handsome doctor who was there for me when I first woke up after the accident. But before that, he was the love of my life. My everything.

Or so I'm told.

I'm not the woman he remembers. I'm just a ghost with her face. An unfortunate remnant of the happily ever after, fairy tale kind of romance we *apparently* had together.

He says he'll wait for me. That he won't stop fighting for us, even if he has to make me fall in love with him all over again.

I think he's right. I *will* fall for him.

But the real question is, can he truly ever love me for who I am *now*? Or will his heart always belong to the memory of who I *used* to be?

Dr. Brooks, an angsty, sexy,contemporary romance, is book 3 in the Billionaire's Club series, but it can be read as a standalone. It features a strong heroine struggling with amnesia, and the protective alpha male doctor who somehow manages to win her heart twice. Download today to meet your new favorite book boyfriend.Mr. Grayson: Please note preorder dates will move up.

∾

Mr. Greyson: Billionaires' Club Book 4

I never should've let my guard down. Especially not with him.

I'm used to being strong. In control. I have to be to run my corporation. So, I should've been able to hold my own against him. Against his relentless charm and devastating good looks.

But I couldn't.

I didn't.

It doesn't matter that our companies are irrevocably tied together, or that being with him is beyond inappropriate. It doesn't matter that he's a known player and I don't tolerate games. It doesn't even matter that he makes me lose my prized control with every heated glance, stolen touch, and dirty whisper.

I *crave* him.

Being with him could cost me everything I've worked so hard to build. But as strong as I am, I can't seem to walk away.

Now, all I have to do is decide whether the cost of following my heart —which is pushing me straight into Alex Grayson's arms—is more than I'm willing to pay.

Mr. Grayson, book 4 in the Billionaire's Club series, is a spicy, office, contemporary romance designed to steam up your Kindle. This book features a sexy, alpha hero and the alpha CEO heroine of his dreams. It also includes plenty of witty banter and a guaranteed happily ever after.

Download today, because you need Mr. Grayson in your life.

CONTACT RAYLIN MARKS

Thank you for reading Mr. Mitchell. I do hope you enjoyed it. You may contact me at

raylinmarks99@gmail.com for anything and I will be happy to get back to you as soon as possible.

All things Billionaires' Club, visit my Facebook page: Raylin Marks